THE MIDNIGHT MEMORY

A JACK WIDOW THRILLER

SCOTT BLADE

Black Lion Media

CHAPTER 1

Before the double barrels of a shotgun were thrust into Jack Widow's face at midnight, a trucker veered his tractor trailer off Interstate 20 and rolled into a truck stop as vast as a Nebraska cornfield. He maneuvered the rig to the back of the sprawling lot, parking in line with rows of slumbering trucks. Truck stops and Nebraska cornfields were familiar territory for him. He'd driven through thousands of both after decades behind the wheel, with tens of thousands of miles behind him. He grew up in Iowa and still lived there. Cornfields were just part of the scenery.

Tonight, the trucker hauled farming equipment—machinery built for corn cultivation. He wasn't sure what the machines were called. They probably had some long factory designation. It didn't matter to him. He saw corn all the time. That didn't mean he understood any of the machines used for it. He wasn't a corn farmer, but he was as familiar with corn as anyone else who lived in the Corn Belt.

This trucker was the outlier among the other trucks in the lot, most loaded with road salt and heating materials, ready to fight off the first bite of winter roads.

Dozens of rows of big rigs hummed quietly as truckers slept through the night. The trucker slipped the rig into a space, switching off everything he no longer needed to keep running while he attempted to get a good night's sleep.

First, he wanted to step out, stretch his legs, grab a bite to eat, and shower.

Before he could do any of those things, he needed to wake the sleeping stranger he'd picked up a few hours earlier on the side of the road.

Normally, the trucker avoided giving rides to hitchhikers, as it was strictly against truck company policy, not to mention his better judgment. However, an unexpected cold front had blown in from the north while he drove along, minding his own business. The weather app on his phone blipped, barely giving a warning. The cold storm front came out of nowhere —the very definition of *unexpected*.

The stranger stood at a highway cloverleaf with his thumb out, shivering from the sudden cold. He gazed wearily at the storm clouds forming overhead. Concern bridged the stranger's face, like he faced impending doom.

The trucker knew something about that.

He had a secret. Before he'd set out on this haul, his doctor had given him some bad news—a bad diagnosis relating to cancer and how much road was left in front of his own life. It wasn't much, according to the lab results. He told no one. Called no one. Not his wife. Not his mother. Nobody. He needed to take a beat. He wanted time to think. Nowhere provides that opportunity better than the open road, except for maybe prison. At least prisoners had more time left than he did.

Not all of them, he thought. Some death row inmates had little time left. They were in the same boat as he was. That's how he felt. Those were the ones he related to. Death row inmates. Like them, he too carried a death sentence, given to him by years of bad habits, and by time and fate.

The trucker just wanted to get out on the road and think—one last time. So he left at the drop of a hat and took a last-minute haul.

His diagnosis explained why he felt more inclined to pick up the stranger, to help the man in his time of need. The stranger stood 6'4", all muscle. The man's face wore a wisdom only seen in those who fought in combat. The trucker saw that too. He recognized it. He had a dead brother who'd served in the military. His brother had that same look of a man who could handle himself. But that came at a price. The price was what he saw over there, fighting a foreign war. It was a price paid in blood, only the tab never stopped coming due.

His little brother enlisted young and served two tours before the war changed him. He came back different. Got angry a lot. On his third tour, he died in a gun battle. The government gave their mother a folded flag and a medal for bravery. That's the word they used: *bravery*.

The trucker had seen violent men and knew that look in their eyes. This stranger was dangerous. A veteran, too—no question. But he lacked that one aspect the trucker's brother had. His brother had gone off to war, but only a broken man came back. He was lost. The light was gone.

Not this stranger. He had a compassion about him. His eyes were full of empathy and kindness. He reminded the trucker of someone else he knew. Not his brother. Not a human either. The stranger reminded him of a German shepherd he'd had as a kid. That dog was loving, kind, but terrifying-looking all at the same time.

Dangerous or not, when they gave him a death sentence, what difference did it make giving a ride to a dangerous hitchhiker?

It wasn't the stranger's look that concerned him. Under normal circumstances, it would've been frightening. He'd been crazy to stop and pick up the guy. Any of his fellow truckers would've questioned his sanity for doing it. But this time, it didn't matter. When you have nothing left to lose, bravery comes easy.

The stranger looked worriedly at the sky. Dark rain clouds filled the horizon. The only thing worse than being stuck on the side of the road in the cold with lingering storm clouds would be if it'd been a snowstorm. Luckily, it was only raining.

Could it have been an act to lower the trucker's guard? Probably not, because winter nights in Nebraska were bitterly cold. No way to fake that. The signs were plain as day—literally.

With the sudden cold front, the chill grew even more severe. The trucker felt the effects from inside his truck before he even thought about stopping.

Plus, the stranger shivered, looking like a man standing out in the cold. Long, icy exhalations vapored out of his mouth as he exhaled. Other drivers passed him by without a second glance. They ignored the guy—pretending he wasn't even there, and for good reason.

The drifter didn't fit the bill for anyone's dream passenger. Every instinct in the trucker's brain warned him not to pick the guy up. Trucking school taught him to keep on driving. He could get fired if his handlers found out.

There was still the fact that the stranger looked dangerous. Nothing would change that. His granddaughter, a high schooler with an obsession with horror movies, might refer to the guy as a real-life Michael Myers.

The stranger was big, several inches taller than the trucker, who was large in his own right. The trucker was six foot and two hundred sixty pounds. The stranger was taller, but maybe thirty pounds lighter. However, the trucker was all fast-food weight, whereas the stranger appeared to be all muscle, like he was carved from stone.

Muscle or not, cold weather freezes everyone. No amount of muscle would protect the man from dying of pneumonia. He couldn't just leave him out there on the side of the road like that.

Still, it was a quandary for the trucker. The drifter was the poster boy for who to never give a ride to. When they taught truckers to avoid dangerous-looking hitchhikers, this guy's picture might've been used in the textbook as *the* example.

However, the trucker was a firm believer in karma and the philosophy of paying it forward. His good nature, terminal diagnosis, plus the sudden cold front and lowering temperatures, forced his hand. *How could he leave the stranger out in the cold? How could he just pretend that he didn't see a man in need? And especially during the holidays?*

A Christmas wreath decorated the grille of the trucker's rig. He believed in Christmas. He believed in spreading love and kindness. Today, he believed in the whole deal. *What choice did he have?* He was going to die. Like those prisoners on death row, he was born again. His faith was rejuvenated. And with that came the lessons of helping others, especially those in need.

So he couldn't just leave the guy stranded out in the cold.

The trucker felt bad. Besides these reasons of his own, the drifter stood out there underdressed and unprepared for the cold weather, like a helicopter had dropped him in with no clue of where he was going. But it was more than that. It was more like he didn't care which way he was going.

Even with all of his personal reasons to pick the guy up, there was a moment when the trucker didn't know if he was going to pick the drifter up or not.

Wind gusted against the windshield, pushing snow across his field of view. He drove up to the point of no return. He either had to start stopping now or pass the guy by.

Against his better judgment and instincts, the trucker took his foot off the gas, switched on the hazard lights, and braked to a crawl. He pulled the truck over, stopping near the shoulder, and offered the stranger a ride. The drifter happily accepted, and they drove off.

They chatted for a while. The stranger gave his name, which the trucker forgot. He heard the guy say it, but it slipped his mind, like forgetting to bring an umbrella on a rainy day. He had a lot on his mind, which he told the stranger about. The stranger listened intently, as if they were old friends. In reality, he listened because it was one of the unwritten rules of the road. A good Samaritan gives you a ride. You'd better feign interest in whatever they have to say. The stranger did it so well that the trucker couldn't tell if it was genuine interest or not. The stranger was sincere, or he faked it well, like the two death notifiers the Army sent to his mother's house with that folded flag.

Eventually, there was a lull in the conversation, and the drifter asked if the trucker minded if he closed his eyes for a while, because he hadn't slept in nearly twenty-four hours. The trucker said, "Go for it."

Within minutes, the drifter fell asleep. He'd slept through the late afternoon and evening, until now.

The trucker said, "Wake up, mister."

Nothing happened at first.

The trucker repeated, "Hey mister. Time to get up." He leaned across the seats and tapped the large man on the arm. The stranger's eyes opened slowly. He blinked a few times. His eyes were red, like the trucker had woken him from a coma.

The trucker unbuckled his seatbelt, took out a clipboard, and began going over his daily checklist, just to give himself something to do while the drifter righted himself and fully woke up.

Eventually, the drifter sat upright in the seat and looked around. He rubbed his eyes and asked, "How long have I been out?"

"You been asleep for several hours."

"What time is it?"

The trucker glanced at his wristwatch and said, "Ten thirty-six."

The drifter looked out the windshield, saw darkness, and realized the trucker meant at night. He'd slept from daylight until nearly midnight. He must've been exhausted.

Widow stretched his arms and rotated his head and neck, getting out the kinks. Afterward, he said, "Thanks for the ride. And for letting me sleep. I needed it."

The trucker didn't look up from his clipboard. He said, "Not a problem, my friend."

"Where are we?"

"A truck stop."

"Yeah, but where are we? What state?"

"This is Nebraska. Shelter County."

Widow glanced out the windows again, saw the sleeping trucks, and the empty darkness beyond. He said, "It looks remote."

"It is. Shelter County's one of the least populated counties in Nebraska," the trucker said, then mumbled, "And that's saying a lot."

"What's the nearest city?"

"City? Nebraska ain't got no cities. Not really," the trucker said, and pointed southeast. "Lincoln's about the only place I'd count as a big city. It's a hundred and fifty miles that way."

Widow followed his pointing finger and saw more darkness on the horizon, and not much else. It looked bleak.

The trucker asked, "You ever been to Nebraska before?"

Widow nodded and said, "I've passed through." However, he thought, *Haven't I?* The truth was he wasn't sure. He couldn't recall ever stopping in the Cornhusker State before. No memories came to mind. Either he'd never set foot in the state before, or he was too groggy to remember. He needed coffee.

The trucker cleared his throat and put down the clipboard. He said, "Well, this is the end of the line. I gotta get some shut-eye myself."

He took the hint and stretched one last time. Then he smiled at the guy and said, "Thanks for the lift." Widow was unsure what he'd do next in the middle of nowhere, Nebraska. But that was *his* problem, not the trucker's.

Widow offered the trucker a hand to shake. The trucker took it and shook it.

Widow said, "Appreciate the ride." He gave the guy a little more goodbye than he normally did for strangers because the trucker had picked him up out of the cold. And the guy let him sleep, which was needed.

"No problem, my friend," the trucker repeated. "It was a pleasure riding with you. Good luck out there."

Widow unbuckled his seatbelt, turned, and opened the passenger door. Before he slid out, the trucker said, "I'll be heading out of here at eight in the morning if you're still around and want to ride along further. I'm going to Denver."

Widow paused a beat. The thought of heading to Colorado in the winter wasn't very appealing. But he said nothing about it. Instead, he thanked the trucker, got out, shut the door, and vanished between slumbering big rigs.

CHAPTER 2

T *oo late for coffee?* Widow wondered.

Answer: *Of course not. It's never too late for coffee.*

Still, Widow did something out of character. He paused at a coffee counter and contemplated grabbing a decaf over regular. Many people assume decaf means no caffeine. Not true. Decaf has around two percent of the original caffeine content. Getting hit by two percent of a bullet will still cause damage. Widow once had a CO who drank a ton of decaf coffee. He used to say: "It's the same great beverage, less *power*."

Widow wasn't so sure about that. He wanted coffee. He always wanted coffee. But he'd just awoken from a decent sleep and didn't need to stay up all night. It was now twenty minutes to eleven—according to the yawning night clerk behind the counter—and decaf felt like the right call.

Widow eyeballed the pot of regular coffee. The smell. The rising steam. The blackness. It called to him like a needle to a junkie. Instinctively, as if his hands were out of his control, he grabbed regular coffee—black, and two cups of it. He paid for them and downed one right there in front of the night clerk's counter. Without pausing, he drank it, crumbled the cup, and trashed it in a bin near the door.

Widow asked the clerk about the nearest town. The night clerk pointed Widow in the right direction and said, "Tent Hills is north down that road."

Widow sipped the second coffee and asked, "How far from here?"

"Five or six miles, maybe."

Widow nodded, thanked the clerk, and contemplated the distance and snowy challenges that lay ahead of him. He figured he could reach Tent Hills in ninety minutes, or less. He could also take his time and stretch it out to two hours. He had nowhere special to be and all the time in the world to get there. Even though it was late at night, he wasn't sleepy anymore. There was nowhere to sleep at the truck stop anyway, except inside a truck, which he didn't have. With nothing more to do, he took the hot coffee and walk to Tent Hills. Maybe he could find a motel there, or at least an all-night diner.

Before Widow could hit the road, he realized he needed a suitable winter coat. Currently, he was only wearing jeans, boots, and a long-sleeved blue flannel shirt with a t-shirt underneath. As he perused the aisles of the truck stop and sipped the second coffee, he found a section dedicated to coats. After sifting through the options, the only coat that fit was a puffer coat so ugly his own mother would've declared it a fashion emergency. But it would have to do—he wasn't strutting down a fashion runway. He just needed to stay warm. However, inspecting the coat, he found something even more vile than its appearance: the price tag. It was in the triple digits.

Widow mentioned it to the clerk before buying it. But the guy didn't give him any sympathy. He simply retorted, "I just work here, man."

Widow said nothing to that and paid for the puffer coat, threw in a pair of gloves and a beanie, and put it all on, setting his coffee on the counter. Satisfied, he left the truck stop with the coffee in hand, headed through the lot, and onto the road to Tent Hills.

What a peculiar name for a town, he thought. Widow had seen a lot of towns with strange names.

Widow walked for thirty minutes north along a deserted road but saw nothing—no town lights beckoning on the horizon as he'd hoped. Aside from the highway streetlights perched high on poles, darkness swallowed the horizon.

The lonely road cut through miles of cornfields. Cornstalks rustled in the stiff wind. Coyotes howled somewhere far off. An owl hooted to the west, its wings so silent that Widow didn't hear it glide over the road.

Snow blanketed the ground, cold and silent. Above, a bright moon hung in a near cloudless sky, casting pale light across the landscape. Night animals rustled through the icy cornstalks.

Widow walked on, encountering no vehicles. No headlights. No hum of tires. Nothing.

The only signs of human life were the occasional farm driveways and aging mailboxes. He couldn't see the farmhouses because they were far from the road. Only their outlines were visible from the street.

Everything was quiet. The night was serene and peaceful, until a sudden shotgun blast shattered the silence, shocking

Widow's ears. Sleeping winter birds launched out of the corn-stalks, startled and spreading out across the night sky.

If the caffeine in the two coffees hadn't jolted Widow awake, the echoing shotgun blast certainly did the trick.

The sound boomed across the sky, making it hard to pinpoint the exact direction it had originated from.

Widow whipped around, looking behind him and slowly back to the front. He scanned the dark sky as he listened for the sound of a second gunshot.

He didn't have to wait long. The second shotgun blast thundered from straight ahead. It ripped through the silence like the last one. The gunshot originated from just over the crest of a hill, straight up the road from his position.

A gunshot in the middle of cornfield country could just be a crow scarer, or a bird banger—a gun that used loud, explosive gunshot sounds to frighten birds away from crops. It didn't really fire projectiles. Crow scarers are all about shock and awe.

But that wasn't the sound Widow heard.

Crow scarers aren't much use in the winter, not in Nebraska. Everything's frozen. There are no crops to protect. And usually no crows to worry about either. Plus, Widow had a lot of experience with firearms. He knew the sound of a shotgun when he heard it. Someone was shooting at something. Or someone. Shooting at midnight out here was unlikely to be for target practice. It could be a local rancher shooting at coyotes. But it could also mean someone might be in trouble.

Widow wasn't the kind of man who could walk on by and pretend he heard nothing. Not when there could be someone in danger. He had to help. This urge he had was like his addiction to coffee. It called to him from deep in his DNA. He couldn't ignore it.

Widow was also a man with priorities. Like the orders of operation in math or standard operating procedures from any military branch, there's an order to things. There are steps to take with a certain order to them.

First on Widow's priority list was always coffee. So he shook the gas station coffee cup to gauge how much was left. Just a little. He shotgunned the rest and set the cup on the side of the road, intending to pick it up later. Widow was no tree hugger, but he wasn't an asshole either. He picked up trash whenever he could, especially if it was his own trash. Of course, his later actions depended on what he'd find at the end of that shotgun blast trail.

Widow jogged forward, following the sound of the shotgun blast. Less than a quarter mile ahead and up a hill, he reached the crest. There, the town of Tent Hills came into view. Widow quickly understood the town's name—beyond the first hill, he saw dozens, perhaps hundreds, of hills. They weren't exactly rolling; instead, their awkward tips made them resemble rows of camping tents in the dark. The town was set among them.

The lonely highway stretched over the hills, disappearing into the distance. Just beyond a couple more miles, the Tent Hills township began. Widow noticed the lights—faint, not because the town was far, but because there wasn't much of a town there at all. It looked tiny.

Then Widow saw an additional light source. It came from a billboard—one of those massive ones way out from the road. It was in an empty field of nothing but cornstalks. The billboard was lit by spotlights aimed at the advertisement on the sign. The ad was for a used car lot, which must've been profitable because the billboard looked expensive. It was huge.

The spotlights lit up the face of the man who owned the car lot. The words on the sign named the man as Mitch Nicely. *COME ON DOWN TO MITCH NICELY'S AUTOMOTIVES. WHERE WE'LL TREAT YOU NICELY!*

To top off the effect of the kind of character Mitch Nicely was, there was an effect added to the image of him. The man wore a cowboy hat and an expensive, tailored suit. The suit was bright yellow, like a freshly husked cob of corn. Nicely gave two thumbs up, a wink, and a smile. The added effect Widow noticed right away was a glint in the man's teeth, like it came from a scene in a movie.

Near the bottom of the hill, Widow spotted the source of the shotgun blast. A figure stumbled around in the dark, clutching a double-barreled shotgun. He waved the weapon at the darkness off the highway shoulder, as if confronting someone.

The giant Mitch Nicely billboard stood tall in the field across from him. The man in the field was angry, cursing at a figure in the darkness. But it was more than that. He was in the middle of a heated argument, a violent situation. Widow watched and listened to the guy. He seemed passionate about defending someone. It sounded like a woman, possibly. The guy was defending a woman he cared about from some unseen enemy standing in the darkness.

There was just one big problem. Widow saw no one there. No one but the used car salesman with the big phony smile.

The guy broke open the shotgun, ejected the spent shells, and dug into the pocket of his coat. He fished out two new shells and reloaded the gun, snapping it closed. He yelled into the darkness again and fired the shotgun. Widow squinted and stared into the darkness. The muzzle flash from the shotgun lit up the darkness for a moment. But it was enough for

Widow to see that no one was there. He saw only a frozen cornfield and the darkness beyond.

Was he shooting at coyotes? Widow thought. *But if he had been shooting at coyotes, then who was he yelling at?*

Widow started to suspect that this guy might be off his rocker. Cautiously, he called out to the guy, "Hey! What're you shooting at?" But the guy didn't respond. He didn't even turn around to face Widow. Instead, he screamed into the void, like he was arguing with an invisible person. It seemed like he couldn't even hear Widow, like he was in another world.

Widow stood there, calculating the odds of getting shot on a dark night in the middle of nowhere, Nebraska. Before this encounter, the chances seemed low. But after running into a stranger on the road—one who fired a double-barreled shotgun at an unseen enemy—those odds skyrocketed.

Carefully, Widow approached the man. He called out, "Hey, mister!"

No response.

Widow walked down the shoulder, keeping his hands out, like he was approaching a wild horse. But the guy didn't see him. He shouted at the stranger again, "Hey, mister! I'm coming up behind you! Don't shoot me!"

Still no response.

Widow moved closer, closing the distance significantly. He stomped with every step, trying to get the stranger's attention while hoping not to get shot by accident. He thought about throwing snow at the guy, but he realized that startling a jumpy stranger with a shotgun, alone in the middle of nowhere, might not be the best idea. The danger tripled if this guy was an escaped mental patient or something.

As Widow drew closer, he saw the man better, and his assessment of the situation changed. He was glad he hadn't startled the man because the guy turned out to be elderly, like in his early to mid-eighties. Jump-scaring a man of that age, who held a shotgun with one shell left in the barrel, never worked out well for anybody.

The old man's hair was thick and disheveled and as white as the snow on the ground. He had sandpaper skin with age spots across his cheeks. His large ears were hidden strategically in his hair. He wore an old, tattered winter coat. And Widow knew the man had pulled two shotgun shells out of one pocket of that coat. Whether it was true, Widow was trained to assume there were more shells stuffed in those pockets. He suspected that he'd have to secure that weapon. More calculations blitzed across his mind.

Besides the shotgun and the unusual behavior, Widow noticed the guy wasn't dressed quite right either. He wore pajamas under the coat, but no shoes, only two different socks. One was black, with a hole in the heel, the other white with holes in the toes.

The old guy pointed the shotgun at the darkness and violently shouted, "Let her go! Or I'll kill you where you stand!"

Widow froze and scanned the darkness, past the old guy. He saw nothing. There was no one there. The old guy aimed the shotgun at the invisible enemy. He trembled, shaking the barrel, which, along with what the old guy yelled, indicated to Widow that the old guy's first three shotgun blasts were warning shots. Context told him the old guy thought he was in a hostage situation, where his enemy was using someone as a human shield.

The old guy confirmed it by saying, "I'm warning you, Enzo!

I'm taking her with me! Don't get in the way, or so help me, I'll kill you!"

Widow stayed quiet. He just stared into the darkness in confusion. He still saw no one.

The old guy shouted, "Please, Enzo! I'll shoot!"

The calculations running in Widow's head stopped—like a Pentagon computer grinding through attack plans. Only one action remained. He had to sneak up on the old man and neutralize the shotgun before the guy shot him by mistake— or hurt himself.

Widow walked casually and not sneakily, as it was obvious the old guy wasn't going to hear him no matter how big and loud he walked. He kept his eyes on the shotgun, taking care not to trigger the guy to spin around and shoot him with it. The closer he got to the old guy, the shorter the range between him and the barrel of the gun.

The old guy continued shouting at a ghost named Enzo. Most of it was incomprehensible, like broken sentences. It sounded like a dramatic and violent scene ripped out of a stage play.

Widow was now just ten feet away, in the homestretch. He continued to follow the old man closely. Five feet. Almost within grabbing distance. But at four feet, Widow stepped on a stick, snapping it underfoot. Although his previous shouts had failed to break the old man from his trance, the sharp crack of the twig instantly did.

Startled, the old guy spun around, saw Widow, and shoved the shotgun in his face. He shouted, "Who're you?" The old guy's features came into view. He had a strong face, sun-beaten skin, high cheekbones, and piercing blue eyes. He wore a face that expressed a life lived hard, like a lifelong rancher's face. No one would ever suspect there had ever been any other kind of life lived in the man's past. Hollywood would instantly cast him as a rancher, if they were making a film set on a Nebraska ranch.

Widow froze, staring down the double-barreled shotgun. Two black holes stared back—one empty, one loaded. *Which was the spent shell and which was the live one?* He had no idea.

Slowly, Widow raised both hands, glancing at the old guy's finger on the trigger, then up at his eyes. Widow said, "Easy, mister! I'm not here to hurt you!"

The old guy shivered. Cold, nervous breaths wisped out of his mouth as he exhaled. He asked, "Who sent you? Was it the Brasis? Was it Enzo?"

Widow said, "Sir, no one sent me. I don't know what a Brasi is. And I don't know anyone named Enzo."

The old guy stared up at Widow slowly, like he was taking in a giant redwood tree. The guy's eyes looked guarded, confused, and terrified—all at the same time.

"You're lying," the old guy said.

"I'm not. In fact, I don't even think I've ever met an Enzo in my whole life."

The old guy stared at him from behind the shotgun barrel. His eyes twinkled. There was a look there. Something unlike what he appeared to be. The old guy may have looked like a rancher, but this look in his eyes said different. There was a hint of something behind them. Something Widow recognized. It was the look of a killer, a man who'd pull the trigger and shoot Widow dead without a second thought.

Widow said, "Move the shotgun away. I don't like guns pointed at me."

The old guy stared at him. That killer-look faded away, as if it'd never been there to begin with. He glanced at the shotgun

—dumbfounded, like he forgot the weapon was in his possession. He stared at the gun blankly for a long beat. Then he looked confused about why he was holding it.

The killer in his eyes reappeared, like he'd been transported back to reality. Only his reality was all in his imagination.

Finally, recognition beamed in his face. He remembered that he'd just been pointing the shotgun at Enzo. Realizing that a ghost stood behind him, the old guy flinched, glancing back over his shoulder. He was terrified that he'd made a grave mistake. He'd turned his back on an enemy from his past, a man he thought was long buried. It was a name that had every right to want retribution.

Widow took advantage of the old guy's distraction. He darted to the right, exploded from the waist, and attempted to swipe the shotgun away from the old guy. But Widow made one big mistake—he forgot the old guy's finger was still on the trigger.

Widow grabbed the shotgun's barrels, but it was too late. Spooked, the old guy shuddered. And a trigger-pull jerked with him. The two dark holes still pointed in Widow's direction. The shotgun boomed between the two men.

The last shell fired at Widow at close range.

CHAPTER 3

MEMORY ONE

Mickey Fog Eyes thrashed around inside the trunk of a speeding '57 Chevy Bel Air as it careened toward Interstate 90—a stretch unofficially called the Chicago Skyway. The ride was anything but smooth. But when you're crammed into a trunk against your will, comfort isn't exactly the driver's concern. Especially when that driver's the one who clocked him in the head with a revolver and shoved him into the trunk.

The gun strike to the back of the head should've knocked Mickey out cold. Instead, it left him dazed, barely clinging to consciousness. Close enough for the driver, though—he'd stuffed Mickey into the trunk and wrapped him in duct tape without a fight.

Leaving Chicago, the car hammered over potholes on Stony Island Avenue, each jolt slamming Mickey against the trunk's metal walls like a fist to his already throbbing head. The Chevy's suspension groaned, its gears whining like the driver had no clue how to work a clutch. The terrible clutch handling could also be attributed to the unusual boots the driver wore. They were Wellington boots, used for walking into wetlands and marshes. Why did he wear them? Mickey didn't know.

The mechanical groans mixed with the fading city noise, a chaotic symphony of 1960s Chicago.

As the Bel Air approached the on-ramp to I-90, the driver swerved, trying—and failing—to dodge the worst craters in the asphalt. Every maneuver seemed to land in another just as punishing to Mickey's head.

Outside the vehicle, the gritty Chicago landscape blurred past them—gray and brown, speckled with neon bar signs and flashes of streetlights reflecting off rain-slick pavements. Trapped in the dark, Mickey could picture every rundown corner, each one disappearing faster than he could register. He knew this side of town like the back of his hand. He'd lived and worked here since moving from Queens five years back.

It was an hour till midnight on a chilly spring night in 1965.

Back in Queens, New York, Mickey had tried to make a name for himself with the local mob guys. But he stepped on too many toes and had to skip town—or risk ending up in the trunk of a car, driven to a bridge, fitted with concrete shoes, and tossed into the Hudson River.

Ironic, that here he was, duct-taped in the trunk of a car with a mobster driving it. It was the very thing he'd avoided by leaving New York City. It turned out to be his fate, after all.

The old Chevy shuddered as it merged onto the Skyway. Wind howled through gaps in the trunk's frame, mixing with the buzz of passing traffic. The ride smoothed slightly as they left the worst of the city's roads behind, but the dull pounding in Mickey's skull didn't ease. Neither did the fear of what awaited him at the end of this ride.

After an hour, the car veered onto a dark, winding rural road. The pain from the initial assault and the rough ride surged, overwhelming Mickey's senses. As his consciousness waned, he slumped into a fitful darkness, barely clinging to awareness.

He awoke sometime later with his hands and feet still bound in duct tape, a strip stretched tight across his mouth. Blood trickled down his face into one eye as he blinked. A sharp throb pounded in his skull. The driver had hit him hard enough to nearly knock him out, but not kill him. Drool pooled in his mouth, held back by the seal of the tape. He swallowed it back and shook his head, trying to clear the daze.

His mind wandered, thinking about how he got his name. He always wanted a cool mob guy name, something like Mickey The Hammer or Mickey Blue Eyes.

But he was Mickey Fog Eyes.

They called him Fog Eyes because he always looked like he was lost in a haze. Not stoned, not drunk—just slow. A beat behind in every conversation. Social cues went right over his head, and when he spoke, he had this awkward, hesitant way about him, like he was feeling around in the dark for the right words.

It made people think his mind was fogged up.

The name stuck.

Mickey didn't get to pick it. The name was given to him by one of the troglodytes who worked for the Brasis.

Not the driver of the Chevy Bel Air. A different guy.

They called him Mad Dom.

His real name was Dominic Rosetti. He wasn't just a guy who enjoyed violence—he thrived on it. Got his nickname after laughing through a beating that should've killed him. At least, that's how the story goes. He took a punch like it was a joke and threw one back like a wrecking ball.

A wild card. But too useful to get rid of.

Strangely, the ride along the rural road was smoother than on the interstate. The calmer terrain and slower movement of the car allowed Mickey's fog to clear. His senses returned in slow, painful waves. His head ached like hell, but it also shook him into realizing one thing—he needed to figure a way out. Fast. Waking up in the trunk of a car was never a good sign of things to come, especially when it belonged to a newly minted enforcer for the Brasi mob family.

Terrified, Mickey studied the inside of the trunk, searching for an escape. That idea went out the window fast.

He should've realized it immediately—there was no way out.

He was a mechanic. He knew cars. And this trunk had no exit but the way he came in. The only way out was for the driver to open the trunk and let him out. And the only way that would happen was if the driver had a change of heart.

Brasi guys were killers. No way around that.

How often did they get struck with a conscience? How often did one of them suddenly decide to let a guy like him walk?

The answer was never.

His next instinct kicked in, and he searched for something to use as a weapon. At some point, the driver—the guy who clocked him—would have to open the trunk. If Mickey could get the drop on him, maybe he had a shot at escaping.

The trunk was mostly empty. A spare tire. A jack. And nothing else.

The jack could work as a weapon, but with his hands and feet bound, it was useless. And even if he could use it, the trunk wasn't big enough to rear back for a proper swing.

Desperation forced him to keep looking, but the reality was bleak. Maybe there was a scenario where he could ambush the driver. But he couldn't piece it together. It seemed impossible.

Maybe a smarter man could figure a way out.

Mickey wasn't that man.

He wasn't the brightest bulb on the Chicago Theatre marquee.

Though slow-witted, he wasn't delusional. He knew his own shortcomings. He'd battled them his whole life. From a young age, doctors had bluntly told his mother he was simple-minded—a label that stung but wasn't sugar-coated.

Mickey barely scraped through high school. Reading never came easy. Words blurred together on a page. His real gift was mechanics—his hands knew their way around an engine better than his mind did around a book. The only reason he passed his classes was by bribing smarter kids to take his exams. It was in machinery and automotive courses he thrived.

Book smart? No. Street smart? Not really. But he had more of that than the other.

And if there was one thing Mickey knew, it was how to talk his way into—and out of—trouble.

His mother used to say, "Mickey's got the gift of gab. He can talk himself into a mess, and right back out of it."

That became the story of his life.

She was right. He had a knack for wriggling out of dangerous situations. The problem was, he was always the one who put himself in them.

It started young. He could talk a bully into a frenzy, then somehow negotiate his way out of getting stomped into the ground. A survival skill. One that only kicked in when he was in real peril.

Working for a mob-owned garage put him in more than a few dangerous situations. One wrong word, one bad joke to the wrong wise guy, and he could end up just like this—tied up in a trunk, on a one-way ride to getting his ticket punched.

And that's exactly where he was heading now.

Mickey worked at Fulton's Garage on Clark Street. Three years without incident. He kept his head down. Kept his mouth shut. Stayed out of trouble. A new trend for him.

Fulton's Garage was mostly legit. Regular people brought their cars in for repairs. But behind closed doors, they also handled boosted cars—stolen vehicles that needed new VINs, fresh paint jobs, or a quick part-out. Mickey was in on it. He wrenched on the stolen cars, no questions asked.

But that wasn't enough. Mickey always needed more. More cash. More action. He couldn't help himself. He enjoyed the nightlife too much. The bars. The girls. Things got expensive for a low-level guy like him. To keep up, he had to take more risks.

So he got himself involved in another side hustle: running betting slips for the Brasis.

Nothing major. They did not trust him with the actual operations—loan sharking, extortion, racketeering. That was for the made guys, like the driver taking him to his death. But gambling? That was easy money.

All he had to do was distribute betting slips at local bars, collect cash, and pass it up the chain. Seemed simple enough.

Until one of those slips ended up in the hands of an undercover cop. Some kind of new gangbusters unit in the Chicago PD.

Mickey hadn't seen it coming. The bust happened fast. The cops knew about his mob ties, but they also knew he was small time. A nobody.

That meant he wasn't worth taking down. They didn't care what happened to him any more than the Brasis did. He wasn't worth turning over any rocks for.

But he was worth using—like throwing shit at the wall to see what sticks. Mickey was scum. He could be thrown at the wall. Maybe he'd stick. Maybe he wouldn't.

The cops gave him a choice: face serious charges, the kind that came with serious jail time, or talk.

Mickey didn't want to talk. Flipping on the Brasis was a death sentence. Everyone knew that.

But he panicked. He couldn't make it in prison either. Going to Stateville in the 1960s for a guy like him would likely be a death sentence too.

Mickey was between a rock and a hard place. Now, trapped in a trunk, he realized the choice had already been made for him. He was about to find out just how much the Brasis thought his life was worth.

Mickey's only chance was to do what he always did—talk his way out of it. But to do that, he needed to know his target.

Who was the driver?

The last thing he remembered was stepping out of the garage, coming face to face with one of Brasi's new guys. Gangly, awkward. A mobster wannabe they called Donnie D. Mickey didn't know why they called him that. Maybe D was short for his last name.

Donnie D was a relatively new face to Mickey. Usually, he dealt with low-level street guys. Then recently, the Brasis switched it up on him, giving him Mad Dom instead. That didn't sit right. He should've known something was up the first time he saw Mad Dom. He should've known they were onto him.

They knew the cops had busted him. That wasn't the worst part.

He really should've known when Mad Dom showed up a second time to collect his cash and give him more betting slips. That was the giveaway. The Brasis suspected him of helping the cops. The second time should've been his sign.

He could've skipped town again. America was a big place. In the 1960s, it wasn't hard to disappear. But he didn't skip town.

The Chevy Bel Air came to a sudden stop at the end of a rural road. Strong winds gusted outside, whistling through cracks in the trunk's seals. Mickey listened. The driver turned off the engine and got out of the car. He heard the car door slam shut. The driver walked back to the trunk. Keys rattled and went into the keyhole. The trunk groaned open.

Mickey saw the driver, his features partially shrouded by the night. What he could see brought the man's remarkable face back to him. He'd seen him on the street, right before the guy whacked him in the head with the revolver.

The driver was definitely Donnie D, one of the Brasi family's newest enforcers. Only was he an enforcer? Mickey found it hard to believe. Sure Donnie D was intimidating, one requirement to be an enforcer. But he wasn't intimidating in the right way. Not like Mad Dom.

Donnie D was only intimidating in an ugly kind of way. Mickey thought that literally. Donnie D was ugly. He had a bent nose, thick eyebrows, and crooked teeth. He had the face of a guy that only a mother would love.

He did have big, piercing blue eyes. That was one thing that stuck out about him, one redeeming feature that attracted the occasional woman to him.

At first glance, he could intimidate because his face wasn't one you'd want to see in a dark alley. But there was something about him that made him all wrong for wise guy work. One of Mickey's talents, the thing that made it easy for him to talk his way out of trouble, was reading people. It only took him seconds to see a flash of kindness in Donnie D's eyes. There was a twinkle of a man with a deep well of empathy there. Only Donnie D's ugly face, broad shoulders, and size gave him the look of a killer. But one glimpse into the man's eyes and Mickey knew he didn't have it in him.

Suddenly, Mickey felt hope. Maybe he could talk his way out of this. Then again, a lot of stone-cold killers were once virgins. They too were once innocent. Would Donnie D pull the trigger when the time came? Something told Mickey he was about to find out.

A full moon beamed across a vast sky behind the driver. Suddenly, the driver shoved the same revolver he'd whacked Mickey over the head with into his face. He followed it with a bright beam from an Eveready Captain, a metal flashlight common in 1965. It was exceptionally relevant for this night as it was thick enough to double as a clubbing weapon.

Instantly, Mickey envisioned being whacked over the head with the flashlight instead of the .38 Special. Given the choice, he'd choose the gun.

Donnie D aimed the flashlight beam at Mickey's face. Mickey squinted and shut his eyes tight to avoid the temporary blindness. The light overwhelmed his senses, triggering pain in his head. He fought against it. In that moment, he desperately wished he had a bottle of Reds to dull the throbbing, or any Barbs for that matter.

Donnie D traced Mickey's body with the beam, checking that his hands and feet were still bound. He made sure Mickey didn't wriggle his way out on the ride. There were no signs that he'd loosened his restraints. So Donnie D lowered the flashlight, stuffing it in his armpit. The beam remained on Mickey. Donnie D reached in with his free hand, grabbed Mickey under the arm, and dragged him out of the trunk, setting him onto his feet.

The chilly night air hit Mickey like a slap as he was yanked onto the gravel roadside.

Suddenly, Donnie D came out with a switchblade. He popped the blade, startling Mickey, making him second-guess his earlier assessment of Donnie D's innocence.

"Stay still," Donnie D barked. He knelt and slipped the blade inside the duct tape binding Mickey's feet. He cut the tape and did the same to Mickey's hands, freeing the man.

Mickey ripped the tape from his mouth, taking deep breaths like they were his last before diving deep into the ocean.

Donnie D stepped back, closed the switchblade and pocketed it. He shone the flashlight into Mickey's face again, then at a trail between two trees that led up over a hill. "Walk!" Donnie D commanded, nudging Mickey forward with the gun pressed into his back. Mickey's shoes crunched over gravel. Each step echoed in the surrounding stillness, the only other sound being the distant lapping of Lake Michigan's waves against a shoreline.

They climbed the hill and came face to face with an amazing sight. The Indiana Dunes loomed ahead, their dark forms seeming to undulate against the starlit sky. Neither man knew that a year into the future, the US government would establish this place as a major national park. For now, it seemed the perfect place to dispose of a body.

"Keep going!" Donnie D barked.

Mickey shuffled forward weakly, his legs stiff from the long ride being folded inside the trunk. His legs moved slowly, but his mind raced. Donnie D was nervous; Mickey could hear it in his breathing, a shaky, uneven rhythm that spoke of a man not sure of his actions. However, Mickey wasn't delusional. He gave his odds of bartering with the man 50/50 at best.

They walked on for several minutes until they reached a secluded spot between two large sand dunes on the beach. The only sounds were Lake Michigan's waves slurping at the shore and the distant calls of nocturnal birds in the cool air. The rhythmic wash of the water contrasted starkly with the tense silence, each wave's persistent lap against the shore only amplifying Mickey's sense of unease hanging in the night air.

Mickey froze. His eyes went huge at the sight in front of him.

A shovel, already stabbed into the dirt, awaited them, stark like a grave marker—his grave. Mickey knew instantly what the shovel was for; Donnie D didn't need to say a word. It was there for Mickey to dig his own grave.

"Donnie, listen—" Mickey started.

"Shut up and dig," Donnie D interrupted, gesturing with the gun to the shovel. Donnie D was new at this, but he spoke with enough confidence to be intimidating and cold all at the same time.

"Please, Donnie. You don't have to do this," Mickey pleaded.

Donnie D fired the gun once. The gunshot boomed and echoed across the wind. The bullet whizzed past Mickey and vanished into the darkness above Lake Michigan.

"Dig!" Donnie shouted, pointing the gun at Mickey. "I won't ask again."

Reluctantly, Mickey slunk to the shovel, yanked it from the earth, and began to dig. The shovel bit into the soil with a soft crunch. He stabbed the ground, starting the hole. He shoveled dirt into a pile—aware that this very pile would soon cover his grave. He repeated this process over and over, each shoveling an unforgiving reminder of the hole's purpose.

After a while, the act seemed repetitive, almost dull—shovel into the dirt, scoop, and dump on the pile. Repeat. It was calming, in a sense. But Mickey's mind was anything but calm. His thoughts spun out of control, desperately trying to weave a narrative that might save his life. He knew, like so many times before, that he had gotten himself into this. And he would have to get himself out of it.

A shallow grave was all that was required. "No need for a six-footer, here. Nobody's ever gonna find him out there in the dunes," Mad Dom had told Donnie D, before he left.

The boss had given Donnie D the chance to prove himself. This was his chance. And it would be his only one. If he failed this test, then he was out. "You'll be lucky if the boss lets you wash his car if you fail," Mad Dom had told him.

Before he set out to grab Mickey, he asked Mad Dom for pointers. Donnie D had tuned up plenty of guys for the boss over the last several months of employment. That wasn't a problem for him. Killing someone in cold blood was a different story. He'd never murdered someone before. But, he needed to do it to become part of the crew as a made man. And he had to do it on his own. No hand holding. They had to rely on him to go through with any hit they gave him. All the Brasis' enforcers went through it. That first kill was a rite of passage, a part of the interview process.

It took Mickey, a man under tremendous duress with average strength, close to three hours to dig a three-foot grave. It could've taken longer, but the dirt was a combination of loose soil and sand from the beach. It was easy to dig.

Mickey wasn't sure how far Donnie D would make him dig. He slowed at the three-foot mark. He tried to talk to Donnie the whole three hours, trying to sway him to the idea of letting Mickey go. Talking to Donnie D was like talking to a brick wall. He showed little emotion. Maybe Mickey was wrong? Maybe Donnie D was a stone-cold killer, after all?

"You don't have to kill me," Mickey said. "Really. I can see it in your eyes. You're not a killer. It would be one thing if I deserved it. If I was one of those kid diddlers or something. But I've done nothing wrong."

"You must've done something," Donnie D said.

"Nothing to deserve this."

Donnie D said nothing. He just stood there, staring, almost stoic. But there was a conflict in his eyes. There was a hint of panic. It wasn't nerves. It was more like a fear that once he crossed this line, he might never come back from it.

Donnie D wasn't a leader. He wasn't a decision-maker. He was a follower.

"I know what you're thinking. I get it. You feel you gotta prove yourself to the boss?" Mickey said. He breathed heavily between words. The hours of digging exhausted him. His knees and back ached from the constant bending.

Donnie D didn't respond. He leaned against a tree stump. The

.38 Special stayed in his hand, aimed at the ground. He stared at Mickey, but said nothing.

Mickey wondered if anyone was even home. Time was running out. The grave was deep enough now to bury him. It was time to be bold. He tried to stay calm, to keep his fear to himself. He said, "Think about it. How will they know? I can disappear—tell them I'm dead. Tell them you went through with it."

Donnie D tilted his head and said, "Keep digging."

Mickey's shoulders slumped. He turned back to the hole and shoveled more dirt onto the pile. He stood in the grave and stared at the ground—his final resting place. He dug more and more, the hole growing deeper with each scoop of dirt.

Donnie D finally pushed off the tree stump. He said, "Okay, that's good." He walked to Mickey and pointed the .38 Special at him. "Toss the shovel out."

Mickey stopped digging. He felt a surge of adrenaline from the fear that this was it—his final moments. He tossed out the shovel and stood in his own grave.

Donnie D walked to him, stopped, and stuck the gun in his face. He asked, "Got any last words?"

Mickey threw his hands up and begged, "No, man! Please! Wait!"

Donnie D paused and waited for Mickey to say his last words. But Mickey said nothing. He stood there trembling, not knowing what to do. Waves from Lake Michigan lapped against the shoreline. The sound filled the silence.

Donnie D thumbed back the hammer on the gun.

Mickey said, "Wait, man! I've got connections. I can disappear. I know people. I can get a new ID and the works. And I got a place to go where no one will ever find me. My stepdad runs a garage in Nebraska. We're close. I can vanish. No one will ever know. Just let me walk, and you can tell them you buried me. Nobody comes out here, right? How will anyone ever know?"

Donnie D said, "I can't do that. I'm sorry." He stared at Mickey, aiming down the barrel. Mickey figured this was it. He squeezed his eyes shut and waited for death. He waited for the gunshot. A long minute passed. But there was no gunshot. Mickey slow-opened his eyes and peeked out.

Donnie D stood in the same position, still staring down the barrel. Mickey saw the whites of his eyes. But he didn't pull the trigger. Instead, his hand trembled, shaking the gun, like he was having second thoughts.

Mickey said, "Please. I know you're not a killer. I know you don't want this."

Donnie D said nothing.

Mickey said, "Just tell them you did it. What? Do you need proof? What proof do you need that you killed me?"

Tears formed in Donnie D's eyes, but he didn't cry. He muttered, "Ring finger."

Reluctantly, Mickey said, "We can do that. Take it. Take my finger. Bring it back to them and just tell them you did it." He stared back past the barrel at Donnie D, his eyes pleading. He didn't want to lose a finger, but it was better than losing his life.

Donnie D said, "I'm sorry. I have to!" He squeezed the trigger. The gunshot echoed out across the dunes and out over the lake. Seconds later, the sound died away. Thirty minutes after that, they pushed the dirt back over the grave. Donnie D patted the dirt with his feet to pack it in.

Ten minutes after that he got back into the Chevy Bel Air and drove back to the interstate, and headed back to Chicago to tell his boss it was done. During the drive back, Donnie D glanced down at a bloody handkerchief in the seat next to him. They wrapped it around the severed finger of Mickey Fog Eyes.

CHAPTER 4

The old man accidentally pulled the trigger. The shotgun boomed in the night's stillness, nearly killing Widow. But a split second before, Widow ripped the shotgun upward and away, forcing the old man's hand. After the boom, he snatched the gun away.

Ripping firearms from guys aiming them at him was something Widow was well-versed in. He ducked down to the right and yanked the weapon up, anticipating the shot and saving his life. The shotgun fired. Widow felt it in his eardrums. Like his fists, his eardrums had developed a thickness, combined with his battle experience, and stopped them from bursting from the close-range gunfire. But his ears rang.

The gunshot echoed over the landscape. Widow couldn't hear it through the ringing in his ears. But it wasn't just him. After the shotgun blast and the muzzle flash, both men stood in a ringing silence.

The old man, though, had been half-deaf before this. He'd already fired three times earlier. That explained why he hadn't heard Widow creeping up behind him—his ears were still ringing from those first blasts. Age didn't help. He was old. His hearing was probably shot long before tonight.

They waited for the ringing in their heads to fade. Widow had been close to a lot of gunfire in his life. Gunfire is loud. It damages hearing—at least temporarily. He was no stranger to it. At least this blast had been out in the open. At close range, a shotgun could be deafening. This one came close.

A double-barrel wasn't some weak balloon pop. It was loud. Thunderous. Unforgettable. It shook most people to their core. But not Widow. And not the old man.

Widow stayed quiet for a long beat, letting his hearing return. He presumed the old guy needed time to recover as well. But he thought, *What the hell are you doing out here alone?*

That killer-look creeped into the old guy's eyes again. Only this time, it appeared terrified, and not selfishly. It was more like the killer feared for the safety of someone else.

What's going on with him? Widow wondered. It was like the old guy had multiple personalities. He slipped in and out of the two different men.

The old guy glanced at the shotgun, now in Widow's hands, and stepped back. He threw his hands up, as if Widow was going to reverse-aim the shotgun, shove it into the old guy's chest, and pull the trigger. He begged, "Please, if you shoot me, let her go first. Just don't hurt her. She has nothing to do with it. It was all me. The whole thing was my idea. I tricked her."

Widow lowered the shotgun, flipped the break-open lever, and dumped the two spent shell casings into his open palm. He pocketed them, left the weapon broken open, and held it one-handed at his side.

Staring at the old man, Widow suspected he wasn't all there, like he was missing a step. Just by looking at him, anyone would come to the same conclusion. He was out in the middle of nowhere, at night, shouting at no one, and shooting at nothing. But it was more than just the bizarre scene. The old man was shoeless, dressed in pajama bottoms, and he had already forgotten that his shotgun was out of shells.

There was one more telling detail about him. In his eyes, Widow saw fear mixed with confusion. Even though Widow had disarmed many men intent on shooting him, this time felt different. Normally, after ripping a weapon away, he responded with extreme violence, a brutal retaliation. He needed to send a clear message: if you point a gun at him, you'd better not miss.

This time, Widow didn't do that. Sure, he was upset about nearly being murdered. His heart pounded from a combination of survival instincts and gas station coffee. *Maybe I should've gone for the decaf,* Widow thought.

His instincts screamed for him to kill this guy. His training pulled him to slam the shotgun across the guy's head. Old or not, losing his marbles or not, the old guy had one personality that was dangerous and unpredictable. Friendly fire or enemy fire was still gunfire. Either way, he was trained to take out threats. And this old guy's killer side was a threat.

But Widow didn't kill the guy. He didn't crush the old guy's head in with the shotgun. Instead, he followed his heart, his empathy, and exercised restraint. This time, he returned to his would-be killer with compassion. Calmly, he asked, "Sir, what's your name?" The response confirmed Widow's suspicions.

The old man stared at him, mouth opening as if to speak, but no words came out. That killer-look faded from his eyes again. Only this time, Widow was certain it wasn't returning anytime soon.

"What's your name?" Widow repeated. Staying calm. Staying cool.

The old guy faltered, the answer seemingly on the tip of his tongue, yet he couldn't quite articulate it. Around them, icy silence prevailed. Fear washed over the old man, doubling as he trembled with the realization of the truth—a truth that terrified him. Finally, he whispered, "I can't remember."

Widow asked, "Do you have a wallet on you? Maybe it's got some identification in it?"

The old guy patted his pockets and said, "I don't think so."

"What about a phone?"

The old guy stared at him vacantly. He asked, "Why would I carry a phone on me? Where would I plug it in?"

Oh boy, Widow thought, and went quiet.

The old guy's eyes darted from side to side, like he was looking for help, a sign, or a landmark that he could recognize. It was useless. There was nothing around them but darkness and highway. Widow wasn't sure if he was completely blank on everything in his life, or if it was simply too dark to see a landmark to recognize.

Widow stayed quiet, carefully trying to think of what to say next.

Suddenly, the old guy's brain switched gears without him, and the fear subsided. He asked, "Do I know you?"

Widow stayed quiet, looking around to see if there was anyone out there looking for the old guy. But he saw no one. No car lights on the road. His ears returned to normal. He listened. But there was nothing. No voices shouting out in the cornfields for the old guy. No search parties. No concerned family members. Nothing.

The old guy asked, "Do you know me?"

Widow said, "I've never seen you before."

"Where am I?"

"You were just standing over there," Widow said, and pointed, "shouting into the darkness."

The old man glanced at the spot Widow pointed to, staring blankly. There was nothing there, just vast, empty cornfields. His expression revealed no recognition, no sign that the location meant anything to him. Then, confusion deepening, the old man asked, "I was? Is that your land over there?" He pointed into the darkness, toward the distant cornfield.

"No, sir. I'm not from here. I was just passing through and saw you on the side of the road."

"Oh, then you don't know where I am?"

Widow had already covered that, but the old guy forgot again. Widow asked, "Aren't you from Tent Hills?"

The old guy's eyes perked up. He said, "Sounds familiar."

"Come on. Let's see if we can retrace your steps. Maybe we can find someone who knows you," Widow said, and reached out to the old guy, like he was going to grab him by the arm, but he didn't. Instead, Widow gestured for the old guy to go toward Tent Hills, leaving the smiling billboard behind them.

CHAPTER 5

The old man slogged through the snow, heading up the road toward Tent Hills. Widow followed, careful not to rush him. Their progress was slow, but soon there was a glimmer of hope. About twenty minutes into their walk, on the shoulder, Widow spotted a set of unusual footprints coming from the direction they were heading. These weren't typical shoe prints but imprints of feet in socks, worn and holey—clearly belonging to the old man. Widow gently steered the old man toward the shoulder, pointed at the footprints, and said, "Those have got to be yours. Let's follow them. They'll lead us to where you came from."

The old man agreed, though he seemed hesitant, as if lost.

They followed the footprints in the snow over the next hill for about twenty meters until a clue emerged. Widow noticed a pickup truck parked on the side of the road, facing the wrong way in its lane. Positioned on the opposite shoulder, the truck confronted them with its headlights on, casting an eerie glow in the stillness. The driver's side door was wide open, and although the engine was off, the soft hum of classic rock music filled the air from the speakers.

Widow noted the old man's footprints in the snow leading back to the truck—clearly, this was his starting point. The thought of the old man driving himself here in his current state troubled Widow. As they passed through the pickup's headlights, the footprints disappeared at the open driver's side door. The original footprint marked the spot where the old guy climbed down from the truck and started his walk out into the frosty night.

Widow led the old man to the driver's side of the truck, stopped, and gestured for him to stay put. He then asked, "Do you recognize this truck?"

The old guy looked the truck over and scratched his head nervously. He said, "Um. Maybe. I'm not sure. I always wanted a truck like this."

Widow went to the truck and peered in. Sure enough. The keys dangled from the ignition. There was no one in the truck and no one around. Widow popped a button on the door to unlock all the doors. He got out and led the old guy to the passenger side door and opened it. "Okay, get in," he said.

"Is this your truck?"

"No. It's yours," Widow said, and thought, *I hope.* It was a safe bet it belonged to the old guy since he drove it here. Unless he had stolen it?

After Widow helped the old guy into the passenger side and closed the door, he circled around the truck's nose to the driver's side. He realized the truck could be stolen—there was no way Nebraska would issue a driver's license to the old man in his current state unless it was from before his decline.

Before climbing in, Widow opened the rear door, placed the shotgun and empty shells on the seat, then moved to the front, slid the seat all the way back—the old guy had it pushed nearly to the steering wheel. He climbed in, shut the door, started the engine, killed the music, and cranked up the heater.

The old guy buckled his seatbelt and said, "Buckle your seatbelt or pay the piper. My son always says that to me."

Widow stared at him and asked, "You got a son?"

"Oh yeah, want to see a picture?" the old guy asked, reaching into his inner coat pocket. He fished around in there for a long minute and came out with nothing. He stared at his empty hand in distress. He searched his other pockets and said, "Oh no. Where did I put my wallet?"

"What's your son's name?"

The old guy paused, stopped searching for the wallet that wasn't on him, and stared out the windshield at the dark, lonely road. He scratched his chin whiskers and said, "Eddie? No, that's not right."

Widow leaned across the center console, startling the old guy. Widow grabbed the passenger side vents and pointed them downward to get hot air blowing into the footwell for the old guy's cold bare feet. Then he popped the glovebox open and dug around inside. He came out with the truck's registration and peeked at the name.

The old guy said, "Billie? No, that's probably not it."

Widow took the registration out, closed the glovebox, sat upright in the driver's seat, and read the name on the registration aloud. He said, "Matthew James Elton."

"Matty! That's his name. Matty...James."

"That makes you Elton?"

"Like the singer? I'm Elton John?"

"I think Elton's your last name."

The old guy paused a long beat and said, "I think I remember my name. It's John."

"Your name's John Elton?"

"Yeah."

Widow smiled but stayed quiet. The old guy stared out the windshield, muttering what he thought was his name to himself over and over. Widow studied the registration. Some US states list the name and address of the vehicle's owner. Nebraska was one of them. He saw the address, didn't ask the old guy if he recognized it. Instead, he accessed the truck's smart computer and started to input the address into the navigation system, but it turned out he didn't have to. The address was already there, listed as Home.

Widow clicked a few icons and the truck's navigation system plotted the route back to Elton's home. It was less than a mile up the road. Widow U-turned the truck around in the lane. No one was coming from any direction. He drove them to the address on the truck's navigation system.

The old guy stared out the window, occasionally pointing at cornfields and whispering, "That looks familiar." But he didn't actually recognize any of it. It all looked familiar. It was cornfields. They all look the same.

Widow drove until the truck's nav system indicated they were coming up on a turn. He stared through the windshield but saw no sign of a turn. He flicked the high beams on and saw the first sign of something other than darkness and cornfields. There was an old, ragged scarecrow up on a pole out in the field on the right.

The old man squinted out the passenger's window and stared at it. He said, "I think I know that gentleman."

The truck's map blinked, telling Widow to turn now. He slowed the truck and pulled off to the shoulder. Finally, there was a sign of hope. The truck's high beams washed over a large black mailbox. Next to it was the entrance to a farm driveway.

Widow pulled into the driveway and took the track slow. Driving along, Widow saw huge farming equipment. A combine harvester rested out in the fields, like a giant sleeping animal. A large tractor was parked near a barn. Animal pens stood around the farm, near the barn. The furthest from the barn was a large round pen, where they could break in horses. Closer to the barn were a chicken coop, a sheepfold, and a goat pen. Widow saw the pens and grazing paddocks, but no animals in sight. They were probably put up in the barn to get out of the cold night.

Dogs barked from inside the house. Widow couldn't see them, but they sounded big.

There was a blue two-story farmhouse with a large front porch, complete with a porch swing dangling from chains at one end. The entire scene embodied the ideal of American country life, as if plucked from a Norman Rockwell painting. It appeared as though the old man had set out with a dream of a perfect family farm life—and unmistakably achieved it.

A porch light clicked on as if someone flipped it on as they were riding up. The dogs' barks woke up the house's residents.

Widow followed the driveway as it curved past the barn's entrance and looped back to the road, positioning the truck's nose toward the exit. The headlights washed over the barn, the farmhouse, and the surrounding cornfields.

Widow parked the truck and asked, "Does any of this look familiar to you?"

The old guy studied the surroundings. Hesitantly, he said, "I… think so. I mean, it might be. But this looks like Nebraska."

"It is Nebraska."

John Elton turned and stared at Widow. He said, "But I live in Chicago."

Widow started to say something to that but drew a blank. Just then, lights switched on upstairs in the house. Widow paused, glancing up at an upstairs window where the lights were now on. A curtain flapped open and quickly closed. A dark figure peeked down. A moment later, more porch lights flicked on.

Widow switched the ignition off, took out the keys, and exited the truck. He stopped in front and stood tall in the headlights.

The farmhouse's front door swung open, light spilling out, and three adult-sized figures emerged. A child-sized figure trailed after them, clinging to the last adult. Inside, multiple dogs barked furiously, as if trying to raise the dead—a crucial part of their role on the farm. Beyond being beloved family pets, these dogs were protectors of the family and livestock, often patrolling the perimeter of the animals' paddocks to sniff out would-be predators like coyotes, snakes, and birds of prey.

Widow's thoughts drifted to Joanie, the loyal dog from the Sutton farm in Missouri. As he remembered her, he couldn't help but think of Nora and the girls, too. He wondered where they were now. Had they stayed in Iron Crossing? Would he ever see them again? Part of him hoped so.

The first figure stepped out onto the porch in front of the rest. It was a man. He called out, "Who's there?"

The man's face came into view under the porch light. Widow saw he looked just like the old guy, only thirty years younger. Widow called back, "Sorry to wake you folks. Are you Matthew Elton?"

Elton stepped off the porch and halted in the walkway leading to the house. He raised a hand to shield his eyes, as if trying to see past bright sunlight, though it was only the truck's headlights. In his other hand, he gripped a handgun at his side. His caution was understandable—it was after midnight in Nebraska, and anything could happen.

Elton squinted against the glare and called out, "I'm Elton. Who are you, coming to our farm in the middle of the night?"

Widow realized he had left the truck's high beams on—a stupid mistake, but then, he seldom drove. The intense brightness blinded Elton, preventing him from seeing Widow or his own steps clearly.

Widow responded, "Sorry about the time and the bright lights, Mr. Elton. It's not my truck. I didn't realize they were on."

"Whose truck is it?" Elton asked, slipping his trigger finger into the shooting position. Widow noticed the quick, slight movement but said nothing about it.

"I think it's your truck."

Apprehensively, Elton sidestepped, trying to find a position where the lights weren't blinding him. He said, "No, my truck's parked by the barn." He didn't glance toward the barn to confirm this because he didn't want to take his eyes off Widow—that would be a major mistake. At this moment, Matty had the upper hand. He had a gun and Widow was unarmed. Giving Widow a moment unchecked could disrupt that dynamic. As the man of the house, responsible for his family's safety, Matty couldn't afford to look away.

Then, one figure behind him stepped into the porch light—it wasn't an adult, but a teenage boy. The boy said, "Dad, your truck's not at the barn." This revelation was like dousing gasoline on Matty's natural protective instincts, setting them ablaze. He had to confirm his son's claim, forcing him to take his eyes off Widow for a crucial moment.

Watchfully, Elton glanced at the barn, saw no truck parked there, and quickly refocused on Widow. Then he raised his gun, pointed it at Widow, and demanded, "Sir, you better start explaining what you're doing with my truck!"

The woman on the porch exclaimed, "Matty!" Her voice was filled with fear, responding to Matty pointing a gun at another man. Matty didn't divert his aim from Widow to acknowledge her. His focus stayed sharply on Widow; the gun firmly trained on him.

Widow stayed calm and still. He kept his hands at his sides. He began, "Mr. Elton, I didn't steal…"

Before Widow could finish, John Elton opened the passenger door and hopped out. Matty froze, watching the scene unfold. Though the headlight's glare prevented him from seeing his father clearly, he detected the movement, heard the door swing open, and the scrape of the old man's feet across the snow. They all did.

John Elton stepped out and away from the truck, looked at his family, and said, "This place reminds me of a farm I wanted to buy with my wife. I think she'll still love it. It'll make a great surprise for her. Is it for sale?"

Nearly simultaneously, the Eltons called to the old guy with various terms of endearment. Matty and a woman standing on the porch called out, "Dad?"

The teenage boy and the child-sized figure said, "Papa?"

Matty Elton lowered his gun and moved toward his father, embracing the old man with his free arm. The children and the woman descended from the porch to join in, crowding around John like a football team in a huddle. They were all dressed in coats over their pajamas, the woman and Matty in house slippers, while the kids were barefoot.

Meanwhile, Widow returned to the truck to switch the high beams to regular lights. Standing back in the softened glow, he watched the family embrace. Thoughts of Nora Sutton and her girls came to him. It couldn't be helped. A wave of longing spilled over him, stirring a deep-seated yearning for a warmth he suspected he might never know again. The moment was brief yet profound, like the thought of a nuclear blast rather than the real thing. Nora's face flashed across his mind—a heartbreaking reminder of what might have been.

Matty left his father and walked to Widow. The truck's headlights revealed more of his details. Matty Elton had his father's ears and thick hair, only his hair was blond and not aged white. He didn't have the same eyes. His were green, probably from his mother.

The rest of the family led the confused old man back to the porch. Matty stopped short of Widow and said, "Oh my God! Thank you so much! Where did you find him?"

"He was out on the road. When I talked to him, he seemed disoriented. So I walked with him awhile, trying to find a clue. I found your truck just up the road from where I encountered him, and just put two and two together."

Matty's face was both grateful, terrified, and embarrassed that he'd pointed a gun at the man trying to return his father to him. He also felt hopeful. The hopeful part injected a question in his mind. He asked, "Did he tell you where we live?"

"I got your address off your truck's registration."

Matty nodded, disappointed. Widow supposed he hoped his father would remember where he lived. Widow got the impression this family hoped for a miracle.

Matty approached Widow and put a hand out to him. Matty said, "Thank you, sir, for getting him back to us. I can't believe it. He's never snuck out like this before."

Widow shook Elton's hand and asked, "How long's he been like this?"

They stopped shaking hands and Matty said, "It's been less than a year now. One day he's normal, and the next he forgets little things. Then it gets worse. The weird part is it seems to happen at night more than in the day. But whenever it happens, sometimes he just forgets where he is. Other times he can't even remember his own name. He forgets who we are. It's..." He paused and sighed. "Hard."

Widow said, "I can imagine. I'm very sorry."

Matty pocketed the gun in his coat and said, "I can't believe we never heard the truck starting up." But Widow wasn't surprised. Ranchers all over the world sleep deeply at midnight because they wake up super early to start their days. It's not that far-fetched to sleep through someone driving off in your truck. Since the old man lived with them, the dogs didn't bark at him because they knew him.

While Widow was speaking, the woman left the old guy with the kids and appeared at Matty's side. She was also blond, but with blue eyes. She was younger than Matty by a decade. She was slender with ivory skin. Her hair was long and straight. She said, "We're lucky Dad didn't run into someone else or off the road and hurt himself."

Matty Elton's face lit up in surprise as the thought hadn't occurred to him. He said, "Yes! Absolutely!"

Widow stayed quiet.

Matty said, "I'm sorry, this is my wife Elsa and I'm Matt Elton."

"We call him Matty," Elsa interjected, and offered her hand to Widow as well.

Gently, Widow took her hand and shook it, giving her a head nod, like he was tipping an invisible hat to her. He said, "It's a pleasure, ma'am. I'm sorry to wake you all at this hour."

"Don't be silly. We're grateful that you brought Dad back to us," Elsa said, and she took her hand back.

Matty said, "Thanks for bringing back my truck, too. And sorry about pointing a gun at you."

"Nothing to be sorry about. It's completely understandable, considering the time of night," Widow said. He paused a beat and added, "There's something else you should know, too."

Elsa asked, "What's that?"

"Let me show you," Widow said, turned, and led them back to the truck. They followed. He opened the rear door, reached in, and pulled out the shotgun. He showed it to them and said, "Your dad was out on the road with this." Widow handed the shotgun to Matty.

Both Elsa and Matty's eyes widened, realizing the danger their dad might've been in if Widow hadn't come along when he did.

Elsa gasped, "Oh, wow!"

Matty, perplexed, took the gun from Widow. "No?" He inspected it. "This is my gun."

Elsa said, "At least it was empty. He could've shot someone with it. Or hurt himself."

Widow grabbed the empty casings and showed them to the Eltons. "He nearly shot me with it," he said. His tone wasn't accusatory or seeking sympathy; instead, it conveyed a serious warning. He wanted them to realize the importance of tightening their firearm security protocols at home.

Both Matty and Elsa's mouths dropped open in shock and fear. Elsa asked, "Are you okay?"

"Yes, ma'am. He fired the shells, but hit no one. There was no one around."

"Except you," Matty said.

"You could've been killed," she added.

Widow said, "No, ma'am. I was never in any real danger. Trust me. I'm just glad I could bring John home to you. He's safe now."

Elsa said, "No more of this sir and ma'am nonsense. Call me Elsa, and he's Matty. No need to go by cordiality. You saved our dad's life. That puts you above a stranger in our eyes."

Widow stayed quiet.

Matty nodded and asked, "What's your name?"

Widow introduced himself, and they engaged in the usual question-and-answer session that ensued whenever people discovered he went by his last name.

Matty said, "Let's get in and I'll drive you back to your truck."

Widow said, "I don't have a truck."

"Really? Your car then," Matty said, looking Widow up and down as if he was taking in Widow's large stature for the first time. "I never would've pegged you for a car guy."

"I don't own a vehicle. I don't even have a driver's license."

Matty and Elsa glanced at each other in disbelief. She asked, "Oh, were you just out walking?"

Widow nodded and said, "I was heading to Tent Hills."

"Where did you come from?" Matty asked.

"From the south."

The Eltons glanced at each other. Elsa asked, "Where do you live, Mr. Widow?"

"I just go by Widow, like in the Navy. No mister required."

"Oh, okay. Where do you live, Widow?" she asked.

"I live where I am."

Matty looked over Widow's clothes, hesitated, like he was about to ask a sensitive question. He asked, "Are you homeless?"

Widow shrugged and said, "Technically, yes, but not in the way you mean. I choose to live this way. I'm a drifter, not a man who's down on his luck. I'm not impoverished. I have a bank account. There's enough money in it to get me by."

They both stared at him, speechless.

Widow added, "I like to think of myself more as a man of leisure."

"So, what? You just go from place to place, walking?" Elsa asked.

"I walk, hitchhike, take trains, and sometimes I fly. It all depends on the situation," Widow replied.

"Huh," Matty said. "Well, I can give you a ride to town."

"That'd be nice."

"Sure, it seems like the least we can do for you."

Elsa tugged at her husband's arm, pulling him away from Widow. She whispered, "Let me talk to you for a minute." Matty looked into her eyes, deciphering the unspoken words that long-married couples often share. The two stepped away to talk in hushed tones. Meanwhile, Widow stayed quiet, his gaze shifting back to the porch where the two boys were leading their grandfather back into the house. They struggled to keep the dogs from bolting outside—two large canines, all white and fur, barking at Widow through the open doorway. He caught only a brief glimpse of them. It was too short for him to categorize the breed. They looked imposing, each easily weighing over a hundred pounds.

A moment later, they stepped back to Widow. Elsa stood behind Matty, who asked, "Widow, what're you going to do in Tent Hills? Do you have family there?"

Widow shrugged and said, "No family. I'll probably check into a motel, take a shower, and wait for morning before I know what I'll do next."

"We'd like it if you stayed with us," Matty said.

Widow stayed quiet.

Elsa said, "We insist on it. It's late at night. It's cold, and the town is still a few miles north. Stay with us. Matty can take you to town in the morning."

Matty added, "It might be hard for you to get a room this time of night in town."

Widow glanced at Matty to see if there was any reservation on his face about this offer. But there was none. It was genuine. Widow said, "Okay. I'll stay. Thank you. I can be out of your hair in the morning."

Elsa smiled and took Widow by the arm, ordered Matty to park the truck and get inside, and led Widow to the porch.

She called out to her teenager and ordered him to put the dogs in their room, which he did. After, she led Widow indoors and introduced him to the kids and to John again, in case he forgot. There were two sons, eight and sixteen, a large age gap, which Elsa didn't explain and Widow didn't ask about. The younger son's name was T.J. and the older was Matthew Adam Junior, but he insisted Widow just call him Adam. He said, "Only my father calls me Junior, whenever he's going to get on my case about something."

Adam called Widow by his last name when meeting him. Elsa corrected him. "It's Mr. Widow to you."

Trying to stick to his preference, Widow said, "That's not necessary."

"I want them to call you Mr. Widow. In this house, we teach our kids to respect their elders," Elsa said.

Widow nodded and didn't argue with that. He knew better than to do that. He too knew a thing or two about being taught proper manners.

For a moment, John seemed to forget Widow's name altogether. He had forgotten Widow since riding with him in the truck and since nearly blowing his head off with the shotgun.

The old guy introduced himself to Widow again, like they were meeting for the first time, but couldn't recall his name. He stood there, stumped, until Elsa gently reminded him. She eased him into it and then introduced John to Widow. She said, "Widow, this is our grandpa, John Elton."

He shook the hand of the man who had nearly shot him to death. John acted like it was the first time he ever laid eyes on Widow. And Widow returned the same response with a newness, like a second chance. Widow seemed to have never met him before. They were only now meeting for the first time. Never had they seen each other before. Never had John pointed a gun at Widow.

It was all a memory for Widow. But it was all a forgotten dream for John.

The inside of the Elton house was warm and cozy. They put Widow in a downstairs guest bedroom. The only other person on the floor was John. He lived in a custom suite on the other side of the house from Widow.

Widow left undisturbed for the rest of the night, except for the dogs. They both sniffed and pawed at his door until they fell asleep in front of it.

Widow showered, brushed his teeth, and lay naked on a king-sized bed and stared at the ceiling.

He thought about how the old guy's name was John Elton—like Elton John's name backward. *Stranger things happen.* Widow knew that for a fact. He had seen a lot of strange things while living a life of constantly being out on the road. He'd have it no other way.

Skeptics might doubt all the strange things he'd seen and experienced. But the more time people spend out in the wild, the wilder things they experience. That fact gave Widow more opportunity than most. Widow lived on the open road. He lived in the wild. He was wild.

Perhaps that was why it'd never work out for him and Nora. Widow wasn't for the stay-at-home life. Maybe he'd been born into a home, but not anymore. He could never go back. Not now. He wasn't the domesticated kind.

Most of the night, Widow stayed awake, thinking. He wasn't much for plans, but sometimes he had to have a game plan for which direction to go. Otherwise, he could end up lost in the middle of nowhere, going nowhere. Or worse, he might end up going in circles, worse than going nowhere. Going nowhere exerts little energy.

Widow changed course. Tomorrow, he'll head south to Texas. He'd been there before. Maybe he'll go southeast to Florida. He'd been there too.

Miami sounded nice. It would be a welcomed change, a stark contrast to Nebraska's cornfields, where he was nearly killed by a shotgun.

He chuckled. Near-death experiences were only funny in the rearview mirror. Memories were funny that way. Funny how they could seem so real, yet be completely misremembered.

Widow thought about that for a minute, lying in bed, until his mind settled and his heart rate slowed. He let his mind drift into his memories. Nights back in Missouri replayed in his head—nights with Nora.

CHAPTER 6

At dawn, a rooster crowed, waking Widow for the day. But that wasn't the only thing that woke him. He smelled something. It came from the house's downstairs, down the hall from him. It smelled enticing. He sniffed the air and his primitive brain instantly identified the aromas. It came from the kitchen. Bacon sizzled in a frying pan. Eggs crackled in oil in another pan. Coffee brewed from a drip machine into a coffeepot.

The smells merged, rising through the corridors of the Elton house, and penetrating the crack under Widow's door. It filled his nose.

The rooster's crow filled his ears. The Elton ranch's everyday early morning events merged to create the perfect morning storm.

It woke Widow. He opened his eyes and glanced out a nearby window as the rooster crowed again. Deep breaths filled his lungs as he stretched in bed, inhaling the aroma of breakfast cooking nearby. Among the scents, two caught his attention. The dominant was the alluring smell of the frying bacon—a favorite for most breakfast lovers. It was a favorite of Widow's, too.

However, Widow wasn't like most. Frying bacon wasn't his all-time favorite early morning smell. It was up there for sure —top ten. But not in the number one slot. That belonged to his greatest addiction. Coffee brewed, and that was what called to him, like a meth addict sitting outside a meth lab. The scent strong-armed him out of bed. Before he realized it, he stood and sniffed the air like a predator on the scent of its prey.

As the rooster crowed once more, a youthful voice from the bedroom above sleepily opened a window and called out to the bird. It was T.J., the eight-year-old, who groggily shouted, "Clucky, shut up!"

Clucky was the rooster's name, Widow figured. Amazingly, the bird responded with a single cluck—not the loud morning crow, but a quiet cluck of acknowledgment, as if recognizing the boy's command. After that, Clucky stayed quiet for the rest of the morning.

Widow dressed in his thrift store clothes, minus his boots and the gas station puffer coat. His boots were parked in a mudroom downstairs, and the coat hung on a hook on the wall above them.

Widow made the bed meticulously, ensuring the room was as orderly as if he were still in the Navy, awaiting a bunk inspection from his commanding officer. Everything was returned to the pristine condition in which he'd found it.

After pocketing his toothbrush from the bathroom, Widow left the guest bedroom. Upon opening the door, two well-trained sentries greeted him. They were positioned just outside. Great Pyrenees brothers—almost twins in their imposing, all-white, furry appearance. They sat at attention, giving Widow looks that blended warmth with watchful wariness.

Effective guards. Economical too. They worked for treats and belly rubs, instead of military pay.

Widow paused in the doorway and acknowledged them. "Good boys," he said.

They responded with low growls, snarling back at him. He stared into their eyes. They held his gaze. Gunslingers squaring off before a duel—two against one.

Adam emerged from his bedroom, already dressed for the day. He descended the stairs and called the dogs by name. They whined but complied, reluctantly abandoning their posts to shuffle around the corner.

"Thanks, kid," Widow said.

"No problem, Mr. Widow," Adam said, paused, and added, "Good morning, sir."

"Good morning."

Adam led Widow from the hall to the kitchen, where the family sat at the breakfast nook by a window. With Widow adding one more to the group, Adam took to the kitchen bar next to his brother. John Elton sat in the nook, next to Matty, and Elsa stood, placing dishes stacked with breakfast foods in front of the men. She turned to see Widow and her elder son enter the kitchen.

Widow said, "Good morning, everybody."

Most of the family responded in kind, including John. Widow watched him. Matty sat next to his father, patiently helping him if he needed it. But John didn't need any help. There was a slight tremor in his hand as he slurped some coffee from a mug, but he managed it on his own.

John glanced up at Widow and said, "It's good to see you again. Thank you for bringing me home last night."

Without thinking, Widow blurted out, "You remember me?" He glanced at Matty, realizing it may have been insensitive to utter the question like that. He didn't know the family dynamics. It was possible that Matty and Elsa had some kind of routine with John.

Apparently, there was no routine. He picked up no signals to feel apologetic or embarrassed. Matty was the one who nearly answered for his father, but he didn't. He waited.

Slowly, John said, "I don't remember much. I'm told I nearly shot you. For that, I'm very sorry. But I remember seeing you in front of the house last night. I remember some things and can't recall others."

Matty said, "Father only just started having lapses in memory."

"I'm good most of the time. It's only sometimes," John said. "Anyway, thank you for helping me out."

"It was my pleasure, sir," Widow said, paused and added, "You have a beautiful family."

John said, "Oh, yes. They're the best." With that, he went back to eating bacon.

Widow sniffed the air and said, "Everything smells good."

"Have a seat. I'll fix you a plate," Elsa said.

Just then, John coughed a few times. Both Elsa and Matty watched him. Time stood still. Matty rubbed John's back, like he was easing the old man back to breathing properly.

A little tetchy, John snapped, "I'm okay. Go back to your breakfasts."

Matty pulled away, leaned toward John, and said, "We're just worried about you, Dad."

Elsa paused a beat, waiting for John to say more. He repeated, "I'm okay." Everyone fell silent for a long minute.

Widow said, "I really should be on my way and get out of your hair. You've already been so gracious to offer me a room for the night."

"Nonsense. Sit down. You must be starving. And I won't take no for an answer," Elsa said. She pointed Widow to a spot at the nook.

Matty scooted in more, giving Widow some room at the table. He beckoned Widow to join. But Widow assessed the legroom, low-level tabletop, and the mechanics it would take for him to squeeze into the nook, and said, "I don't think I can fit there. I'll stand at the bar, next to the boys."

Matty put a forkful of scrambled eggs down, and called for one of the boys to volunteer to move to the nook with them. The boys hissed and moaned as younger generations often do. Young people don't like to have their routines interrupted by a sense of civility. Then again, neither do old people. But one of them had to do it. So the brothers argued for a moment about who would give up their seat.

T.J. made the point that he was already comfortable and eating, while Adam had only just sat down. Adam claimed he was taller than T.J. Therefore, he would also be cramped in the nook, even though he was shorter than both his father and grandfather, who both fit in the nook just fine.

T.J. said, "You're not tall! Stop pretending!"

"I'm five-ten, dweeb!"

"In your dreams! You're barely five-seven! You only pretend

to be five-ten so you can feed your delusion that Catie Bosewicky would ever date you."

"Shut up, you little turd. Catie Bosewicky isn't my type!" Adam said. Which was both true and a lie. Catie Bosewicky was everybody's type—homecoming queen, head cheerleader, the works. But Adam already had a girlfriend. The rest of the Eltons just didn't know about her. He planned to keep it that way.

Matty said, "Junior! Stop arguing with your brother and join us!"

Adam gave his brother a sideways look, which was returned in kind. Defeatedly, Adam eased off the stool. But Matty said, "T.J., you too!"

"But Dad, I'm already eating! Why do I have to move?"

"Get over here and don't make me ask twice!"

With that, T.J. obeyed his father, picked up his plate, juice and silverware, and followed his older brother over to the breakfast nook—sitting with the other men in his family.

Widow thanked the boys, and took up one of the abandoned bar stools. He scooted the other stool over a bit, just to give himself enough room to squeeze in. He made himself comfortable, watched Elsa, and smiled. He tried not to ogle the food, but the fresh coffee was harder. He nearly salivated staring at the pot.

Elsa made a big plate with a bit of everything, pulled a fresh set of silverware out of a drawer, and set it all down before Widow. He thanked her. Then, with a tactical hint, he remarked on how good the coffee smelled. It was a clear ploy, but his love for coffee ran deep enough to warrant any maneuver—after all, all's fair in love and war.

Elsa smiled and offered him a cup. He accepted it—black— which he gulped down in seconds. She asked if he wanted another. Widow replied with a big, "Yes, ma'am! Please!"

Elsa poured him another. This time, Widow slowed down on drinking it, so Elsa could get her own breakfast going. She made herself a plate and sat at the bar next to him. They chatted while they ate. Occasionally, their conversation spilled over into the nook with the men.

Widow learned that Elsa and Matty both grew up in Nebraska. All the local boys chased after her, and she admitted to dating the football team's quarterback. They were a popular couple, elected king and queen of the homecoming dance junior and senior year. She was also at the top of her class in high school. Then she revealed that the reason she was at the top of her class was because Matty tutored her in the one subject she was no good at—math. She credited him for making her valedictorian. Over the years of tutoring sessions, she grew quite attached to him.

Eventually, she tried college, making it one entire year before deciding it wasn't for her. Meanwhile, the star quarterback went off to a different college on a football scholarship, which led to their breakup.

Toward the end of her second semester, she felt rudderless. "Like I was just going through the motions, spinning my tires," she told Widow. "I had no goals to graduate. Where all my friends wanted to be lawyers and doctors, I just wanted to live on a farm again." Elsa turned in her chair and glanced at her family.

She said, "Totally by accident, I bumped into Matty at the quad. He went to the same university as I did, and I didn't even know it. He asked me to dinner. We went and never looked back."

"Mom, we've heard this story a million times!" T.J. interjected and rolled his eyes.

Elsa waved him off, turned to Widow and went back to her breakfast. She and Widow continued their conversation, sharing surface level information about themselves. Sometimes their conversations invited the breakfast nook part of her family to add their two cents.

Whenever Matty gave an opinion on something, he'd offer his father the chance to weigh in, like he was trying to keep John a part of reality. Occasionally, John would respond and sometimes he'd ignore them all and stick to his breakfast. But the whole time he seemed to know exactly where he was and who he was speaking to. There was no sign of the confused, lost man Widow had met the night before. Today, John seemed put together and all there. He trembled here and there, but he was an old man. It happens.

Elsa asked Widow questions about his life and background. He gave her the usual stuff, leaving out that he had been a SEAL and an undercover NCIS agent. He just mentioned he was in the Navy for sixteen years before becoming a drifter. Of course, the boys overheard that and asked loads of questions about what life was like on the road, where he didn't have to answer to anyone. Where he could go, where he pleased. T.J. was interested in where the Navy sent Widow. And he asked about different jets and ships Widow had seen. His knowledge of various military hardware was pretty good. When Widow asked him how he knew a lot of it, he said, "Video games, dude."

Elsa corrected, "T.J. It's Mr. Widow."

"Sorry, Mom..."

"And?"

"Mr. Widow," T.J. said, after she stared at him in a way that reminded him of his own mother, which seemed like ancient history now.

More time passed, along with three cups of coffee, which was slow for Widow. But he didn't want to assume he could help himself, and he certainly didn't want to bother Elsa to get him more. So he acted content with what he had.

Widow never spoke directly to John, but observed him. At breakfast, John seemed nearly like a different person. He was still slow, and forgetful, but he knew his name and his son and his grandkids. He engaged in the conversation enough to show that he had his wits about him. He didn't seem like a guy who had some kind of dementia. *It must be early onset*, Widow thought.

The Eltons treated Widow like a guest. Just sharing breakfast with them, he saw their love for each other. They were what many would consider the dream family. When Matty had introduced John to Widow, the old guy acted as if it was the first time they were meeting. The gap in his memory was definitely authentic. He looked at Widow as anyone would a total stranger. John got through the entire breakfast without a hiccup. There were no signs of him having any kind of memory or cognitive issues.

After finishing his breakfast, T.J. asked permission to go outside with John to play among the animals. John smiled at this. His face lit up, like playing with his grandson was his favorite activity in the world. It seemed to be a normal thing between them. They stared at each other. John winked at T.J., like they both shared the same mischievous thought.

Elsa resisted the idea, probably because of what John had done the night before. But Matty asked T.J. what he planned to do. T.J. said they were just going to pretend to ride the tractor. Reluctantly, Matty agreed but warned T.J. to stay away from the horses and leave the tractor turned off. Then he told them to feed the chickens while they were out there. The kid agreed and led his grandpa by the hand away from breakfast. A long moment of them putting on their boots and winter coats passed, and they exited the house. Widow saw them walk by a big window on their way down the porch.

After T.J. and John were gone, Adam got up, cleaned his dishes, walked through the kitchen's doorway, and said, "I'll see you guys later."

"Hold on, mister," Elsa said. "Get your butt back here."

Adam slumped back into the kitchen and curtly asked, "What?"

Alone at the breakfast nook, Matty stared at his son and said, "Don't talk to your mother in that tone!"

Adam took a deep breath and said, "Sorry, Mom."

Elsa asked, "Where're you going?"

"Robbie's picking me up," Adam glanced at the time on his phone and said, "in like two minutes."

Matty said, "She asked you where you're going, not who you're going with."

"We're going into town. A bunch of the guys are helping set up for the Husk-Town Showdown."

Widow arched an eyebrow and wondered, *What's the Husk-Town Showdown?*

Matty said, "Don't you have homework?"

"Dad, it's Sunday. I did my homework on Friday. Besides, you know we're off school till Wednesday." The whole town was off for the next couple of days. The Husk-Town Showdown technically started the next day. But today was the last day to prepare for it. It was the day that most of the last-minute work got done.

Matty nodded, like he'd forgotten, when really he wasn't paying attention. Not a hundred percent. He was running at fifty percent this morning. It had been a long night for him, too. After he got his father into bed, and Elsa got the kids back to sleep, Matty stayed up half the night worrying about his father. As well as he worried about Widow, a menacing stranger that they'd just invited to sleep in their guest room in the middle of the night.

Elsa said, "Okay, hon. Be back by dark. And call us and check in later."

Before Matty could add input, his son was already out the kitchen, shouting back a goodbye, and putting his shoes on in the mudroom. A vehicle sounded a horn from the driveway and Adam was out the front door seconds later, before his parents rethought the whole endeavor.

Elsa got up from the counter and joined her husband at the nook. They invited Widow over. He finished the remains of his second plate, which was two forkfuls for an average man but barely one for Widow. He left the plate, took the coffee and single bacon strip, and joined them at the nook. The bacon strip was gone before he sat down.

At first, Widow hovered over their table, eyeballing the bench, which he doubted he could squeeze onto comfortably. If he got down on the bench, it would force his knees to jam up under the table, hitting the bottom of the tabletop. If he moved the wrong way, he'd lift the table up off the ground, like a car jack under a truck.

Matty saw the dilemma and kicked a chair out for Widow. Widow opted for the chair, and simply kept his legs out from under the table.

The three of them chatted. The Eltons heard more about Widow. They learned the things he was comfortable sharing with strangers. Leaving out ninety-nine percent of his past, he gave them pleasant snippets of his life as a drifter. It was the basic same stories he shared daily because as he met new people, they always asked the same questions.

They had a good time chatting, making the time fly by. The early morning marched onward. The sun melted most of the snow from the night before. The twilight of spring marked North America. Today's forecast was sunny and warmer than yesterday.

Matty and Elsa finished their breakfast, coffee, and conversation. They both got up from the table at the same time. Matty stretched behind his chair. Elsa took both their plates to the sink.

Widow didn't wait to overstay his welcome. He got up from the table with Matty and chugged the rest of his coffee. He brought his plate, silverware, and empty mug to the sink. Elsa took them, thanked him, and told him not to worry about it.

Elsa asked, "Want anything else, Widow?"

Widow eyed the coffeepot, saw it was empty, and decided not to burden Elsa with making a new one just so he could have one more coffee for the road. He said, "No, ma'am. Thanks for the hospitality, but I'd better be going."

Elsa said, "Matty can give you a ride into town."

Matty leaned on the bar top with one hand, glanced at his watch, and said, "Sure. I gotta go into town for some feed and other things, anyway. But why not hang out here? I need an hour to get ready and make a list."

Widow pondered the proposal for a moment. He was grateful for the bed, shower, and breakfast, and especially for the coffee, but he was ready to get on his way. He didn't want to stand around for another hour. So he said, "I appreciate the offer, but town's only, what? Another couple of miles that way?" Widow pointed north.

Matty said, "That's right."

Elsa asked, "Are you sure you don't want to wait?"

"Not necessary. Thank you for everything, but I'm going to get back on the road," Widow said, and made his way out of the kitchen, and to the mudroom. Both Eltons followed him, thanking him again for what he'd done for John. Matty thanked him for returning the truck, too.

Widow got his boots and coat on and headed out the door, leaving the Eltons to their lives. At least, that's what he thought.

CHAPTER 7

Outside, clusters of clouds roamed fast across the sky, blotting out bright sunbeams. Long, dark shadows danced across the landscape. Beyond the clouds, the outer edges of the sky glowed bright blue.

Widow stood on the porch and gazed out across it all—the rolling tent-shaped hills to the north, the flat plains to the south, and the Eltons' ranch. It was spectacular, in an idyllic Grant Wood American Gothic painting sort of way. The ranch conjured a sense of family life, something missing from Widow's own life. Although he didn't plan to change the way he lived, it was a lie for him to say he didn't think about a life like this. If the right woman came along, he could imagine a scenario where he could fall in love and fall in line. It wasn't hard for him to reach back that far to think of a woman to convert him. He instantly thought of one—Nora—and the girls, back in the Ozarks.

Widow thought about Nora's last words to him. "We could go somewhere. Together. We could take the girls," she'd whispered to him. Should he have gone with her? Would it have worked out for him?

The answer was, probably not. Questions lingered in his mind anyway, like an idea or a fantasy that gnaws at you. For a while, there might be a sense of peace, a sense of happiness. But how long would it last?

Widow was cursed with the desire to roam. It clung to him like a deep, dark secret that one can never forget or ignore.

Farm animals fussed, making sounds from pens spread across the yard, mostly concentrated around the barn. Goats baaed, chickens clucked, and horses neighed. Clucky the rooster circled the hens as they fed, like a general observing a ragtag band of troops, an all-female platoon of feather fighters.

Widow smiled at the thought and stepped off the porch onto the grass. He got to the driveway and started down it. He passed the dormant tractor. He saw no sign of T.J. and John. He hadn't seen them at the barn and thought nothing of it as he continued.

Suddenly, Widow heard shouting and noise coming from behind the barn, out of the round pen. He stopped and looked. The old man and his young grandson were in the round pen with a horse, exactly where Matty had warned them not to be.

John petted the horse while T.J. fed it a carrot. The animal chomped the carrot to bits, dwarfing the kid. Following the carrot's obliteration, T.J. petted the horse's snout, and John rubbed the animal's back. The horse neighed, as if happy and docile.

Out of Widow's earshot, T.J. asked his grandpa if John still had what it took to break this bronco. John responded, "I can handle it. He's pretty tame now." He paused and then said, "Let's give him a ride."

"But Dad said not to," T.J. warned.

"Who?"

"Dad."

"Oh yeah. Well, what does he know? I've been breaking horses since your old man was in diapers. I think I can handle this gelding," John said, then climbed onto the back of the bronco without a saddle or stirrups. It impressed Widow because the old guy didn't seem as frail as he had the night before. The old man's brittleness must have been a side effect of his cognitive ailment. His frailness depended on what state of mind he was in.

The bronco seemed okay with the whole thing. It glanced back at the old man once and did nothing.

John said, "See? Nothing to worry about. Come on up with me."

T.J. tried to climb up with him, but without a saddle and no stirrups, he couldn't quite get on the horse with his grandpa.

T.J.'s attempt to climb up stirred the wild side of the horse, like it had only been lying in wait. Suddenly, the bronco reared, raising its two front legs into the air, balancing on its hind legs. It neighed loud and violent, like thunder cracking over an open plain.

The sudden movement threw John off balance, his grip slipping. The old man clung to the bronco's mane with all his strength. The bronco towered over T.J., engulfing the boy in an enormous shadow.

T.J. threw his hands over his face, as if the horse was going to stomp down on him. He shouted in terror. The bronco's muscles tensed, nostrils flared, eyes wide with panic. Hooves slammed down, kicking up dirt as the bronco bucked hard, trying to shake John loose.

The bronco came down, barely missing the boy. Then it stormed violently into the round pen. It bucked and heaved, running in circles and zigzags. John clung on for dear life. The animal kicked and galloped madly, wildly.

Widow glanced at the house and shouted, "Help!" hoping Matty and Elsa would hear him and come running out. He knew little about horses. Maybe there was a trick or a command to get it to calm. Only Matty or Elsa would know the answer to that. But Widow didn't wait for the Eltons to respond. He sprinted away from the driveway, toward the round pen. He hurried past the house, the animal pens, and the barn.

The bronco galloped out into the round pen. Frozen in fear, T.J. cowered in the center. John clung on, crying out like a kid riding a roller coaster for the first time. The bronco reared again and then bucked. Miraculously, John stayed on.

Widow hurdled over shrubs and a tree stump. Running toward the round pen, he steamrolled through a pile of loose hay.

The bronco planted its hooves and locked eyes on the shivering boy. Then it charged. John held on, shouting for T.J. to run. But T.J. froze and shuddered. The bronco galloped down on him, seconds away from trampling him into the ground.

Widow passed the last animal pen and stepped onto an old wagon parked near the round pen's fence. He hurtled over the gate, landing in the snowy mud.

John shouted for the boy to move, to dodge the barreling out-of-control horse, but T.J. couldn't. He stood there, frozen in terror. He breathed heavy. His asthma kicked into overdrive. His heart raced as he struggled to breathe.

Widow charged.

The bronco closed in on T.J., who shook and cried, still unable to move, still struggling to breathe properly. The horse exhaled hot breaths as it ran at him. The horse was seconds away from trampling the kid into the ground when Widow shoved T.J. out of the way onto his butt.

Widow, standing tall at six-foot-four and weighing two hundred thirty-five pounds of grit and real-world muscle, faced the bronco—a thousand pounds of powerhouse mass and wild muscle barreling down on him. Just before impact, Widow reared back a fist, swung a colossal right hook, and sidestepped. He punched the horse, smashing his fist across the horse's snout and into its eye.

The punch rocked the bronco, sending it off course. The horse stumbled forward, went down, and crashed onto the ground, kicking up snow and mud.

The fall hurled John from the horse's back. The old man hit the dirt hard, rolling to the side. Although he hit the ground, it was lucky that the horse didn't roll over the top of him, crushing his brittle bones into dust.

Widow stayed where he'd thrown the punch, surrounded by a dust-up of snow. He twisted at the waist, watching the bronco to ensure it didn't come back at him. The animal stayed down for a long moment, shuddering its head from side to side as if dazed. Slowly, it rose to its feet. The bronco, disoriented, raced away from them after shaking off the dirt.

Widow paused a beat, waiting for the animal to charge again. It was instinctual. He was used to enemies coming back for seconds. He'd never had to fight a horse before. A memory of a horrifying grizzly bear flashed across his thoughts. He got shoved into a pit with one. He survived that encounter. That memory was still pretty fresh in his mind. But the horse wasn't an enemy. It wasn't a predator coming after him. It was a wild animal, doing what wild animals do.

Finally, Widow relaxed, but then the hurt set in. Pain swelled in his fist, striking a match and lighting a fire within his nervous system, scrambling the message from his pain receptors to his brain. As the adrenaline faded, his fist felt like it was on fire. He inspected it, turned it around, and opened his hand. The pain in his knuckles and bones was intense, though his hand wasn't visibly mangled or bent out of shape. No fingers obviously broken.

Widow forced his fingers to extend, but they resisted because of the pain. He closed his fist and tucked it into his armpit to dull the throbbing.

Widow looked at T.J., who stood up and tried to speak but struggled with his breathing, reminding Widow of sailors he'd known with asthma.

Suddenly, Elsa ran into the round pen, Matty close behind, both in their socks. She reached her son, inhaler in hand, embraced him, and administered several puffs. T.J. took long, slow breaths as he recovered.

After a couple of seconds, T.J. breathed unassisted. Elsa hugged him tightly, while Matty joined in, embracing them both. They also admonished him for disobeying their explicit warning not to mess with the horses.

"You could've been killed," Elsa said.

"What were you thinking?" Matty asked harshly.

Widow stepped to where the horse had thrown John. He eyed the bronco, keeping the creature in view. The animal stayed in the farthest quadrant of the pen, returning Widow's gaze with snarls and huffs. Its stare held recognition, anger, and fear—like it had locked eyes with a predator in the wild and knew to steer clear.

John was hunched over, his face buried in the dirt. Widow grabbed him and gently turned him over. The old man stared up at him, winced in pain, and said, "I think my ankle's broken." He pawed at his right ankle.

"Any other pain?" Widow asked.

"Just my ankle," John replied, wincing. The sun blasted across his face, causing him to squint and ask, "Who are you?"

Matty darted over, stood beside Widow, and helped get John to his feet, asking, "Dad, are you okay?"

John stared at Matty for a long moment, as if he recognized him but couldn't place him.

Matty gazed into his father's eyes—lovingly but terrified—and asked, "Dad?"

Father and son stared at each other, the power of family unable to snap John out of the degenerative cognitive disease eroding his memory. It was heartbreaking to watch. Worse than the pain in Widow's hand.

Finally, John's eyes lit up, and he said, "Matty, I'm okay."

Matty smiled, tears welling in his eyes. He hugged his dad, but John blenched in pain, not from his ankle this time.

"What is it?" Matty pulled back.

"It hurts," John said, grabbing at his ribs.

Widow suspected John might have cracked a few ribs—or worse—given his age and the fact that he'd been tossed from a bucking bronco. The man was eighty-five years old. Countless senior citizens, younger than him, had broken bones from far less violent falls.

"Oh, God! Okay. We'll have to get you to the hospital," Matty said, trying to help his father to his feet, but John groaned in pain. Matty glanced at Widow, asking, "Can you help me with him?"

Widow pulled his hand from under his armpit, glancing at it. It was definitely out of commission for the moment. But he didn't complain. He didn't refuse. Keeping it closed and tucked close to his abdomen to stifle the pain, he moved to John's left side and nodded to Matty.

Together, they lifted the old man. Widow ducked down to balance the height difference. Elsa ran to the truck, unlocked the doors, and they loaded John inside. Widow rode shotgun, while Matty drove to the hospital in Tent Hills.

Widow kept his injured hand tucked under his arm. He never mentioned it.

CHAPTER 8

Sheriff Bill Easton arrived at the Tent Hills General Hospital on a hit-and-run call, which signified a busy day in his quiet county. One reason he worked law enforcement in this county was because it was quieter than the big cities. Some might say it was boring, but that's exactly what he wanted. As a war veteran who served in Iraq, he wasn't looking for the rest of his life to be filled with looking over his shoulder for IEDs and armed combatants.

His police career didn't start so safe and quiet. He began working in Dallas, which was filled with lots of action. Some guys liked it. He didn't. So he transferred to Salt Lake City for a year. It was quieter than Dallas, but still too dangerous for his taste. After that, he had no intention of dealing with large populations again, not for the rest of his career. Not if he could help it. He'd been shot at in Iraq. And he'd been shot at in the line of duty a few times. Dodging bullets wasn't something he ever wanted to experience again.

Easton parked his sheriff's SUV, an all-black Chevy Tahoe with Police etched down the side in gold, in a spot reserved for some doctor called Wakefield. Easton was pretty sure the guy didn't exist, because he knew most of the people in Tent Hills, at least by face. And he'd never seen this guy before.

The sheriff got out and entered the emergency room. A set of double glass doors slid open for him and sucked shut behind him. He walked into the hospital like he was part of upper management. A security guard half-assed saluted him, like they were both back in the military. Only the guard had never served. Easton knew because he'd checked the guy out. He checked out a lot of the citizens of his county. He knew many of them by name, at least the ones around Tent Hills. The people he didn't know, he could usually guess what family they were from. That was partially why he figured the mysterious doctor from the reserved parking space didn't exist. There were no records of the name. At least, not any criminal ones, or any in his police database. That wasn't confirmation of the name being fabricated by the hospital, but he was certain of his hunch.

Easton greeted various hospital staff, who all knew him. Some names he knew offhand and others he only knew their faces. He made his way to a reception desk. There was a woman with a childhood scar on her forehead behind glass. She talked on a landline phone, but paused her conversation to greet Easton. She said, "Good morning, Sheriff."

Easton returned the greeting and said, "Morning. Don't get off the line for me. Just tell me, where am I going?"

The receptionist smiled and pointed to the elevators and said, "Fourth floor, Rooms 401 and 403."

"Two rooms?" Easton asked.

"Yeah, there are three injured."

"Three? Oh, boy. I didn't know that. I thought it was only Mrs. Walsh? I guess it's gonna be a busy morning."

"Oh, not Mrs. Walsh. There ain't nothing wrong with that old bird."

"There's not? I'm here for her. I thought a truck side-swiped her car?" Easton asked.

"Oh, she's here all right. But there's nothing wrong with her. Nothing new anyway," the receptionist said and smirked. The scar on her forehead widened with her facial expression. "She claims to have a headache. Someone hit her car? I know nothing about that. I wasn't talking about her. I'm talking about the Eltons. Most of their family's here. I figured you were here to see them."

"What's going on with them?"

"The old man's hurt bad."

Easton's facial expression perked up. He asked, "What happened to him?"

"The family said a horse threw him."

Easton's interest waned. He said, "That's not a crime. Old John shouldn't be riding horses to begin with. Unless he ran into Mrs. Walsh's car with the horse, then it ain't my department. We only deal in crimes and traffic accidents. Was he riding the horse on the road?"

The receptionist leaned in across the desk. She looked both ways, like she was making sure no one was listening. She said, "They're saying a horse threw him. And he looks like a horse threw him…"

"But?"

"He looks like a truck had hit him. I saw wicked bruises on him as he passed through here. He's got a black eye. The word is there's some broken bones too."

"Isn't he like eighty years old?"

"He's eighty-five, according to his paperwork."

"Black eyes and broken bones are exactly what you get when you're eighty-five and thrown from a horse," Sheriff Easton said, paused a beat, and followed it up with a sideways look at the receptionist. "Are you supposed to be reading people's private paperwork? Ain't that a violation of the law?"

"I was curious."

"Right. Well, that old fool shouldn't be riding horses, anyway. Not at his age."

The receptionist said, "Sure, but..."

"But what?"

"I mean, he could've gotten those injuries from a horse. Or maybe he got them another way," she hinted conspiratorially.

"What do you mean?"

"I'm not making any accusations here. I'm just wondering something..."

"What?"

"Is it possible, maybe, there's some abuse going on?"

Easton's eyebrow furrowed. Suddenly, his interest piqued. This receptionist was nosy, but she normally didn't make stuff up. He leaned against the counter, inching his face toward a hole cut out in the glass for the receptionist to pass things back and forth to the public. Easton never understood why there was this glass partition between her and the public. But there it was.

He asked, "You suspect that Matty Elton is abusing his father? Hogwash!"

"Not Matty, but what about his brother?"

"What brother?"

"The big guy that came in with them. John Elton has broken bones and a black eye. But his other son also has injuries. He came in with fractures in his hand, like he punched the hell out of something."

"What other son? I never heard of another Elton son."

"I think that's who he is. It was in the manner they acted around him. I couldn't imagine who else he could be. He must be part of the family. I ain't never seen him before. And this is a small town. I've seen everyone."

"You sure he wasn't a stranger? Or a friend?"

"No way! They treated him like family, like they'd known him forever. So I assumed it was John's other son. Maybe he was a cousin or something. I don't know. I think they were covering for him," she said.

Easton contemplated this information, thinking about what to say next. Before he could, she added, "The guy was tall and massive, all muscle, like an NFL wide receiver kind of way and not a lineman."

The sheriff nodded along.

"He also looked unkempt too," she added.

"Unkempt?"

"Yeah, his clothes were dirty and ridiculous. He didn't match at all. He looked like he got them from a bin."

"A man's fashion sense isn't a crime."

"It's more than that. He seemed dangerous too."

"In what way? Was he mean to you?"

"No. He was polite, well-mannered. I might describe him as stoic. But he was scary in a certain way," she said, pausing another beat. "And not just his size. 'Cause you know one of my grandsons plays football. He's like a big teddy bear. This guy seemed dangerous, deadly," she said, putting a finger to her lips like she was trying to think of the right words. "You know what he makes me think of?"

Easton stared at her blankly.

She said, "Like a man who just got out of prison. The clothes, the muscles, the way he exuded danger. That's what he makes me think of. In fact, Sheriff, it wouldn't surprise me if he was a man on the run.

CHAPTER 9

E aston eased past the doorway to Mrs. Walsh's hospital room, trying to avoid her gaze.

Walsh was a nosy local, always convinced she had a crime to report to him. Everything was a red alert, call-the-police kind of event with her. If Girl Scouts were selling cookies in her neighborhood, she'd question them why they were there. She'd report them to the police if she thought they would do something about it. She didn't actually behave this way in life. But she fantasized about it often.

Walsh was also a conspiracy theorist—every small town has at least one. She was what the kids called a Karen. Every small town had one of those, too. Mrs. Walsh doubled as both —a double agent of annoyance and ignorance rolled into one person.

These days, it seemed like Karens were multiplying. Easton blamed the internet and social media. Back when he was a patrolman in Dallas, he'd encountered them daily. He could clock them from a block away, just because he'd gotten so used to dealing with them, which made sense in a way. Why do the police usually show up somewhere? Because someone called 9-1-1. And there were only two types of 9-1-1 calls: actual emergencies and non-emergencies. What kind of person calls 9-1-1 for a non-emergency? Karens do.

If he counted on two hands, the number of times he'd had to respond to a 9-1-1 call over a dispute that didn't involve a crime, he'd run out of fingers. If he had four hands, he'd run out. If he had six, he'd still run out.

Karens were always crying wolf. It was best to live and work in a place with fewer of them. Tent Hills was such a place. But he could never escape them completely. In the natural balance of society, there was always at least one.

Ninety-nine times out of a hundred, she exaggerated, mistook innocent acts for crimes, or completely made up her stories. And the one time there actually was a crime, she saw Billy Horton, a local teenager, spray-painting graffiti on a wall outside the local hardware store. The store owner forced the kid to repaint the damage and declined to press charges.

Walsh had some screws loose. Being a little off-kilter, plus the boredom of small-town life, could make a woman like her drum up drama that didn't exist before. She was known for it. Easton could have warned her to knock off this sort of behavior. But what was the point of that? Even he got bored with the slow and safe county he'd chosen to police. As annoying as she could be, Mrs. Walsh was entertaining.

Slipping past Mrs. Walsh was easy because she faced one of his deputies from a hospital bed. Her back was to the door. A female deputy was taking Mrs. Walsh's statement, writing it all down on a notepad. The look of boredom stretched across her face. Boredom was a part of the job when you work in a small town. That was Easton's favorite part, but it didn't work for everyone. Younger, more action-hungry deputies, like the one sitting with Mrs. Walsh, were hoping for a real crime to happen.

Easton signaled to the deputy to come out into the hall. Then he stepped to the opposite side of the doorway and waited for her.

The deputy closed her notepad and asked Mrs. Walsh to wait a moment, then she went out into the hall to report to Easton.

The deputy's name was Daisy Bloom.

At twenty-six years old, Bloom wasn't Easton's youngest deputy, but she was the only female. Bloom was tough. If she hadn't been, Easton wouldn't have hired her. However, she was also inexperienced, which made her green in his eyes.

To look at her, her youth and inexperience weren't the first thing people noticed. Typically, they zeroed in on her looks. Her skin condition.

Faint, ghost-pale patches mapped half her face, along her neck and down her arms. She had developed vitiligo at a young age. It wasn't contagious. It wasn't dangerous. Just the kind of thing people stared at, but never asked about. Easton never brought it up, not even in her interviews. He told his deputies not to bring it up, either. They obeyed. And she never spoke of it with them.

Even with it, she was runway-model beautiful. Long legs. Strong frame. High cheekbones like she'd been drawn by someone who didn't like soft edges. People in town looked twice when she walked in a room. Then they kept looking.

Bloom stood at average height but had an above-average build. Partly from boredom and partly from feeling like she had something to prove, Bloom was built like an Olympic swimmer from training more than she needed to. She was slender in that deceptive way where she looked unthreatening until she got a suspect in a chokehold. Although many areas had outlawed chokeholds, Nebraska continued to debate the topic. Until they were banned, she'd deploy them.

It wasn't her first tactic, but she would use it when necessary.

He was protective of her, more so than his other deputies. Not that she reminded him of his daughter, who no longer talked to him for various reasons. It was more like she reminded him of having a daughter.

Bloom had only had to take a suspect down once with the chokehold.

She encountered the guy in a traffic stop. She ran his driver's license, found it suspended, and saw that there was a warrant out for the guy's arrest. When she tried to take him into custody, he resisted, knocked her taser away, and grappled with her. Bloom's patrol car recorded the whole thing on the dash cam. It took place outside of the suspect's car.

Bloom had stopped the guy for a broken taillight before running his license. She called it over the radio. Easton heard it from his radio and ordered her to wait for backup. Eager for some real action, she ignored the order and asked the suspect to get out of his car. He stepped out, and she tried to put on the cuffs. He threw a jab at her, and things spun out-of-control right there. It was all in the dash cam footage.

Easton admonished her for disregarding his order. But he didn't make a big fuss about it. He had taken her off of street patrol for the past month. That's how she ended up here, taking Mrs. Walsh's statement. A punishment worse than many others he could've given her.

The other deputies saluted Bloom for the act, like she was a hero. They nicknamed her Hamilton, as in Linda Hamilton from Terminator 2. That was the one where Linda Hamilton buffed up because the first movie changed her completely.

Still, Easton saw Bloom as Linda Hamilton from the first Terminator, a defenseless woman who needed protecting. It wasn't as blatant as all that. But it made Bloom feel that way. She had to tell him once that she wasn't a maiden in distress. "I can take care of myself," she'd said.

Even though Bloom proved herself tough, Easton came down on her for letting the situation get to that point in the first place, which was his right and obligation to do. She had disregarded his orders.

He responded to her, "Orders are there for a reason."

"If I were one of the others, you'd allow me to take him down myself," Bloom retorted.

"The others are all experienced deputies."

"They're all men too."

"And they would've obeyed orders, too."

She said nothing back to that. And so Easton kept a watchful eye over her.

Leaning against the hospital's hallway wall, Easton asked, "What's she saying?"

"She insists a vehicle ran her off the road last night. She hit a ditch. The airbag deployed, smashing her in the face, and rocking her jaw."

"She telling the truth?"

"This time, I think so. I looked at her car."

"You looked at her car already?"

Bloom said, "Sure. It's parked outside."

"She drove it here?"

"Yep."

"How's it look?"

"There's some front-end damage to the grille, and the airbag deployed. But it drives fine, obviously."

"Did she recognize the car that nearly ran her off the road?"

"It was a pickup truck, a crew cab. Dark color."

Easton said, "That narrows it down to every household in the county."

Bloom nodded.

"Then she's telling the truth this time?"

"I think so."

"She get a look at the driver?"

"No. Too dark and fast, or so she says."

Mrs. Walsh called out from the room, "Daisy, is that Bill? Send him in, will you? I could use some cheering up."

Easton rolled his eyes.

Bloom smirked and said, "Earlier she looked disappointed when I walked through the door instead of you."

"Uh-huh."

"She even called you handsome."

Easton palmed his face in his hand.

Mrs. Walsh called out, "Oh, Bill? Is that you out there?"

Bloom said, "Sounds like she wants to talk to you, not me."

"Just finish up with her and find me down the hall," Easton said, lowering his voice to a loud whisper.

"Why're you going up there?"

"Might be an actual crime worth investigating."

Intrigue flamed in Bloom's eyes. "Really? What is it?"

"Don't know yet. Might be nothing. I'm going up there to find out."

"I wanna go."

"No. You stay here and deal with her."

Bloom sighed and asked, "Do I have to?"

"Yes!" Easton said and paused a beat. "Just make sure you get her story and make her feel heard. Then you meet me up there."

Bloom shrugged and went back into the room. Easton walked to the elevator. It opened as he approached and two doctors got off. He nodded to them, but he didn't recognize one of them.

He got into the elevator and turned around to face the doors closing. That's when he realized one doctor was someone he'd never seen before. He called out behind the two doctors. "Dr. Wakefield?"

But the doors closed before he could see if one doctor turned around to his name.

CHAPTER 10

In room 403, a nurse with a mischievous, schoolgirl smile finished casting Widow's right hand. He never flinched. Not even when she accidentally scraped his bad wrist with the edge of her casting scissors. It was a simple mistake—a muscle spasm in her arm, combined with an uncommon nervousness from being so close to a man like Widow.

The moment it happened, she froze in panic, like a barber accidentally cutting off the tip of a client's ear. Her mistake didn't rise to the level of a bloody ear tip, but to her it was unforgivable, a cardinal sin. Not as bad as if she'd been a surgeon, or a barber, but still unbecoming for someone of her profession.

She stopped and stared at Widow with apologetic eyes, frowning away the schoolgirl smile. She waited for his reaction, for his justified anger. But he did nothing. No flinching. No reaction. No burst of anger. Nothing.

Widow acted as if he hadn't noticed the mistake. She raised her eyebrows, surprised. He had to have felt something. That was for damn sure. She'd seen Widow's x-rays. The bones in his hand showed painful damage. Nothing broken, but close enough to the edge to see over it. Certainly, the damage was enough for him to feel pain.

Widow hadn't seen his x-rays—hadn't even asked about the results, which she couldn't give him, anyway. Hospital policy said a doctor had to deliver the official diagnosis to patients. Not the nurses or aides. No passing comments about any diagnosis until a physician made it official. Until then, Widow sat on a hospital bed, cool as a slab of stone, like pain was something he didn't have bandwidth for.

Widow never brought it up, figuring someone would explain eventually. His right hand was banged up pretty bad, but he was lucky—no breaks. That part he figured on his own. He'd fully recover. In time. He figured that part too. So why make a big fuss about it?

In that moment, she waited for what seemed like a long second, waiting for him to react to the scissor scrape. But he didn't react. He did nothing but stare at her and smile.

It was unreal. She knew it had to hurt like hell. And yet, he didn't flinch. Not once. Not with the accidental scrape. Not even when she took his hand to clean and cast it.

Straddling the line between playfulness and professionalism, the nurse with the schoolgirl smile said, "This must've really hurt."

Widow acted like it was nothing, made her wonder if he was even human.

But then he spoke, and she understood.

It wasn't just toughness.

It was the morphine.

Widow breathed deep, feeling dazed. He joked, "You should see the other guy." His words came out a little slurred.

"I thought the other guy was a horse?" she asked, smirking— she already knew the story.

"Is that why he refused medical attention?"

"He did?"

"Yeah," Widow said, grinning a crooked smile. "He said: Neigh."

It wasn't the best time to be cracking corny jokes. That thought flickered in the back of his mind. But he didn't care. He chalked it up to the morphine—same as the nurse probably had. The jokes kept coming. He couldn't stop them if he tried. He wasn't one hundred percent in control anymore. He was riding in the copilot seat of his own mind. The morphine had the stick.

As far as painkillers went, morphine did its job. The sharp, white-hot pain he'd felt walking in had dulled to a distant throb—or maybe he was just too numb to care. The side effects reminded him of his early days in the Navy. Back when they passed around the occasional marijuana cigarette below deck—just a few puffs among bored sailors blowing off steam. Morphine gave him that same slow grin, that same warm buzz.

Only heavier.

He felt almost guilty for feeling that good.

Still, it wasn't anything to call the DEA about. The buzz wasn't dangerous. Just enough to take the edge off the pain and knock the seriousness out of the moment.

No big deal.

Lame or not, the schoolgirl-smiling nurse giggled at his horse joke—but stopped when an ER doctor stepped into the room. This wasn't the same guy he'd seen when he first arrived. Not the same doctor who initially inspected his hand. This was a new guy.

Older. More stern. He had that traditional small-town doctor demeanor—all business, no room for nonsense. He looked like the kind of guy Widow imagined on an old educational poster, plastered to the wall of some outdated medical school hallway. More chestnut. More first-image-in-your-head kind of doctor. His thick hair was parted on the side, gray at the temples. He wore a crisp, stiff white coat. An expensive pen poked out of his breast pocket. The doctor looked at the nurse and asked, "What's so funny?"

No expression on his face. No smile. But no judgment either.

"Nothing, doctor," the nurse said, clearing her throat—just in time, because Widow was priming to repeat his corny, morphine-induced horse joke. She knew this doctor wouldn't find it amusing. He'd find it annoying, which wouldn't bother Widow—he didn't work with the guy. He never had to see him again. But she did. She backed off to a corner and carried her schoolgirl smile with her.

The doctor didn't say another word to her. He focused on Widow, introduced himself, and said, "I'm just starting this shift. Playing catch-up. I gotta ask—did the previous doctor explain your diagnosis to you?"

Widow went quiet, like he was thinking it over. He wasn't. He was still amused by his talking horse joke, but he didn't want them to know. He composed himself.

The no-nonsense doctor seemed to notice, anyway. Still no judgment. He waited patiently. The guy would've made a fine medical officer—or a flight surgeon on Air Force One, maybe. But not a very good party guest.

Finally, Widow said, "Don't remember."

The no-nonsense doctor nodded and pulled one of those pens out of his coat pocket—only it wasn't a pen. It was a penlight. He asked Widow to hold still, then shone the light into his eyes, checking his pupils. He flicked the beam from one eye to the other. Afterward, he slipped it back into his coat and turned to the nurse.

"How much morphine did you give him?"

Widow giggled and muttered, "Morphine. Mor... phine. More like—More PLEASE."

"I didn't give him any," the nurse said. "The other doctor did."

The no-nonsense doctor frowned, disappointed. He sighed, like the damage had already been done. "Hand me his chart."

The nurse passed him the clipboard. He studied it. His eyes slowly widened.

"Why did he give him so much? It's significantly higher than the standard dose. More than what's recommended. This dosage is enough to treat a horse."

Widow giggled again. He whispered, like it was a secret, "Neigh."

The schoolgirl-smiling nurse covered her mouth, trying not to burst out laughing. The doctor scoffed—just slightly. Then he said something to her out of earshot, probably a quiet jab about the previous doctor.

He spoke again, this time like Widow wasn't in the room.

In a sense, he wasn't. Part of him was out in space somewhere.

"I think the other doctor decided he needed more because…" the nurse said, glancing back at Widow. "Look at him. He's bigger than the standard patient."

The doctor nodded. His brow creased as he processed her justification. He stared at the chart for a long second, questioning every word on it—something he did often. The staff was used to it. Finally, he set it aside, surrendered to the situation, and refocused on Widow.

Widow stared at him with a stoned expression—one that was both stone-cold and just plain stoned.

"All right, Mr. Widow, let's be clear here," the doctor began hesitantly. But the professional in him pushed him through. "You've sustained what's known as a boxer's fracture." He glanced at Widow's face and locked in, waiting for Widow's reaction.

Widow smiled slowly and idly, like a comment was forming, another side effect from the morphine. He quipped, "But I'm no boxer? Am I?" He paused and motioned with his good fist. "Step into the ring!" He followed the gesture with the cast one. Pain jolted from his injured hand, sending the message to his brain. Widow's brain wasn't wired the same way as other men. Whereas the modern man's moved out of the cave, leaving his lizard brain behind, Widow's was built different. That old primitive man's brain remained with him, passed down through his genetics. Some might say his family tree never evolved properly. And they might be right, but it helped him from time to time.

His primitive brain fought the effects of the morphine. The sudden pain from his cast hand ignited his brain's response, firing adrenaline through his body. And like that, he was suddenly more sober. He shook off the drug-induced dazed feeling, not completely, but enough to regain control over his words.

The nurse said, "Be careful, Ali!"

Widow slow-nodded and said, "Sorry. You're right. I think the drugs have impaired me. But I'm okay."

Silence. Both the doctor and the nurse gave Widow some time to recover from the pain in his hand. Finally, he said, "Sorry, Doc. Continue, please."

The doctor said, "Mr. Widow, a boxer's fracture is a serious thing. It means there's a small crack in the metacarpal bone leading to your little finger. It's minimal, which is good. But it's still severe—and it can be painful until it heals."

"How long, Doc?" Widow asked, sounding deflated because he'd have to stay in a cast and rely on his good hand.

The doctor relaxed, smiled, and said, "I understand you punched someone?"

"Not a someone. I punched a horse. It's a long story," Widow said, knowing it wasn't a long story, not really. He just didn't want to recount the whole thing. He feared the morphine would get some words in that he didn't want to say. He'd said enough.

"I saw the sheriff's deputies outside. Thought maybe they were here for you," the doctor said.

Widow peeked through the gap between the doctor and the nurse, out the door and into the hallway. In that exact moment, like it was scripted in a stage play, a man in a deputy uniform walked past the open doorway. He glanced in and made eye contact with Widow. It was only a second, but it happened.

The doctor interrupted and said, "I want you to take it easy. No boxing anymore, horses or men or any other animals. Okay? Let's say you're down for the count for the next while. No hitting, no lifting—just lots of thumb twiddling and channel surfing, or you'll be right back here again. Got it?"

Widow nodded. "How much time are we talking?"

The doctor paused, looked at Widow's cast, and said, "Six weeks in the cast. Leave your number with the nurse. One of the staff here will call you to check in to make sure it's healing right."

"I don't have a phone," Widow said.

The doctor sighed. "We'll call the Eltons' house then. That's where you're staying?"

He wasn't staying anywhere. He almost said that, but kept his mouth shut. That answer would only lead to more questions. Truthfully, Widow wasn't planning on sticking around at all. Not for one more day. Not one more hour. Much less would he be around in six weeks. He was thinking of going somewhere warmer. Maybe he'd head down to Southern California. He could just stop in a clinic and have the cast removed when it was time. Or do it himself. Both were a real possibility. But knowing exactly where he'd be in six weeks was an impossibility. Widow didn't know where he'd be tomorrow or the next day. He could be gone forever at any moment. That's how he lived his life.

The doctor explained that Widow needed to keep the arm elevated and try not to overuse it. He prescribed him a short supply of oxycodone for the pain and 800 milligrams of ibuprofen to help with inflammation. He gave it all to Widow with instructions on how many times per day and eating it with food.

Before the doctor left the room, he dismissed Widow's story about the horse, saying, "I suggest using your words next time, Mr. Widow, and not your fists. Violence never solves anything." Wise words. Widow had heard them before. He'd even said them before to the men under his command back in the Navy. But he knew it wasn't true. Not one hundred percent of the time. Just look at the American Civil War. Words didn't free the slaves. Violence did. Sure, there are words on paper—important words too. There's the Thirteenth Amendment, which was equally important.

But violence came first. Without it, where would history be?

Violence would come again to answer his next problem. Only Widow didn't know it yet.

CHAPTER 11

Leaning against the wall, Easton sipped hot coffee from a Styrofoam cup, just out of sight of Widow's hospital doorway. He waited for Bloom without a care in the world—the way an old ranch dog waits in the truck for his owner. Patient, but ready for the next thing.

He liked waiting. It bothered some people. Not him. It was time to himself—a perk of the job. He liked the silence. The peace.

Easton knew Bloom would be awhile. Mrs. Walsh was nothing if not the kind of person who loved giving an earful to any—and every—soul who'd listen. Minutes passed, slow and methodical, like the universe had dropped into low gear. A clock on the wall showed it'd been more than fifteen minutes, then twenty.

After twenty-five long minutes, Bloom slow-backed out of the room. Not walked out—backed out, like she'd accidentally walked into a mountain lion's den and didn't want to lose eye contact while trying to get away. Never turn your back on a mountain lion. Always back away slowly, keeping eye contact. Turning your back told the cat you were prey. Bloom had seen it in an animal documentary on a flight once.

She held eye contact with Mrs. Walsh, same as she would the lion. She nodded along to the old bird's monologue, like she was in total agreement. Then, at the right moment, she side-stepped before finally turning away from the door. She turned the wrong direction at first, facing away from Easton. She stopped, glanced around, and didn't see him. Nurses, doctors, and staff filled the halls, going about their routines, paying her no attention.

Easton came off the wall and whistled to her. It was some-thing he did to all his deputies to get their attention. Annoyed the hell out of them. But that was part of his charm, with love. They looked up to him, like a father figure. He returned the affection. His deputies were important to him. He had his favorites, naturally. Behind closed doors, he'd kick their ass when they needed it. Not in full view of the public. He was a professional. He had to keep up the appearance that he had full faith in his deputies. In front of the townspeople, he always had their backs.

Easton was good at whistling. One of the many time-wasting skills he'd learned, occupational hazard from being the sheriff of a town with little crime. Among his deputies, he was known for it. Not that Tent Hills was crime-free. Nebraska had its own problems. Tent Hills wasn't immune. Catching criminals—and keeping them caught—was another story.

In a place like Nebraska, things got trickier. Rural country people kept to themselves. What city folk called "off the grid" was just life out here. Cops are part of the government. And people out there didn't like the government. They didn't trust it. They especially hated cops poking around. Didn't matter if they wore a badge or brought coffee and good intentions.

People in his county liked their personal business to stay personal.

Tent Hills was mostly peaceful. Happy, even. But every community has its underbelly. Tent Hills was no different. The real trouble didn't brew in the town center. For passersby, the town looked quaint, friendly. It had that small-town charm that city folk only saw on postcards.

The underbelly, the criminal element, lived further out. There was an area to the north, toward South Dakota. The locals called it The Scarlands. Easton didn't know who named it. He had no clue who was the first to think of it. Didn't matter. The name fit. It wasn't printed on any map, but speak it out loud and any local would know exactly where you meant.

Unfortunately, it was where many of the lower-income families lived. Folks who couldn't afford to be closer to town, but also couldn't afford to leave. They weren't the down-on-their-luck types. Not most of them. They were the families whose sons had the long rap sheets. They dealt in everything from petty crime to armed robbery to cooking and distributing meth.

Old, rundown double-wides stretched across acreage nobody wanted. Overgrown gravel driveways, rusting trucks, and satellite dishes pointed toward the sky like hope. A few good people out there, sure. But it was also where most of the county's crime brewed. Many investigations ended there too. Sometimes with an arrest. Sometimes not.

The Scarlanders protected their own. Besides hating cops, they hated snitches even more. One could say they had their own sense of justice, but there was no justice out there. It was survival of the fittest.

The deadliest offenses that plagued his county were drugs. Mostly meth, but some other stuff came out of The Scarlands too. Unlike in much of the West, marijuana was still illegal in Nebraska, with medical marijuana being the exception. Even then, getting caught with weed was only a misdemeanor offense. It came with fines. Not a big deal. Easton didn't even press his guys to look for it. In fact, he suggested they ignore it, unless they needed it as an excuse to claim probable cause. He left it to their discretion if they wanted to cite someone for smoking. More often than not, the possession of it was used as a tool to get to probable cause, and that was it.

Easton liked to think the gap between major crimes in his county stretched wide. That most days were quiet for a reason.

But he wasn't stupid. Was it quiet because there were no crimes? Because the meth labs stopped all operations? Or did the silence mean something else? Did it mean that the meth business was busy? It was booming.

Easton read the state reports. He followed the headlines on the news app that came pre-installed on his phone. He could've deleted it. Could've ignored the headlines. He could've buried his head in the sand. But that wasn't him. It wasn't his character.

A lot of the bigger crime, like the meth industry, didn't start in The Scarlands. The criminals who lived there were small on the grand scale of things. They were low-level, local dealers and cooks.

Easton couldn't turn his back completely on the outside world, no matter how much he wanted to. It was too danger-ous. What happened in other states often rippled all the way through his quiet county.

Easton had a higher education, both in school and from the streets. So he knew that just because his office didn't see every crime didn't mean they didn't happen.

Nebraska sat nearly dead center in the US. That made it part of every major distribution route—for drugs, for human trafficking, for anything illegal that needed to move fast and quiet. I-80 cut through the state like an open vein. It pumped in meth by the kilos. There was a prominent human trafficking industry too. I-80 also was pivotal for that as well. Girls were moved out in the dark. Never to be seen again.

Nobody in Tent Hills talked about it. They lived in their quiet little town, blind to their role in it. But the truck stops weren't just for diesel and coffee anymore. They were hiding places. Wolves among sheep. Major criminal networks slid through in silence—unchecked, unnoticed.

One of those state reports Easton read estimated that for every one thousand trucks that passed his town along I-80, one hauled something illegal. They had ties to one of the big criminal industries. Typically, this was drugs or trafficked girls.

Easton had come here to escape such worries. But there was no escape. This was the world now. He couldn't solve the world's problems. His responsibility was limited to Tent Hills. Still, it kept him up nights.

Not the crimes he saw. The ones he didn't.

Fortunately for him, I-80 ran far to the south. He got little spillover. Tent Hills wasn't exactly built on any major thoroughfares. Still, drugs and human trafficking had to move north too. Transporters sometimes veered off the beaten path —either to dodge police checkpoints and weigh stations, or because their GPS routed them along quieter roads. And sometimes, they passed through Tent Hills on their way to Canada, or wherever. It happened.

Easton saw Bloom, lost and searching for him. So he whistled.

Bloom heard it, spun around, and saw Easton perched at the opposite end of the hall. She pocketed her phone, where she'd been pretending to take notes—just an act to keep Mrs. Walsh thinking that she was actually listening. Her boots scuffed against the tile like sneakers on a racquetball court, loud in the silence.

Their eyes connected. She walked to Easton, who bounced up from the wall. He nodded toward the open door between them. She glanced in through the doorway, saw Widow, and did a double take, like a hiker walking a trail, glancing to the side and unexpectedly seeing a grizzly bear. She continued past the door, came to Easton, and slowed.

He said, "You're up again. Go talk to the man."

"That guy? In there?" she asked, pointing at Widow's room.

Easton nodded.

"Why me? Because I'm a hot chick?"

"You got it. You'll get further with him than I will."

"What if he's dangerous?"

"Desk attendant thinks he is." Easton shrugged. "Look, the guy's a stranger here. He's suspicious. He's in the hospital. I'd like to know who he is and why he's in my town."

"Plenty of strangers come through. You're not going to know them all."

"True, but they don't look like this guy. I've never seen him before. Have you?"

She shook her head. "I'd remember him. No doubt about it." She said it with a hint of excitement in her voice.

"Wait. You like him?"

"I don't know him."

"But you're swooning."

"I'm not swooning. It's just… He's not bad to look at is all. Scary-looking, but attractive in that biker, bad boy sort of way."

Easton nearly rolled his eyes. He said, "Just keep your cop instincts switched on and your gun nearby. The guy came into the ER with the Eltons. His hand is all busted up, and I'd like to know why. He broke it, hitting something. Plus, old man Elton's smashed up pretty bad too, from what I hear."

"How bad?"

"I don't know. That's why I'm not talking to him with you. The Eltons are in another room. I'll check in with them. See what they got to say about it."

"Are you talking about John? Not Matt Elton?"

"I heard it was the old man who's all beat up. The one who's in his nineties."

"That's John. He's in his eighties. His birthday's in June," Bloom said.

Easton eyeballed her and said, "That's why you'll go far in this business."

"What?"

"Memorizing details like that. It shows a genuine concern for the population, a necessary skill of any detective worth his salt."

Bloom smiled. She wanted to be a detective one day. Of course, she'd have to move to a bigger town, possibly to a city like Lincoln. But she was okay with that. She'd come to Tent Hills because Easton was the only person to give her a chance.

She had to cut her teeth somewhere.

"Thanks," she replied.

Easton glanced at a passing doctor. Not recognizing him, he asked, "What's that doctor's story?"

"I think he's an orderly, not a doctor."

Easton glanced at the man again. "You sure? I guess he is. They all wear scrubs. Who can tell the difference?"

"I don't know him, anyway. I don't know every person who lives here. It's not possible. Just the notable ones—who stick out."

"What makes you think old man Elton sticks out? I don't even know much about him, and he's been here since long before I took office."

"That's why, sir. There's not much to know about him. He's lived here for decades, yet he's never made a splash. He's quiet, reserved. He keeps to himself. Stays out of trouble. A quiet man is a man with secrets."

"Hmm," Easton grunted, like he'd heard that phrase from somewhere, but couldn't place it. An old movie, perhaps?

Bloom glanced at Widow again. She craned her head, sneaking a look through the open door. Widow sat upright on the hospital bed—calm, quiet, and built like a concrete truck, his cast freshly set. But there was something off about him. Something that didn't seem to fit. It was his smile. He grinned from ear to ear. He appeared giddy.

Easton asked, "So, what do you think?"

"He looks dangerous. But he's giggling."

Easton glanced. A puzzled look came over his face, like now

he too was confused. He shrugged and said, "You're the one always complaining that I'm overprotective of you."

"Compared to the boys, you are," she said. She kept her eyes on Widow, shuddered, and wondered if Easton was right to worry.

"So? Here's your chance to take a risk."

"But… he's huge."

"You got a gun. And I'll be down the hall."

Bloom swallowed hard and withdrew from staring at Widow. Her hand instinctively brushed against her holstered gun. She asked, "You got anything on the official story?"

"Supposedly a riding accident."

"Horse or motorcycle?" she asked, knowing the Eltons had horses, but this dangerous stranger looked like he might ride motorcycles. Maybe he's part of a gang? He's got the tattoos for it.

Easton nodded. "Horses. That's what the lady at the front desk told me."

"The receptionist? She gossips about everything. She's about as reliable as Mrs. Walsh."

Easton shrugged again and said, "Broken clocks are right twice a day and all that."

Bloom nodded reluctantly. "Okay. So what're we looking for?"

Easton sipped some of his coffee and said, "Just go in and feel the guy out. Get his story. I'll talk to the Eltons. We meet after and see if their stories match up."

"Okay," Bloom agreed and split away from him.

Easton paused a beat and peeled off the wall, and headed down the hall, disappearing around a corner. Bloom approached the door to Widow's hospital room, rested a hand on her holstered gun, and took a deep breath. She paused, closed her eyes, and pictured quick-drawing in case she needed to. But she was thrown off guard as suddenly the door opened and the nurse and doctor exited the room.

She backed away, letting them pass. They nodded to her.

Inside, Widow glanced up. A euphoric expression washed over his face as he came down from his morphine high. He glanced around the room, lost in a daydream. The staff asked him if he had someone to take him home. They mistook his answer to mean that he was too high to be discharged. He told them he had no one, and he lived nowhere. He was all alone. But like Easton, they presumed because he came with the Eltons, he was likely one of them.

In the end, they let him have the room for another hour until the morphine effects wore off.

Widow didn't complain. He knew he was impaired. He was grateful for their concern. The morphine wound down, and he knew it because the pain in his injured hand wound up.

At one point, his cast arm slammed into a side table as he turned to see who was standing at the door. Before he could register who it was, the sting from the so-called funny bone ignited through him. The lingering morphine in his system didn't help. The shock kicked his adrenaline into overdrive and shook him nearly out of the feeling of euphoria he'd been feeling. He clamped his eyes shut tightly to stop himself from crying out in pain. It took a long second.

Bloom stood halfway through the doorway, staring at him. She saw him hit his cast, and she paused, feeling his pain, as most humans on earth would. She entered the room, leaving the door open behind her like it was some kind of safeguard that might protect her, in case things went sideways. *If he tries something, I can always scream*, she thought. However, stepping closer to him, her backup plan went out the window. Even in the cast, the guy looked dangerous, just as the desk attendant downstairs had described to Easton.

The room smelled like antiseptic and wet plaster. She glanced around, checking the corners, which she tried to make a habit of for every room. It didn't matter if she was breaching or simply walking into a new room. Fluorescent lights hummed above her. By the time her eyes returned to Widow, he was staring at her—wide-eyed.

He stared at the deputy standing inside his door. She stood around 5'6", a hundred forty pounds, including significant muscle in her shoulders, and thick legs. Long dark hair bunned up tight in the back of her head. It reminded him of his mother's hair, which was thick enough to fill a bucket.

A nameplate over her left breast read the name: Bloom. But Widow hadn't noticed that, not like he usually would. Not like he did ninety-nine percent of the time. He hadn't noticed because he couldn't get past one distinguishing feature Bloom had. She was both white and black, but not like a person of mixed race. It looked like a cartographer had painted an old-world map of what sailors thought the continents looked like in dark ink over a white woman. And she was absolutely stunning because of it.

Widow tried to speak. Tried to say something. He choked, like he was starstruck. The deputy's appearance was unforgettable because of her skin. Whatever was going on with it gave her a special kind of look. Sleeve tattoos covered Widow's arms, like tapestries recounting the violence of a past life. So he knew a thing or two about getting inked. He'd sat in tattoo chairs all over the world. This deputy's skin coloration, though it seemed perfectly planned, wasn't ink. It was real. And she was absolutely beautiful for it.

Bloom stood there in an awkwardness she'd grown accustomed to. All her life, people stared at her because of her condition. A person newly minted with her skin condition would've been offended. But not her. People always stared at her. She did what she always did and waited for them to take it all in.

She waited for him to get the words out.

Eventually, Widow gave up trying to string together whatever sentence he wanted to say. He simply blurted out, "Hi."

Bloom stayed professional. Routinely, she said, "Hi. My name's Daisy Bloom. I'm a sheriff's deputy." She inched further into the room, getting closer to his bedside, but staying out of reach. Something primal deep inside her told her to stay back. But her training told her not to show fear. It taught her to stay in control of the situation, to show confidence. So she cracked a smile and said, "I'm sure you guessed that already by the uniform."

Widow suddenly forgot the sting in his funny bone. He paused a long beat, realizing that his morphine high was nearly gone. It was a combination of time passing, adrenaline from hitting his cast elbow on the table, and the pain in his fracture.

He also realized he was leering at her. So he shook it off, staying quiet, waiting for Bloom to say more. But she waited for him to interject. They sat there in the silence, until Widow nodded once. She stepped further into the room, as close as she dared, and stopped. Widow noticed her hand resting near her gun, like she meant it to look casual. She pretended to be confident, sure of herself, and not intimidated. Widow saw right through it. He knew the signs. He'd learned the same cop postures long ago, in another life.

She was a cop, and a nervous one at that. He didn't know why. He didn't know why she was there. But he certainly didn't mind. He could think of worse things to give attention to, like the pain in his hand.

Bloom said, "What's your name?"

"Widow."

She stared at him sidelong, waiting for more.

Widow stayed quiet.

Bloom asked, "Are you a biker? Is that one of those biker gang names? Like Spider?"

Widow cracked a smile and said, "It's a military thing. Jack Widow is my name. But no one calls me that. Just Widow."

"You were in the Army?"

"Navy, ma'am."

"Oh. Cool. I never served. I thought about it before. Back when I was deciding on what to do with my life."

"You made the right choice."

"Think so?"

"I do. I don't envy servicepeople today. Back when I joined, the enemy was more clear-cut. We knew who the bad guys were. Service to country meant service to good. We've always sworn to defend the Constitution against enemies both foreign and domestic. When I was in, the enemies were more foreign than domestic. Nowadays, it's not so clear. Too many enemies from within."

"You watch a lot of the news? I don't. No time."

Widow shook his head. "No. I don't own a TV. I read newspapers from time to time. But I hear from people what's going on. And I see the headlines at checkout counters across this country. You don't have to be blind to see things aren't great. I'm just saying I'm glad my time wasn't so hazy."

Bloom stood there, unsure what to add to that.

Widow said, "Daisy Bloom? That's quite a name."

"Yeah, it's my mother's."

"Daisy?"

"No, Bloom. My father took off when she was pregnant with me. So she gave me her last name. Daisy comes from flowers. She's obsessed with flowers. She's kind of hippie. My two sisters both have flower names—Rose and Lily."

Widow nodded, as an image flashed in his mind of two little girls he'd met with flower names. Somewhere out there, Nora Sutton was working to rehabilitate her husband, while raising two spirited little girls. A smile crept across his face, just thinking of them.

"What happened to you?" Bloom asked. Widow shook off his thoughts and returned to reality. The pain in his hand eclipsed the sting in his elbow from his funny bone strike. The morphine had nearly completely worn off. He sat straight up in the bed and threw his legs over the side. Only now was it dawning on him he was in a hospital gown. He forgot they'd made him put it on—hospital policy.

A cool draft reminded him of something else. He was naked underneath the gown and Bloom got a glimpse of enough of him to tell her the same information. He glanced up and saw her frozen. Their eyes locked for a long second before she broke away and stared at the wall.

"Oh, sorry. I saw nothing," she said in embarrassment.

Widow put his feet on the floor, ignoring the cold tile. He stood up and stretched. "I'm sorry. I forgot I wasn't wearing pants." He glanced around the room. "Where are my clothes?"

Bloom saw a pair of jeans hanging from a shower rod in the bathroom. "I think they're in there." She pointed.

Widow thanked her, walking slowly past her to the bathroom. She darted out of the way, turning with him to keep facing him like a deep-sea diver keeping eye contact with a great white shark.

Widow stepped into the bathroom, keeping the door open. He pulled the hospital gown off. Bloom caught another glimpse of more than she bargained for from the backside of the gown, which flapped open. She turned around, ignoring her training to not take a suspect like him out of her sight.

"You were asking me something?" Widow called from the bathroom, slipping his clothes back on, underwear first. At one point, he glanced at the mirror and noticed Bloom look at his backside and then turn around.

Bloom couldn't ignore her training any longer. *What if he had a gun in there, with his clothes?* she wondered. She turned back around to face the open bathroom door, but sidestepped to give him privacy. She said, "I was stopping by to introduce myself, and ask you why you're here."

"In this town? I gotta be somewhere."

"What brings you to the hospital? I see you're wearing a cast? What happened?"

Widow stepped out from the bathroom, still barefoot and shirtless. He wore jeans, buttoned and zipped up.

Bloom stared at him. She couldn't help but stare, like someone staring at the sun for the first time. It was amazing, but dangerous to do. She was caught in a momentary trance.

Widow's shoulders and chest were plastered with thick muscle, like plates of NFL armor. His washboard abs bore the kind of hard muscle that millions of people struggle to crack in the gym every day of the week.

Like his upper body, they looked like more armor, forged over a blacksmith's fire. If a Major League Baseball player slammed a Louisville slugger into his stomach, Bloom wasn't so sure the bat wouldn't snap in half.

Widow put his shirt on, pulling it down over his body, breaking her trance. He stepped into the room, glanced around, and found his socks and shoes nestled under a chair. He dumped himself down in the chair and put them on. Never looking at her, he answered her question. He told it straight, recounting that he'd stayed the night with the Eltons. He told her about seeing their son in danger, about the charging horse. He'd had no time to think, only to react, which he did on instinct. He took a swing at the horse, hitting the animal's snout, which nearly broke his hand. At the end of it, he looked at her and said, "That's it. That's the story."

She stared at him intensely and asked a question he didn't expect. "Are you a bodybuilder or something?"

It took him off guard. He blushed, without knowing it. It was only a moment, but it had happened. He wondered if it was a tactical move from Bloom. Maybe she knew how beautiful she was? Maybe she knew how young she looked? How green she seemed? He wondered if she took advantage of it and was trying to lower his guard by playing to his ego. It was a tactic that certainly would work on most men. And it worked on him, too. It was just that he had nothing to hide. So keeping his guard up against her was unnecessary.

Widow said, "Never had any interest in that sort of thing."

"I'm sorry. I shouldn't have asked that. I just… You're built like someone who body builds. It was a stupid question."

"Not at all. I don't even go to the gym. Like I told you, I don't live here."

"Where do you live?"

"I don't live anywhere. Therefore, it makes no sense for me to have a gym membership."

"So you're homeless?"

Widow shrugged. "I don't like to say that because it comes with a certain negative connotation, implying I'm a homeless person, living on the streets. I'm a nomad."

A violent nomad, he thought, which was one nickname for SEALs. But he didn't want to say that to a cop. She'd only hear the word violent, and think the worst about him.

"So, are you staying here long?"

"Not long. I'll probably leave today."

"So soon? Just like that?"

Widow finished with his shoes and stood up, picking up his coat. He said, "Maybe right now." He paused a beat, thinking hard about adding one thing. Which he did. "You can tell your boss I'm no threat. No crime's been committed here. Not by me. And I'll be out of his town by this afternoon."

"My boss?" she asked, wondering, *Does he know Easton?*

"Yeah, the sheriff who's been standing out in the hallway for thirty minutes."

"You know about that?"

Widow cracked a smile and said, "Tell him to work on his stakeout skills." And he walked past her slowly to the door. He stopped. "It was a pleasure to meet you, Deputy Bloom."

She started to speak, but hesitated. Widow nodded and walked out of the room into the hallway. She called behind him. "Before you leave town…"

Widow stopped and faced her.

"Can I buy you a drink?"

That got his attention. One eyebrow lifted, just barely, like she'd said another left field thing he hadn't expected.

"Really?"

"Yeah. Why not?" she said inadvertently. Easton had given her a mission. She didn't want to mess it up. What if there was something criminal about Widow? This could be her chance to shine. "I mean, of course."

"Like a date kind of drink?"

She smiled. "It's to thank you for what you did for the Elton boy." She glanced at his cast. "You nearly got your hand broken. I think you deserve more than just a hospital bill."

"It was expensive," he said.

"So let me take you out? Tonight?"

He didn't answer. Thinking about if he really wanted to stick around. He'd barely seen the town so far. But he'd gotten a faraway look at it from the road last night. And from what he saw, there wasn't much to it. What would be the point in sticking around? But the answer slapped him across the face. It was for Bloom. Widow had a longstanding rule: never turn down a beautiful woman with a gun.

Sensing his hesitation, Bloom added, "I know a place. Live music. Cheap beer."

"Cheap beer?"

"It's good though. Plus, they serve Runza."

"Runza?"

She smiled, showing him white, but slightly crooked teeth. He liked her smile. The slightly crooked teeth gave her smile character, more than most. She said, "It's like a breaded pocket filled with beef, cabbage, onions. You gotta try some. It's a Nebraska staple."

Widow looked skeptical. But he slow-nodded and said, "Sounds... fun."

"That's a yes?"

He held her gaze. "Sure. Yes. Let's do it."

"Great. I'll pick you up tonight, at eight?"

"I don't know where I'm staying."

"Then I'll give you the address. You meet me there."

"What's the place called?"

"Outer Limits. On the north edge of town. Council zoned it out there to keep it off the main drag. It keeps the peace around here, like separation of church and fun. It keeps the barflies away from the churchgoers."

"There's no bars in town?"

"There are, but this one gets rowdy. The others are more like pubs. This one has live music. People get out of control."

Widow nodded.

Bloom said, "Yep. It's the most packed spot in the whole county. Local bands play for little pay or just free beer. Nothing fancy. But I like it."

"Where's the police station?" he asked.

She gave him a look and asked, "Why? You going to file a complaint against me?"

Widow smiled and shook his head. She gave him directions.

"I'll meet you there at eight instead," he said. "You can drive us to the Outer Limits place." With that, he turned away and left the floor, leaving the hospital.

She stood in the room a second longer, pulse ticking faster than it should have.

Then she went to meet Easton.

CHAPTER 12

In Room 401, the Eltons waited in stiff chairs—the kind with worn plastic arms and thin vinyl cushions that weren't meant for comfort, just holding worried families while they waited for news that could change everything. An orderly had brought in an extra chair for Matty. Elsa sat in the visitor chair that came standard with every room. The only family members missing were John and Adam. Otherwise, this was it—the entire Elton family tree.

The hospital staff had assigned the room to John, not T.J., which felt backward to everyone because John wasn't even in it. John came in with them, obviously. But the staff came in and took John out soon after he checked in.

An hour ago, a nurse came in with an orderly pushing a wheelchair—one squeaky wheel that announced their arrival long before they appeared. The Eltons heard it echoing down the hall. The orderly helped John into the chair while the nurse stood by, professional and efficient. Then the orderly wheeled John out without ceremony. They vanished into the fluorescent-lit corridors, headed for tests. X-rays. CT scans.

The works. The kind of thorough examination that either means nothing or means everything.

The first thirty minutes had been all about T.J., which was how it should've been. The boy had nearly been trampled to death.

"Are you okay?"

"I'm fine, Mom."

"Are you sure?"

"Yes."

"Really sure?"

"Mom, I'm fine."

Elsa asked him several more times, each question wrapped differently but containing the same fear. T.J. answered the same way every time—patient, exasperated, knowing his mother needed to hear it more than he needed to say it.

Matty didn't ask as much. It split his worry down the middle like a bullet cleaved in half—half for T.J., half for his father.

The second thirty minutes, they spent questioning T.J. Then scolding him. The inevitable shift from thank-God-you're-alive to what-were-you-thinking.

"What were you thinking?"

"Why didn't you listen to me?"

"I told you to stay away from that bronco."

"You better hope your grandfather's okay."

"You're grounded until further notice, young man. And I mean it this time."

That went on until the words ran out and T.J. sat on the hospital bed in silence, staring at his hands like they held answers to questions he didn't know how to ask. He looked far away. Distant from his parents. The time-tested silent treatment. He'd perfected this tactic over the years. Adam had taught it to him one summer afternoon when they'd both been in trouble for something they absolutely did, but wouldn't admit to. Cry a little. Not too much. Just enough to show you're sorry without overdoing it.

"If you overdo it, oversell it, they won't believe you," Adam had told him. Being the oldest gave him an unfair advantage, which he didn't mind using on his kid brother. Adam liked the way T.J. looked up to him. The kid would follow him into the sun if Adam led the way.

T.J. was better at it than his brother ever was. Being the baby helped. Being actually scared this time helped even more. Only T.J. wasn't scared for himself. Sure, it rattled him. But deep down, he feared for his grandpa. John was the oldest Elton and T.J. was the youngest. They bonded on a different level. His grandpa was more than family. He was his best friend. His partner in crime.

Halfway through the second hour of waiting, the tactic worked.

Elsa called him over first, wrapping him in her arms and squeezing him like she could protect him from the world through sheer force of will. Eventually, Matty snapped out of his anxiety-induced trance. He looked at his son. Placed a hand on T.J.'s shoulder. With a straight face, he told him he was glad his son was okay.

But T.J. saw past it. He heard something behind Matty's words. Something in the back of his voice that told him his dad was guarding how scared he was. The only other time T.J. remembered his dad acting this way was when Adam fell off the roof a few summers back. Adam and Matty were up there re-shingling with some workers. Adam took a step too far to the right and plummeted over the side. Broke an arm and cracked a rib. The bone in his arm poked through the skin. Adam passed out from the pain. T.J. remembered how his father acted then. Panic mode. They ended up at this same hospital an hour later. His dad told him there was nothing to worry about. But he had that same look behind his eyes. Same tone behind his voice.

T.J. dropped his silent treatment tactics. Once his father hugged him, he realized how worried Matty was about his grandpa. Not just worried. Terrified. That scared T.J. more than anything. His dad was his hero. Nothing scared him. But this did, which meant this was serious.

Over the next hour, they sat in silence. Hospital sounds filled the hallways beyond the door. Fear spread through all three of them. The longer the medical staff kept John out, the darker their imaginations grew. At one point, T.J. couldn't hold back anymore. He cracked and cried over his grandpa—actual tears this time, not the tactical kind. His fear of being grounded had turned into fear for his grandpa. Then guilt. He buried his face in his hands and sobbed.

Elsa put an arm around him, squeezing his small frame into her chair with her. "What's wrong?"

He blurted it out. "It's my fault Grandpa's hurt." He wrapped his arms around his mother and buried his head against her chest. "I tricked him. I'm sorry. I should've listened."

"It's okay." Elsa rubbed his back like she used to do when they watched Saturday morning cartoons together. "It was an accident."

"Your grandpa's tough," Matty added, glancing at T.J. and

half-smiling. "Tougher than all of us. Toughest guy I ever met. He'll be okay."

"You're not worried?" T.J. stared at his dad with big, glassy eyes. He already knew the answer.

"Of course I'm worried. But your grandpa's stronger than the average grandpa. He's going to pull through." Matty paused. "I know it." Doubt crept into his voice despite the words.

He locked eyes with Elsa over their son's head. She saw the truth on his face—the worry lines deeper than usual, the tightness around his mouth, the way he swallowed hard before speaking. He was more worried than anyone else in that room. More worried than she'd seen him since his mom died.

After another half hour, their spirits improved when a nurse in green scrubs popped her head in. "He's doing fine. Just running a few more tests."

"You guys are being thorough," Matty said.

"Yes, sir." She left before there were more questions.

T.J. felt better after that. They all did. He moved on to another topic—Widow. A distraction for everyone. "Widow saved my life, Mom."

"Mr. Widow," she corrected him.

"Mr. Widow saved my life."

"I know he did. He's a good man." Elsa sensed there was more coming. T.J. had that look on his face like he was dancing around a question. She knew her boys better than they knew themselves. Including Matty.

T.J. paused. "Do you think he can stay with us? A little longer, I mean."

THE MIDNIGHT MEMORY wait

Elsa glanced at Matty. He stared back, his face blank.

Silence.

They owed Widow. That was undeniable. He'd saved T.J.'s life this morning. Maybe saved John's life last night too, finding him wandering the roads with a loaded shotgun and foggy confusion. The debt was real and heavy.

But Widow was still a stranger. A drifter. A dangerous man. Possibly a troublemaker. The kind who brought trouble with him?

"He could work for us," T.J. suggested.

"We can't afford another worker right now," Elsa said. "We've got as many people as we can handle."

"Not now," Matty added. "It's the middle of winter. There's no work to do. Maybe if he comes back in the summer, we could talk about it."

That quieted T.J. on the topic. It lasted about twenty minutes. Then he asked again.

The Eltons gave him the same answers. Too many workers already. No work in winter due to frozen ground, and the animals huddled for warmth in the barn on the longer snow days. Spring, summer, and fall were when they needed extra hands. This was the dead season. The waiting-till-spring season.

T.J. sighed dramatically and changed the subject.

Elsa checked her phone. She texted Adam: We're at the hospital with Grandpa. There was an accident. He's been hurt. We're waiting for more info. Call me.

No response. No read receipt, which meant he hadn't seen it yet. But he would. She didn't mention it to Matty. He had enough to worry about.

An hour later, a doctor with a familiar face entered the room. He was new, but familiar. Different from the one who'd seen them earlier. This was the same doctor who'd treated Widow, though none of them knew that. They'd seen him before. But none of them could recall his name. He wore a fresh white coat. The other one had mustard on it from a lunch accident he had. So he'd changed it.

A clipboard was tucked under his arm. "Hi folks. I'm Mitch Russell. I've got an update for you," he said and smiled.

The Eltons stood. Elsa squeezed Matty's hand, reminding him he wasn't alone. She hadn't squeezed his hand like that since his mother died five years ago. Time had a way of speeding up as you got older. The days turn to weeks to months to years to decades. At the beginning of life, it seems eternal. At the end, it seems like the blink of an eye.

Matty stared at the doctor. He fought back tears, like they waited in the wings for the worst news.

Dr. Russell launched into it. "Let's start with your son. T.J.'s tests all came back fine. Clean bill of health for him. Nothing wrong with the boy." He glanced at T.J. and cracked a smile. "You're a lucky kid."

T.J. asked, "What about my asthma?"

"You still got that. But no worries. I'm going to hook you up with a refill of some new stuff," Dr. Russell said, tousling T.J.'s hair. He was too old for it. He knew that. But he didn't complain.

"What about John?" Elsa asked.

Russell nodded at them empathetically and said, "That's a different story. But he's lucky too. No broken bones. Being thrown from a horse? At his age, that's honestly a small miracle. Mild concussion. Bruised ribs. Nothing that won't heal with time and plenty of bed rest. And I wouldn't recommend any more horse-breaking for him."

"That wasn't supposed to happen," Elsa said.

"I'm surprised he agreed to do it," Matty mumbled.

But Russell heard him. Russell asked, "Is it possible he forgot?"

Matty started to explain the night before, but stopped. He didn't want to talk about the details in front of T.J. He asked, "When can we see him?"

Russell paused a long beat. He half-whispered, "About that. Can I speak with you for a moment? Privately?"

He glanced at T.J., making it obvious.

Matty turned to Elsa, gave her a look from their shared Rolodex of looks that meant something to the other and no one else on Earth. As in many long marriages, they'd formed a language of their own. It included certain looks.

Elsa knew instantly what to do. Message received. Loud and clear. She squeezed T.J.'s shoulder, pulled him close. "Hey. Let's go down to the cafeteria. See if they have ice cream."

T.J. agreed without argument, which told Elsa he understood more than they wanted him to. He knew the signs when adults were going to talk about something that was above his eight-year-old paygrade.

They left. The door whispered shut.

The doctor turned to Matty. "Your father is stable. Physically, he's going to be fine. We're running a few more tests to be certain, but I'm confident about that."

"But?" Matty prompted, seeing on Russell's face there was more to say.

"But there's another issue. A concerning one."

"What's that?"

"I asked about the horse situation because I wonder if it's possible he forgot. Like he's confused. He's showing signs of cognitive decline. Possibly significant."

The words hung in the air for a long, quiet moment.

Matty said nothing. Couldn't say anything. He feared something like this. Last night it hadn't been that big of a deal, because he hadn't faced the reality of his father's decline. But he should have. He knew that now.

The night before, Matty might've been more confused about the event than his dad. It was the middle of the night. A stranger showed up at his house with his confused father. It was a confusing situation. And Widow's a very intimidating man. It didn't even dawn on him to question it further. Guilt crept in again. Matty blamed himself. He knew what had happened. He should've taken his dad to the E.R. this morning, instead of going about his day as business as usual.

He didn't think enough about the night before. None of them did. They failed to ask the right question: Should we take John to the hospital?

"It's his memory. Right?" Russell asked. "Has he been behaving strangely? Forgetting where he is? Stuff like that?"

Still fighting the denial, Matty said, "He's eighty-five. Isn't some memory loss normal at his age?"

"To a degree, yes. But could it be more than that?"

Matty stood there. Silent. Unable to come to grips with something he already knew.

Russell recognized the signs. Sometimes his job required him to treat not just his patients, but their families, too. So he gave

Matty a necessary push. He said, "For a moment, he had trouble recalling my name."

"You just met him today though," Matty said.

"Not so," the doctor said. "I've met him many times before. I've known your father for years."

Matty furrowed his brow. "Really?"

"Sure. I see your dad every other Saturday at the Nicely Center. We play dominoes. There's a whole group of us. Your dad's one of the regulars. Has been since the center opened." He paused. "He tells the same dirty jokes over and over."

The comment broke Matty from his spell. His shoulders lowered. The stress lowered. And for the first time, he smiled. "Yeah. I've heard them all," he said and paused. "I thought he was hanging out there with all old guys."

Russell said, "I'm younger than your dad, but I like going there. I get to see my patients outside the examining room. When you're someone's doctor and also their domino partner, they trust you more. Drop their guard. Makes me a better doctor." He paused. "Plus, I'm genuinely friends with a lot of them. Including John."

Matty nodded slowly.

Russell asked again, "So, anything you want to tell me? Is he having episodes of any kind? Forgetting things?"

Matty nodded and told him everything about the night before. About John stealing the truck at midnight and wandering off. He hesitated before mentioning the shotgun, but he did. Told him about Widow finding his father on some back road, about John yelling at someone who wasn't there—carrying on full conversations with ghosts only he could see.

Russell's eyes widened, and he stroked his beard. He stayed poker-faced. On the inside, his concern deepened. This could be worse than he suspected.

"What does it mean?" Matty asked.

"It means we need to keep him here overnight for observation. See how he does through the night, then regroup tomorrow."

Matty swallowed hard. "Okay. I understand." The words came out automatically. "What happens now?"

"Oh, you can see him. He's asking for you," Russell said, turned to the door, and stepped out into the hall. He stopped and waited, giving Matty space.

Matty stood there for a long moment, mouth slightly open, staring at nothing. His world was changing fast. Too fast. The ground beneath his feet felt unstable, like walking on a frozen lake in spring when you're not sure if the ice will hold.

Will it hold? he thought.

The doctor didn't rush him. Just stood there in the hallway, quietly.

Finally, Matty pulled himself together—that's what his father would've done—and joined Russell.

Russell led the way, and the two men headed down the hall together.

CHAPTER 13

On the second floor, in a different wing of the same hospital, Easton stood by a window with one hand shoved in his pocket and the other holding his near-empty coffee, watching the parking lot like it owed him answers.

Early afternoon sunlight slanted through the glass, painting the hall behind him in harsh light that showed every detail of the room behind him—including where the hospital custodians forgot to dust.

Easton had stopped by Room 401 earlier to talk to John Elton, but the old man wasn't there. Just his son, daughter-in-law, and their younger boy. Easton didn't want to speak with them yet. Not until he talked to John first. He found it best to speak directly with potential victims without their loved ones around. It was better to get the truth straight from the horse's mouth, so to speak, without influence from others. Matty loved his father. No question about that. Everyone who lived in Tent Hills would attest to it. But did he love his brother, too? If this Widow guy was his brother? Would Matty lie to cover for the guy? The answer, Easton didn't know. But it wouldn't surprise him.

Easton passed their room. He wanted to talk to the old man first. Get his version of events before anyone could coach him.

Easton asked an orderly, who he'd cited with traffic tickets more than once, where they'd taken John. The guy pointed Easton to the second floor. Which indicated that John's injuries were being taken seriously. The expensive machines resided on the second floor. CT scanners. MRI machines. The kind of equipment small hospitals couldn't afford to use without good reason.

Easton thanked him and headed to the elevator.

Dr. Russell—a doctor Easton actually knew—came out of a room a few minutes later, probably headed to speak with the Eltons upstairs. Easton caught him in the hall.

Russell confirmed he was headed back to the fourth floor. He asked why the sheriff was interested.

Easton told him part of the truth. John Elton showed up in the hospital all beaten up with a giant stranger in tow. All the same information the desk receptionist had gossiped with him about, minus the theories or opinions about it. Russell didn't mention Widow. So Easton asked him.

"Well, you know I can't talk about Mr. Widow," Russell said, smiling a practiced doctor smile. "Doctor-patient confidentiality."

"Right."

"I'm headed to speak with the Eltons now. Want to join me?"

"Nah. I'll meet you back here. I want to talk to John first."

Russell paused. "Okay, but Bill—I'd prefer if you wait for us. John's a patient. There's something going on with him. But I can't talk about it. I just need to insist that you don't interrogate him without his son present. Got it?"

Easton stared at him. This was the first time Russell had ever pushed back against his authority. First time any civilian in Tent Hills had, except for the local judges. But judges were different. Court orders were different. He'd never had to answer to doctor's orders before.

Russell's response was so left field, Easton retorted, "Whatever you say."

"I mean it. You're the sheriff, but this is my hospital. I have an obligation to protect my patients' well-being. Even from the law. So please. Wait here. I'll be back with Matty. Okay?"

"Fine," Easton said and shrugged.

"All right. Good."

Easton nodded and walked back to the window. Russell disappeared around the corner.

Easton glanced after him and finished his coffee, tossing the cup in a wastebasket. Then he pushed away from the window and moved toward the door to John's room. Quiet on the linoleum. Checking over his shoulder in case one nurse had been told to keep him out. But their backs were to him.

He slipped into the room and found John Elton sitting up in bed, staring at a TV hung on the wall. The Price is Right was on. It was an ancient episode too. It had to be. Bob Barker was hosting, and he'd been off the show for a long time, dead now too. Easton couldn't remember how long ago. The TV volume was turned all the way down. The closed captions were on the screen.

The old rancher looked smaller than Easton remembered. Diminished by hospital gowns and fluorescent lighting in a way that age alone couldn't accomplish. The setting put everyone in a new light.

John turned his head. Saw Easton. No surprise on his weathered face. Just tired recognition.

John Elton wasn't a particularly attractive man. In fact, if a witness had described an elderly, frail man who sat more on the side of ugly than not, Easton would know exactly who they were describing.

"Bill? What're you doing here?" John asked and scooted up in the bed.

"Mr. Elton." Easton moved closer. "How you feeling?"

"Like I got thrown from a horse." John's voice carried dry humor. The kind that came from a man who'd been injured enough times to know the difference between bad and worse. And this wasn't so bad. He'd faced worse before. "Which I suppose I did."

"Is that what happened? You fell from a horse?"

John nodded. Slow. Careful. Like the movement cost him. "Shouldn't have been on that bronco. Not at my age. I knew better. Just didn't listen to that internal voice. Guess I was trying to impress my grandson. You know?"

Easton grabbed a visitor's chair, pulled it closer to John, and sat. The chair matched the ones that the Eltons sat in upstairs. The frame creaked a quiet little sound from his weight. "Mind if I ask you some questions?"

"About what?"

"What happened?"

John said, "Not much to tell. It's like I said. I got thrown from a horse, is all."

Easton nodded and asked, "What about last night?"

Something shifted in John's face. Confusion crept in around his eyes. "Last night?"

"You don't remember?"

John stared at him. His expression went blank like he'd been asked his name, only to just realize he couldn't remember it. It confused Easton, too. The old man blinked several times and said nothing for a long moment. Easton didn't interrupt him. He let John try to recall it. But nothing happened. There was no expression of recognition in his eyes. John tried to remember. But there was nothing. It was like trying to clear fog from a windshield, only the mist kept coming. "No. I don't remember last night. What happened?"

"You took your son's truck. Drove off the ranch around midnight."

"I did?" John looked genuinely lost. Like a man just waking from a coma. "Where'd I go?"

"That's what I'm trying to figure out. A stranger found you on the road. Out past the county line. Big guy. Brought you home."

"Widow." John's confusion cleared from his face, like sunlight breaking through storm clouds. He recognized the name. "Yeah. I met him. He's a good guy. Saved T.J. this morning. He saved him from that bronco. Now I think about it. He saved both of us."

"How so? Tell me about that."

"Yeah. T.J. was on the horse when he shouldn't have been. My fault for letting him talk me into it. Kid's got a gift for getting what he wants." John paused. His eyes went distant. Then he said, "Anyway, the horse threw both me and T.J. I guess that's why I'm in so much pain." He touched his bandaged ribs and grimaced. "Next thing I know, I'm on the ground. T.J.'s standing there frozen. The horse got a wild look in his eyes. And he charged at my grandson." He trailed off, like what he was about to say was completely insane.

Easton waited a long beat, giving Elton time to answer. When he said nothing, Easton asked, "Then what?"

"Oh. Yeah. The bronco charged and it would've run my grandson down too. If not for Widow. He came out of nowhere. I didn't even see him run into the pen. But he was there, standing between the charging bronco and my grandson. Widow punched that horse right in the face. He broke his hand doing it. I've never seen anything like it. The horse went down like it'd been shot."

Easton leaned forward. Elbows on his knees. "You remember all that? You sure that's how it happened?"

Elton nodded.

"But you don't remember last night? Don't remember taking your son's truck?"

"No, sir." Elton looked down at his hands. At the lines and scars of decades of ranch work. "It's funny. You see these lines on my hands?" he asked and showed Easton the aged lines on his weathered hands.

Easton nodded.

"I can remember back before I got these. I can remember how I got each of them. All the time spent breaking horses and growing corn. All the days with my wife." Elton paused. "But last night. It's all blank. Like it didn't happen. Like somebody erased it."

Just then, someone cleared their throat, and Easton noticed two men standing in the doorway.

Dr. Russell walked in with Matty behind him. Both men stopped when they saw Easton sitting by John's bedside. Elton's features lit up when he saw his son.

Russell said, "Bill. I thought we agreed you'd wait."

"I did," Easton said, standing. "Felt stupid waiting out there. So I came in. Mr. Elton is my friend too."

Russell nodded and glanced at John, then at Matty. "John, Matty, mind if I discuss John's condition with the sheriff present? I can ask him to leave."

Matty glanced at his father. John shrugged and said, "Doesn't matter to me."

"Go ahead," Matty said.

Russell stepped to the bedside. Just then, his phone buzzed like a pager. He checked it and pocketed it. He didn't make a face to indicate if it was important or something that could wait. He said, "Physically, you're banged up, John. Bruised ribs. Mild concussion. Deep tissue bruising. But nothing that won't heal with time and rest."

"When can I go home?" John asked.

Russell paused. "That's what concerns me. Your memory lapse from last night. The confusion about events that just happened. We'd like to keep you overnight. Run some additional tests."

"Tests for what?"

"Look, John. There's no easy way to say this. You're an old man. It's possible you're showing early signs of cognitive decline."

The words hung in the air. The room went quiet except for distant monitor beeps and muffled conversations bleeding through the walls.

Matty stared at his father, trying to keep the same straight face he did for his son. But this was different. It was far more impossible to hide his true fears in front of his father.

John asked, "I have dementia?"

"I can't diagnose that at this time," Russell said, choosing his words carefully. "But we should monitor you tonight. Run some tests while you're sleeping. Brain scans. Sleep studies. Blood work. Get a clearer picture. We can reassess tomorrow."

John stared at his hands for a long moment. When he finally spoke, his voice was low and quiet. "Okay."

"We'll take good care of you," Russell said. "Don't worry. If everything goes well, we can have you back up and busting broncos in a matter of months." He chuckled. No one else did. "Well, not really. But you can play dominoes."

John nodded and smiled, but didn't laugh. Matty fought back tears, but didn't cry.

Russell's phone buzzed again. He ignored it. Then his name came over the hospital's PA system. It was muffled through the walls, but they all heard it. He turned to Easton. "Bill, if you have more questions—"

"I'm good for now."

Russell nodded and left them.

Easton stood there another moment. He watched the Eltons not quite looking at each other. Both of them processed this new possibility and how it might change everything in their lives. Finally, Easton looked at Matty and then at John. He said, "I'll be in touch if I need anything else."

Easton walked out into the hallway. He took out his phone and texted Bloom that he'd wait for her in the parking lot.

CHAPTER 14

The afternoon sun beamed down across Tent Hills, both the town and the hills themselves. The hilltops cast shadowy points across the landscape. Even with the worst of winter to come, the temperature was warmer today than the night before. The local forecast called for sunny days and cold nights.

Widow wouldn't have known any of that because he didn't own a TV or a phone to check the weather app. He owned a toothbrush, which was shoved into a pocket at that moment. Technically, he owned the clothes on his back, and he owned a lifetime of memories. Not much else.

Widow squinted in the sunlight. He saluted, like he was standing in front of a C.O., and used the salute to shade his eyes from the sun. He scanned ahead of him, saw the street, and crossed the hospital parking lot, unzipping his puffer coat because it was warmer outside than he'd expected. The cast on his hand was bulky and awkward. Not something he was used to, but also something he'd worn before. More times than he could remember. One memory that came to mind was a time when he rode Empire Builder out of the Pacific North-west and headed east. It was a beautiful train ride. Scenic. But somewhere along the way, the train he rode derailed and flipped. He woke up handcuffed to a hospital bed. They'd put a cast on his hand then, too.

Widow walked on. Much of the snow from the previous night had melted away. Even from this morning, when the Eltons first took him to the hospital, it had melted away.

The concrete was damp in places from melted snow. Widow's boots squeaked quietly over the sidewalk pavement. Behind him, the E.R.'s automatic doors hissed closed. An ambulance pulled up with lights flashing, but no sirens. A couple of paramedics parked it and hopped out. They walked to the hospital casually. No patient came out the back. They must've been using the lights to speed through midday traffic.

Widow stepped off the sidewalk and tracked through the lot. The morphine had faded away. Now he felt fully alert and sober. The price for that was the intense pain from his knuckles. It hurt more than when his hand was broken in that train derailment.

The doctor had given him a prescription for Percocet, ten tablets, and told him to keep the cast dry. He was supposed to keep the cast on for six weeks.

Widow walked past a sheriff's SUV, an all-black Tahoe, clearly marked as Police. It was parked in a reserved doctor's parking space. The SUV sat empty, but the windows were cracked. A radio crackled inside.

Widow didn't catch what was said. But he doubted it was Bloom's vehicle because of what rested on the dash. A white cowboy hat was parked in between the windshield and the dashboard. It was in pristine condition. He figured it was a safe bet it wasn't her hat. He could be wrong, but he wasn't. That was made clear three seconds later when he rounded a corner of parked trucks and saw what must've been Tent Hills' entire police force.

Ahead of him and two rows over, a cluster of police SUVs idled together. Bloom stood in a circle outside the vehicles, talking to the town sheriff and two other deputies. The three men all dwarfed her in size. Bloom struck him as tough as nails, but she was small compared to the men she worked with. Like Widow's mother, Bloom was small in size, but big in stature.

All four wore the same uniform—dark tan shirts, with clip-on ties to match, and tan khakis. They wore the same gun belts and same shoes. Each wore a pair of aviator sunglasses, except for Bloom. Two of the deputies were subordinates to the sheriff. They were obvious. They looked so much alike that they could've been interchangeable. They wore the same bored expressions. The kind that came with the territory for small-town cops. However, Bloom and the sheriff didn't look bored. They appeared to be discussing something important.

Widow kept walking. No reason to change course. And every reason to avoid them. In his experience, avoiding cops was always the best course of action. Even though he used to be one. Technically. These days, Widow avoided cops more than he did sketchy people he saw on the street. Gangs and criminals, Widow could deal with. They didn't carry a badge. They had no shield to hide behind. No authority over him.

Bloom spotted him before the others. Her face lit up. She waved.

Widow waved back.

She shouted across the lot, "See you tonight!"

Widow smiled, nodded, but kept moving. He wasn't going to stop and chat with her because of the other cops. Widow had seen this show before. Many times. Small-town cops were bored, looking for something to do. They often paid a lot closer attention to outsiders than city cops did. And he was an interesting outsider to pay attention to. Interesting to small-town cops, anyway.

Not that he had anything to hide. Better to err on the side of caution.

Widow made it another ten yards before Easton's voice carried across the parking lot. Confused, he ignored it. Easton spoke in the kind of tone that demanded answers. It was a tone he was all too familiar with. A reel of past commanding officers played through his mind.

"Wait? What?" the sheriff asked, confused.

Widow kept walking. Whatever conversation happened behind him wasn't his business. And he wanted to keep it that way. He aimed to stay out of it.

CHAPTER 15

Bloom watched Widow walk away. She teetered on the edge of a trance. Lost in thought. There was something about the way he moved. He walked with what she called swagger. It was his confidence. It made her smile.

Widow walked out into the street, turned on the sidewalk, and vanished behind a line of snowy trees.

Easton and the other two deputies stared at her.

"Why're you seeing him tonight? For what?" Easton asked.

Bloom's smile faded. She'd come off too excited. She dialed it back.

"You told me to get a read on him."

"I meant talk to him. Get some information. Feel him out. Not go out on a date with the man." It came out aggressive and overprotective.

One deputy, mid-thirties and cocky, smirked and pushed off his cruiser. "I thought you were a lesbian? That's what you told me when I asked you out."

The other deputy, older but not wiser, grinned. "She turned you down because you're ugly."

Laughter erupted between the two. The kind that came easy in parking lots with nothing but time and bad jokes to fill it.

Bloom rolled her eyes, unoffended. She was used to it. "My personal preference is none of your business. But even if I were gay, I'm not blind. That's a real man."

The younger deputy's mouth fell slack. "Oh, and I'm not?" He took it personally, but kept it to himself.

"Shut up, Jimmy! You two go back to work!" Easton barked and snapped his fingers twice. Fast. Like he always did when he wanted to shut them up.

The laughter stopped. Jimmy and the other deputy straightened up. They exchanged glances, still grinning.

"Okay, why don't you two get out of here?" Easton said. They lingered a second too long. "Go on. You got routes to patrol. Get going. Fun's over."

Jimmy and the older deputy got into their SUVs, engines already running. One after the other, they pulled out of the lot. The older deputy went one way. Jimmy turned the other.

Easton waited until they were gone. Then he turned back to Bloom. The humor had drained from his face. All business now.

"Are you sure about this?"

Bloom uncrossed her arms and planted her feet shoulder-width apart. Easton noticed.

"Think about it like I'm going undercover. What better way to get close to him, to get information, than go out with the guy?"

"Who said anything about going undercover? I asked you to talk to the man."

"I made a judgment call. I think you're right. He's dangerous. It's worth taking a close look at him."

"This is a bad idea."

"I can handle myself."

Easton grunted at that. He'd heard it before.

"I know you can handle yourself against a normal guy." He gestured in the direction Widow had walked. Just a quick flick of his head. "But that ain't no ordinary drunk local who steps out of line because you pulled him over. That guy's something different."

"I can see he looks dangerous."

"No. You don't understand. I've seen it before. It's not that he looks dangerous. That guy is dangerous. He doesn't just look it. He is it."

"That doesn't make him a criminal."

Easton said nothing to that. "You get his name?"

She stared at him blankly. Blinked several times. Her mouth opened. Closed. Opened again. "I forgot to introduce myself. Damn. I've got no idea what his name is."

Easton pointed at her chest. At the silver badge pinned on her uniform above her left breast pocket. "He knows yours, though. It's on your name badge."

Bloom's face flushed. Her hand came up to touch the badge. Like she was confirming what he already knew. "I can't believe it slipped my mind."

"This is the kind of thing I'm talking about. You know nothing about this guy, except that he looks dangerous." He shook his head. Slow. Deliberate.

Bloom's embarrassment faded. Her lips curled into a half-smile. The hard shell returned. "Relax, Dad. I'm kidding. His name's Widow. Can't believe you thought I didn't get his name."

Easton stared at her. Not amused. Not even a little. "Ha ha. Funny. You know I hired you for your sense of humor. You know what?"

Bloom said nothing.

"Maybe I should get Jimmy on this instead? He has seniority over you after all." He looked dead serious.

"What? You've got to be joking?" she blurted out and stared at him.

Easton paused a beat. He let the silence pass between them. The wind picked up. Cold. Cutting through their uniforms.

He pulled his jacket tighter. "Yeah, I think Jimmy should go on that date instead of you. He'll look good in a tight skirt. Don't you think?"

Bloom stared at him. Relief and irritation washed over her. "What?"

"You are going to wear a tight skirt, right? You gotta entice the man if you want to get information out of him."

"I beg your pardon?"

Easton looked over the rim of his aviators at her. "I can also be funny. See?"

Bloom smiled. "You really had me going."

Easton smiled a crooked smile. It was rare to see, but he did it sometimes. He had a real deadpan sense of humor.

"When you get the chance, run his name through the data-base. See what you find."

"Which database? The state? FBI?"

"All of them."

"You think he's got a record?"

"A man like that has surely had his run-ins with the law."

Bloom nodded. Making mental notes. This was her shot. Her chance to prove she was more than just a deputy who wrote speeding tickets and broke up bar fights.

"Okay. I will. Don't worry about me. I'll be fine."

"Yeah, right." Easton pointed at the holstered gun on her hip. "Take your sidearm with you tonight."

"Sure. Whatever you say, boss."

Easton went quiet for a long moment. He glanced back at the hospital buildings, over the parked vehicles. The white walls. The clean windows.

"The hospital's going to keep Mr. Elton overnight for observa-tion. The doc thinks he may have something wrong with his brain."

"Like what?"

"All he told me was Elton's showing signs of cognitive decline."

"That's too bad. I like him. He's a sweet old man."

"We all grow old."

"What's he got? Alzheimer's?"

"Maybe. Or maybe it's dementia. But whatever." Easton tipped his sunglasses back further on his nose with one finger.

"Sounds like with whatever he's got, he slips in and out of old memories. Like he's reliving them. Which makes me question the story about the horse."

"What story?"

"Apparently, this Widow guy punched a horse."

Bloom stared at him sideways. "What?" She thought about Widow's cast.

"They're saying the whole reason they're both in here is Elton got thrown from a wild horse they're trying to break. The kid too. The kid was on the ground, and the spooked horse nearly stampeded him. But Widow came out of nowhere, stood in the way, and punched the horse off course. Mid-stampede."

"What the hell?"

"Yeah. It's ridiculous."

"He is wearing a cast."

Easton shrugged. "Yeah, well also Elton had an episode last night, which he doesn't remember. He stole his son's truck and drove it a few miles from their ranch. Apparently Widow found him out there shooting a gun and arguing with someone who wasn't there."

Bloom stared wide-eyed. "That sounds insane."

"Yeah. I know."

"Could it be possible?" she asked.

"Anything's possible. Few people were on the road last night. Elton's lived here for decades. Maybe his whole life. He probably knows these roads in a way that doesn't require much brain power. Second nature. I suppose he could've stumbled out of the house, confused, got into the truck and drove out there."

Bloom said, "I read once about a sleepwalker from New York. He woke up in the middle of the night, got dressed, took the train downtown and tried to enter the building he worked in. He woke up the next morning fully dressed, holding his briefcase on the steps of the building."

"Weird. Well, then I guess it's possible." Easton nodded. "Just be skeptical of your new boyfriend. Don't believe everything he tells you."

"Trust, but verify?"

"Not even that. Trust nothing he tells you."

Bloom let out a breath. Long. Slow. "I guess I'll just take him out and find out what I can."

"What?" Easton asked.

She stared at him.

"What's that sigh for?"

"I just hope this leads to something. I'm ready for something more. More responsibility. I want to get out of here one day. Be a detective in a big city somewhere."

Easton had heard that before.

"You want more action." His voice shifted. "Most detective work is boring and methodical. Building a case. It's not like the movies."

"Are you making me a detective now?"

"We've not had a detective here in years. There is a spot open."

"But are you making me a detective?"

"Eventually, I gotta fill that spot."

Before he could say another word, Bloom leaped on him. Her arms wrapped around his neck. Hugging him before she could stop herself.

"Oh, thank you! Thank you!" she said into his shoulder.

"Slow your jets!" Easton eased her away from him. He glanced around the parking lot, making sure there were no witnesses to her outburst. And just then, like clockwork, Mrs. Walsh stood on the sidewalk, her hand covering her mouth.

Easton stepped back from Bloom. They both looked at Mrs. Walsh. Easton waved to her and called out, "Hello, Mrs. Walsh."

She said nothing. She lowered her hand, closed her mouth, and walked to her car. She glanced back a few times before she got in and drove off.

"She's going to tell the whole town that we're doing something inappropriate." Easton shook his head.

Bloom said, "That old bird needs to get a life."

Easton moved on. "I'm not doing anything yet. This is a chance to prove what you got. If there's something here, I expect you to investigate and find it."

"What if there's nothing? What if Widow's clean? And everything is as they claim it is?"

"There's something there. I got a gut feeling."

"What if there's not?"

"Then it's good practice for you." He paused. "All right, go to work. I've got a lot to do myself."

The wind picked up again. Colder this time.

Easton turned and headed toward his cruiser. Bloom followed

and stopped at hers and got in. She watched Easton pull out of the lot before she let herself smile.

She could make detective. She just had to prove herself first.

She opened her police computer, attached to the dash, and accessed the database. She typed in the name: Jack Widow.

The screen loaded. Then it showed results. But there wasn't much. Nearly nothing, in fact.

No driver's license. No address. No criminal record. No social media. No digital footprint at all.

It was like Jack Widow didn't exist.

Which was impossible. Everyone existed somewhere. In some database. On some server. In some file.

Bloom stared at the screen. At the empty search results. At the man who'd punched a horse and carried himself like he didn't have a care in the world.

Who are you, Widow?

She'd have to dig deeper. Make some phone calls. She didn't want to ask Easton for help. She wanted to prove she could do this on her own.

CHAPTER 16

Widow walked into downtown Tent Hills mid-afternoon, one hand in a pocket, the cast swinging by his side, bulky and awkward. The sun hung lower in the sky than earlier, casting shadows across the pavement. Some stretched into eerie shapes—abstract forms that seemed to follow him from another dimension. Several times along his walk, he wondered if a lingering side effect from the extra morphine was paranoia.

The realization of having such a thought told him that paranoia was definitely a side effect from the morphine.

The main street ran straight through the center of town, lined on both sides with historic brick buildings that looked like they'd been standing since the early 1950s. Colorful wooden awnings stretched out over the sidewalks. Old-fashioned streetlamps stood at regular, planned intervals. Paint chips peeled off some of them. Others were still solid black without scratches or imperfections. None that Widow could see.

Widow passed a crowd of people standing around talking to one man. At first, Widow thought it was the mayor or something. The small crowd around the man treated him like he was some high-status politician—too small to be the president, but mayor fit.

Then Widow got a look at the guy. Big, expensive yellow suit, same bright white smile, only without the sparkle. It was Mitch Nicely, the used car salesman from the billboard.

He stood with a small team of his employees. They handed out placards that hung from a vehicle's rearview mirror, like a handicap placard. Nicely and his team shook hands with locals. Nicely saw Widow through the crowd. He noticed Widow had no placard. Before Widow could break free from the man's eye contact, they stood face to face. Nicely reached out a hand for Widow to shake.

Reluctantly, Widow took it and shook it. But something immediately struck Widow. There was something unusual about the man's hand.

Nicely smiled a big smile—all white teeth. He saw Widow noticed his hand. The man only had four digits on the hand Widow was shaking. Three fingers and one thumb. One of his fingers was nothing but a stump near the knuckle.

Nicely said, "That missing digit always stumps people when I first meet them." He chuckled at a joke he probably told a thousand times.

"Sorry, I didn't mean to seem weird about it."

"Oh, it's perfectly all right. It happens to me every day. It makes for a great icebreaker."

Widow released the guy's hand.

Nicely said, "I pride myself on knowing everyone who lives here. I've never seen you before. A guy as big as you, I think I'd remember. I'm Mitch Nicely. What's your name?"

Widow told him.

"Well, Mr. Widow. What kind of car guy are you?"

"I don't own a car."

Nicely's eyes lit up bigger than they were on the billboard. "That's a stroke of luck. For me, I mean. I'm the man you need to come see. What kind of car you interested in?"

Nicely looked Widow up and down, judging him by his outfit —the ugly puffer coat and all. Then he added, "We take bad credit."

"I'm not looking for a car."

"Of course not. You're too big for a car. You need room. Something bigger. We're stocked to the gills with top-of-the-line pickups! Ford! Chevy! What's your poison?"

"I'm not interested."

"Huh. Well, that's okay. If you change your mind, come see me." He tried to hand Widow a placard.

"No thanks. I have nowhere to put it." Widow thanked him again and left him standing there, placard in hand. It was only a few seconds before Nicely was already talking to his next target.

Downtown Tent Hills had the kind of architecture that looked good in postcards and tourism brochures, which seemed to work because there were lots of pedestrians. Numerous vehicles were parked along street parking. All had Nebraska plates, but Widow sensed that most weren't from here. For one thing, he was pretty sure he'd already seen the entire Tent Hills police force. They didn't have the manpower for a population this size. Not on a regular basis.

This suspicion was confirmed when Widow passed a row of parked Nebraska State Patrol cars, each with an expensive Police Interceptor Utility package, including the push bumpers mounted on the front grille and heavy-duty steel wheels designed for high-speed pursuit.

Several state troopers stood around the back of one vehicle, drinking coffee and shooting the shit. One of them had a trooper hat resting behind him on the roof of his cruiser. The others kept theirs on, like it was regulation to take them off. Two of them leaned against their cruisers. They all glanced in Widow's direction. One of them tipped his hat at him, saying either "hello, civilian" or "I'm clocking you as a person of interest."

Widow didn't know which it was meant to be. He suspected the latter. Or maybe it was both. He didn't return the gesture. He turned on the next street to get out of their view, and out of their crosshairs.

That street was short. It led to another street, less busy than the main drag, but still busy. Widow doubted the town saw this many people most days of the year. But something was different today. The whole town was setting up for something. Widow could tell by the activity. By the banners being raised across the street. By the vendors positioning food trucks and trailers along the curbs. By the locals hustling back and forth, carrying rolls of extension cords, folding tables, and boxes of supplies.

Every business along the curb and storefront seemed to take part in the setup. It reminded him of what Adam had mentioned at breakfast. Widow had been so distracted he forgot about it, which was understandable. So far today—if you count the day starting one second after midnight—he'd nearly been shotgunned to death, punched a horse, taken morphine, gotten a cast on his hand, and been asked out by a younger woman with a badge. For a guy who lived carefree, he had a lot on his plate suddenly.

But there it was. The answer to what was going on. The thing the Eltons spoke about at the breakfast table that morning.

An enormous banner hung across the street, suspended between two streetlamps. The words on it ranged from small to big. It was printed in bold red letters on white fabric. The whole thing spelled out: *Welcome to the eleventh annual HUSK-TOWN SHOWDOWN FESTIVAL!*

Another banner, smaller, advertised it took place all day Monday this year. A sign staked in the ground under the banner, near the sidewalk, revealed the surrounding streets would be closed to vehicle traffic for the festival.

Widow kept walking, observing everything as he went. He didn't have to weave around the sidewalk foot traffic. The pedestrians moved out of his way willingly, like he was a bull shark swimming upstream in a river.

Widow kept his cast-free hand in his coat pocket. The cast on his other hand waved alongside him. It felt heavier than it should have, but he'd get used to it. It was strange. Even with the cast, hand injury, and the shotgun scare in his face the night before, the day was shaping out to be a good one.

His day consisted of the locals of Tent Hills getting ready for their annual corn festival tradition. Which was in the beginning of winter. He didn't know why.

The festival setup unfolded around him like a small-town choreography everyone seemed to know by heart. Maybe there was a festival director, or an elected board who oversaw everything. He wasn't sure. Neither would surprise him because it all gave the impression of a coordinated effort, like hosting the World Cup, only on a much smaller scale.

A local band unloaded equipment from a van near what looked like a makeshift stage constructed from plywood and two-by-fours. All the band members were over forty with long hair. Two had mullets—long in back, thin on top.

The street was still open to traffic for today. Cars drove through slowly, careful not to hit anyone or run over the power cables snaking across the pavement. But tomorrow, the entire street would be shut down. The entire downtown would transform into a pedestrian zone. Music would play from the stage. Kids would run wild between the game booths. Adults would stand around drinking beer from plastic cups, pretending they enjoyed being out in the cold. *Was there a no open container law in Nebraska? Or the county?* Widow imagined there probably was. But the cops would most likely overlook such infractions. Especially when he imagined everyone would break that law.

Widow kept walking until he spotted a bookstore on the other side of the street. It drew his attention and before he knew it, he was headed over to it. He crossed the road, waiting for a group of teenagers jammed into a Honda Civic to pass. He stopped outside the store.

A store sign above the door read: *CHAPTER & VERSE & COFFEE BOOKSTORE* in faded gold letters on a green sign. They did the sign that way on purpose. It gave it an old Manhattan bookstore vibe, like the whole thing was painted decades ago. It was obvious because there was a coffee shop attached to the store. It was one of those big brands that everyone knew. Not the big kid on the block, but the next rung down the ladder.

It wasn't a coffee he remembered trying before. But he wanted coffee, he liked books, and he had time to kill. His date with Bloom was later on. So why not stop at a place that offers books and coffee? Two birds dead with one stone kind of thing.

CHAPTER 17

Large windows at the storefront displayed a mix of new release books, both fiction and nonfiction. Widow recognized the big-name authors, but not most of the others. He thought about the last book he'd read. It wasn't bad. But it wasn't memorable either. It was a book with a lot of high praise on the cover. It was one of those self-help gurus. Normally he didn't go for that kind of grift, but a former SEAL, like himself wrote this one. He'd tried it, but mediocre writing, compounded by even worse advice, made it forgettable. He wasn't even sure he finished it. He'd left it on a bus stop bench in Kansas.

A chalkboard propped on an easel outside the door advertised *COFFEE INSIDE* and *FREE Wi-Fi* in neat, hand-drawn letters. Although the coffee part was obvious. He guessed having it double obvious was a marketing tactic. It seemed to work because there were many people perusing the book aisles and even more walking out with hot coffee from the counter.

Next to the bookstore's entrance, a patio area popped out onto the sidewalk. It was mostly empty except a pair of teenagers who faced the other direction. They held hands and did the whole young love thing.

Widow pulled open the main door and stepped inside. A bell chimed overhead, one of those old-fashioned bells on a string, which he figured was more to match the old hole-in-the-wall bookstore ambience than it was to alert the staff to a new customer walking in.

That morning at the Elton's ranch, he'd been awakened by two of his favorite smells in the world—fresh-brewed coffee and frying bacon. But now he realized there was another smell he loved as much as those two. That smell, combined with the scent of coffee from the coffeeshop, hit him just as hard as the breakfast smells at the Elton's. It was the smell of fresh coffee and old books, from the used book section. The paper and old wood. It was a combination unique to bookstores that also served coffee.

The bookstore was small but well-organized, with a comforting, lived-in feel. Bookshelves lined the walls from floor to ceiling. The coffeeshop area occupied the front corner. Round tables scattered throughout the space, all of them occupied. Several customers sat and stared at laptops, looking like they were hard at work. Others chatted. And a few buried their heads in books. The customers indoors nursed their coffees out of oversized ceramic mugs.

Behind the counter near the entrance, a young woman with dyed green hair pulled back into a tight ponytail looked up and smiled. She had piercings in her face and overcomplicated eyeliner. It seemed to bother a pair of women standing in front of Widow. They ordered and the moment she turned her back, they made comments. When she returned with their orders, they smiled to her face.

Widow came up next. She smiled at him with a big, warm smile. "Welcome in. Can I get you something to drink?"

Her piercings didn't bother him. He had extensive sleeve tattoos on both arms. Plus, he was in the Navy. He couldn't count the number of sailors who pierced various parts of their body after they got out.

Live and let live was his motto. It always seemed to be that last part that so many people had a problem with. Let live. Or in the words of Violet: Mind your own beeswax. Or was it Poppy who'd said that? He couldn't remember. One of them said it back on that dying farm in Missouri.

"Sir?" the girl behind the counter asked. He drifted off into his memories for a moment.

"Coffee. Black," Widow said.

"Small, medium, or large?"

"Large."

"Sure thing. That'll be six-fifty."

Six-fifty, Widow thought. Coffee sure had gotten very expensive since he first started the nomad life. Then again, everything had.

Widow pulled out two five-dollar bills and set them on the counter. The barista turned and walked to a back counter to pour his coffee. He glanced around the bookstore while she worked. The place was cozy and welcoming. No wonder it was crowded. Worn hardwood floors creaked underfoot. Mismatched furniture looked like it had been collected over years from thrift stores and estate sales. Local artwork hung on the walls between the bookshelves. Paintings of Nebraska landscapes. Photographs of cornfields at sunset.

The girl handed him a large coffee in a big ceramic mug with the face of a cross-eyed cat on it. Widow took it and tried the coffee. It was good. Better than the gas station coffee he'd had the night before. Widow waved off the change and thanked her.

He walked around the bookstore, down the aisles, and browsed the books. He searched through the sections for a long time. He drank the entire coffee and still found nothing to read. Not that there were no books that caught his eye. The problem was he found loads of books that appealed to him. He didn't know what to pick. A lot of readers would just take them all home. Widow had no home. There was no rule for books. Not for him. But he limited himself to one at a time. Because Widow had no home, no bookshelf—he couldn't buy all the books he wanted. Whatever books he bought, he had to carry with him. Widow didn't like to carry more than he needed. And he didn't need twenty books.

After he bought his second cup of coffee, he stood in some aisle staring at the backs of books. Everything sounded interesting.

A group of teenage girls saw him standing there. They stayed at the end of the aisle, giggling over something. Finally, one of them, a redheaded girl with dark eyeliner and a Van Halen t-shirt, approached him. She asked if he needed a book recommendation.

At first, he told her he was okay. Then the entire group came up to him and asked him the same question. He asked if one of them worked there or something.

A blonde one scoffed at the question, like she was offended. But then she retorted, "Ew! No way!"

Another one said, "You're thinking of Ester Marrow. She's the only loser who'd work in a place like this."

Widow frowned, but didn't respond to that. He wasn't about to get into an argument with a group of teenage girls. At first, he nearly told them that working around books was a dream job. Millionaires, adventurers, and inventors were created from reading books. But he kept it to himself.

Widow could take on multiple big guys all at once in hand-to-hand combat. But talking to a group of teenage girls? He was out of his element.

The blonde one, who Widow established was their leader, asked him again if he was looking for a book to read. Widow paused a beat. He didn't want to engage with them. But he was looking for something to read. So he said, "I'm looking for a quick read. Like a thriller. You got a recommendation?"

The blonde said, "Mister, I got the best recommendation." She signaled to the redhead, who walked by Widow, stopped at the J's—where the authors whose last name began with the letter J were. She knelt and grabbed a book off the shelf and handed it to Widow.

Widow looked at the cover. A fancy knot on a tie strung across the cover. It was over various shades of dark blue. He knew a lot of knots from being in the Navy. And navy blue was his color. He'd never heard of the author before. But words over her name read: #1 New York Times Bestseller.

Widow flipped the book over to read the blurb, but the blonde covered it with her hand. She said, "You want to go in blind. It's got tons of twists and turns."

Widow stared at her. She removed her hand.

"Trust us, mister," the redhead said.

The other one added, "The back spoils too much. It's an awesome read."

Widow shrugged and lowered the book, kept it in his hand. He was looking for something to read. This was a thriller book. It was in the thriller section. It sounded as good as any. So, he thanked them and headed to the register.

He stopped halfway through the store and glanced back at the pack of teenagers. They were giggling and staring at him.

Widow paid for the book and took it to the coffee side of the store to find a seat to read. The inside was still full. So, he headed out to the patio, which turned out to be small but efficient. There were five metal tables with matching chairs. A metal railing separated the patio from the sidewalk. A single overhead heater was mounted on the wall. It kept the space warm despite the afternoon chill.

Only one table was occupied. It was the young teenage couple he'd seen earlier from behind. Because of the festival, all the town's teenagers were running free today.

From this angle, Widow got a look at the young couple. It was Adam Elton and some girl wearing a coat over a work uniform. It was for the bookstore.

They sat at a table near the far corner. The girl sat across from him. They were holding hands across the table, talking quietly, smiling at each other the way young couples do when they think no one's watching. The girl was pretty. She had dark hair and big blue eyes. However, she was timid and meek, like a person who didn't like the spotlight to be on her.

Widow chose a table on the opposite side of the patio, far enough away to give them privacy but close enough to the railing that he could glance up from his new book and watch the street and the festival setup continuing outside.

Widow loved to read books whenever he could. For him, getting lost in a good book was what the kids call peak. But Widow was also a former SEAL. His instincts forced him to glance up from time to time. He had to check his surroundings. He had to know where the exits were. It was engrained in him, like breathing.

Widow sat down, set his coffee on the table, and cracked open the book.

Adam glanced up and noticed Widow. Recognition flashed across his face, followed by something that looked like awkwardness, like he'd been caught in a lie.

"Hey, Mr. Widow," Adam said.

"Hey," Widow replied.

Adam glanced at the girl, then back at Widow. "This is Ester. Ester, this is Mr. Widow. He's the guy I told you about. He helped my grandpa out last night."

Ester smiled politely. She was younger than Widow had initially thought. Sixteen, maybe seventeen at most. "Nice to meet you, Mr. Widow," she said shyly.

"Ester Marrow?" Widow asked. He saw her nametag peer out from under her coat. She was the girl that those teenagers had mentioned. She worked at this bookstore.

An awkward silence settled over the patio. Ester glanced at Adam. The two of them looked at Widow, wide-eyed.

Ester asked, "Do I know you, sir?"

"Oh, no. I heard some kids talking. They mentioned a girl who works here is all," Widow said.

"They were?" she asked. She looked nervous about it.

That's when it dawned on Widow. Those girls referred to her in a negative light. They weren't friends with her. They were another term that kids used these days—mean girls. Widow regretted mentioning it. He said, "Oh, yeah. It wasn't anything bad. I overheard one girl say something to the effect of: I wish Ester Marrow was working. She'd be able to help me pick out a book."

Ester paused a beat. She glanced at Adam. A surprised expression swept over her face. She said, "That's weird."

"Maybe it's some friends of yours." Widow shrugged.

"I don't really have any friends," she said, and looked down for a long moment, like sadness had kicked her down a peg.

Widow stayed quiet. It reminded him about how far out of his element he was. The last time he'd had to deal with teenage drama, he was a teen himself, though he'd seen brief instances over the years.

Adam shifted in his seat. "So, uh, you just hanging out? Exploring the town?"

"Something like that. Saw the sign for coffee. I've got some time to kill, so I thought I'd stop here and read a book all afternoon."

"Oh. Cool. Yeah, this place has pretty good coffee. Best in town, probably."

"What're you killing time for?" Ester asked, quietly.

Widow placed his cast over the book he bought, concealing the book cover. He said, "I'm going out for a drink later with a friend."

Adam asked, "I thought you were new here? Didn't know anyone?"

"Oh, yeah. It's just a woman I met today."

Ester's demeanor changed, and she seemed suddenly intrigued. She asked, "Is it like a date?"

Widow smirked. It was automatic. *I sure hope so*, he thought. "Nothing like that. It's just this cop I met. I used to be a cop of sorts. I think we're just going to have a drink and talk... About cop stuff."

Adam seemed interested by the cop part. But not Ester. She saw Widow's smirk. She smiled. Then something dawned on her. She asked, "You have a date with Daisy?"

This question seemed to distract Adam from his questions about Widow's past. He was all ears now.

"I don't think I should speak about it," Widow said.

"It has to be her," Ester said.

"How do you know that?" Adam asked.

"She's the only woman cop here, Lenny."

Adam stared at Ester playfully. Then he looked at Widow. "I think she's calling me stupid. She does that sometimes. I don't know who Lenny is. But I think she means Einstein. Like: good thinking, Einstein."

Ester shook her head. "You don't get it. It's not just you. It's all the men in this town. Nobody gets me."

Widow said, "He's got the right idea. Calling him Lenny is just the same as the Einstein quip. In spirit anyway."

"You know who Lenny is?" Ester asked.

Adam stared at Widow, hoping for him to enlighten Adam about the meaning.

Widow nodded and said, "It's Steinbeck. Lenny's from Of Mice and Men."

Ester seemed surprised. Adam looked dumbfounded, like he couldn't believe Widow read books, much less remembered a classic.

Widow changed the subject. "How's your grandpa? I'm surprised you're not at the hospital."

Ester's face perked up. She asked Adam, "Hospital? What happened to your grandpa?"

Adam glanced at his phone, which rested on the tabletop. "Yeah, he had an accident this morning." He turned to Widow. "I spoke to my mom a little while ago. Everything's okay. They're going to keep my grandpa overnight. But otherwise he's good. I'm going to head over there after this."

Widow nodded.

"My dad said you saved my grandpa's life again. Thank you so much," Adam said.

"Don't mention it."

"I should buy you a coffee or something."

"Not necessary. You just enjoy your day. I'll leave you two alone," Widow said. He sat back in his chair, lifted the book, and cracked it open. He began reading.

Adam and Ester stared at Widow more confused than ever. Their eyes dropped to the book cover, mouths agape like they were a step away from shock.

They gawked at the book cover Widow read. The book title was *Fifty Shades of Grey*.

CHAPTER 18

Ninety minutes passed. Or maybe it was closer to two hours. Widow wasn't sure because he'd lost track of time. In the first hour, the book he read bored him—mostly. But he kept going. He didn't have any hard lines when it came to books. Some people don't read past a certain number of pages if they're not sucked right in. Widow could get behind that philosophy.

He got up once to get a refill of coffee.

Those teenage girls walked by the sidewalk once. They sneered at Ester and Adam. Then they saw Widow sitting in the back. The blonde girl came to the railing and said, "Hey, mister. You like that book?"

They were talking to Widow. But he didn't know it at first. The book started very boring. But now he was engaged in it.

"Mister?" the blonde mean girl said.

Widow looked up. He sweated bullets, like he'd been engaged in an intense fist fight with an equally skilled opponent.

"How do you like that book?" she asked.

Widow stayed quiet. But the look of discomfort on his face said it all.

The mean girls laughed at him and walked on. He could hear their laughs for another block.

Adam and Ester stared at Widow. He lowered the book, glanced at the cover. He looked at them. "This isn't a thriller, is it? This is an erotic romance."

Ester giggled and said, "It's a smut book."

Widow stared at the book jacket. Then he opened it and read the reviews inside the flap. The word *tantalizing* was used a lot. "It is?"

"Yeah. Everyone knows that. It's famous," Ester said.

Widow stared at it.

Adam asked, "What do you think about it?"

"It's poorly written and overly dramatic."

"But you're still reading it?" Ester smiled.

"The sex scenes are really something," Widow said, blushing.

Widow closed the book and looked up. He'd been pranked. By teenage girls. In a small-town bookstore in Nebraska. This stung worse than some of the punches he'd taken in combat.

Widow shook his head, almost smiled despite himself.

Ester said, "Those girls are dicks. Don't pay them any attention. I don't."

Widow nodded and reopened the book. He sipped more coffee and kept reading. He'd already paid for it. He still had to kill time. Might as well keep going.

Adam and Ester kept talking, enjoying each other's company.

The afternoon wore on. The sun continued its track across the sky. The temperature started dropping steadily, transitioning into the cold night ahead. Widow was about halfway through the book when movement on the street caught his attention. It wasn't the locals setting up. It was something else. Something in his primal brain told him to pay attention. He glanced up, stared over the book.

A rusted pickup truck pulled up to the curb across from the bookstore. The engine was loud, rumbling like it had a hole in the muffler. The kind of truck that announced itself before it arrived.

Four guys sat inside. All of them looked to be in their early twenties. Rough around the edges. The kind of local boys who'd peaked in high school and then never left town or did anything meaningful afterward. Widow knew the type. He'd met the same kind of guys all over the world. He'd met the same type back in his own school days. Years after school, he'd met the same type when they were grown men. They were the kind of guys who were usually up to no good, which didn't bother him as long as they kept it to themselves.

The driver was the oldest of the group. He had a buzz cut that screamed he was a skinhead, or skinhead adjacent. Tattoos crept up his neck from under his collar. He sat behind the wheel with one arm hanging out the window, staring at the patio like something there offended him. It wasn't Adam and Ester. They were both white, as was Widow.

Widow had to be the target of the driver's disdain. It made sense. Widow had experienced this phenomenon countless times before, in countless small towns. Some locals never accepted outsiders. Sometimes it was the local cops. Sometimes it was the local tough guys. And sometimes, it was the guys who represented the local chapter of white nationalists.

Of course, he didn't know that for sure. A buzz cut wasn't proof that the driver was white nationalist or some other local gang based on hate. But it wasn't just the shaved head that pointed to his deduction. All three of them had the same buzzed heads.

The tattoos backed up his suspicion as well. They all sported neck and face tattoos. Probably many more under their winter clothes, Widow suspected. Tattoos weren't conclusive evidence either. But these were specific tattoos. He couldn't see the detail on most of them because they sat in a truck across the street. But he made out two of the tattoos. One was the Iron Cross on a guy's neck. The second guy had 100% tattooed in big, black block letters right on his cheek. It was big and obvious. 100% meant one hundred percent white. It told others he was pure blood, one of those insane things white nationalists were obsessed with.

Widow recognized these symbols easy. Over a long under-cover career, he'd seen them before. He'd seen many others, too. But not the one carved into the driver's neck. That one was new to him. However, he identified it as white nationalist because it had one thing he recognized. Right in the center of the tattoo on the driver's neck, Widow made out the swastika. That told him that the rest of it was some kind of Aryan-American thing.

Widow wanted to read his book, smut or not. He'd gone too deep to turn back now. But he couldn't concentrate on it because his primal brain focused on the guys in the truck.

The driver stared in his direction, seemingly never even blinking. The other three in the truck watched the same patio with the same expressions of personal offense. Each of them had the same rough appearance as the driver. The same dead-end future was written all over their faces. Two of them drank beer straight from the can.

Widow guessed these boys had all done time. Petty stuff, probably. But they'd been inside the walls of a prison before. No question. They were straight out of central casting for the roles of nameless thugs.

Widow watched them carefully, but without staring. He had countless years of experience doing this very thing. From their point of view, he was reading a smut book. But really he watched them back. They didn't get out of the truck. Just sat there with the engine running, talking to each other and occasionally glancing at the bookstore, at the patio, and in his direction. It seemed like they were watching him, making it hard for him to concentrate on the only good parts of the book, the sex scenes.

Embarrassed by it or not, Widow was locked in now. He was committed to the book. He wanted to read it, but the crew in the rusted truck drew his attention away from his goal.

On the patio, Ester checked her phone and said something to Adam. He nodded. Neither of them noticed the guys in the truck. Ester stood up from the table and leaned across to kiss him. It was nothing long, but not fast either. It sat somewhere in the middle of a peck on the lips and a scene from his book. Which was a big gap.

After the kiss, Ester turned and headed back inside the bookstore. She stopped at the patio doors and turned to Widow. He glanced at her. She said, "It was nice to meet you, Mr. Widow."

"Nice meeting you, Ester."

She paused a beat, holding the door open. "If you want to swap that book out, just come to the counter and ask for me. I'll help you."

"Thanks. But I'm far into it now," he said, holding up the book to show her the thickness of the pages he'd read so far.

Ester giggled. "Okay, sir." She went inside, off to work her night shift.

The guys in the truck watched the whole thing. The kiss. The girl's interaction with Widow. All of it. But Widow studied their reactions. Trying to get a read on them. What did they want? There was something there. Something he wasn't picking up on. Especially from the driver. The guy was angry. It was more than just some disgusting political ideology. Widow got the sense that it was more than personal. There was something fundamental he wasn't seeing.

One passenger in the back said something that made the others laugh, but it wasn't a friendly laugh. The driver didn't laugh. Instead, he tightened his jaw, clenching his teeth. He seemed to stare at Widow, like he had a particular beef against him.

Adam sat back down and pulled out his phone, completely oblivious to the truck or the guys inside.

About ten minutes later, another teenager showed up on the sidewalk, just over the railing. He came from around the corner. He found a gate and stepped onto the patio with them. He was about Adam's age, maybe a year older. Taller. Heavier. Wearing a jacket with the local high school's mascot on it. Widow got a look at the back. It was a jacket representing the school's band.

"Hey man, you ready to go?" the friend asked Adam.

Adam looked up, pocketing his phone. "Yeah, let's roll." He stood up and shivered. He wore only a sweater, but not for long. He grabbed his jacket off the back of a neighboring chair and pulled it on. He greeted his buddy with some kind of longstanding handshake followed by a series of high and low fives. They hugged at the end, like best friends his age often did.

Widow presumed this was the same kid who had picked Adam up from the ranch earlier. If so, then they had just seen each other earlier in the day. But they greeted each other like two long-lost friends would. That was the thing about being a teenager. Time felt like forever. The passage of time was slow. But the time seemed longer than it would later on in life.

The two friends headed past the gate.

Widow set his book down and kept his attention on the street. He tracked Adam and his friend as they exited the patio and stepped onto the sidewalk.

Suddenly, the rusted truck's horn blared, loud and aggressive.

Adam and his friend both snapped their heads up, like the sudden, violent truck horn woke them out of their little worlds. They saw the truck and the guys inside. Their facial expressions changed instantly into concern. Fear replaced their carefree demeanors in less than a second.

The rusted truck lurched forward and screeched to a stop in the middle of the street, right in front of Adam and his friend. All four doors opened, and the skinheads piled out. They moved with the coordination of a pack of blind wolves. Clumsily and stiffly they marched to the boys, leaving the truck parked in the street and the doors wide open.

The driver led the way. The other three followed close behind, spreading out to box Adam and his friend in.

"Stay put, Elton!" the driver shouted, crossing the street. They stopped for another vehicle to go by. It bought the two boys a quick second before the skinheads were on top of them.

It was at that moment, Widow realized they weren't watching him at all. These skinheads were parked over there the whole afternoon to watch Adam. But why?

Adam froze on the sidewalk. Terror swept over his face. His skin turned as white as the sheets these boys probably had in their closets with eye holes cut out, waiting for the night they could burn a cross on some poor family's lawn.

Adam's friend grabbed his arm, panic in his voice. "Dude, we gotta go. Let's run. Right now. Come on!"

Adam stared at his friend, his voice quiet but resigned. "They'll just come after me later if I run."

"Man, screw that. I'm not sticking around for this."

"Just go. It's fine. I'll handle it."

The friend looked at the four guys crossing the street. Then back to Adam. "Sorry, man. I can't do this." Then he turned and bolted down the sidewalk, not looking back.

Adam stayed where he was. He froze with fear. He could run and he should've. But they knew where he lived. Where he went to school. Where his girlfriend worked. He couldn't run forever.

Widow set his book down and watched, waiting to see more before he interjected himself. It looked bad from where he sat. But he'd been wrong before. He was wrong about these boys watching him.

The four guys surrounded Adam on the sidewalk. The driver stepped right up into Adam's face. He shoved a finger into Adam's chest. The others surrounded Adam. They towered over him. Widow nearly lost sight of Adam in the circle.

"I thought I told you to stay away from her," the driver said. He didn't shout, but his voice carried far enough for Widow to hear everything.

Adam didn't respond. He swallowed hard, trying to find his words, trying to stand tall, to not show fear. But he was afraid. Terrified. These guys weren't schoolyard bullies. They were dangerous. Some of them had done time. Not for murder, but once you've done time for petty crime, what's next? You either quit or step up to crimes with longer sentences. Murder was on that list.

"You deaf?" the driver continued, standing close enough to Adam's face he could spit in his eyes. "I told you to stay the hell away from her. But I also told you that was your only warning. What do I have to do to you to get you to understand me?"

Adam tried to speak. The words came out strangled—barely audible.

"What's that?" the driver said, cupping a hand to his ear and leaning in, like he dared Adam to repeat it.

Adam took a deep breath, and went for it. He blurted it out. Meekly, but it came out. "She's her own person. She doesn't belong to you. She can make her own decisions."

Widow stayed where he was, just to see how this played out. He wanted to see how Adam handled it. But he wasn't going to let it get too far.

This was a classic fight over a girl. It might've been on the street in Tent Hills, but it was no different from something that happened every day across the world. Men fought over women all the time.

However, this was different. Much different. The driver cocked back, fast, and punched Adam straight in the gut. Adam folded over, falling to his knees. He dropped his backpack on the ground and held his gut. Trying to breathe, he winced.

A pedestrian and a vendor about ten feet away from the whole incident stepped forward, like they were going to intervene. But two of the other skinheads stepped between them. They stared at them. One of them opened his coat to show something to them. The pedestrian and the vendor froze in place. The object the skinhead had revealed changed their tune in a split second. And the pedestrian and vendor returned to where they were. They turned their backs on Adam and the four skinheads, like nothing was happening.

The object was a revolver shoved into his waistband.

"The hell she is. She's my sister. And I'm telling you—you don't talk to her. You don't look at her. You don't even think about her. You got that?"

Ester was this guy's sister. It all clicked for Widow. You can't help who you're related to. And Ester had a skinhead brother.

Adam said nothing. He couldn't.

Ester's brother said, "Now, I done told you this before." He grabbed Adam by the tuft of his hair and pulled his head back. He reared another fist up, showed it to him.

Widow stood up. The metal chair scraped against the concrete. It was loud. All four guys turned to look at him. So did Adam. Ester's brother kept Adam's hair in his grip and his fist balled up, ready to strike.

Widow set the book on the table and stepped forward. He stopped just on the patio side of the railing. He stared at the four boys.

Ester's brother asked, "What? You got something to say?"

Widow just stood there, staring back at them. His ice-blue eyes pierced through each of them to the bone. He knew it because he'd used it as an intimidation tactic many, many times in the past.

"Well?" the brother asked.

Widow stayed quiet. He just stood there, near the railing, and stared at them.

The one with the revolver shoved in his waistband stepped around the others. He asked, "You got a problem? Or you want a problem?"

The skinhead opened the flap of his jacket and showed Widow the same gun he'd shown the pedestrian and vendor. The revolver was a snub-nose .38. He thought the threat itself would do the trick. It had always worked before. But he couldn't be more wrong.

Widow stayed quiet and waited.

Another skinhead joined the one making the threats. He stood right beside him. They waited for Widow to react.

Nothing. Widow didn't react.

The two skinheads glanced at each other, like no one had ever not gotten the hint before. The skinhead with the revolver stepped closer, and the second one followed him.

The first one pulled the gun out and shoved it in Widow's chest. He glanced around at the street and the windows into the bookstore. Widow realized he was looking not just for witnesses, but for witnesses filming them with their phones. Today everyone had a phone with a decent camera on it. If these boys all had records, the last thing they wanted was to have their faces on camera shoving illegal guns in someone's face.

Widow changed ownership of the gun. In a violent outburst, Widow snatched the weapon from the first skinhead. He held it in his cast-free hand, his grip around the cylinder. He jerked his hand back, and stuck the skinhead dead center of his face. The guy's nose *cracked*. A bone broke. No question, because everyone heard the snap. Blood squirted out of three places on the guy's face. He reacted like a little kid getting their first tooth yanked out. He screamed and cried, cupping his nose to stop the bleeding.

Before the second skinhead could react, Widow leapt over the railing, not even scraping it with his boots. He reversed the .38 and pressed it into the second skinhead's face. The muzzle pushed into the guy's nostril. Widow lifted the gun up in such a way that the second skinhead's face tilted up with it. The guy tried to reach for it, like he was going to shove it away.

Widow snapped the hammer back and said, "Leave it or I'll blow your nose off."

The skinhead put his hands up to surrender. In a muffled voice, he begged, "Don't shoot me, man! Please! Don't shoot!"

"Shut up! Get away from the kid!" Widow ordered. He walked toward them, leading the second skinhead with the snub-nose barrel, and the guy's fear of having this psycho blow his nose clean off his face.

Ester's brother and the remaining skinhead shuffled backward, putting space between them and Adam.

Widow asked, "Any more guns among you?" He figured there were, but there was also a good chance there weren't. Because felons can't legally possess guns. And he would bet money that his original presumption that each of these boys was a felon was correct. They could get illegal guns, like this one. And they clearly had the means to get them. But illegal guns cost money. They weren't cheap. Often they were marked up significantly from the store price because of the risk. The snub-nose was a cheap gun, when purchased legally.

Widow imagined that an illegal gun dealer, no matter how low level he might be, would take one look at these boys and know they couldn't afford the good stuff. So, he'd offer them the cheap guns, the inventory that was harder to offload. Naturally, he'd overcharge them for it. Widow guessed a gun like that would run $500 legally. That price went way up for these boys from their local illegal gun dealer. Widow guessed it'd be somewhere in the range of $2,000. These boys together, all four of them, could combine their resources and come up with that.

"We ain't got no more guns," the third skinhead, who'd said nothing up till this point, responded.

"Well then, gentlemen. I guess your business here is concluded."

The skinheads just stared at Widow, except for the first one. He stayed on his knees, cupping his nose, and crying.

Widow glanced down at him. He waved the gun to the others. "What're you waiting for? Help your friend up and get the hell out of here."

The others eased past Widow like he was a sleeping lion. They gave him a wide berth. Ester's brother stayed where he was, standing over Adam. Widow said, "Get away from him."

Ester's brother eased away, keeping his eyes on Widow.

Widow walked to Adam and stood between them. He kept the gun pointed at Ester's brother. "Whatever," the brother said finally, trying to save face. He pointed a finger at Adam. "This ain't over. You hear me, Elton? Stay away from her, or next time it's gonna be a lot worse." Then he looked at Widow. "You can't protect him forever, mister."

"You'd better hope I don't see you messing with him again," Widow said.

Ester's brother turned and walked back toward the truck. His crew followed, helping the first one up. His nose was broken. He cupped it, agonizing in pain the whole walk to the truck. The boys climbed back into their pickup truck, slamming the doors shut one by one.

The engine revved unnecessarily loud. Then the truck peeled away from the street and roared toward Main Street, disappearing around a corner.

Widow lowered the gun and pocketed it. He offered Adam a hand. The kid took it and stood up. He breathed hard. His hands trembled. And his knees shook.

"You all right?" Widow asked.

"Yeah. Yeah, I'm fine. Thanks. Seriously, thank you. I don't know what would've happened if you hadn't..."

"Don't mention it."

"So, that's your girlfriend's brother?"

"Trent Marrow is his name. He's in and out of jail. Just like their dad. Apple doesn't fall far from the tree, I guess," Adam joked.

"Sometimes. But that's not always true. Ester seems like a special girl."

Adam's eyes lit up. "Oh, she is! She's nothing like those two. She's like her mother, I guess. I'm not sure. Her mother took off when she was little."

"Sorry to hear that."

"I'm not sure she left out of choice. Ester thinks her dad threatened her, probably beat her every day. Eventually she had enough."

"Why didn't she take Ester with her?"

"I guess you just saw the reason. Trent's just like his dad. Ester's dad threatened to kill her if she left with the kids."

"How do you know that?"

"Ester saw it. She was thirteen."

Widow nodded, but stayed quiet.

"Her mother left the week her dad got out of jail the last time. She should've taken the kids when he was inside." Adam stopped, realizing he was probably sharing too much. He looked worried, like he'd betrayed Ester, betrayed his parents. "Please don't tell anyone I told you. Don't tell my dad about this. They'd completely lose it if they knew Trent and his crew were hassling me."

Widow nodded. "I won't say anything."

"Are you sure?"

"I know how to keep a secret. Believe me."

"Thanks, man. I really appreciate it."

They returned to the patio railing. Adam seemed like he was about to say something else, but then his eyes drifted to the table where Widow had been sitting. To the book lying cover up, pages down on the table, opened to the page Widow was on. His expression changed from grateful to confused to amused.

"You're still reading that dirty book?" Adam asked, unable to stop himself from grinning.

Widow followed his gaze to the book. Back to Adam. He smiled. "I told you. I've got to kill some time."

"See you around," Adam said, still grinning as he turned and headed down the sidewalk. His hands had stopped shaking. He walked with a little more confidence.

Widow went back to the patio, climbed over the railing, and returned to his table.

He sat down. Picked up the book. Opened it back to where he'd left off.

And kept reading.

CHAPTER 19

Hours passed, turning the late afternoon into a cold Nebraska night. The bookstore's front door chimed as Ester Marrow stepped outside into the night side of Tent Hills. Dark already. Winter meant the sun died early. By five-thirty, darkness swallowed everything. The temperature had dropped twenty degrees since the mid-afternoon. From the mid-fifties down to the low forties. Her breath came out in small puffs of white vapor.

She pulled her jacket tighter and walked down the sidewalk, crossing the street, and passing vendors covering up their exhibits before the morning festivities. She reached a half-empty parking lot, where she'd left her dad's truck. Her footsteps echoed on the asphalt patches between, crinkling over the snowy areas.

She walked to her daily driver, a beat-up nineties Ford F-150 with rust eating through the fenders like skin cancer. Primer spots covered the doors where someone had tried to fix the body damage and given up halfway through. The truck wasn't hers. Nothing was hers. But Clayton, her father, didn't need it anymore. The state had revoked his license years ago after his third DUI. Maybe his fourth. Ester had lost count.

She climbed into the cab. The seat was cold and the old leather torn. Springs poked through the upholstery on both front seats. She had a solution for that. She pulled an old bed comforter from out of the footwell, where it had slipped when she slid out earlier, and covered the front seat. The bedcover served two purposes, really. It covered the springs poking through the leather. And it lifted her up higher, which helped her see over the dashboard. She drove better when she sat up higher.

The truck's interior smelled like stale cigarettes and motor oil. Not from her. She didn't smoke. Her dad did. Even though he wasn't supposed to drive, he did sometimes. Not far enough to get pulled over by one of Sheriff Easton's guys. He drove around the trailer park, mostly over to one of his drinking buddies who sold him pot. Her dad had no job, but he always had money for drugs and beer. He got it from running small-time, petty crimes around The Scarlands. A lot of his dealings involved running a low-level crystal meth operation.

Ester turned the key. The pickup's engine coughed once. Twice. Finally turned over with a grudging rumble. She let it idle while she checked her phone.

A text from Adam. *I had a run-in with Trent.*

She typed back. *Great. I'm sure I'll get an earful from him at home. You okay?*

I'm okay. That Widow guy stepped in. I think he's some sort of super soldier or something.

Interesting. A super soldier who reads smut.

Ester didn't respond. She put the phone down and stared out the window. She waited for the truck to warm up. She knew from driving it for a year that if she tried to drive immediately after starting it, it would die somewhere on the way home. And the last thing she wanted was to be stranded on the road in the winter between Tent Hills proper and The Scarlands. It was only five miles out of town, but still. The men who headed out that way from Tent Hills weren't the kind of guys she wanted stopping to help her. She was a teenage girl on the verge of womanhood. A lot of the kind of men who visited or lived in The Scarlands were the kind of men a teenage girl didn't want to be left alone with. Her only other option would be to call her brother. She'd rather walk.

Another text from Adam appeared. *I miss you.*

She smiled. Typed back a heart emoji. Then locked her phone and shoved it in her coat pocket.

The good news about her drive home was that once she left downtown, she could pick up speed. Her ride home took less than thirty minutes.

She backed the old truck out of the parking space, and left the lot. She turned onto the street and headed home.

The road home took her out past the last working streetlight. Past the grain silos that looked like tombstones against the dark sky. Past an abandoned gas station with its windows boarded up and into The Scarlands.

She knew when she entered The Scarlands because she came to the beginning of a collection of double-wide trailers scattered across acres and acres of packed snowy dirt and dead grass. Countless families who couldn't afford better. Most of them are on government assistance. Most of them were one paycheck away from homelessness. Most of them hooked on meth and other cheap narcotics. All of them stuck.

She dreamed of the day that she could just leave. She had to escape this place. Escape her fate. The local kids born here usually ended up dying here. They came from nothing. They ended up with nothing. Not her. No way. She was gone the moment she graduated high school. She just had to last another semester, and that was it. Then she was free.

Ester turned in to one of the trailer parks, following the slow speeds and the winding road. She pulled up to the trailer at the far end of the park. The one with peeling siding the color of old mustard. The one with the sagging porch held up by cinder blocks. The one with the Confederate flag hanging in the front window like a warning sign. Not her flag. She hated it. But Clayton liked it. Her brother liked it. Her whole life, the two of them claimed it was her heritage. Which was funny to her because the Confederate flag represented the Confederacy, the South, which Nebraska was not.

Her father didn't hang the flag because of heritage. Ester knew what it really represented. She'd learned about the American Civil War in school. They taught her what that fight was really over. She'd read the books. She knew.

Ester killed the engine and sat for a moment. She didn't want to go inside. This was the worst part of her day. Usually, she'd park the truck and sit in it for as long as she could get away with. She never wanted to go inside. Every time she opened that door it felt like stepping back into the prison that was her home life. This was her cage. But what choice did she have? The law forced her to stay there until she was eighteen. Plus, she had nowhere else to go. Not yet. Someday she'd save enough money. Buy her own car, or steal her dad's truck. It's not like he'd call the cops over it. More than hating people who differed from him, darker skin color or whatever stupid reason he had to hate, her father hated cops. Nothing compared to his hatred for the law.

Many people in The Scarlands hated the cops. It was one reason Sheriff Easton stayed out. Sure, they came around when there was a major reason to be here. Someone called 9-1-1, or they were investigating a major crime or something. But mostly, they stayed out.

Ester didn't know exactly where she'd go when she was old enough. But she'd drive away forever. Colorado maybe. Or California. Somewhere far from Nebraska. Somewhere, nobody knew her.

That dream kept her going.

For now, she had to go inside. She killed the truck's engine and grabbed her backpack off the other seat and climbed out. The cold slapped her face. She walked up a set of rickety wooden steps, skipping the middle one because of a wicked crack in the middle. She stepped over it like always and got to the front door and froze, like something deep down in her stomach told her to stop. She felt like she was being watched.

She looked to her left and saw him. A man leaned against the corner of her trailer. The darkness shrouded him. He puffed on a cigarette, lighting up part of his face. The man stood around six feet tall. He wasn't that old, but his hair faded away like he was forty years older than he was.

She said, "Hello?"

He said nothing. Just puffed on that cigarette, staring at her. He took the cigarette out of his mouth and licked his lips, continuing to stare at her, like a predator watching its prey.

Ester opened the front door, which wasn't locked. It never was. She opened it and stepped inside.

The living room was small and cluttered. A couch with stuffing bleeding from the cushions sat against one wall. A ratty old recliner held together by duct tape sat opposite. The TV was the newest thing in the trailer. It was a large flat screen. It blared some reality show. Empty beer cans littered the coffee table. Cigarette butts overflowed an ashtray.

At least the kitchen was clean. But that was only because she was the one who cleaned it.

Clayton Marrow sat on the couch. Tall and lanky with weathered skin and a thick graying beard. He wore old jeans and a flannel shirt with the sleeves rolled up. His forearms showed a faded SS tattoo. Prison ink done with a needle and pen ink. He looked up when Ester entered. His eyes were bloodshot.

"You're late," he said. "I've been waiting for dinner."

"I'm not late. I just got off work."

"Whatever." He took a pull from a beer can. Crushed it. Tossed it into a pile on the table. "Grab me another one, would ya? You can make dinner while you're in there."

"Sure, Dad," Ester said. She went to close the door behind her, but a big boot stopped it cold. She looked up. The creepy man from the outside stood there in the doorway. His boot shoved inside, stopping her from closing the door.

She stared at his features. He was big and rough-looking. His head was buzzed on the sides. The top didn't need to be. Like her brother's friends, he had prison tattoos creeping up his neck. SS bolts. A swastika behind his ear. A Confederate flag on his cheek. He smiled at Ester. A smile that made her skin crawl. He smelled of beer and cigarettes, like her living room.

Clayton stood. Swayed a little. Drunk already. "Look who just got out," he said. His words slurred together. "It's your uncle Crick."

Not her real uncle. Boyd Crick was his full name. He had recently been paroled after doing five years for armed robbery. The guy was another friend of her father's from his prison days. And, like her father, he was a part of the Aryan

Brotherhood. Or one of those prison gangs. No question. Ester had never met this guy before. That didn't matter. She didn't like him. She didn't like any of her father's friends.

"Hey, sweetheart," Crick said. His voice was smooth. Too smooth. Like oil on water. "You sure grew up nice."

Her eyes opened wide. She didn't remember meeting him before.

His eyes traveled up and down her body. Lingered too long on her chest. Her legs. She felt a naked vulnerability even though she was fully clothed.

Ester forced a polite response. "Hey. Nice to meet you."

"Crick's gonna be staying with us for a while," Clayton said. He grabbed an open beer from off the coffee table, shook it, and heard some left in the can. He chugged it. "Till he gets back on his feet. Gets a job. You know."

Ester nodded. She started toward the hallway. Toward her room. Toward safety.

"Hold up," Clayton said.

She stopped and turned.

"Aren't you gonna fix us some dinner?"

She stared at him. "I just got off work. Fix it yourself."

Crick laughed, a wet sound that made her think of phlegm. "Wow. You let her talk to you like that?"

Clayton shrugged. Didn't seem to care. "She's like her mother. Girl, don't speak to me that way." His words slurred.

Ester sighed and said, "There's some TV dinners in the freezer. I really am tired. I gotta get up early tomorrow."

What he said about her mother hurt. It always hurt. Her mother had vanished when Ester was young. Just disappeared one day. Never came back. Nobody knew where she went. Or maybe they did and nobody told Ester. Either way, she was gone. And Clayton blamed Ester for it somehow. Like she'd driven her mother away just by existing. But it was his own fault that she left.

Ester ignored them. She walked down the narrow hallway. Past the bathroom with its broken light fixture. Past Trent's room with its door covered in band stickers and holes punched in the drywall. The smell of old marijuana cigarettes hung in the air. Her tiny bedroom sat at the end. It was the smallest room in the house, except for the bathroom that she shared with her brother. But at least it was a sanctuary.

She went inside and closed the door behind her. The door didn't lock. It never had. She'd asked Clayton to fix it a hundred times. Begged him. But he never did. Said she didn't need privacy. Said only girls with something to hide needed locked doors. Sometimes he'd give her a speech about how he never had privacy in prison.

Her room was small. Barely big enough for a twin bed and a dresser. The walls were bare except for a calendar she'd gotten free from the bank. The floor was cheap carpet worn thin in spots. But it was hers. The only space in the universe that belonged to her.

She dropped her backpack on the floor and peeled off her work clothes. She pulled on an oversized t-shirt and left her underwear on. Her usual sleepwear. The trailer's heat worked well enough—one of the few things that did. She enjoyed sleeping bundled under the covers.

She climbed into bed with her phone and a book from her work. It was a fantasy book with a badass female protagonist.

She'd read half of it already. It was good. She loved it. It was the perfect escape from her little world.

She texted Adam on and off for the rest of the night. She read until her eyes got heavy. The words started to blur together. She set the book on the floor beside her bed, locked her phone, and plugged it in to charge.

She closed her eyes and fell into a deep sleep, filled with dreams of escaping Tent Hills, The Scarlands, and her dire family situation.

Hours passed.

The trailer went quiet. The TV was still on. It played some old movie that was calming enough because it was back in the days when movies were about characters and dialogue. There were no explosions and ridiculous people in comic book costumes. Voices mumbled and faded. Trent came home at some point. She heard his truck pull up. She heard him and her father have words. Then Trent got back in his truck and sped away. He was probably going to stay the night at one of his girlfriend's places. He had a few of them.

Clayton fell on the couch and went back to sleep. His snoring rumbled, echoing through the house.

Ester drifted off again. Her phone slipped from her hand onto the bed beside her. She fell back into her dream world.

Sometime later Ester stirred. Her first reaction was that her room had gotten cold. She felt the air on her skin. It was her legs and bottom. Everything below her waistline was exposed to the cold air. Somehow, her covers had uncovered her lower half. Which was weird because she'd fallen asleep bundled up, like she usually did. It was like a ghost tossed the covers aside, revealing her thighs and legs to the cold.

Suddenly, she realized something.

Something woke her up. It wasn't like something touched her or she heard a noise. It was more like a feeling, like earlier when she felt Crick watching her. She wasn't fully awake, just caught in that space between sleep and consciousness. Something felt wrong. So, she opened her eyes, squinting them, peeking out into the darkness. Just slits. She kept her breathing slow and deep, like she was still fast asleep.

She wasn't alone in the room. Through her lashes, she saw a figure standing in her doorway. Dark. Still. Watching her.

It was Crick.

The door to her bedroom was no longer closed. It was wide open. He stood in it. Saying nothing. Just staring at her in the darkness. Her heart hammered in her chest. Hard enough she thought he might hear it. She forced herself to stay still. To breathe steadily. To keep pretending she was asleep.

He made a sound. Low. Guttural. Like an animal. Like something strange. She heard rustling. Movement. Fabric on fabric. Then she realized what he was doing. The fly on his jeans was open. He watched her while pleasuring himself.

Terror flooded through her. Cold like ice water in her veins. She wanted to scream. To run. To grab something and hit him with it. But fear paralyzed her. Fear kept her frozen. Her eyes squeezed almost shut, like they wanted to close. Her body wanted her to close them, to go back to sleep. To escape into her dream world.

But she couldn't. She had to stay awake and alert. She had to watch, to make sure he stayed at the door. She wanted to scream. But she couldn't. Would her dad help her, anyway? Maybe. Maybe not. Would he believe her? Probably not.

Trent would help her. But he was gone.

All Ester could do was lie there, frozen. Her body was rigid under the covers. Barely breathing.

The sounds continued. Crick's breathing got heavier. Faster. Ragged.

Minutes felt like hours. Like days. Like an eternity stretched out in the darkness.

Finally, he stopped with a grunt. A sigh. Then silence.

He eased into the room. His footsteps were soft on the thin carpet. He hovered over her bed. Looming. Blocking out what little light came through the window. She could smell him. Sweat and cigarettes.

He leaned down, but not too close. He kept enough distance to not breathe on her face, but close enough to smell her hair.

"I hope we get to spend some time together," he whispered. His voice was soft. Intimate. His words were gut-wrenching. Horrifying. She cringed, but stayed still, her eyelids just open enough to see him.

He hovered there for a long minute, then he straightened. He wiped something on his pants, zipped them back up, and walked out. He closed her door softly, but not all the way. Just enough. Like he wanted her to know he could come back anytime. That nothing could stop him. That the door didn't matter. Nothing stood between him going further next time. Any time he wanted.

Ester lay there, shivering. She grabbed the blankets and pulled them back up over her legs and bundled up tight inside them. A tear trickled down her face. She sobbed quietly. She pulled the covers over her head, afraid to look out again. She feared he'd be back tonight. She couldn't sleep now.

She finally drifted back to sleep. The rest of her dreams played out like nightmares.

CHAPTER 20

Bloom stood outside the police station under the glow of streetlights. The time was eight o'clock at night on the dot. Night air blew across the parking lot. It felt cold but not unbearable, not as she expected the next night would be. To her, this was pretty good weather for winter.

The best part of wearing it tonight, for her, was the fact that she still looked good in it.

Bloom's hair sprouted around her face, big and curly, in that way that eighties' women paid to have done. The eighties were the decade of the big, teased hair look. She was born later, but she really missed her decade. Her natural hair would've been a big hit back then.

Bloom waited for Widow. She looked up and down the block, but saw no sign of him—just other cops and pedestrians.

Two familiar deputies walked past her from the parking lot—Jimmy and Rollins—both of them older than her and both married. They were the same two she'd seen earlier in the hospital parking lot. Now she saw them again. Together.

Which made sense because they were practically joined at the hip. Sometimes she wished Easton would hire another female cop, one that she could get along with as well as these two did. They acted more like grade school boys than cops.

The deputies did a double-take at her as they walked by. They stared at her standing there. They had nearly walked right past her, as if they didn't recognize her at first.

If only I could be so lucky, she thought.

"Wow, Bloom!" Jimmy stopped walking and stared at her, mouth agape for a long second before he closed it. Almost like he wanted to make a show of it.

Rollins grinned. "What're you trying to do? Find a date?"

"Yeah," Jimmy said. "Rollins and I just tossed a couple of guys into the drunk tank. Maybe you can start there." The two of them chuckled like a pair of fraternity bros.

Bloom didn't miss a beat. "Funny joke, Jimmy. Too bad you're not as good in bed as you are at telling jokes. Truth is, I'm waiting for your wife. I heard she's slept with all the guys already. She's bored with them too. So I thought I'd show her a good time. You know? Show her what's she's been missing."

Jimmy's face went red. Rollins laughed, then stopped when Bloom looked at him.

"You too, Rollins. Your wife's probably tired of you by now. I'll visit her next."

That shut them both up. They mumbled something under their breath to each other and headed inside. Jimmy jerked the station door open and stormed through it, as if his feelings were hurt. Rollins followed. The hydraulic closer at the top forced it shut painfully slowly behind them.

Bloom smiled to herself. It was the small, everyday victories with the guys on the force that made this job fun sometimes.

Footsteps approached from the shadows at the corner of the car lot. They differed from the passing pedestrians. Heavier. She heard the boots clicking on concrete and looked in that direction.

From out of the darkness, Widow stepped over a concrete curb, transitioning from the sidewalk and into the lot. He threaded between parked police cruisers. He wore the same clothes as earlier. Only he'd ditched the blue flannel some-where. Now he just wore the same jeans, the same gray t-shirt under that ugly, gas station puffer coat. The cast on his hand looked stark white under the lamplight. He moved with that same hardened confidence she'd noticed at the hospital, like a man with nothing to prove. Rare in her experience. It was one thing about him that intrigued her.

"Sorry, I'm late. I got caught up in this book I'm reading and lost track of time," Widow said, smiling at her. He looked her up and down. Nothing lingering. Nothing too uncalled for. "You look great."

He looked long enough to take her in, but short enough to stay out of creep territory. She liked it, so much that she did something unexpected to them both. She hugged him. She wrapped her arms around him, got up on her toes, and planted her head against his chest.

It took Widow off guard. He froze for a long second, then he hugged her back.

Bloom backed away. "Sorry. I don't know what came over me."

"Don't mention it."

She glossed over it and glanced at the time on her phone. "You're not late. Maybe five minutes. But that's nothing. It's not a matter of national security or anything."

"My truck's over here," she said, pointing the way.

Widow nodded and motioned for her to lead the way—the universal *after you* gesture. Bloom walked ahead through the lot toward a Silverado parked at the far end. She'd worn tight jeans today for a reason, and she knew Widow would notice as he followed behind her, which he did. She didn't complain.

The truck was lifted with running boards on both sides and painted midnight blue. Not quite navy, but close enough that Widow appreciated it. Like a sign from the universe.

Bloom opened the driver's side door and climbed up.

Widow followed and got in the passenger side. First, he took the paperback he'd been reading from out of his back pocket, so he wouldn't sit on it. He shoved it into the inside pocket of his ugly puffer coat.

Bloom glimpsed it. "What're you reading?"

"Nothing. Just a book." He got in and dumped himself down in the seat and slid it all the way back to fit his legs in the footwell. He closed the door. The truck's cab smelled like cold leather and mint air freshener. A little green tree hung from the rearview mirror, spinning slowly.

Bloom wondered what book it was for a second, but quickly let it go.

"Nice truck," Widow said.

"Thanks. But you should see my payments."

Widow paused a beat. A question occurred to him, so he asked it. "Where did you get it?"

"Nicely's Automotive. It's owned by this guy who dresses like corn on the cob. He's always wearing a big yellow suit."

"Yeah, I saw his billboard and then ran into him."

"I'm not surprised. He's a town fixture. Plus, that's how he sells so many cars. He squeezes every second of meeting a new face. It must work. He's got a huge car lot." Bloom started the engine. It growled to life with a deep rumble she loved. She backed out of the space, pulled out onto the road, and headed north through town.

They drove past last-minute festival preparations. A few workers high on ladders strung lights across Main Street. Others set up barricades for tomorrow's parade. Vendor booths lined the sidewalks, covered with tarps for the night.

"You going to this festival tomorrow?" Bloom asked.

"I wasn't planning on sticking around. But maybe."

"It's pretty small-town stuff. Corn-eating contests, corn pie judging. Nothing fancy. But we like it. It brings the community together. Plus, it drives up tourism just before the harsh winter kicks in."

Corn pie? Widow thought. He didn't ask. He didn't even want to know. "Sounds fun."

"Are you a country boy or a city slicker?" she asked, faking two different accents—from the stereotypical, Hollywood impression of a slow rural person, to a stereotypical, Hollywood impression of a know-it-all city dweller.

"I'm a bit of both. I suppose. I grew up in a small town, but the Navy took me all over the world."

They drove past closed storefronts—hardware store, bank, insurance office—all dark and locked tight. They passed the last streetlights of downtown Tent Hills, where the blacktop turned to forgotten pavement. And continued on.

"Where we going?" Widow asked. Rolling hills lay ahead in the darkness. The lights were sparse—little neighborhoods and scattered farms. Streetlights past the main drag were set up high on poles. Half were out. The other half flickered.

"This is what the locals call The Scarlands," she said.

"Interesting name. Why do they call it that?"

"I guess because if you look at it on a map, you see the long, jagged cuts of the topography. They look like scars. At least, that's my best guess."

Bloom noticed him watching the citizens of the Scarlands. "It's kind of sad, isn't it?"

"Why do you say that?"

"You know. These are impoverished families. They turn to crime often because of their circumstances."

"You guys investigate a lot of crime here?"

"Sadly, this is where a lot of clues lead. We make most of our arrests here. Other than that, we try to stay out of their lives. Easton's policy," Bloom said.

"Easton?"

"Sheriff Easton."

Widow nodded, and said, "I saw him in the parking lot with you today."

"He's a good cop. Good man too."

Widow stayed quiet, just watched the people as they watched him pass. They weren't driving in an official police vehicle.

However, something told him they all knew Bloom's truck. Probably knew all the deputies' personal vehicles.

They drove on until they came to a gravel road. Bloom slowed her truck. A single building stood in the center of a gravel parking lot. The lot mirrored the shape of a baseball diamond, only bigger.

A squat concrete building rested in the center, on the pitcher's mound. The building was brick, painted all white with a black roof. Neon beer signs glowed in the barred windows. Bud Light. Miller. Coors. A wooden sign over the door in faded red letters read: The Outer Limits. Underneath, someone had spray-painted: Abandon All Hope. Probably meant to be funny, so the owners kept it.

A couple of motorcycles were parked near the door. Widow wasn't sure if it was smart to ride on the roads during a Nebraska winter, but there they were. Pickup trucks filled the rest of the lot. F-150s and more Silverados and Rams, all caked with muddy snow and road salt on the tires.

Music thumped from inside. The style was called country rock, a combination of rock songs with country music backdrops and themes. This one twanged the steel guitars. The exact song that played was hard to tell from outside. It might've been a jukebox or an actual live band. Widow couldn't tell that either.

Along the way to the bar, Widow noticed a familiar face— unforgettable because the guy wore a nose splint. The splint held his nose in place after Widow had broken it earlier in front of the bookstore. One of the skinheads. One of Trent Marrow's friends. Trent's truck was outside, and now here was one of his crew.

The skinhead with the broken nose talked to a group of other white guys. None of them had the telltale signs of being of his political beliefs. No swastikas or Aryan tattoos. He was the only obvious skinhead. But they all stared at Widow.

Bloom said, "Don't pay any attention to those losers. They always stare at me when I come by. They're white supremacists."

"All of them?"

"No. Just that one with the…" She trailed off. "Huh. Looks like someone broke his nose. He probably said the wrong thing to the wrong guy."

"Yeah, I bet he did."

"Most of those boys aren't like him. Maybe two of them are on the fence."

"Good to hear."

"Still, it makes me nervous they don't shun him. Kick him out of their friend group."

"Why don't they?"

"It's a small community, Widow. You can't go around ignoring everyone."

Widow stayed quiet. He kept his gaze on the skinhead with the nose splint. The skinhead stared back at him—trembling. He dropped his beer bottle. It hit the gravel. Beer streamed out. The guy's jaw dropped.

As Widow and Bloom passed, the guy scrambled away, nearly falling down twice. He vanished into the bar.

Widow said nothing about it. But he kept an eye out for any sign of retaliation. He doubted they'd try anything in front of Bloom. They all knew she was a sheriff's deputy.

Bloom asked, "You like live bands?" This answered Widow's question about the music.

"Sure," he replied.

"Good thing, because that's what they got going on tonight." Bloom drove them into the lot and parked at the far end. Widow figured it was probably to avoid the locals getting too close to her truck. She killed the engine, and they got out.

Stiff wind slapped them again, harder out here where nothing blocked it. It blew straight across the plains, gaining momentum like a runaway freight train.

Bloom led the way. They walked through the parked trucks, toward the bar. He noticed something out of the corner of his eye. He stopped and stared at a particular truck parked near the road. It was Trent's old pickup. No mistake about it. It had the same Frankenstein features—the different-colored driver's side door, four different tire brands, and the missing tailgate.

Widow still had the gun in his pocket. He stepped in front of Bloom and pulled the bar's heavy door open. Warm air rushed out, thick with cigarette smoke and the smell of fried food and domestic beer. The music was loud, but somehow it had seemed louder from the parking lot.

They stepped inside.

The bar was packed. Locals mingled with outsiders, here for the festival. Farmers, ranch hands, and trailer park people were all drinking and having a good time.

A three-man band jammed on a small stage in one corner. They played love ballads and rock covers, but in country style. And one of them played a steel guitar. He set it down occasionally to pick up either an electric or acoustic guitar. It depended on what the next cover song called for.

People were playing pool in the back. The bikers sat at the bar drinking whiskey straight from a bottle. Women were scattered throughout, some alone and some with their men. A bunch of them appeared to be on the clock, looking for dates for the night.

No sign of Trent or the other skinheads. Maybe they were there. Maybe not.

Bloom said hello to a few locals and led Widow through the crowd to a table in the corner. They sat away from the crowd. Both of them put their backs to the wall so they could see everything. Widow liked that about her.

A waitress came over. Young, maybe twenty-two, with blonde hair pulled back in a ponytail. She chewed gum and had a tired look about her, like she'd had enough of this shift already. She and Bloom were on a first-name basis. Bloom ordered a beer out of a bottle, and Widow ordered the same.

She came back with the beers and started them a tab.

"You like the bar?" Bloom asked.

"It's got character, that's for sure."

"Yeah. I like that about it. It's the real people of a county like this one. It's honest. No pretense. Just people drinking and trying to get through another day."

Bloom raised her bottle and said, "To real people." Widow raised his. They clinked their bottles and drank.

"So," Bloom said. "Tell me about yourself."

"Didn't you already look me up on your computers?"

Bloom smiled and said, "You know I did."

"And?"

"Not much came back. I got some indication you were in the Navy. But the DoD responded with a bunch of bullshit."

"What do you mean?"

"Their response seemed like a nothing-to-see-here kind of thing. Which tells me you're a lot more interesting than you let on."

"What am I letting on?"

"There's a lot more to you."

"Is that why we're here? Easton put you up to taking me out? Getting to know me? See if I spill some secret about myself?" Widow took a pull from his beer.

"No. I mean." She paused a beat. "Yes, but I asked you out because I want to know you. Personally. It's nothing to do with Easton."

"He doesn't buy the story about the old man and punching the horse, does he?"

Bloom shrugged. "Can you blame him? It sounds crazy."

Widow showed her his cast. "It doesn't feel crazy. It hurts like hell." He took another pull from the bottle.

"Now that I think about it. Should you be drinking on pain meds?"

"What pain meds?"

"Didn't they give you something for the pain?"

"They gave me a prescription. I didn't fill it."

"Should you?"

Widow glanced at his cast. First one side. Then the other. "I'll be okay."

"Why'd you help John Elton? The other night on the road?" Bloom changed the subject. "I think most people would've kept walking."

Especially since he nearly shotgunned me to death, Widow thought. But didn't mention it. "He needed help." He shrugged.

"That's it?"

"That's it."

"But why you? Why did *you* help him?"

"It's a compulsion. I can't walk away from someone like that."

Bloom smiled, and they ordered more rounds. Hours passed. She told him about moving to Tent Hills for her job. Easton was the only sheriff willing to hire her. She wanted to make detective someday but had to prove herself every day in a department full of men who treated her like she didn't belong. But not all the time.

Widow told her about some of his time in the Navy. He shared highlights that were public information. He left out all the nonpublic information.

At one point, they got to talk about her skin. She brought it up. She gestured to the patches of lighter skin on her face. "How come you never asked me about this?"

"Vitiligo?" Widow asked.

"You know what it is?"

"Never seen it before. Not in real life."

"Most people stare."

"Doesn't bother you?"

"I think you're one of the most beautiful women I've seen. Definitely the most beautiful woman I've ever seen with vitiligo."

"I'm the only woman you've seen with it. You just told me that."

"See, there you go." He smiled. They laughed and talked for another hour.

Later, they ordered more beers. And Bloom asked, "You hungry?"

"I could eat."

She flagged down the waitress. Widow thought she was going to ask for menus. Instead, she ordered for them. "Two Runzas." The waitress took the order and disappeared into the crowd.

"What's a Runza?" He asked.

"It's a Nebraska thing. Beef and cabbage and onions wrapped in bread. German recipe, maybe Russian. I don't really know. But it's good. You gotta try it."

"Sounds good."

After a while, the food came out, hot and steamy. Widow waited for Bloom to take a bite and then he followed suit. "Not bad," he said.

"Told you," she said, covering her mouth while she ate.

They ate and talked. The crowd around them came and went. People ate. They drank. They danced. Eventually, it got late and people started clearing out. The band took a break, and the bar got quieter for a while.

Bloom leaned back in her chair. "I'm having a good time. It's been a while since I had this much fun just talking."

Widow stared back at her.

She smiled and then realized she'd lost track of time. She glanced at the time on her phone. "Damn. It's getting late.

Wish I could stay out all night with you. But I gotta get going. I have to work early tomorrow. It's the Husk-Town Showdown."

"Yeah. We'd better get going." Widow felt the call of nature and added, "I need to go to the boy's room before we leave."

"Yeah, me too. I'll meet you at the bar after. We can pay the tab there."

They stood up. Widow followed her toward a sign for the women's bathroom. He didn't see one for men. They got just outside the door for the women's room and stopped. He looked at her, confused. "Where's the men's?"

Bloom smiled. "Oh, I forgot. The men's is outside. Through there." She pointed at an exit that went out back of the bar.

"Outside?"

"The men's room is an outhouse. It's straight out back there."

Widow shrugged and went through a dark hall and pushed open the exit. He glanced back at her. She held open the women's bathroom door and said, "Meet you at the bar and we'll leave."

Widow stepped outside, behind the bar. The music thumped, shaking the rain gutters on the side of the building. Small windows near the roofline were steamed over from all the bodies and alcohol inside.

Widow passed a pair of dumpsters and a stack of pallets.

The men's room was an outhouse attached to the building, old gas station style. It had a concrete floor, a single toilet, and a sink with rust stains on the faucet. It only spit out cold water. There was no knob on the hot water side. A bare bulb flickered from the ceiling. No light cover. Moths danced beneath it.

Widow went inside and did what he'd come in to do. He washed his hands. The water ran a tint of brown at first, then clear. There were no paper towels, just one of those hand dryers. It barely blew any air.

Widow pushed open the door to find a group of men waiting for him—the skinheads.

Trent and the three skinheads from the bookstore stood in a loose semicircle, blocking his path back to the bar. Their breaths came out in white puffs like bulls in cold weather. Their eyes were red from a long day and night of drinking. They stood there with bad intentions.

The first skinhead, the one Widow had smashed in the face with the .38, stared at him over the new, shiny splint he'd gotten during a hospital visit. His nose looked swollen and bruised under it.

Trent grinned. "Remember me?"

"I remember." Widow nodded.

"You made me look like a bitch in front of my boys today."

Widow stayed quiet.

"That's not cool," Trent said.

"That right?" Widow asked.

"We want what you stole from us," another skinhead said.

"What would that be?"

"You took my gun!" Trent said.

"Yeah!" the splint-nosed skinhead said.

Widow reached into his pocket and pulled out the snub-nose .38. He held it up in the dim light of a streetlight overhead, so all four of them could see it clearly. "You mean this gun?"

The splint-nosed skinhead gulped. The others tensed and their eyes locked on the weapon. Trent took a half-step back before catching himself. The second skinhead, the one Widow had shoved the barrel up his nostril, went pale, like he was reliving the event.

Widow smiled. "Why're you afraid? Because I'm armed?"

"How do you know we're not armed?" one of them asked.

"If you were armed, you would've pulled your guns on me already," Widow said.

Silence. None of them spoke. They just stood there, dumb-struck. All but Trent, who looked like he was at least attempting to hide his fear.

"Tell you what." Widow cracked open the cylinder with his thumb and tilted the revolver. Five rounds dropped out and hit the concrete with metallic pings that echoed through the cold night air. The bullets rolled in different directions, and one stopped a few feet away from Trent's boot. "I'll give you a chance."

Widow snapped the cylinder closed and slid the empty revolver back into his pocket. He looked at Trent, then the others, going from face to face. "You want the gun back? Come get it."

Trent clenched his jaw. His face flushed red. Then he smiled.

"That was stupid, mister," he said.

"Yeah! Real dumb!" another added.

Widow waited.

The skinheads did something they thought was smart for once. They moved in together. Same time. No coordination. No choreography. No years of practice under their belts.

The first skinhead came from Widow's left and swung wildly with a haymaker. There was no technique behind it. No real skill. It was all arm and no hip rotation. Sure it'd be effective against a guy who'd never been in a fight before. It might work on the schoolyard. But this was no schoolyard. And Widow was no regular fighter.

Widow danced back easily. The haymaker flew by. The second skinhead came in from the opposite side—fast, but clumsy. Widow gut-punched the first skinhead. He folded forward.

Widow danced behind the guy and pushed into the second one. The first skinhead's haymaker slammed into the second one's face. They both toppled over in a violent heap.

Trent stayed back, trying to look like he was waiting for his turn. Really, he was frozen. And Widow knew it.

The other two skinheads scrambled back to their feet. They ran at Widow, throwing a flurry of punches. Widow blocked one with his cast, which hurt like something crazy. He ducked from the other's second haymaker attempt. Widow realized this guy only knew haymakers, only he didn't even know them because he could never land them.

Widow danced back and killed the haymaker guy's feet out from under him. He hit the gravel hard. Widow stepped close and crashed a boot into the back of the guy's head. Not full force. He wasn't trying to kill the guy.

The first skinhead was on the gravel. He tried to get back up, to get back in the fight. And Widow stomped just hard enough to crash into the gravel. But not hard enough to jam bone fragments from his skull into his brain. The guy's head bounced once off the gravel. He spit out a couple of shattered teeth and then it was lights out. The guy blacked out.

Widow now stood with Trent and splint-nosed skinhead at his front. The second skinhead scrambled back to his feet. He stood behind Widow.

Widow looked over his shoulder back at him. Then back to Trent and the splint-nosed skinhead and back at the second one. He waited to see who was next.

To his surprise, it was the splint-nosed guy. None of them had a gun. Widow knew that part. What he hadn't accounted for were knives. The splint-nosed skinhead flicked open a three-inch blade from out of his pocket. He growled like a wild animal and came in for an attack.

Widow stepped left. The skinhead stabbed downward. Widow danced inside of the skinhead's stabbing arc and drove his cast-free fist into the skinhead's floating ribs in a short, compact punch that traveled maybe eight inches. Widow put his whole body behind it. Something cracked under Widow's knuckles. The force of the blow stumbled the skinhead back several paces. He toppled back gasping and clutched his ribs. His face went flush from the pain.

Widow went in for a follow-up. But the splint-nosed skinhead reacted out of fear. He stabbed again, wildly. Widow dodged two stabs, but put his cast up to block one. The knife stuck Widow in the arm. It pierced the cast and got jammed in his bone.

Widow winced in pain. It was quick. He had no time to bleed. But the blood came. It streamed down his cast. Within seconds, his whole cast was blood red and cracked from the knife.

The second skinhead saw an opportunity and took it. He scrambled behind Widow and grabbed him from behind, trying to lock his arms around Widow's torso in a bear hug.

He tried to pin Widow so Trent could step in. This skinhead was strong, cornhusker strong. But Widow was stronger.

Before the guy could get Widow's arms to budge, Widow slammed his head backward fast and hard. He headbutted the guy full on the face. And another nose cracked and broke. The guy let go of Widow instantly.

Widow didn't wait. He reared back like a footballer going for the scoring kick, and booted the guy square in the nuts. The second one went down faster than the last one.

Widow added another stomp for good measure. This time he stomped on the second skinhead's nuts, the same guy who was already down because of an injury down there. The guy squealed, writhing around on the ground, holding his groin. Widow hoped the guy didn't want to father any kids anytime soon.

Either way, the second skinhead was also down for the count.

The splint-nosed skinhead had to be the bravest out of them, or the dumbest. Because he kept going. Widow had given him a chance to run away. After stabbing him in the cast with that knife, he should've taken it.

The splint-nosed skinhead came in swinging. Widow swatted his swings away and threw a colossal straight cross right into the guy's face. Once. Twice. And a third time.

The skinhead's splint nose cracked all three times like a walnut. Warm blood sprayed across Widow's face and clothes. It ran down into his collar. The skinhead staggered backward with both hands covering his face. Blood sprayed from between his fingers and dripped onto the gravel.

The skinhead screamed in sheer agony. His words were completely garbled. "You broke my nose again!"

Widow popped the guy straight in the face with a quick jab for a fourth time. The jab slammed into the guy's hands, cracking his nose once more. He released his nose. His face was more garbled than his words. Bone and skin and metal dangled from the mangled heap that used to be the guy's nose.

"You broke my nose again!" the guy garbled.

Widow reached out and grabbed it. He twisted the mangled mess just enough to get the guy's brain to send him into shock. Widow released him. The skinhead collapsed right there between him and the only one left standing—Trent.

Widow stood over the mangled-nose skinhead. He jerked the knife out of his arm, slipping it through the cracked and bloody cast.

Widow looked at Trent. He said, "What about you?"

Trent glanced at his broken crew. Fear flickered across his face. It took him a long time to decide because he was too drunk and too stupid to process what he'd just witnessed.

Widow stood there breathing deeply, not from exertion but from the adrenaline coursing through his veins and from the pain shooting up his arm like electricity. He looked down at his right hand. Blood covered his knuckles and blood stained what was left of the cast. Fragments of white plaster littered the ground like broken teeth.

Three men lie around him in various states of agony.

Widow looked back to Trent, locking eyes. Widow showed him the empty gun from out of his pocket. He reached it out toward Trent. "You still want it?"

Trent threw up his hands, like he was blocking Widow from throwing the gun at him. "No... man. No. You keep it."

Widow reared back like he was about to throw a live grenade and threw the gun far out into the darkness, into a frozen cornfield. Then he turned to walk away. He didn't turn back around to see them. He kept walking.

Back into the bar.

Back to Bloom.

CHAPTER 21

Widow walked through the bar's back door, bloody and bruised. Bloom had paid their tab already. She waited for him at the women's room. She came to him, concerned about what had happened. He lied to her and told her he fell. She asked about the cut in his arm. He told her he must've hit a jagged rock when he hit the gravel. She believed him and helped him to the truck. They drove off. Bloom sped the whole way. Widow wrapped his crumbling, bloody cast in bar towels. They worked pretty well at keeping blood from dripping on Bloom's seats.

The streets were pretty empty. The time was closing in on midnight. Small towns quieted down long before that. They made it to the hospital in no time.

Bloom pulled into the hospital parking lot and shut off the engine. It was the same lot they'd left hours ago. The night was darker and colder, like they'd driven from one movie set to another.

Widow looked out the windshield at the hospital. Bright lights glowed from inside. The emergency entrance sat to the left. They were parked near the front, not far from where

Easton had parked earlier in a doctor's reserved parking space.

A few cars were scattered throughout the lot, but not many. One of them was the Eltons' truck. It was still there in the same spot as earlier. It was parked just a few rows over from them.

"Looks like the Eltons are still here," Widow said.

Bloom followed his gaze. "The doctors wanted to keep Mr. Elton overnight for observation."

Widow stayed quiet.

They got out and headed inside. Widow held the bar towels tight around the bloody cast. The automatic doors sucked open and warm air rushed out. The smell of antiseptic and floor cleaner hit them. A custodian mopped the floor. A "wet floor" sign stood behind him.

A few people sat in the waiting area. They looked tired and sick. The nurse at the front desk looked up as they walked in. They checked in with her.

Bloom didn't know the nurse's name. But the nurse knew Bloom's. She knew she was a cop and fast-tracked them to the front of the line. The people in the waiting room groaned like they should be top priority. But none of them was bleeding from a knife wound.

They waited at the counter and a second nurse showed up. He took them back around a corner and down a corridor. They passed empty rooms and closed doors. Nurses passed them. A pair of doctors made their rounds together like they were tag teaming the various emergencies. It turned out that the younger one was shadowing the older one. Some sort of training program. The hospital was quieter at night, but there was still life in it.

They reached the emergency treatment area. The second nurse took them into an empty room. Widow sat on the bed and the nurse removed the bar towels and got to work on the cast.

Widow had to get stitched up. At one point, the nurse commented it was some bad luck that he fell on such a jagged rock. He noted the rock must've been as sharp as a knife. He said it with skepticism.

Widow replied that it certainly was some bad luck. The nurse also remarked how strange it was that Widow had blood on his face, but not cuts on his face. Widow replied, "It must've splashed up from the cast, when I hit the ground."

The nurse just nodded to that. The nurse cleaned Widow's wounds, then applied the stitches. After that, he wrapped Widow's hand in fresh bandaging and then started on the new cast. He wet the casting material and wrapped it around Widow's hand and wrist. He did it layer after layer. The material was warm at first, then it cooled and hardened.

The entire process took twenty minutes. Bloom watched from the wall and said nothing. She just watched.

They did the whole thing without morphine this time. Which was an oversight, or because this nurse didn't believe Widow's story. Either way, Widow's hand hurt like hell. But he stayed quiet about it.

When the nurse finished, he said, "Keep it dry. Don't punch any more walls."

"He fell," Bloom said.

The nurse nodded. "Right. Well, Mr. Widow, try not to fall so hard." The nurse gave him the whole spiel about coming back and getting the cast removed in six weeks. After, the nurse looked at Bloom. "You keeping an eye on him?"

"Trying to."

"Good luck with that." The nurse packed up his supplies and left them in the room. He told them to wait and one of the doctors would swing by to check on Widow, before they could discharge him. The door closed behind him. Widow and Bloom sat in silence for a moment. The room was quiet except for the hum of fluorescent lights overhead.

Widow looked at his new cast. It was white and clean. Finally, he said, "You really don't have to stay here with me."

Bloom pushed off a wall. "I'm not done with our date."

"You're not angry?"

"About what? You fell. Accidents happen," Bloom said, and yawned.

"What about work tomorrow? You need to get home and get some sleep."

Bloom opened her mouth to answer, but then her phone rang. She pulled it out and looked at the screen. She sighed and said, "It's Easton. I gotta take it."

Widow nodded and stood up. "You do that. I'm going to swing down the hall and see if I can find the Eltons. I want to check on John."

"Okay, I'll meet you there," she said, and stepped out the door. She walked out into the hallway.

Widow followed behind her, turning and going the other direction. He heard her voice fade as she moved down the corridor. He stopped and looked at his cast. He flexed his fingers. It hurt. Pain shot through his hand like never before. He stopped moving his fingers.

The hall stretched in both directions. It was quiet and empty, minus Bloom at the other end. Widow wandered down the hall, away from her. He passed closed doors and darkened rooms. The hospital was different at night. It was quieter, with more shadows and less movement. He headed for the elevator to get to the fourth floor, to room 401, where John had been earlier.

The elevator opened on the fourth floor. Widow continued on. He kept walking and passing rooms. He read the room numbers. It seemed like he was getting close. Most of the rooms were empty, but a few had sleeping patients inside.

Then he saw room 401.

The door stood half open, and the room was dark inside. Only the glow from medical equipment and the light from the hallway filtered in. Widow stopped, stepped close to the opening, and glanced inside.

He saw a figure in a chair near the window. The figure was slumped over and asleep. He snored heavily, like he'd not slept in days. It was Matty Elton. He sat there with his head tilted back and his mouth open.

Widow didn't see Elsa or T.J. He didn't know it, but they'd taken an Uber home earlier in the day. No reason for Elsa and the kids to sleep in the hospital. Matty wanted to. He wanted to be there for his father.

Widow looked at the bed. It was empty. The sheets were pulled back and messed up, like someone had gotten out of bed recently or been dragged out.

Widow stepped inside the room, staying quiet. The room smelled like hospital—antiseptic and old air. He moved past Matty and checked the bathroom. The door was open, and the light was off. He flipped it on. The bathroom was empty. No sign of John anywhere.

Widow turned back to the room and looked around. But there was no sign of him. There was no note and nothing else. It was like John had gotten up and walked out.

Widow walked over to Matty and put a hand on his shoulder. He shook him gently at first. "Hey."

Matty didn't wake, so Widow shook him again. This time he shook him harder. "Matty. Wake up."

Matty's eyes fluttered and opened. He looked up at Widow. He was confused and disoriented. It took him a second to place where he was and who Widow was.

"Widow?" Matty sat up straight and rubbed his eyes. "What're you doing here? We thought you left?"

"Matty, where's your father?"

Matty rubbed his eyes again. "What?" He looked at the empty bed and his face went pale. It was slow at first, because of his disorientation. But after a long moment, his eyes shot open and his mouth fell agape.

"He was … He was right there. I just—" Matty stood up too fast and stumbled forward. He caught himself on the chair. "Where is he? Dad?" he called out.

"The room was like this when I came in. You don't know where he is? Did someone come get him?"

"I don't know. He was in bed, sleeping. And I must've dozed off." His voice rose with panic. Widow saw it in his eyes too. He saw fear and guilt stirring up in Matty, like this was his fault. Matty had fallen asleep and lost his father again.

"Okay. Stay calm. Let's go look for him. I'll help you."

Matty's breathing got faster. "Where do we go first?"

Widow said, "We need to call security. We need to—"

Matty's eyes darted around the room, panic-stricken and terrified.

"Matty. Look at me." Widow put his cast-free hand on Matty's shoulder.

Matty stopped and looked at Widow.

"We'll find him, but you need to stay calm. Panicking won't help."

Matty took several deep breaths and nodded. He steadied himself.

Neither man noticed the time. But a big digital clock hung on the wall. Blood red numbers glowed in the dark.

The clock read exactly midnight.

CHAPTER 22

MEMORY TWO

The fertility doctor's waiting room smelled like antiseptic and aging magazines. Donnie D sat in a plastic chair near the door. The seat was hard and cold. He shifted his weight and tried to get comfortable, but comfort wasn't really the problem.

A clock on the wall ticked loud enough to make him aware of every passing second. He counted them. Alessandra had gone through a green door with a frosted glass window thirty-seven minutes ago. A sign hung near the door that read: Staff Only.

A nurse's shoes squeaked on linoleum somewhere down the hall.

Donnie D stared at a magazine on a side table. It was a copy of *Life Magazine* from May 1965. The cover pictured a US soldier in Vietnam. That was months-old news by this point. He didn't pick it up. Current affairs and politics didn't interest him. Plus, he was on the clock. Protecting and chaperoning Mr. Brasi's wife was his highest priority. He just sat there and waited, watching the door for any potential threats he needed to track. It was all he'd been doing since Enzo Brasi hired him, after he passed his test. Back in May, he was supposed to kill Mickey Fog Eyes, bury him outside the city. He'd let Mickey go, but none of Brasi's guys knew that. The severed bloody finger sold the lie.

Three other women sat in the waiting room. They wore coats and cardigans against the October chill outside.

They looked to be in various stages of pregnancy. One rubbed her belly in slow circles. Another knitted something small and yellow, presumably for her unborn baby. The third just stared at the same spot on the wall, lost in whatever thoughts pregnant women think about.

It was all a mystery to him. This wasn't Donnie D's natural setting. He stuck out here more than an undercover cop at a card game.

None of the women spoke to him. In fact, they made it a point to avoid eye contact with him. He didn't know exactly why. It might've been the .38 special he had holstered in a shoulder rig under his jacket. But he wasn't sure they could even see that. It could've been the run-of-the-mill reasons—his looks.

Whatever the reason, he was glad about it. Donnie D wasn't much of a people person. That wasn't his strong suit. He was better at not talking. No one wanted to hear his opinions, anyway. No one but Alessandra, the boss's wife. She was nice to him. They became friends in the last several months. He liked to think so. He never crossed the line or anything. Mr. Brasi would murder him for that. He told him so himself the day he hired him for the job. He also told him to be nice to her, just not too nice. Which got a laugh from the other boys, who sat around a poker table, taking friendly bets. A few others stood around the room, talking business. But they all joined in to laugh at Donnie D.

One of them even remarked, "Boss, you really think Donnie D would ever have a shot with Mrs. Brasi?"

"Yeah, boss?" another joked. "Donnie D wouldn't have a shot with a blind hooker on payday!"

The fellas laughed at that. Everyone but Donnie D and Enzo Brasi himself. Enzo shouted at them for it. "Shut up, boys! Don't speak of my wife like that!" Even though Enzo shouted, this didn't terrify them. Everybody knew that when Brasi was quiet, it was the time to worry. If Enzo gave one of them the silent treatment, that's when things got scary.

Enzo was always angry. He was always yelling at one of them. That wasn't new. It was when he went quiet, that someone ended up dead.

"Sorry, boss," one said.

"We're just having a laugh at Donnie D's expense."

"Yeah, we don't mean nothing by it."

Donnie D felt out of place in the fertility doctor's office, like a bull in a china shop. He didn't belong in a place like this. This was a place families came, that families were planned. Donnie D wasn't the family type. At least, he didn't think he was. But who knew what was in store for him down the road?

Everyone changes. Everything changes.

Donnie D's face wasn't the friendliest face in Chicago. It wasn't the meanest either. There were guys on Enzo's crew who possessed more terrifying features than his.

After waiting for nearly an hour, the door with the frosted glass finally opened and Alessandra stepped out. She wore a cream-colored dress that came to just below her knees with a navy-blue cardigan over it and white gloves. She was a vision out of a dream in his nightmare world. Her dark hair was pinned up. A pair of pearl earrings glinted under the office's fluorescent light.

She looked beautiful, as she always looked beautiful to him. But right then, she looked broken. Defeated. Not like her normal cheery self. But the moment she stepped out from behind the door and into the regular world, a façade washed over her face, like a mask. She smiled big, like nothing was out of the ordinary. She was just the happy wife of a mobster. Nothing to see here.

Donnie D knew better. He'd been driving her around five days a week to all her medical appointments, taking her shopping and out to brunch with her friends for more than six months. Sometimes he chaperoned her five days a week. Sometimes less. But one thing was true. He knew her very well. Some of the other guys in Enzo's crew thought he spent too much time with her—more than Enzo himself.

Alessandra knew it too. Since they'd been spending so much time together, she'd grown attached to him.

Of course, Enzo Brasi wasn't stupid. He and his twins ran one of Chicago's biggest organized criminal empires. You don't become successful evading the law for decades by being blind and stupid. Sometimes he'd ask Alessandra about Donnie D. She'd learned from previous experience it was always best to feign ignorance. Her husband could be insanely jealous. And for no reason. That's why her last driver had vanished one day. He was a long-trusted enforcer for Enzo's brother. He came highly recommended. He was nice, too. She liked him, but not romantically. He was just pleasant to be around.

One day Enzo caught her smiling at a joke the guy made. Enzo didn't like that. She knew it the same way the driver knew it. Enzo went quiet. He said nothing about it. He never questioned her about it. The next day the driver had vanished. Gone. Like he never existed. She never knew what happened to him. That was before they hired Donnie D.

The entire crew never spoke that driver's name again. And neither did she. She tried to imagine that he'd been transferred to Elena's guys. She ran a completely different territory from her brothers. They all did. They separated their Chicago territory into three sections. It made it much easier to run their business. Maybe her former driver was working a different territory.

But he wasn't. His corpse was rotting away under the waters of Lake Michigan. A pair of concrete shoes keeps it anchored there.

Alessandra's experience had taught her that even though she really had zero physical attraction to Donnie D, it didn't matter. Enzo's jealousy was only overshadowed by his ego. She had to constantly belittle Donnie D to her husband. She made quips, making fun of how ugly Donnie D was. Or how crooked his teeth were.

Eventually, she learned she could manipulate Enzo to helping Donnie D. So she started making negative comments about how poor Donnie D was.

She'd say to Enzo, "Do you pay these guys? Can't he afford nicer clothes?"

She'd say things like that. It worked too. Enzo started paying Donnie D more money. He hooked Donnie D up with store credit at some of the finest stores in the city. Enzo ordered Donnie D to go shopping for himself.

Alessandra would say to Enzo, "Darling, I can't be seen in public with a guard who looks like he lives in a gutter. I'm your wife. Your property. When people see me, they think of you. They think of the Brasis. It's terrible for our image for my guard to look like Donnie D. Can't you do something about it? Clean him up? Give him better clothes?"

It worked like a charm. Before she knew it, Enzo had given Donnie D enough to buy new clothes and get better haircuts. Enzo even bought Donnie D a new car. A 1965 Cadillac Sedan DeVille. Black. Brand new. The thing was a boat on wheels, but it looked expensive and that was what mattered. She convinced Enzo that she had to be seen in a nice, new American car. Not that old '57 Chevy Bel Air.

It all worked. Enzo fell for it. The downside of it all was she couldn't tell Donnie D her scheme. She couldn't tell him she did it for him. Was she attracted to him physically? The answer was no. But did she trust him? Did she feel safe with him? That was a different answer entirely.

Donnie D may not have known she did all that for him. But that didn't mean he was stupid. He knew her as well as she knew him. He knew her better than her own husband did. Maybe not physically, but in all the other ways. In all the ways that matter, Donnie D knew her. He saw her—the real her.

When she stepped out into the doctor's waiting room, she knew one thing for sure—that her mask didn't work on him. Not now. They were too accustomed to each other.

Donnie D stood from the chair, scraping it against the floor. He stepped toward her. She saw him. Her façade crumpled, like dust falling off a corpse. It hurt them both that he knew she'd gotten bad news. She couldn't hide it. Not from him.

Alessandra recovered fast. She straightened her spine, lifted her chin, and smiled. She walked past him toward the exit, whispering, "Let's go."

Donnie D followed. Rain hammered on the pavement

outside. The wind gusted, cold, blowing the rain diagonally. She pulled her cardigan tight to shield herself from the wind.

Donnie D told her to stay under an awning. He ran out into the street, splashing through rain puddles. He retrieved their car and came around to pick her up. He got out with an umbrella, popped it open, and escorted Alessandra to the car. He opened the rear side passenger door for her, and she slid onto a long cushy bench seat.

Donnie D closed the door and scrambled back around to get into the driver's side door.

Alessandra wiped tears from her face. He saw it as he slid in behind the wheel. She smiled, pretending they were raindrops.

Neither spoke about it.

Inside the car, the silence weighed heavily between them. The rain hammered on the windshield, but it was the silence that chipped away at Alessandra's mind.

Donnie D knew not to ask questions. He knew not to push her hard. He wanted to. *God help me*, he thought. He wanted to pull over, get in the back seat with her, and hug her. He wanted to tell her it was all going to work out. But he knew better. If he pushed it. If he said the wrong thing. She'd tell her husband, and he'd end up at the bottom of Lake Michigan.

So, he pulled into traffic and drove. Enzo had told him to take Alessandra to this appointment and bring her straight home after, with no stops and no detours. When Enzo gave orders, he expected them followed blindly. Donnie D had seen Enzo himself put out a cigarette on a man's eyeball for talking back. The Brasis didn't give second chances.

Donnie D glanced at her. She stared out the passenger window with her gloved hands folded in her lap. She didn't move and didn't speak. Even in her sadness, she was the most beautiful thing he'd ever seen. But he could see the sadness in her. She was a woman trapped.

knew better than to ask about what the doctor had said. Whatever he'd told her, it wasn't good. That much was obvious. And if she wanted to talk about it, she would.

But she didn't.

They drove through downtown and past storefronts and office buildings. They drove past people under umbrellas, hurriedly walking through the rain to their destinations. They drove past the whole world, going about its business, while Alessandra's world fell apart on the back bench.

Donnie D came to an intersection and stopped. He glanced right in the wrong direction. The wrong road. But that road led them to a place that Alessandra liked to go. He glanced at her in the rearview mirror. A car behind them honked its horn to get Donnie D to move forward, which he probably should've done. But he didn't.

Right there he made a decision that would change their lives forever. It involved ice cream. Was it a stupid decision? Maybe. It was definitely the kind of decision that got men killed. The kind of decision that got men killed slowly.

Donnie D turned right instead of going straight. Away from the route that led back to the Brasi estate. Away from Enzo. Away from everything that made Alessandra's life feel like a prison sentence she couldn't escape.

She noticed. "Where are we going?"

"It's a surprise."

"Enzo said—" she started.

"I know what he said." Donnie D drove on, staring at her in the rearview.

"He'll be angry."

Angry was an understatement. Enzo Brasi didn't get angry. He got even. He got medieval. He made examples out of people. If she said one word about this, Enzo would make an example out of Donnie D.

"We're already late. He won't suspect anything. Besides, we won't take long."

Alessandra asked, "What kind of surprise?"

"You'll see."

She smiled and didn't argue. The look on her face changed to one of hope. It was fleeting, but for that one moment, she had a deep hope that she dared not say out loud. She hoped they would keep going. She hoped that she'd never have to tell Enzo the news that she'd still not gotten pregnant.

Donnie D drove to the edge of Little Italy and kept going. He drove to a small ice cream parlor on Taylor Street. It had been there since before the war. It had a red-and-white striped awning and a hand-painted sign. The smell of waffle cones baking drifted out onto the street. They could smell it even through the rain and the windows.

Donnie D parked on the street and shut off the engine and turned to her.

Alessandra stared out the window, wide-eyed. "Ice cream? It's autumn?"

"You like ice cream, right?"

Alessandra stared at the parlor and a small smile danced at the corners of her mouth. "You know I do! It's my favorite thing in the entire world. I had you take me to get ice cream at least once a week this whole summer."

"Is that the last time you had any?"

"Of course. It's too cold for it now."

"Then it's been too long," Donnie D said. He got out, went around, popped open the umbrella, and opened her door. She stepped onto the sidewalk and smoothed her dress, standing close to him under the umbrella's protection. The rain thrashed around them.

She whispered, "What if someone sees us?"

"They won't. It's raining too hard. Besides, if they do, so what?"

"I'll tell Enzo I ordered you to take me here," she said and smiled up at him. He gazed, locked into her smile for a long moment, then led her to the ice cream parlor. They walked across wet pavement and entered the parlor. An old copper bell above the door jingled when Donnie D pushed open the door. Inside, the parlor was empty of customers. An old man stood behind the counter. A teenage boy swept the floor in the corner. He was his teenage son.

The old man looked up. He had a thick Italian accent and white hair slicked back with pomade. "Welcome, welcome! I'm so happy to see you. There's been no business today."

Alessandra smiled and greeted the owner. Donnie D closed the umbrella and leaned it by the door.

The old man asked, "What can I get for you?"

Alessandra stepped to the counter and studied the flavors behind the glass. "There are so many flavors to choose from. I see chocolate, vanilla, strawberry, pistachio, lemon, and is that mint chip?" She pointed at a gallon of mint green ice cream.

The store owner nodded and said, "Plus we got plenty of toppings to choose from. What's your favorite, signorina?"

"Strawberry." Donnie D said, without hesitation.

Alessandra stared at him, shocked he remembered her favorite. Shocked, he ever paid attention. Even Enzo doesn't know the answer to that question. Or care to know.

She agreed with the choice and told the shop owner that was the flavor she wanted.

He replied, "Then you'll have strawberry." He began scooping it into a cone for her.

"Two scoops," she added. He smiled and complied.

Donnie D ordered the same for himself even though he preferred chocolate. The old man scooped their cones with practiced efficiency and handed them over with a smile. Donnie D paid, and they found a corner table, near the window. They sat and licked their cones.

Outside, the gray clouds covered the sky. The rain hammered relentlessly against the shop's large glass window. Alessandra licked her ice cream and closed her eyes for just a second. When she opened them, tears streamed down her face.

Donnie D froze. He didn't know what to do. He'd never been good with crying women. Hell, he'd never been good with any women, but especially not crying ones.

"Alessandra—" he whispered, holding his cone away from him so it wouldn't drip on his clothes.

"I can't give him children." She stopped herself from saying more. She couldn't finish.

Donnie D stayed quiet. He just sat there holding his ice cream cone.

"He's going to kill me." She whispered, wiping her eyes with the back of her gloved hand to stop her tears from smudging her mascara. "I can't do the one thing a wife is supposed to do."

He stared at her. Questions on his face.

"I can't bear his children."

"Well… There's more to life than that. He married you for you. Not just for children."

"To him it was the most important reason to marry me. It was the only reason."

She wasn't wrong. Donnie D had heard Enzo talk about having sons. About legacy. About building an empire and having someone to pass it down to. It wasn't just talk for him. It was obsession. Enzo talked about it the way he talked about money and power and blood. The Brasi family had ruled Chicago's underworld for two generations. Enzo intended to make it three, and four, and five. He needed sons for that. He needed heirs. A wife who couldn't provide them was useless to him, and useless things got discarded by the Brasis.

"What's wrong with you? Why can't you have kids? The doctors can't help you?" Donnie D asked.

She shook her head. "That's the thing. It's not me."

Just then, he realized. He got it. Donnie D saw the truth. It wasn't her. It was Enzo. If he couldn't have sons, he'd blame her. His ego would never let him believe for a second that it was him. No mobster would. Not in those days. He'd blame her. He'd always blame her.

Donnie D looked at her. Another slow tear streamed from her eye. He did something out of line. He did something he never should've done. It wasn't impulse. But it was second nature. It was instinct. He brushed the tear from her face.

"I'm sorry," he said, and withdrew his hand.

"Don't be." She slowly turned to him. Her green eyes met his. She smiled at him with a smile that could level an army. "You're the only person I trust. You're the only man who—" She trailed off.

"What?" he asked, hesitantly, knowing he was ringing a bell that couldn't be unrung.

"Never mind."

"Tell me."

"You're the only man I've ever felt safe around."

Donnie D felt something like a knife twist in his chest. It was a feeling he knew as the thing he felt just before he lied to someone he loved. "I'm just doing my job."

"No. You're not." She moved her chair closer. "You see me. Really see me. Not what I'm supposed to be. Not what Enzo wants me to be. Just me. As I really am."

"I never met a woman who—"

"Who what?"

"Talks like you before."

The ice cream melted down the side of Donnie D's cone, and he didn't notice. He couldn't look away from her.

"Is that a good thing?" she whispered.

"I like it. I like you."

She eased closer to him. "I like you too." And then she kissed him. It was sudden. Abrupt. Unplanned. Perhaps it started from a deep sense of desperation. Perhaps it came from a single moment of longing for something real. Something better than her life built of lies. She was sabotaging herself. Sabotaging her life.

She expected him to pull away. She expected him to tell Enzo. But he didn't. He kissed her back. Their ice cream dripped on the table. They didn't care. His free hand went to her cheek. He caressed it. The kiss was the kiss to end all other kisses for the rest of their lives. And they both knew it. Right there. And right then.

For a long, long series of moments, the whole world disappeared. Enzo didn't exist. The Brasi family didn't exist. Her impossible situation didn't exist. There was just them. Two people. No one else.

Alessandra pulled back first. She stared at him with wide, big green eyes, shocked at what she'd just done and terrified of what it meant. She'd put him in grave danger. She was as good as dead already. But now, she'd marked Donnie D for death as well. A man who was kind to her. A man who wanted nothing but her happiness.

"I'm sorry. I shouldn't have—" she started to say.

Donnie D kissed her again, softer this time. When he pulled away, he kept his forehead pressed against hers. "Don't be sorry. I've wanted to do that since I first saw you. Since you first spoke to me, like I was more than I am."

"We can't do this," she whispered. "We shouldn't do this."

"I know."

"Enzo will kill us if he finds out."

"I know that too." He kissed her again anyway. It was too late now. He could've walked away seconds ago. That would've been hard, but possible. But not now. Not after he'd tasted her lips and felt her heart race to the beat of his own.

They kissed for what seemed like forever. They threw away their melting ice creams and walked back to the car in silence, all but the pounding rain.

Donnie D drove her home and took the correct route this time. When they pulled up to the Brasi estate, Enzo stood on the front steps with his arms crossed. He'd been waiting.

Alessandra sat in the passenger seat this time. She touched Donnie D's hand as it shifted gears. It was brief, so brief that anyone watching would've missed it. She whispered, "I need you."

Then she got out and walked to her husband. She smiled, hugged him. He tried to kiss her, but she lied and told him she might have a cold.

She glanced back at Donnie D. One time. It was quick. It looked like a goodbye glance. But he saw in her eyes something more. She spoke to him with that glance. She told him to wait for her.

There was more to say.

More to their story.

CHAPTER 23

Widow and Matty moved along the floor, looking in various rooms, calling out for John. No answer. No sign of the old man. Matty left Widow near the elevators and went to a nurse's station. He found a nurse and explained that his father was missing. She called security.

Widow told Matty to wait for security. He would go on and check around himself. He left him there with the nurse. Widow walked the halls. They stretched out darker and quieter than before. Most of the patients were asleep. At midnight the hospital switched over to its all-night graveyard crew, which meant that security went down to a minimal number of probably two or three guys tops. The graveyard shift meant fewer eyes that could be on the lookout for John.

Most of the lights were dimmed for night shift. Emergency exit signs glowed red in the shadows. Widow moved quickly but methodically through the hallway, checking the whole floor. He went room by room. Each door he opened revealed the same thing—sleeping patients or empty beds, but no sign of John.

Widow spotted a camera near the elevator, but none anywhere else on the floor. To save money, they probably only put them where they needed them. Watching the elevators was a good way to clock everyone who came and went. He checked the emergency exit—no cameras there. Probably more at the first-floor entrances, and that was it. He left, figuring the cameras were security's problem.

Widow went down the fire stairs. In the stairwell, he saw no sign of John. He went back down to the first floor and ran into Bloom. He told her what had happened. She took him to another nurse's station. It was empty. No staff in sight. Bloom grabbed a phone, dialed zero, and got a guard at the security desk. She identified herself and brought them up to speed on the situation.

Widow only heard her side of the conversation, but that was what he deduced from it. She hung up and said, "Security's been notified. They're checking the exits at the street level. If he walks out of the hospital, they'll stop him. He also said they rolled back the cameras at the exits first. Apparently, they only record when there's movement. Makes it easier to scroll through hours of records because of the notifications. He said they've had no recordings of an old man leaving the building."

Widow nodded. "Then he's gotta be here somewhere."

"Where could he have gone?"

"I don't know. But we'll find him."

"Think we should split up?"

"Yeah, for now."

"Security's got the first floor covered. The only way in and out has a guy at a desk. Let's stick to the top floors. I'll take two and three, you go back to four. I'll meet you up there."

Widow nodded and went up the fire stairs to the fourth floor, leaving Bloom to check the third floor thoroughly. Widow stepped off the stairs. He heard a ding from the elevators down the hall. He hightailed it to the lift to find an orderly coming off, pushing a cart.

"You see an old man in a hospital gown wandering around?" he asked the guy.

"No, but I saw security down on two, looking for him. But I've not seen him. As far as I can tell, the patients are all asleep."

Widow nodded and left him there, moving back along the fourth-floor hallways. He stuck his head into each room, checking bathrooms and looking behind privacy curtains, but found nothing. He searched for nearly fifteen minutes. He was running out of places to check.

Widow checked an empty broom closet, then he saw movement across the hall. Through a window in a door, someone stepped from one side of a room to another. He heard voices. He stepped to the door and looked inside.

Bloom stood in the room at the foot of the nearest hospital bed. She had her phone out, opened to a notepad app, like she was talking notes for an investigation. A doctor stood near her, reading a chart.

Two men lay in hospital beds. The first one had bandages wrapped around his head and bloody gauze packed into his mouth where teeth used to be. The second had his nose taped and splinted, both eyes blackened and swollen nearly shut. A cold pack iced down his groin.

Widow recognized them from the bar. They were two of the guys from Trent's crew. The ones he put here less than a couple of hours ago—less than that. One was the guy he'd kicked in the groin, and knocked out some of his teeth. The other was the one he broke his nose with a reverse headbutt to the face.

The one with the broken nose talked to Bloom, gesturing with his hands like he was describing something tall. "He was a big guy, built like a tank. I never seen him before."

Widow pushed the door open and stepped inside.

Both men locked eyes on him. They went silent. The one with the broken nose froze mid-sentence. His swollen eyes went wide, and what little color remained in his face drained away. The other one, the one missing teeth, physically recoiled, like a vampire to a crucifix. He pressed back into his pillow like he wanted to disappear into the mattress.

Widow held their stares for a long second. His expression said nothing, but his eyes said everything.

Widow glanced at Bloom. "Did you ask them about John?"

Bloom glanced between Widow and the two men. She'd caught the fear. Impossible to miss. And the realization hit her like a ton of bricks. They were describing Widow.

Widow knew she knew, but what would she do? Would she take the statement? Arrest him? He wasn't sure.

"I had to stop searching for a moment. These gentlemen were just about to give me a statement. They claim some guy attacked them. I gotta take this down. It's my job too." Bloom said. She turned back to them. "You were saying? Big guy attacked you. He was built like what?"

The one with the broken nose swallowed hard. His eyes flicked to Widow, then back to Bloom. "I, uh... Actually, my memory's hazy. Not sure what he looked like."

"What?" Bloom glowered.

"We're mistaken. Yeah. I remember it different from him. I remember it was several guys. Never seen them before," the other one said quickly, his words garbled through the gauze. "It was a stupid bar fight. Don't need to make a thing of it."

Bloom said, "You've got a broken nose. Your buddy's missing teeth and has a concussion. That's assault. But I need a straight story, guys."

"Yeah. I think it was out-of-towners. I can't remember exactly. Sorry. It's all fuzzy," the broken-nose guy said. He looked in Widow's direction. "We don't want any trouble."

Bloom stared at them, clearly not buying it. She looked at Widow again.

Widow shrugged and looked at the two men one more time. They couldn't meet his eyes. Bloom put her phone away and shrugged.

"Have you seen an elderly man?" Widow asked them. "White hair, hospital gown. He might look confused?"

They both shook their heads fast.

"What about you?" he asked the ER doctor.

"She already asked me that. I've not seen him. I got my hands full between these two and the other one down the hall." The ER doctor looked at Bloom. "And stay out of his room. He's sedated. Can't talk to you. He's not giving any statements to the police or anyone else for a long time."

Bloom asked, "What happened to him?"

"Someone tuned him up good. His face is messed up."

"He going to be okay?" Widow asked, feeling a little guilty.

"Sure. He's going to be fine. Eventually. I expect in a year, he'll make a full recovery. After a couple of surgeries and some physical therapy."

The two skinheads gulped and stared at Widow. Both of them never wanted to see him again.

Widow nodded to the doctor and stepped back into the hall. Bloom followed. The door swung shut behind them.

In the hallway, Bloom stopped him in the center of the corridor. She asked, "How did you injure yourself again?"

"I fell."

"Really?"

Widow stayed quiet.

" 'Cause just before you walked in, those guys were spinning a tale about a large man who beat the shit out of them. You wouldn't lie to me?"

"I'm sorry."

"I don't like being lied to."

"You going to arrest me?"

"For what? According to those losers, some out-of-towners attacked them. And I bet if I look more into it, it'll turn out they tried to jump somebody back at The Outer Limits. That person wasn't planning to be a victim and defended himself."

"Thank you," Widow said.

"Besides, no one's going to believe them about one man beating them up. Honestly, I wouldn't believe it, except..."

"Except what?"

"I met you. And now I think it's possible."

Widow stayed quiet.

Bloom grabbed him, reached up, and kissed him on the lips. He kissed her back. She said, "You lie to me again and I will arrest you. Got it?"

"Yes, ma'am."

She backed away and said, "I already checked this floor. How about the fourth?"

"No sign of him there."

"I checked with security just a few minutes ago. They can't find him either. Where the hell did he go?"

Widow glanced at an exit sign in front of the fire stairs. "We should check the roof." They went up the fire stairs and climbed to the top. Widow pushed through a door with a warning not to exit to the roof. Bloom followed. She stopped it from closing behind them and wedged a brick between the door and the jamb. It was on the ground, just outside the door, like that was what everyone used the brick for.

The wind howled across the flat roof. Thin clouds covered the night sky. Over the horizon, Widow saw the rolling hills.

Widow's eyes adjusted and he saw silent air conditioning units, ventilation shafts, and pipes. Steam rose, puffing out of a small stack. The vapors rolled across the roof, low and haunting.

"See anything?" Bloom asked.

At the far edge near a low wall, Widow saw a figure. He tapped her shoulder. She looked too. They stared at the figure.

John Elton stood on his crutches near the ledge of the roof. He stood too close to the edge. One wrong move and he'd go flying over the side. His hospital gown flapped in the wind and his white hair moved like wheat in a field. His eyes were wide open, but Widow and Bloom weren't sure if he was there or not. He stared down at the parking lot four stories below.

Widow and Bloom moved slowly. Running might startle him, forcing him to fall or maybe even jump off the side.

"Mr. Elton," Bloom called out in a calm, steady voice.

No answer.

"John, can you hear me?"

John didn't turn around. He just stood there, swaying on his crutches.

"John," Widow said. "It's Widow. We met last night. On the road. Remember?"

Elton mumbled something. They couldn't hear him.

Widow moved closer.

Bloom grabbed his arm. "Careful."

Widow nodded and gestured for her to circle right, and he'd walk straight up the line to Elton. They could try approaching him as if they were trying to catch a bird on a ledge—slowly and steadily.

As he got closer, Widow tried talking to John. But it didn't seem like he was listening. Widow realized John was in the same state as he'd been the night before, at midnight.

Widow crept slowly over the roof. He glanced at Bloom every thirty seconds. She kept his pace. But she stayed out of Elton's view, approaching him from behind.

Halfway across the roof, Widow listened. John spoke up this time. He said, "She's gone." Tears streamed down his face.

"Who's gone?" Widow called out.

No answer.

"John! Who's gone?" Widow repeated.

John swung around to stare at him, like the night before. Only this time, he looked at Widow like he was conscious. But there was something off. There was something there that wasn't there the night before. John seemed like a different man. His eyes seemed different, like another man lived in his body.

"Who's Alessandra?" Bloom called out. "My wife. She was his wife first. But we ran away and got married." John's voice cracked. But it also sounded different. It sounded like someone else's voice. He spoke with an accent. Widow placed it as some kind of urban Italian, Chicago maybe.

Widow and Bloom exchanged a look.

"We were going to start a new life together. Just the two of us," John said.

"Mr. Elton, your wife's name is Jane," Bloom said gently. "Remember Jane?"

"Alessandra." John shook his head. "Her name was Alessandra. He was going to kill her. I had no choice. No choice."

Widow inched closer.

"I can't remember. I can't—Everything's mixed up. It's all wrong."

"Maybe it's the medication. The doctors are helping you. It's probably the meds they're giving you. It's making you a bit confused." Bloom moved in closer than well, keeping sync with Widow. One of them would reach him. One of them would grab him and get him down safely. They had to before this took a wrong turn.

Bloom raised her hands out to Elton. "Mr. Elton, you remember me? I'm Daisy Bloom. I'm with the sheriff's department."

No recognition on his face.

"John, I need you to come away from the edge," she pleaded with him.

John took another step closer to the ledge, and one of his crutches wobbled on the gravel. Widow's muscles tensed. He was fifteen feet away—close enough to rush John if he had to, but not close enough to guarantee he'd reach him in time. And if he rushed him, and lost balance, they both could go over the edge.

"I killed him. I killed Enzo Brasi. Shot him in the head. He deserved it." John paused a long beat. "I killed him." John dropped one of his crutches. It fell over the side, off the roof. It tumbled from end to end and clattered on the parking lot concrete below.

Bloom stopped moving and looked at Widow. Her expression said everything—*was this a confession? Was this real?*

"John," Widow said. "Why don't you tell us about it? Come away from the edge and we can talk."

"No talk. I have to end it. If I talk about it, they'll come for me. They'll come for Matty. For the boys. For everyone," he said, seeming to slip in and out of two different people. His accent changed just as much. It switched between John now and whoever else he thought he was.

"No one's coming for anyone," Bloom said. "You're safe here."

"I'm lost without her." John's voice broke completely. Tears streamed down his face. "I'm so lost. I don't know who I am anymore. I don't know where I am. I don't know—"

The roof door burst open as Matty ran through it. "Dad!" he shouted. "Dad, don't!" Matty froze there in the rooftop doorway. He stared at his father. Tear streamed down his face too. Worry flushed his cheeks.

The sudden movement, and sight of his son, startled John. He turned at the sound, but the movement was too fast. His last crutch slipped on the gravel and his balance shifted. His arms windmilled as he stumbled backward, teetering toward the ledge. The crutch went over the side first. John Elton started to follow.

Time slowed down. Milliseconds felt like an eternity. John's whole body pinwheeled, like he was about to go over the side.

Widow moved without thinking. His legs pumped and his boots hit the roof hard. He covered the distance in seconds. He punched his cast-free hand out to grab John's arm just as the old man's body started to tip over the ledge. He grabbed it and fell onto the gravel.

The momentum pulled Widow forward. White-hot pain exploded through the cast and up his arm from slamming onto the roof. He slid across the roof to the edge, like a batter sliding into home plate. Searing pain shot through Widow's body.

But Widow didn't let go. John's weight dragged him forward as the old man dangled over the edge. Four stories of nothing but air separated him from the parking lot below. His hospital gown flapped and his legs kicked.

Suddenly, John's alter ego was gone. The old man was back. He shouted in utter confusion about what was happening.

"Hold on!" Widow gritted his teeth. His cast-free hand gripped John's wrist while his cast pressed against the roof's edge for leverage. Every muscle in his body strained.

Bloom and Matty rushed over to help. They reached the two men. Bloom grabbed Widow's belt and Matty leaned over the side and grabbed his father's other arm. Together, they pulled.

Widow ignored the pain shooting through his cast hand.

They all pulled and heaved John up and back onto the roof. All four of them collapsed afterward. John landed on top of Matty, Bloom fell to her knees, and Widow rolled onto his back to stare up at the night sky.

Widow's cast hand throbbed. The freshly plastered cast was cracked clean through. Blood seeped out from underneath. The knife wound had reopened. One of his stitches had popped. He's had to get the whole thing done again.

John sobbed in Matty's arms. He was so confused about what was happening. Matty held his father and rocked him like a child. "It's okay, Dad."

"I'm sorry," John said between sobs. "I don't know how I got up here."

Bloom sat next to Widow and looked at his hand. "We need to get you back inside."

Widow sat up. His head spun for a second before clearing. "I'm fine."

"Your hand's bleeding."

"I noticed."

Matty looked up, his face pale. "Thank you. You—You saved him again."

Widow nodded.

Security arrived, piling through the door. Two guards burst through the roof door. They helped John to his feet. They walked him back inside and Matty went with them.

Bloom stayed with Widow. She helped him up, and they made their way back down the stairs with Widow holding his cast hand against his chest. More blood trickled out, covering his t-shirt again.

Widow had his cast redone for the second time that night.

An hour later, they left the hospital, Bloom driving and Widow in the passenger seat. His stab wound was restitched and a new cast plastered over his hand. The ER doctor gave him some good painkillers. He took them this time.

Widow asked to be dropped off at a hotel. But Bloom told him that was nonsense.

"You can't get a hotel now. This isn't New York City. This is Tent Hills. The hotels have all closed for the night. There's no checking in after midnight. Not here. There's not going to be anyone at the front desk till six a.m."

"Of course."

"Even if they were open, they're all booked. Husk-Town Showdown tomorrow."

She drove through empty streets. A few houses still had lights on, but most were dark.

"So where to, then? Where are you dropping me off?" Widow asked, relieved when he suddenly realized they'd passed the sheriff's station already, which meant she wasn't dropping him off at the jail.

"You can stay with me."

Widow looked at her. "You don't have to do that."

"Where else are you gonna sleep? Under a bridge?"

"I've slept in worse places."

"I'm sure you have. But not tonight. Tonight you're staying at my place. On the couch. And you're keeping that cast dry and elevated like the nurse told you."

"Yes, ma'am."

Silence stretched between them for several minutes until Bloom asked, "What was with the different accent? You think he has a personality disorder or something?"

"I have no idea. Never seen anything like that before."

They spoke no more about it. But both of their minds raced with questions.

They drove the rest of the way in comfortable silence. Bloom's house was a small ranch-style home on the east side of town. She parked in the driveway and killed the engine.

"Home sweet home," she said.

They got out and walked to the front door. Bloom unlocked it and flipped on the lights. They removed their coats and hung them on hooks near the door. Then came their shoes. They kicked them off, leaving them in a row of Bloom's neatly placed shoes.

The inside was neat and simple, with hardwood floors, a couch and TV, and a small kitchen through an archway. The place looked like a comfortable, worn-in home.

"Make yourself comfortable," she said. "Bathroom's down the hall. Guest bedroom's got boxes all over the bed. So you're on the couch."

Widow stayed quiet.

She looked at him and said, "What? You're not sleeping in my room. Not tonight. Not our first date."

"First date?" he asked.

Bloom smiled and said, "Play your cards right and maybe there'll be another one. For now, there's the couch." She pointed to the living room.

"Couch is fine."

"I'll get you blankets and a pillow."

She disappeared down the hall, took too long to just be grabbing a blanket and a pillow from a hall closet. Widow sat on the couch and felt his muscles relax for the first time all night.

Bloom returned with blankets and a pillow, like she said. Only she also came back out in a man's oversized t-shirt and no pants on. Presumably she wore panties, but Widow couldn't be sure because there was no sign of them. The shirt covered that area.

She wore no bra. That was one thing he could be sure of. It was very obvious. Also, it was something amazing. He wasn't going to complain.

Bloom set folded blankets and a pillow on the arm of the couch, next to Widow's cast. "Need anything else? Water? Food?"

"I'm good," he said.

She stood there for a moment like she wanted to say something else. Instead, she yawned a long, tired yawn. She said, "Goodnight, Widow."

"Goodnight, Bloom."

She disappeared down a hall. Widow heard a bedroom door close. The house fell quiet.

Widow tugged his socks off, removed his jeans and blood-dried shirt. He folded it all up and placed it on the floor, near the sofa. He kept his underwear on and clicked off the light. He lay down on the couch, unfolded the blankets, and pulled them over himself. His cast hand throbbed and his body ached.

Outside, the wind rattled the windows. Somewhere in the distance, a dog barked.

Widow closed his eyes and let sleep take him away to dream.

CHAPTER 24

The greatest smell in the world—coffee—woke him before the cat did.

Widow opened his eyes from a dream with a whirring motor in it. Only the whirring motor was something else, something from the real world. Orange fur filled his line of sight. He blinked twice to make sure he was seeing correctly and let his eyes adjust to the new morning, to the new surroundings. Green cat eyes stared back at him. The whirring motor in his dream was actually not a motor at all, but a purring cat. The animal sat on his chest and stared back at him while it kneaded the blanket with its claws. A small bell on its collar jingled with each movement.

"Morning," Widow said to the cat.

The cat purred louder and meowed at him once.

Sunlight cut through the windows and laid bright rectangles across the hardwood floor. Shadows stretched across the floor, created by the corners of living room furniture. The house was quiet. Just the cat purring, a coffee maker gurgling in the kitchen, and the low hum of the refrigerator. Bloom's place. He remembered now.

Widow glanced at his newest cast. His hand throbbed with a dull ache that wouldn't quit. He ignored it. He suppressed the pain, another capability he'd learned in the SEALs. Pain's only temporary. Victory is forever. Accomplish the mission, and they'd give him a medal. Think about the pain, and he only magnified its effects. Pain distracts from the objective.

Widow shook off that old SEAL programming and sat up slowly. The cat stopped purring. It stopped kneading his chest and jumped down. It landed softly on a rug before padding across the hardwood toward the kitchen. Widow ran his good hand through his hair and looked around. Everything was exactly as it had been the night before—neat, simple, and lived-in.

A paperback book sat face down on the coffee table. It was his smut book, as the teenagers called it.

"Morning," Bloom called from the kitchen and stepped into the doorway from the kitchen to the living room. Already dressed in her uniform—dark tan shirt with the sheriff's department patch, tan khakis, duty belt loaded with gear. Her hair was pulled back in a ponytail, and her badge caught a glimmer of morning light.

This was the second time he'd seen her in uniform. The first time, she didn't have those aviator sunglasses like the men had. Now she did—folded and tucked into her shirt pocket.

Bloom walked into the living room carrying two coffees. The mugs were both sports teams. She sipped out of one of them. The other piped steam out the top. Both coffees were black. She sat on an armchair near the sofa and set a coffee for Widow down on the coffee table.

"Morning," Widow said.

"I hope you like coffee. It's black. If you want cream or sugar, you'll have to go to the store." Bloom sipped more of her coffee.

"Black is perfect. Thank you," Widow replied and sipped the coffee. The blanket slipped off him.

Bloom stared at him and then glanced back over her shoulder to see his folded clothes on the floor, tucked just under the couch. She said, "You really made yourself at home."

Widow sipped the coffee, felt a draft, and realized he wasn't wearing any clothes except his underwear. And she saw it all. It hit him all at the same time. He nearly choked on his coffee and said, "Oh, sorry. I forgot." He set the coffee down and pulled the blanket over his legs.

"Don't cover up on my account." Bloom smirked behind her coffee mug. She sipped more as well. Then she stared at his book. She reached out and flipped it over. She looked over the cover and made a face.

"I didn't know you were into this sort of thing."

"I'm not," Widow said.

"It's your book."

"I mean I never was before." He explained to her about the mean teenage girls at the bookstore. That he was searching for a thriller. They tricked him into reading this one.

She replied, "But you're still reading it?"

"It's bad. No question. But…"

"But what?"

"It's sort of hard to put down."

"To each his own. I don't judge." She sipped more of her coffee.

Widow set the coffee down on the table. He stood and slipped his jeans on quickly. He buttoned them up and latched the belt. Then he folded the blanket, setting it on the arm of the couch with the pillow on top. The cat weaved between his legs and meowed. Widow said, "I like your cat."

"That's Ranger," Bloom said. "She likes you too." Bloom stood and walked into the kitchen. She came back out without the coffee. "So what's the plan? Sticking around or moving on?"

Widow considered it. He hadn't thought that far ahead. Never did. One town to the next. One day to the next. That was his life.

"Don't know," he said. "Should I?"

Bloom shrugged. "Festival's today. You know, the Husk-Town Showdown thing. Main streets will be shut down for the parade, so you'll have a hard time getting a ride out. We don't get a lot of through traffic."

"Bus?"

"Couple times a week. Not sure when the next one comes through." She paused, swallowed, and went for what she wanted to say. "I'd like to see you again."

"Me too," he said. "I'll stick around. I want to stay to check on the Eltons, anyway. See what's going on with John. Make sure he's going to be all right. No reason to leave now," Widow said.

She smiled. "Good."

Bloom checked her phone for the time and grimaced. "Listen. I gotta go. I'm already running late. Today's all hands on deck. The festival brings in lots of people, and Easton wants extra patrols."

Widow stood, holding his coffee like he was going to return it to the kitchen. But he froze. He asked, "Is there time for me to take a shower?"

"I really gotta go." She paused, thinking. "You know what? Just go ahead. Lock the door when you leave. Okay?"

"You sure?"

"Yeah." She grabbed her keys from a hook by the door. "Don't go through my stuff."

"Wouldn't dream of it."

"Uh-huh." She opened the front door and paused. "There's food in the pantry. Eggs and bacon in the fridge if you want breakfast. Help yourself."

"Thanks."

"See you later, Widow." She smiled at him, slipping the sunglasses on her face.

"Have a good day."

The door clicked shut behind her. She locked the deadbolt with a key. Her truck started in the driveway, pulled away, and faded into the distance.

The house fell quiet.

Widow finished his coffee and rinsed the mug in the sink, setting it in the dish rack. The shower was quick. Hot water, steam, and Bloom's body wash that left him smelling like flowers. He didn't mind because it smelled like her. He wrapped his cast in a plastic bag from under the sink. When he stepped out, he felt almost human again.

Widow dried off with one of her towels. He wiped steam from the mirror over the sink and brushed his teeth with the pocket toothbrush he always carried. He rinsed the sink when he was done and got dressed in the same clothes with the dried blood on the shirt. He'd have to find a store in town to get new clothes.

Ranger appeared and rubbed against his legs.

Widow crouched down and scratched the cat behind the ears. "Take care of her." He told the cat; in case he never came back.

Ranger purred and meowed at him once.

Widow stood and gathered his things. His passport. His money. His bank card. His smut book. He stuffed them into his pockets and walked to the front door. He made sure it locked behind him and stepped out into the morning.

The sun was higher now. The air was warming up. *Good day for a festival*, Widow thought. He could already hear faint music in the distance.

Widow walked toward town, wondering if he'd ever spend another night in Bloom's house.

CHAPTER 25

The Tent Hills Sheriff's Department was nearly empty when Bloom walked in. Morning light streamed through the glass doors, bathing the reception area in golden light. The deputy working the front desk had the sun directly in his face. He had to wear his sunglasses just to see. It happened every morning.

Deputy Harris sat at the front desk with coffee. He looked up as Bloom walked in and nodded a good morning to her.

"Where is everyone?"

"You're a little late. Most of them are already out there at their assigned posts." He sipped his coffee. "Gonna be a madhouse around here today."

Bloom walked past the desk toward the back offices. The station was quiet. Just the hum of fluorescent lights and Harris answering calls.

Her desk sat in the corner near a window overlooking the parking lot. She dropped herself down in a chair and booted up her computer. The screen flickered to life.

She'd said nothing to Widow about last night. About Elton. Or the names he said. But that didn't mean they weren't lingering on her mind. She couldn't stop thinking about Widow finding Elton, lost, out in that field, waving around a shotgun and shooting at ghosts. That was how Widow described it. Last night she'd witnessed Elton's behavior. He'd had some kind of episode, like he was reliving a memory and not just remembering it.

The names he mentioned: Alessandra and Enzo Brasi. They stuck with her all night. The names didn't leave her either. By morning, she kept thinking about them. Especially that name Elton repeated on the roof.

She opened a browser on her desktop PC and searched for the name: Enzo Brasi.

The results loaded within seconds. She clicked the first one. It was the Chicago Tribune, 1966. She found a headline titled: Mob Boss Enzo Brasi Missing.

She scrolled on and found other headlines with follow-up to the story.

1967: One Year and Still No Sign of Brasi

1971: Supposed Mob Family Still Can't Find Brother

She scrolled through several more until she found:

1985: Mob Brother Found Dead

Bloom read through it. It read short and direct:

Enzo Brasi, known associate of organized crime, found dead with three associates. Buried in a mass grave near new land development.

Brasi, and three of his enforcers, were shotgunned to death and dumped in one mass grave. No suspects. No arrests.

She clicked on another.

1966: Wife of Missing Mob Boss Vanishes

Alessandra Brasi, wife of the missing Enzo Brasi, also reported missing. Family believed she'd been abducted. Possibly killed. No leads.

The article included a black-and-white photograph. Alessandra was a beautiful woman. She had dark hair and sad eyes.

Bloom stared at the photograph. John Elton had mentioned the name Alessandra on the roof too. He said something about starting a new life with her. Then he said she was gone. But he also said she was his wife. But his wife's name was Jane. Bloom remembered her. She had died shortly after Bloom first got hired on and moved to Tent Hills.

Could this be the same woman? she wondered. What does Elton have to do with Enzo Brasi?

She kept reading. More articles. The story stayed consistent. The FBI concluded that Enzo Brasi had been murdered in what appeared to be a professional hit. He, along with three of his enforcers, was shotgunned to death. They were dumped in a mass grave. His wife Alessandra vanished the same night. Her body was never found. The case went cold.

Bloom leaned back in her chair. She thought about John Elton on that roof at midnight. He'd mentioned the name Enzo Brasi. He spoke with a Chicago accent that wasn't his normal speech. He went on about Alessandra. The mention of her name seemed to upset him.

If John's episodes were flashbacks to real memories—if they weren't just confused fragments or something he saw on the news decades ago—then something connected John Elton to this sixty-year-old cold murder case. A real mob boss named

Enzo Brasi had been killed in Chicago in 1966. And his wife, Alessandra, had vanished the same night without a trace.

John Elton, standing on that roof at midnight, had mentioned both names.

Was it just coincidence? Dementia mixing up old news stories? Or was there something more?

Bloom needed to find out. She felt the call of a real mystery. This could be the case that would put her on the map. It could get her that detective promotion. She had to know more.

Bloom tried the Nebraska State Police database. She found nothing on Enzo Brasi. She tried the Chicago Police Department archives. She found nothing beyond the news articles. Except one interesting detail. Enzo was the youngest of three siblings. The suspicion had always been that the Brasis ran their criminal enterprise together. All three of them. They cut their 1960s Chicago territory up into three slices, each of them running a slice of it.

So far she'd read about a lot of hearsay, a lot of low-level arrests, but not one conviction or charge against the siblings. Nothing ever connected them to any of their supposed crimes.

Bloom tried the FBI database.

She got one result. A case file from 1963 to 67. She clicked it and got a critical warning:

ACCESS RESTRICTED — CLASSIFIED

She scowled at the screen. Why would the FBI classify a sixty-year-old mob murder? She tried her credentials again. The system denied her.

The front door to the station opened. Heavy footsteps echoed through from the front of the station. Deputy Harris scuffed the floor, like he'd backed out of his seat and stood up for whoever had just entered the station. Harris greeted someone. A moment later, that someone walked back through the foyer, the hall, and the bullpen. They were headed straight for her. She leaned forward to see past Jimmy's cluttered desk.

It was Easton. He walked toward her, removed his cowboy hat and held it in hand. His face flushed red from standing out in the cold for a long period.

"Bloom! What're you doing here? Why're you not at your post?"

"Sorry. I'm doing some research. I lost track of the time."

"Research?" He stopped behind her and looked at the screen. "On what?"

She filled him in. She told him what had happened on the hospital roof last night. She explained John Elton's episode at midnight and described the names he kept repeating—Enzo Brasi and Alessandra. She mentioned how he'd spoken with a different accent, like he was someone else entirely. She told Easton she'd looked into it and found the names were real. A Chicago mob murder from 1966. The wife vanished the same night. All of it. The only thing she left out was Widow and the skinheads. She didn't want to lie to Easton. But luckily, he never asked why she and Widow were back at the hospital.

Easton squinted at the headlines on her screen. "Huh. Interesting. What about your boyfriend?"

Bloom felt her face flush. "Widow's not my boyfriend. I took him out to investigate him. Like you suggested."

"That's why he spent the night at your place?"

She spun around. "What? How do you know that?"

"Deputy Miller saw you after midnight, leaving the hospital with Widow in your truck."

Bloom rolled her eyes. Of course, Miller saw her. She couldn't get away with anything in a town this small. Everybody knows everything about everyone. She said, "He slept on the couch."

"Not my business." Easton set his hat on her desk. "Now, get out there to your post."

"What about Elton? Or this Enzo guy? Or his missing wife?"

Easton crossed his arms. "John's got dementia. Could be something he saw on TV."

"What if it's not? What if the Brasi family's looking for John? Like he had something to do with the murder?"

Easton's face went serious. "You got ten minutes. Then I want you at your post." He paused. "But call the FBI. I bet if you mention the file, someone will call us back." He picked up his hat and headed for the door. "Keep me in the loop."

"I will."

Easton left.

Bloom called the FBI's Chicago field office. After two minutes on hold, an agent came on the line.

She explained the situation. She described how it sounded crazy that an elderly man was having flashbacks at midnight. But he kept mentioning names from their cold classified murder case.

The agent went quiet for a long beat. "Someone will contact you within twenty-four to forty-eight hours."

"Forty-eight hours?"

"That's the best I can do. Protocol." The agent hung up.

The line went dead.

Bloom hung up. Forty-eight hours. By then, the festival would be over. Widow might be gone. But at least she would get some answers.

Bloom logged out of her computer and left the station.

The festival sounds were louder now. Music echoed from downtown, and voices and laughter carried on the wind. The parade would start soon.

But as she walked to her patrol SUV, she couldn't stop thinking about John Elton on that roof. Tears had streamed down his face. He felt something real, a real memory. Not something from some old TV show he saw. Elton spoke in someone else's voice, like a completely different person. Maybe he had something to do with killing Brasi.

Sixty years was a long time to keep a secret like that. It was long enough for people to forget. It was long enough for memories to fade.

But even forgotten memories can come back to haunt you. And if the Brasi family was still out there, she wondered if they'd forgotten.

Bloom started her patrol car and pulled out of the lot.

For now, she had a job to do. Her questions would have to wait.

CHAPTER 26

The rain-worn dock creaked beneath their weight as Tony Donovan sat with his grandson and watched the fishing line disappear into the dark water. The water reflected the dark clouds above. There was no rain today. Not this morning. Not yet.

Donovan hoped for clear skies all day. It was a sliver of his birthday wish. He wanted his family to enjoy the whole day outdoors.

The lake stretched out before them, calm and glassy under the cloudy sky. Somewhere far across the water, a boat's engine hummed faintly, but otherwise the world was silent.

"Grandpa, why do we have to throw the little ones back?" his grandson asked. It was a valid question. The boy was seven years old with sandy hair and his mother's hazel eyes. The two of them sat on chairs on the dock. Each had a fishing pole, cast out into the lake. A drink cooler rested between them.

"Because they need time to grow," Donovan said. "You catch

them too young and they never get the chance to become big and strong."

"Can we eat them?" The boy was full of questions. But that's the nature of young boys and girls. They start out with loads of questions. Then, by the time they're teenagers, they think they have all the answers.

"You don't want to eat those. They're too small. That's why we catch the big ones. Be patient. There'll be big ones too."

The boy thought about this and nodded like it made perfect sense. He nodded like they were equal sports anglers, talking about the ins and outs of the sport. Donovan smiled and ruffled the boy's hair.

Behind them, up the hill, voices and laughter drifted down from the backyard. The rest of the family had gathered for the party they'd insisted on throwing despite his protests. Eighty-eight years old today, and they wanted to celebrate with cake and candles and all the fanfare he couldn't care less about. But that was his family. They always came first. And they always got what they wanted. It didn't matter about his wishes. If they wanted to throw him a huge birthday party, then that's what they did.

It was funny for him. He thought back to a time when he was the man. He'd been a special agent in charge at the FBI. He gave the orders back then. He ran a mob task force at the Chicago field office for decades. He started out at the bottom and rose to the top. Agents used to jump when he said jump. Now, his family ruled his life, which was fine by him. No matter how much he complained, deep down he loved it.

Donovan retired from the FBI twenty years ago, bought this lake house, and spent his days fishing and reading and trying not to think about the cases he'd worked. Most days it worked. Some days it didn't.

Footsteps thumped down the wooden steps from the house to the dock, walked across a footpath, and finally clumped over the dock's boards. Donovan turned and saw his grand-daughter running toward them with her oversized knit sweater flapping in the breeze. Her grandmother, his wife, knitted the sweater too big on purpose. She told their daughter that the granddaughter would grow into it.

"Grandpa! Grandpa! Mom said to tell you that there's a phone call for you."

"Well, who is it?"

"Mom just said to tell you there's a man on the phone for you!"

Donovan figured it was one of his friends or distant relatives calling to wish him a happy birthday. It was probably someone who didn't send a card. "Tell him I'll call him back, sweetheart. Grandpa's spending time with you kids today. No time for phone calls."

"Mom says it's important. She said the guy says he's FBI."

Donovan's grandson looked up from his fishing pole and asked, "Grandpa, weren't you in the FIB?"

"FBI," Donovan corrected him. "It's called the FBI. Okay, you keep watching the floats for us. I'll be back." Donovan put his fishing pole into a holder with a weighted bottom. It was a nifty device that held a fishing pole in place so anglers could set their poles aside, freeing their hands to do other things, like drinking beer.

Donovan stood and took the girl's hand. "All right, let's go see what he wants."

They walked up the dock, took the footpath cut through his backyard, and climbed the steps together to the house. Her small youthful hand in his old weathered one. At the top, his son-in-law stood on the patio with a beer in his hand talking to other family. Donovan passed the girl off to him and leaned down to kiss her on the forehead.

"You stay here with your dad."

"Okay, Grandpa."

Donovan entered through a sliding glass door into the kitchen where his wife stood at the counter arranging food on a platter. She looked up and smiled when he entered, and he kissed her on the cheek as he passed. The phone sat on the counter next to the refrigerator. He picked it up and pressed it to his ear.

"This is Donovan."

"Tony, it's Jerry Nicks." The caller said it like Donovan was supposed to know him.

The first person Donovan thought of was Stevie Nicks. Still, he searched his memory for the name. No luck. He couldn't place it. "Sorry, do I know you?"

"Sorry, I'm a senior agent with the Bureau. At least I am now. We met years ago. I was brand spanking new, back then. I don't blame you for not remembering me."

"Nicks. Yes, of course. I remember." Donovan lied and forced a chuckle. "With a name like that, who could forget? So, Agent Nicks, it's nice of you to call me on my birthday. Didn't hear from you guys last few years. I thought you forgot. Director Lamb used to call me to wish me a happy birthday, and that stopped suddenly. Did you guys get a new policy?"

"Sorry, sir. No, Lamb's been retired for a while now. Actually, I didn't realize it was your birthday. Happy birthday."

"Thank you. But Nicks, if you're not calling me about my birthday, what's the call for?"

Nicks cleared his throat on the other end. "I need to talk to you about an old case. One you worked back in the sixties."

Donovan's grip tightened on the phone. This might be bad because the FBI never called him about old cases anymore. "I worked a lot of cases in the sixties."

"This one involves organized crime out of Chicago. The Brasi family. Specifically, it's about Enzo."

Suddenly, Donovan felt a cold burning in his chest, like a ghost from the past reached up from the depths and grabbed him. That sudden cold feeling turned to blistering ice, and he froze there for a long second.

"Hello? Sir, are you there?"

"Hold on a second," Donovan said and glanced at his wife. He smiled at her, so she wouldn't see the terror on his face. He walked out of the kitchen, into the living room, up a couple of flights of stairs to his study on the house's third floor, far out of his family's earshot. He closed the door behind him and sat down at his desk. "So, Agent Nicks. How can I help?"

"I assume you remember Enzo Brasi?"

"I do."

"Yeah, so this was your case. Enzo was murdered, and it went unsolved."

"Still is," Donovan added. "Unless that's why you're calling. You guys solve it?"

"Well, as far as the Bureau's concerned, it's closed, dead in the water for decades. Ancient history now. Most of the people involved are gray or dead by this point." Nicks paused. "Still, you know how the Bureau is. If they can solve an old case like this, one that has a certain sexy appeal to it, they'll resurrect the dead just to charge them with old crimes for the credit." Nicks chuckled.

Donovan didn't laugh. "So Nicks, my family's literally preparing for a birthday party for me. What can I help you with?"

Nicks cleared his throat again. "We got an inquiry from a small-town sheriff's department in Nebraska. Some place called…" Donovan heard paper shuffle as Nicks checked his notes. "Tent Hills."

"Never heard of it."

"Yeah, well. They've got an elderly man there who might have a case of dementia or something. Anyway, he's been saying things. Apparently. This comes third party from a deputy there. The old guy's making claims."

"Okay. What kind of claims?"

"He says he killed Enzo Brasi."

Donovan closed his eyes. After sixty years, it was all coming back. "How can I help?"

"I'm sorry for disturbing you on your birthday." Nicks waited for a response, but Donovan stayed quiet. "I'm sending a local agent out to Tent Hills from Lincoln. I'd like to ask you to assist him if he needs you."

"Oh? I've not been in the field in decades. I don't know if that's a good idea."

"There's no need for you to go anywhere. I just ask that you keep yourself open to phone consultations. Talk to my agents on the phone. Steer them in the right direction. If they have questions, they can call you for answers. That's all."

Donovan was glad Nicks couldn't see him. His brow sweated. His skin turned ghostly white. But he kept it together and said, "Sure. I'd be more than happy to talk to your agent. I'll give whatever help I can."

"Thanks, Tony. I really appreciate it."

They hung up, and the line went dead.

Donovan set the phone down and stared at the wall. His mind raced. Tent Hills, Nebraska. That was the place they went. He knew it because he'd helped them escape. Just like he'd helped Mickey Fog Eyes. He helped them reinvent themselves. He hadn't spoken to them in decades. He forgot about them mostly—Donny DeLuca and Alessandra Brasi.

As far as Donovan knew, they were still in Tent Hills. Nicks mentioned an old man with dementia making claims. Could that be Mickey Fog Eyes? Could it be Donny D.? After sixty years of silence, the secret was coming out.

A knock on his study door made him jump. Donovan stared at the back of the door.

"Dad?" His daughter pushed the door open and peeked inside. "Hey, Dad. I know you're on the phone. Oh, you're off now." She looked at her father. "Come out here and join your family. We're all here for you."

Donovan said nothing. He stared into space.

"Dad? We're ready for you outside."

No answer. He continued to stare.

"Okay, Dad. I know you didn't want a cake. But we got one anyway. The kids really wanna see you blow your candles out. We're going to start soon. So come on out."

Nothing.

"Dad?!" She stepped closer, concern in her voice.

"Not now," Donovan mumbled.

"But the kids are waiting."

"NOT NOW!" he shouted. The words came out louder than he'd intended.

His daughter's eyes shot open. Her father hadn't yelled at her like that in decades. Not knowing what to say, what to do, she backed away and shuffled out the door, hurt and confused. Donovan realized what he'd done and called after her, but she was already gone. He grimaced and stood up from his desk.

Donovan walked past the desk to a framed portrait hanging on the wall—a painting of Franklin D. Roosevelt. He lifted the frame away from the wall and revealed a safe behind it. His fingers worked the combination from muscle memory, and the safe clicked open.

Inside sat his old service weapon, a stack of cash, and in the back corner, an old burner phone covered in dust. He pulled out the burner phone and pressed the power button. Nothing happened. The battery was dead.

He found a charger in a desk drawer and plugged the phone in. It took a minute before the screen flickered to life. There were only a couple of numbers saved in the contacts—all fake names he'd created decades ago.

Donovan dialed the number and held the phone to his ear. It rang once. Twice. Three times. But then an automated voice came on. The line was disconnected. He hung up and tried the other one. This one went to Alessandra. He got the same outcome. Disconnected. He tried the final one. It went to Mickey Fog Eyes. Or whatever name he gave himself now. And it was the same result.

Too much time had passed. They'd all moved on with their new lives.

He hung up and set the phone on the desk, not sure what to do next. His hands trembled. He left his desk and walked over to a bar cart in the corner and poured himself a big glass of whiskey. He drank it in one swallow and felt the burn spread through his chest.

Less than ten minutes passed when a voice shouted up to him from the front of the house. It was his wife. "Honey?" she called to him.

He ignored her. A few moments later, her shoes clopped on the stairs, and she opened his study door. She stuck her head in.

He said, "I know about the cake already. I'll be down in a minute."

"No. This isn't that. There's some men here for you. They're FBI."

Donovan froze. That was impossible. He'd just hung up with the FBI. They wouldn't call and send agents to his house. Not on the same day. Not this fast.

Footsteps echoed from the stairs and out in the hallway from his study. His wife froze as she realized she hadn't given the men permission to follow her into the house or up the stairs.

Four large men appeared in suits behind her in the doorway. He didn't recognize them. But one thing he knew for sure was they looked nothing like FBI agents. They looked like wolves in expensive clothing.

"These gentlemen say they need to speak with you," his wife said.

Donovan forced a smile. "Thank you, honey. I'll take care of it. Why don't you go out back with the family? I'll meet you out there in a little bit."

She paused there for a long moment, like she didn't want to leave him alone with these men. Then she left and closed the door behind her. The four men stepped into the study and spread out. One stood by the door. Another walked to the window and looked out. The third approached the desk with his hands in his pockets. The fourth stood in front of the door, like a barrier preventing it from reopening.

The man at the window stared down at the lake, the dock, and the backyard. He saw a large concrete patio below.

Going by age and intimidation factor, he was in charge. He was the shortest of the men, but he seemed to be the giant of the four. He had a presence about him. He reminded Donovan of one of his favorite actors—Ed Harris. This guy had a similar build. Similar features: bald head, piercing blue eyes, and same powerful stance. The one difference was this guy had a big scar cutting through the side of his lips.

He spoke with a Chicago accent. He said, "Tony, we're not with the FBI."

"I figured that."

"You know who we are with?"

"I have some idea."

"Good. That makes this easier." He looked down from the window, over Donovan's concrete patio. "That's a long way down. Think a man could survive that fall?"

Donovan stayed quiet. But under the desk, he clenched his fists. He had that gun in the safe, behind his FDR painting. The safe was still open. But he was eighty-eight years old and seated. Could he make it to the gun, shoot these four men, before they got to him? Impossible. His old knees hurt just from the potential rainy weather. There was no way he could outrun them either for the same reasons. All he could do was talk.

"Cut the shit, why don't you? We both know you work for the Brasis."

"You took a lot of money from my bosses. For years, they paid you to look the other way while we conducted business. Now, I didn't work for them back then. As you can tell, I'm old, but not that old. Not like you."

Donovan stayed quiet. The large man by the desk stepped behind him, put a hand on Donovan's shoulder, locking him down in the chair.

The guy at the window turned and faced Donovan. He said, "You're half right. And I'm half lying. You see. I do work for the family. But there's more to it. My name's Vito Brasi. Enzo was my uncle. Elena's my mother. And Elio is my other uncle. I work for the family now. I never met my uncle. He vanished the year I was born. So, you see, I take finding his killers more than just some assignment from my employer."

Everything became slow, nearly euphoric for Donovan. He felt the room get heavy. Vito glided over to him, like a phantom floating across the room.

Vito stopped just a foot from Donovan's face. That's when he noticed it. All four men wore gloves, and not the kind for cold weather. They wore plastic crime scene gloves, the kind used to prevent leaving fingerprints and DNA at crime scenes to negate any chance of crime scene contamination by investigators.

"It's my mother, you see. She's sick. Her ailment has put her in a wheelchair. She can walk, but it's difficult. She's dying.

And it's a slow, painful death. Not something a son wants to see." He turned, looking at the open safe. He walked over to it, saw the gun, and reached in and grabbed it. He took it out and examined it. The gun was a Smith & Wesson 1076, a 10mm handgun that held nine rounds. He felt the weight in his hand.

"This a nice gun. This your service piece?"

Donovan shook his head. "They make you turn that in when you retire." He gulped.

Vito didn't point the weapon at him, not exactly. But he held it, finger in the trigger housing, barely touching the trigger. He did it in such a way that he almost appeared to be caressing the trigger. He moved to the desk, sat on the corner and faced Donovan. The gun's barrel pointed near Donovan's legs.

"My whole life, my mother's always wanted one thing above all. She talked endlessly about it. It was so damn annoying when I was young. To have your mother talk about the same thing over and over. Know what that was?"

Donovan shook his head.

"She wants to know who killed her baby brother. She wants them to suffer. She wants justice done. Know what kind of justice I'm talking about?" He stared into Donovan's eyes.

Donovan gulped again and said, "I can imagine."

"It used to annoy me. Like I said. But now, I think about my mother in the afterlife. I want her soul to rest easy. She can't rest until Enzo's killer faces such justice."

Vito stared at Donovan a long, long second. Then he motioned for one of his guys to bring something over. The man pulled a laptop from a bag and set it on the desk, next to

Vito, in front of Donovan. He opened it and pressed a few keys. The screen came to life.

Donovan's legs felt weak. He sank into his chair as the man behind him moved his chair to face the screen. The other pulled a gun from his jacket and held it casually at his side—a reminder of what would happen if Donovan tried anything. Now, he faced two guns.

The laptop screen flickered. It rang. There was an incoming video call. Vito clicked to accept the incoming call. It connected. Two faces appeared—an elderly man and woman with the same aged features and cold eyes. Twins. Donovan recognized them even though he hadn't seen them in decades.

Elena and Elio Brasi. The older siblings of Enzo.

"Hello, Tony," Elena said. Her voice was pleasant, but aged, like an actress who used to be somebody, but now spoke from years of cigarette smoke. "It's been a long time."

Not long enough, Donovan thought.

Elio leaned forward on the screen. "We heard you received a call from the FBI today. About our brother."

"I did." Donovan ran the scenarios in his head. The Brasis' men were here so fast. Way too fast. He figured they must've been listening in on his phone lines, waiting for Nicks to call. Somehow they'd gotten word before he did. They must've had a new guy on the inside. A new FBI agent was on their payroll, keeping them in the loop. Same as he used to do, decades ago. He should've never helped Mickey Fog Eyes escape. The moment he opened that door, it set him up to help Donny DeLuca and Alessandra do the same.

"And what did you tell them?"

"Nothing. I said I'd help if they needed me."

"Of course you did." Elena smiled. "You've always been so helpful, Tony. You helped Mickey Fog Eyes disappear after our brother sent Donnie D to kill him."

They knew about Mickey. Donovan's last hope of talking his way out of this died right there. And he knew it.

"Did you help Donnie D and that whore escape after they murdered Enzo? Is that what you did to my brother?"

Donovan's mouth went dry. "I never betrayed your brother."

"You didn't help them escape after killing our brother?"

Silence.

"I…" he paused a beat. "I didn't know they killed him. I only thought I was helping Alessandra escape your brother. They fed me a story about Enzo threatening to kill her for not giving him a son."

"So what?!" Elio shouted. "So what if he was? That was his right!"

Elena said, "Calm yourself, brother."

Elio said nothing.

Elena said, "We know you helped them. You were sloppy."

Donovan began to speak, to deny it, to lie, anything, but Elena raised a hand.

"Show him," she said.

Vito pulled out his phone and scrolled through it, then held it in front of Donovan's face. The screen showed a website for a used car dealership. An enormous billboard above the lot featured a smiling man with the name Mitch Nicely printed in bold letters.

Donovan recognized the face immediately. Mickey Fog Eyes, alive and well and selling cars in Nebraska, apparently.

Vito scrolled to another link. This one showed an old news clip from twenty years ago—a local TV interview about a horse ranch. The video was muted, but Donovan could see the family lined up in front of a barn. Two couples. The older man and woman stood in the center with their son- and daughter-in-law beside them.

The scroll at the bottom of the screen identified them as John and Jane Elton, along with their son Matty and his new wife, Elsa.

But Donovan knew their real names. Donnie DeLuca and Alessandra Brasi. There they were, in the flesh. They had made it. They really escaped and created a life for themselves. The truth was Donovan had done very little to help them. He really just helped with some fake names. Not that hard back in those days. And he mostly looked the other way, kept the FBI off their trail. That was all. Essentially, all he had to do was nothing.

Vito pulled the phone away and pocketed it. He smiled with that scar across his lip, opening up as he did. It made his grin even more devilish than it already had been. Donovan slumped in his chair. He was caught. He was done. After sixty years of keeping this secret, they'd caught him in it. He'd kept the secret so long that he actually forgot about it.

They were going to kill him. He knew that as much as he knew the sun would set. It was an undeniable truth.

No point in lying or fighting them. "I helped them escape because your brother was a maniac," Donovan said. His voice was quiet but steady. "He deserved to die. And I'd help them again."

Elio's expression didn't change. He fumed in anger. But he stayed composed. "We hoped you'd be more repentant. But it doesn't matter. You committed the sin, and you'll get the punishment either way."

The screen went black.

Vito stared at Donovan; gun still aimed near Donovan.

Donovan asked, "Are you going to kill me with my own gun?"

The man behind Donovan released his shoulders and stepped back. Vito shook his head and pocketed the gun. The third man closed the laptop and picked it up and went to the door, stood next to the other three.

"Your family's beautiful," Vito said. "Your wife, your children, your grandchildren. It would be a shame if something happened to them."

Donovan's head snapped up. "They have nothing to do with this."

"That's up to you." Vito walked to the window and looked out at the backyard again. He saw the family gathered down there. "You have a choice. You can die here, now, where we can see you do it yourself. Or we can kill everyone in this house. Your choice."

Donovan stood on shaking legs. The three men at the door watched him closely. He picked up his glass, pointed to the bar cart, and asked, "Can I make a drink first?" Fear washed across his face, like a dead man walking.

Vito nodded, and Donovan walked to the bar cart and poured another drink. This time he didn't gulp it down. He held it in his hand and stared at the amber liquid.

"How do I know you won't kill them anyway?" he asked.

"You don't. But if you cooperate, they live. If you don't, they die. That's the deal."

Donovan slammed the whiskey down his throat and swallowed hard. He set the glass down on the cart. He walked to the window, stood next to Vito, and looked out at his family. His wife was laughing at something his son had said. His grandchildren were running around the yard playing tag. They were happy and safe and completely unaware of what was happening inside the house.

He'd spent sixty years protecting Donnie D and Alessandra. He'd helped them escape, helped them start new lives, kept their secret. And now that secret was going to kill him.

But at least his family would live. He hoped.

"Give me my gun. I'll do it now."

Vito shook his head. "I'm not giving you a loaded gun. Think I'll hold on to it. As a keepsake."

"How then?"

Vito gazed up at the ceiling. Then he looked back at the window. "An attic entrance maybe?"

"Sure," Donovan said.

"You got a window up there, something that leads out to the roof, maybe?"

Donovan swallowed hard again. He tasted the lingering flavor of aged whiskey. He nodded yes to that question.

"Then lead the way," Vito said.

Donovan turned away from Vito and walked to the door. The three men followed him out of the study and down the hall. They stayed behind him as he pulled down a ladder from the ceiling. It led to the attic. He climbed the ladder to the attic. Vito followed.

Donovan went to a window and opened it. It was tight, as it hadn't been opened in ages. He felt the cool air rush in. Behind him, Vito stood and watched in silence.

Donovan thought about calling out, about warning his family, about fighting back. But it was useless. His choice was already made. No turning back now.

Vito said, "Go on."

Donovan climbed onto the windowsill, eased out onto the roof. He looked down at his family four stories below.

"I'm sorry," he whispered to no one.

Then he jumped.

Vito watched him fall and slam onto the concrete. The distance may not have been far enough to splatter a younger man. But Donovan was elderly. His bones were more frail. He splattered on the concrete. Blood and sinew sprayed across the birthday cake set out on a table he barely missed. The cake had white frosting. Now it was splattered in crimson blood and flesh.

Satisfied, Vito and his guys left the attic and the third floor. They heard the screams from the backyard. They heard Donovan's wife crying out his name.

They walked downstairs and out the front door while the family wailed and cried out in horror and shock. No one saw them leave. No one saw them get into a black SUV and drive away.

They drove for an hour, back to just outside of Chicago. Finally, they arrived at a private hangar at a small airport. A sleek private jet sat on the tarmac with its engines already running. Two elderly figures waited for them. One stood. The other sat in a wheelchair. They were Elio and Elena Brasi.

The three men boarded the plane, and the door closed behind them. The jet taxied to the runway and lifted into the sky.

The plane flew high above the clouds. The flight manifest might've labeled their destination as Las Vegas, but that's not where they were heading.

They flew to Nebraska.

CHAPTER 27

Widow hiked the shoulder of the road into Tent Hills as the Husk-Town Showdown Festival parade got underway. He wasn't from there, but finding his way around was easy, even after only one day. He just followed the crowd sounds and the beating of drums and the guitar strums from the event's live music. The louder the crowd, the closer to downtown.

Widow walked until he hit downtown, weaving through crowds of people. The main street had been blocked off to vehicles with road barriers and orange cones. State troopers stood posts at various intersections. In some cases, Widow saw police cruisers parked on street corners, with no officers around. Due to both the local sheriff's department and the state police being spread thin, manpower was limited. Parking unmanned police cruisers strategically throughout the town was a good way of showing police presence without actually having men posted everywhere.

Crowds of people, both locals and tourists, lined the streets. Family-oriented street vendors were everywhere. Widow saw local artists doing cartoon drawings of people, festival-goers played carnival style games, and there was plenty of street food.

Along the parade route, whole families gathered on lawn chairs while little kids ran around with cotton candy and yellow balloons in the shape of corn on the cob. Everyone wore winter clothes. Some took off their heavy coats and hung them on the backs of lawn chairs. Others tied them around their waists, keeping their sweaters on. Many people just wore pullovers, as the weather might vary from cold to freezing throughout the day.

The air smelled like fried food and diesel exhaust from the tractors idling at the staging area. The weather was cold but clear. The sun hung bright in the pale blue sky. The wind had died down to almost nothing. The winter cold held. But the day felt warmed by the sun. It wasn't perfect festival weather. But it was about as close as it was going to get.

At one point, the live music stopped for a high school marching band. They marched the streets with the parade. Behind them came a float decorated with cornstalks and a banner. Later in the morning, Mitch Nicely, wearing his famous yellow corn suit, waved with his four-fingered hand from the back of a brand-new pickup truck from his lot. The truck's price and a short, punchy sales slogan were written on the truck's windshield in bright pink marker.

Nicely's truck pulled a float on a trailer. Young, attractive girls threw candy into the crowd from it. They were all dressed in some kind of corn-on-the-cob bikinis. A portable heater was bolted to the floor and switched on to keep them warm. None of the girls seemed to mind the cold. Big smiles were plastered across their faces, like they were grateful for the opportunity.

Widow threaded through the spectators and walked past the parade route. He'd never been one for sizeable crowds. He had nothing against them. It more went back to his own personal motto of live and let live. The let live part translated to mind your own business and leave people alone to mind theirs. Widow enjoyed being left alone. Large crowds weren't the place to be alone. That was the very point of a large crowd, to be around a lot of strangers.

Standing around watching floats wasn't his thing. But there was another thing that motivated Widow to get out of the crowd. He needed coffee.

The bookstore and coffee shop combination he'd been to the day before sat on a corner two blocks away. So, he walked there. The patio looked closed. The chairs were upside down on tables and the gate to enter was roped off. But the bookstore looked open. Widow pulled the door open and entered. The same old-fashioned bells on a string chimed as they had the day before.

The place was virtually empty because of the festival. But the coffee shop was still open too. The same barista from yesterday looked up from behind the counter as Widow entered the store. He threaded past bookshelves and went to the coffee counter. The barista greeted him, recognizing him. Widow ordered coffee, paid, and took his coffee to a table by the window. He hung his puffer on a chair, sat down and watched people pass by outside. Most headed toward the parade. A few stragglers walked in the opposite direction, just as uninterested in the festivities as he was.

Widow pulled his smut book out of his puffer coat pocket and started reading, picking up where he'd left off—on a graphic sex scene. He hoped no one saw the cover of the book, but he also didn't care what others thought. He had started this smutty read, and he was going to finish it.

After a half hour passed, the bookstore's main door opened, and the old-fashioned bells chimed again. Widow glanced up, coffee nearly to his lips, and froze, seeing a face he recognized. Adam walked in. Bags half-circled under his eyes, like the kid hadn't slept all night. Widow imagined the whole family didn't sleep much. Their grandfather was losing his grip on reality, which understandably broke their father up. Matty was still at the hospital when Widow and Bloom left last night.

Widow imagined Elsa was the only one on the ranch trying to keep the kids on a normal routine. She probably slept very little last night as well.

Adam entered the bookstore and walked around, going from aisle to aisle. Seeing it was empty; he ignored the coffee area. He searched everywhere for something or someone. Presumably, he was searching for Ester. He went to the main counter and spoke with one worker behind the cash register. They spoke for a minute. Adam looked visibly worried. The worker told him one thing. And Adam reacted animatedly, like it wasn't the answer he wanted to hear.

Widow had seen this same sort of reaction in public many, many times. It was a scenario where he couldn't hear what was being said. Not exactly. But body language and volume of voices said it all. The most common place he saw such an exchange was the airport. Usually, a passenger yelled at some airline counter clerk because their flight was delayed or some similar issue. The airline clerk tried to keep the peace, telling the customer that it was out of their hands or they could compensate them for their troubles. Things like that.

Only this wasn't a situation where Adam was an unhappy customer. This was something else. Eventually, the bookstore clerk spoke loud enough for Widow to hear the end of the conversation. Like one of those unruly airport fliers, Adam wouldn't take no for an answer. He grew loud and frustrated with whatever answers the clerk gave him.

The bookstore clerk raised his voice. "Adam, I told you! I have no idea where she is! She's not scheduled today! Whatever Ester's doing outside of the store is none of our business! Now, buy something, or leave the store!"

Defeated, Adam backed away from the counter, and out of the conversation. His shoulders slumped and his face turned to the floor. He stepped back onto the street.

Widow closed his book and grabbed his coat off the chair. He threw it on, picked up his coffee, and went out the patio door. Widow stuffed the smut book deep into a pocket in his coat. He stopped Adam on the sidewalk— the same spot where he'd broken a skinhead's nose the day before. "Adam?"

The kid froze, hands in his jacket pockets. He turned and saw Widow. "Oh, hello, Mr. Widow."

"What's wrong?" Widow asked.

Adam shook his head. "Nothing."

Widow said, "Come on. I can see something bothering you. What's going on?"

Adam looked at him and hesitated. Then he said, "It's Ester. She was supposed to meet me here this morning, and she never showed."

"Maybe she got held up."

"She's not answering her phone, either."

"You sure she's not ignoring you on purpose? Women do that sometimes." *Men too, probably*, he thought. He'd never done it. Not to his memory. What he knew for sure was that whenever a love interest ignores your calls, it's normally not a good sign. But he said nothing about that.

"Has that happened to you before?"

"Sure. Plenty of times. It happens to us all."

"No. I don't think Ester would do that. Not unless it was something bad," Adam said with certainty. "She would never stand me up like this. Something's wrong. I can feel it."

Widow studied Adam's face. He was genuinely worried. That worry might be justified. "Maybe we should go look for her," Widow offered. He had nothing else going on. And he didn't want to bother the police with something like this. Not on such a busy day for them. Not when he and Adam had no proof of something that would warrant police intervention.

"We can't go to her house."

"Sure we can. I'll go with you."

Adam shook his head. "I don't think that's a good idea. Her brother might be there. Plus her dad is kind of worse. He's a drunk, and won't do anything. But he doesn't stop Trent and his buddies from messing with me. I think he's got some jail buddy staying there. Ester doesn't like him."

Widow knew that Trent's skinhead buddies were out of commission for the time being. Trent wasn't so bad. He might be there. But Widow doubted the guy would try anything while he was around. Not after what he'd seen Widow do to his buddies.

Widow said nothing about it to Adam. "Sounds like you could use some backup. I'll go to her house with you. Nobody will mess with you. I promise. I won't let them."

"I don't know." Adam scratched his head.

Silence fell between them for a long moment.

"Tell you what. Let's save her home as a last stop. That way we don't kick a hornet's nest if we don't need to."

"I guess that would be okay."

"Let's start with what you know. Where's the last place you saw her?"

"Here. Yesterday."

"She worked yesterday. Where did she go when she got off work?"

"Straight home."

"You sure?"

"Absolutely. We texted on the phone all night. She went to bed in her trailer."

"Trailer?" Widow thought about the trailer parks he'd seen in that place that Bloom called The Scarlands. On the way to The Outer Limits Bar, Widow saw large swaths of trailer parks. "She lives out in The Scarlands?"

Adam looked surprised Widow knew the terminology. "Yes."

"Okay. You said you texted her last night. What's the last thing you talked about?"

Adam paused a long beat, like he was thinking about it. "Nothing too out of the ordinary. Dad drunk on couch. The usual."

"What about this prison buddy you mentioned?"

"Yeah, she didn't like him. She mentioned he was creepy. But that's also not unusual for her home life. It's awful. But her dad's always got some strange prison buddy or friend from the past staying over there."

"She didn't say anything else about him?"

"Nope. She went to bed last night, and that was it."

"No word from her this morning?"

Adam shook his head.

"Okay. What about, is there anywhere she might go?"

"She only goes home, to school, and here."

"What about a hangout spot?" Widow asked.

"Hangout spot?"

"Yeah. Where do local teenagers go? Someplace the parents don't know about? Someplace where she can be alone today?"

Adam's eyes shifted away. "We have a place like that. But, adults aren't supposed to know."

"I'm not going to tell your parents."

Adam thought about it for a moment, then nodded. "Okay. Yeah, there's a place."

"Let's go there."

They left the bookstore. Adam led Widow down the block to a parked Ford F-150, painted red, white, and blue, to match the US flag's stripes. Chrome accented the truck. Widow stared at it as Adam took out the keys.

"My buddy let me borrow his wheels today," Adam said, and shrugged. They climbed in and Adam started the engine.

They pulled out onto the street and headed away from downtown, off into The Scarlands.

They drove through town and away from the parade route. Adam took all the right streets to avoid the parade, cops, and the pedestrians. That was a perk of living your whole life in the same small town.

The streets got quieter as they left the downtown area behind. A while later, they came to the edge of The Scarlands, before the rows of trailer parks began. Adam turned onto a dirt road that led out past empty fields and abandoned farmhouses.

"So, what's the deal with you and this girl?" Widow asked.

Adam's face flushed. "What do you mean?"

"You like her?" Widow asked, making small talk. He'd already seen their display of public affection the day before. He did that cop thing, questioning someone in order to gain information to build a case. In such cases, it was always important to get the witness to admit to whatever Widow was driving at, in plain English. If Adam was dating Ester, then he needed to hear the boy say it. It helped for context to understand the situation.

"Yeah. I mean, we're more than friends."

"Are you serious about her? If you're not, that's okay. You guys are young. It's okay to just have fun. You got your whole lives to figure out the serious stuff."

Adam checked his side mirrors and continued on down the dirt road. They passed more abandoned farm driveways and dead cornfields. "I love her."

Widow glanced at him. "You sure about that?"

"Yes, sir. I am."

A face flashed across Widow's mind. He said, "She know that?"

"I think so. I hope so. I don't know." Adam gripped the steering wheel tighter. "I never told her. Should I tell her?"

That face stared back at Widow in his mind. A smile, a kind of warmth, radiated from the woman's face, flashing across his memories. "You should. If that's how you really feel, then tell her. Don't let the rest of your life go by and you never told her."

"What if she doesn't say it back?"

"Doesn't matter. Tell her. Let the chips fall. Wherever they land, play from there." Widow paused a beat. "She like movies?"

"Yeah. Well, she doesn't like new stuff. She says it's all recycled crap. Remakes and sequels. But she likes old movies."

"Next time you go on a date, say you go to your ranch or whatever, find a certain old movie and watch it with her. See how she reacts to it. If you both like it, then tell her."

"What movie?"

"It's called Casablanca." Widow smiled, thinking about his own experience with that movie.

Adam repeated the name of the movie to himself, committing it to memory so he wouldn't forget.

They drove in silence for another few minutes before Adam turned off the dirt road and onto an even rougher path that cut through a cornfield. The truck bounced over ruts and rocks until they crested a small hill.

On the other side, the field opened up into a clearing. In the center stood a massive oak tree that looked like it had been there for a hundred years. Around the base of the tree were lawn chairs, a makeshift fire pit, and an old tire swing hanging from one of the lower branches. A creek streamed through the field about fifty yards away. It babbled, echoing a low, seductive sound. The ruins of an old barn sat at the edge of the clearing.

Widow smiled, looking at the whole scene because it brought back memories of his teenage years, and the secret meetup he had with his friends. It was a set of abandoned train tracks. It was overgrown with grass and forgotten by the town he grew up in.

This was similar, the kind of magical place where teenagers went to drink beer and smoke weed, with no one bothering them. It was a place where friendships were forged in the fires of youth.

They saw an old pickup truck parked in the old barn. It was out of the way, and hidden from the path. But it was there.

Someone was there. A figure faced the other direction, swinging away from the tree on the tire swing.

Adam parked the truck and killed the engine. They got out and walked toward the tree. Widow could see it was a girl sitting on the tire swing with her back to them.

"Ester?" Adam called out.

The figure on the swing didn't move. She just froze there.

They walked closer. Widow could see her more clearly now. Long blond hair pulled back in a ponytail. Shoulders hunched forward. She was crying quietly.

"Ester, are you all right?"

Ester turned her head slightly, but kept her face hidden. "Go away. Leave me alone."

"What's wrong? What happened?" Adam asked.

"Just go away. Please."

Adam looked back at Widow with helpless eyes. Widow gestured for him to wait where he stood.

Widow walked to Ester. She felt him behind her and stopped swinging. "Ester, it's Widow. I know it's not my business, but Adam's just worried about you. We just want to make sure you're okay."

"I'm okay. Please, leave me alone."

Widow glanced around. "I don't think it's safe to leave you out here. I know you kids spend time out here. But being out here all alone while the town cops are too busy to help you if you need help may not be the smartest thing."

She said nothing.

"Mind if I just stick around? We'll stay back at Adam's truck. We just want to make sure you're safe out here. Would that be okay with you?"

Ester didn't turn to look at them. "I guess that would be okay."

"All right. If you need anything, we'll be here. We're just going to sit back over there." Widow left her there and told Adam to follow him. They went back to the truck. Widow got the rest of his coffee out of the cab and went over to the lawn chairs. He had a seat. The chairs were a good distance from Ester. Widow figured they were safely out of earshot.

Confused, Adam followed him over and sat in a chair. "Now what?"

"You love her, right?"

"You know I do."

"Well," Widow said, and glanced at Ester on the tire swing. "Sometimes, you gotta give them space. Be patient and understanding. She'll talk to us when she's ready."

Widow and Adam sat there for the rest of Widow's coffee. Adam broke the silence first. The wind rustled through the oak tree, whistling through the branches. Ester swayed gently on the tire swing, her back still to them.

Widow said, "Nice place you guys got."

Adam shifted in his chair and glanced around, confused.

"I'm talking about your family ranch."

"Yeah. My grandpa started it. Horses mostly. Quarter horses. Some paints," Adam said.

"Good animals." *Maybe not the Bronco that tried to run me down*, Widow thought.

"They are." Adam paused. "We grow corn too now. To supplement. Or it started that way."

Widow studied the kid. "Why supplement? Looked like your dad's got a solid operation."

Adam's face changed, like a heavy memory settled across his mind. "We do now. Wasn't always that way."

Widow waited.

"Few years back, my grandma got sick. Real sick. Cancer."

The word hung in the air between them.

"I'm sorry to hear that," Widow said.

"Grandpa stopped running things. He stayed with my grandma at the hospital. Then had her moved back to our house. He took care of her every single day. My dad took over the ranch. So my grandpa could just focus on grandma."

"How'd that go?"

"Okay at first. But she got worse. Medical bills kept piling up. Insurance didn't cover half of it." Adam looked down at his hands. "Dad had to sell off pieces of the business. Horses. Equipment. Some land. Stuff like that."

Widow stayed quiet.

"Eventually, we had to find another stream of income. Corn was the natural thing to grow. We had the land for it. So, that's what my dad did. That's what turned things around financially. Corn saved us."

Widow stayed quiet and stared at him.

"My grandma died anyway. And Grandpa never came back to work. He just stopped. My dad had to rebuild everything. The corn was the best way to make profits. So it stayed. We still raise horses, of course. But not nearly as many as we did when I was a kid."

Widow drained the last of his coffee. "Your dad sounds tough."

Adam smiled at that. "He had to be." Adam stared at Ester. Widow saw something about the kid in that moment. He genuinely loved her. He really meant it. Some call it puppy love or first love. But Widow knew from experience it can be as real as any other.

They sat in silence after that for a long time, watching Ester on the swing. The oak branches creaked overhead. After twenty minutes, Adam stared at his phone, which was something his generation did. Widow didn't approve of it, but that's the way of the world now.

Widow finished his coffee and set the empty cup down on a pile of empty beer bottles. *What's the difference if he left it there or not?*

Finally, Ester glanced back over her shoulder at them. Widow stayed quiet about it. But when she did it several more times, he nudged Adam. "Hey."

Adam looked at him. Widow nodded in Ester's direction. "Now go over to her."

Adam looked at Ester. She glanced back at him fast and then away from him.

"You sure?"

"Yes. That's your signal. She wants you to go to her."

Adam got up, fought his nerves, and walked over to her. She turned away from him at first, like she didn't want him to see her. Adam looked to Widow.

Widow mouthed to Adam. "Gentle. Be patient."

Adam talked to her and whatever he said must've worked, because she hopped off the swing and hugged him tight. They held each other for a long, long time.

Widow waited.

Ester kept facing away from Widow. Adam left her there and walked back to Widow. He said, "Hey. So, she wants to know that you won't overreact when you see her."

"Overreact?"

"Yeah, she says she doesn't want you to do anything."

Widow stared at Adam, confused. "Like what?"

Ester glanced back at Widow fast and looked away again. Just then he realized. It was him she didn't want to see her. Not Adam.

"Like what you did yesterday to her brother's friends."

"I'm not going to beat her up. If that's what she's worried about," Widow awkwardly joked.

"I think she's serious. It's not about her, but what you might do to someone else. And she doesn't want you to tell Ms. Daisy."

Widow shrugged.

"Mr. Widow, she wants you to promise not to hurt anyone."

"Okay, I promise."

"He promised. It's okay. You can turn around," Adam called to her.

Ester eased off the tire swing, turned and lifted her head. Widow saw her face for the first time. She had a black eye. It was nothing severe enough to need to go to the emergency room over, but bad enough that it was already turning purple. Widow had punched a lot of people in his life. He'd been punched a lot, too. So much so that it became easy for him to recognize the leftover wounds from every type of strike. And Ester's black eye wasn't a jab or haymaker or hook. It looked like a backhand slap more than a punch.

Widow's face stayed calm, composed. But he clenched his fist. "Who hit you?"

Ester looked past Adam at Widow. "You promised. You weren't going to do what you did yesterday to my brother's friends."

Widow thought about it. He realized she had no idea about Widow's second fight with Trent and his guys. She was only thinking about what she saw yesterday in the street in front of the bookstore.

"I won't hurt anyone unless they provoke me. Now, who did this to you?"

Tears streamed from Ester's eyes. She wiped them away and sniffled, like she'd already been crying for a while. "It was my dad's friend. He's a creep. He watched me sleeping last night. I woke up, and he was just standing in my doorway staring at me. I think he…" she trailed off.

Widow waited. Adam asked, "He what?"

She looked at Adam. Shame flushed across her face, like she didn't want him to know.

"Tell us," Widow said.

"I think he was pleasuring himself."

Adam said nothing. He just took her hand and held it.

Widow asked, "What else?"

"This morning he tried to... he tried to make a pass at me. He grabbed me, pulled himself toward me. I pushed him away, and he hit me. I kicked him... You know. In the balls."

Good girl, Widow thought. "Did you tell your dad?"

"He doesn't believe me. Or he doesn't care. I don't know which is worse." She wiped her eyes with the back of her hand. "My brother would've done something. But he wasn't there. Not sure he'd believe me now. So, I just ran away after that. I didn't know where else to go."

Widow stepped forward and reached a hand to her chin. He raised it and inspected her black eye. "This will heal in a few days. You should get some ice on it, though." He released her chin and said, "I think you need to tell the police. Let them handle it."

"No. No police."

"You shouldn't ignore this. This time you got away. But what happens next time?"

"No police. I don't want them involved."

Widow stayed quiet.

"I'll be eighteen soon. I graduate high school next year. After that, I'll go to college or something. But I'll get out of here and never look back."

Adam looked down at the ground hearing that. She didn't mention what would happen to them. And he didn't ask. How could he? It would sound selfish. But Widow noticed.

"That's still a long time. A lot can happen in six months. I think you should tell someone. You can talk to Bloom. She'll help you. I'm certain of it."

"I don't know. I think it's better if I just keep my head down for a few more months."

"I don't think you should be there," Widow said.

"Maybe I can stay in my truck for a while," Ester said.

"No way. I know. You can stay with us," Adam said.

Ester looked at him. "Are you sure? Your parents would be okay with that?"

"I'll talk to them. I think I can convince them."

"Won't they tell the cops?" She asked.

"I'll make sure they don't."

"Won't your dad eventually notice you're not home?" Widow asked. "I'm not familiar with this kind of thing, but what if he calls the cops? He could cause the Eltons a lot of problems potentially."

"My dad wouldn't call the cops if his trailer was on fire. He'll notice I'm gone, but he won't care. My brother might. But I can handle him," Ester said, jumped into Adam's arms and wrapped her arms around him. "Oh, Adam! If they'll let me stay at your house till I graduate, it would be so amazing!"

Adam gulped, like he was just realizing now he had to convince his mother. Widow saw it. Ester didn't—she was too excited to have a safe place to stay.

Widow didn't like her choice to leave the police out of it, but he understood it. He'd run away from home when he was about her age. He joined the Navy and never looked back. Then again, maybe he should have. He watched his mother die. That turned out to be the first time he saw her in sixteen years, and the last time he ever saw her.

"What about my stuff?" she asked. "Plus, I'll need my makeup to cover up this black eye. I can't walk around with it. People will ask questions."

"Let's go to your trailer. I'll go with you. We'll get your stuff," Widow said.

"Mr. Widow, you promised you wouldn't hurt anyone," Ester said.

"I won't. I'll just take you there. Make sure you got no problems getting your stuff," Widow said.

They were all in agreement. Widow rode with Ester and Adam followed behind. They drove to her trailer.

Her trailer park was a collection of single-wides and double-wides arranged in crooked rows. Ester led them back to the end and parked in front of her trailer.

Ester's trailer sat at the end of the last row. She pulled up and parked her old truck in the gravel driveway. Her brother's truck was gone. *Probably out with his friends somewhere,* she thought. Widow knew he was probably at the hospital visiting his buddies. Not out drinking with them. He knew at least one of them would be drinking from a straw for three months or more.

She said, "My brother's not here. So we don't have to worry about him, at least."

"I'm not worried about any of them," Widow said. They hopped out of her truck. Ester told Adam to stay behind. She tried to ask Widow the same, but he refused. He was going inside with her no matter what.

They went up to the porch. She stopped and said, "The place's a real mess. Please don't judge us."

"I won't."

They entered the trailer.

The place reeked of stale beer, cigarette smoke, and something chemical—*probably meth residue,* Widow figured. Dirty dishes were piled in the sink. Empty beer cans littered the coffee table. The carpet was stained and worn through in places.

Two men sat in the living room. The older one was slumped in a recliner with his head tilted back and his mouth open. He had a beer gut that hung over his belt and thinning hair slicked back. His eyes were glassy and unfocused.

Widow was stunned by how off the mark he'd been. He knew she had a poor home life, but he had no idea it was this bad.

The guy on the recliner was Ester's father. It had to be. They had the same eyes. The same jaw. Plus, Trent looked a lot like him, only twenty years and a long prison stint younger.

Whereas the other guy looked nothing like either kid. The other guy sat on the couch. He was maybe early fifties, with a scraggly beard and prison tattoos crawling up his forearms. He wore a sleeveless shirt despite the cold weather. His eyes were sharp and alert, tracking Ester and Widow as they entered. This had to be the one who gave Ester the shiner.

Clayton Marrow, Ester's father, stirred in his chair at the door opening. He blinked slowly, like he was having trouble focusing. "Ester? That you?"

"Yeah, Dad. I'm just here to get some stuff."

The other man stood up from the couch. He was maybe six-two with the wiry build of a guy who'd spent years in prison doing push-ups and pull-ups. His eyes locked on Widow. "Who's your friend?" he asked Ester.

"None of your business," she said.

"You bringing strange men into your daddy's house now?" The man took a step forward, around the coffee table. He knocked a couple of cans off the edge. They clattered against each other on their way down, sounding like cans hanging from a car with the words "Just Married" stenciled on the rear window. "That ain't right."

Widow stayed quiet, with his hands at his sides, ready for whatever these two might try.

Clayton tried to sit up straighter in his chair. "Ester, who is this?"

"Just a friend, Dad. I'm getting some clothes and then I'm leaving." Ester shifted nervously.

"Leaving?" Clayton's voice rose. "Where you think you're going?"

"I'm staying with a friend for a few days."

"The hell you are. You live here. You ain't going nowhere."

Ester said nothing. She froze in fear.

Widow turned to Ester. "Go pack your bag. I'll wait here."

Ester looked between Widow and the two men, then nodded and hurried down the narrow hallway toward her bedroom.

The other man stepped closer. "I asked you a question. Who are you?"

"No, you asked her a question. And she's got nothing to say to you."

"Is that right? You speaking for her now?"

Widow stayed quiet, clenching his fists. He started to count to a hundred in his head, just to keep himself from crushing this guy's face in.

"Ooh. I understand what's going on. You into her?" The man chuckled. "I understand that, friend. I'm sorry about our little misunderstanding. I didn't know she was spoken for."

Widow kept counting.

Clayton Marrow seemed completely confused about what his friend was talking about. Which didn't seem to matter anyway because he was nearly three sheets to the wind from drinking too much or smoking or snorting or shooting up too much. Or all of the above. None of it would've surprised Widow.

The other man took another step forward, inching closer to Widow. Twenty-five. Twenty-six. Widow counted.

The man asked, "You got a hearing problem? I'm talking to you."

Widow didn't move. He just stared back with cold eyes with deadly intent behind them. Finally, he stopped counting and asked, "What's your name?"

The man's face twisted in confusion. "What?"

"Your name. Full name. What is it?"

"Why you wanna know that?"

"I want to remember it."

"Remember, it for what?"

"For when I see you again." Widow stared down at the man. The trailer went quiet. The man's jaw clenched. He trembled. It was fast. He recovered fast, trying to make it seem like he wasn't scared. But Widow had seen it.

The man asked, "That a threat?"

"You too scared to tell me?" Widow took one step forward. Just one. But something in his body language changed. His shoulders squared and his weight shifted. He didn't look angry, just ready to kill. And he was.

The man stared at him for a long moment, trying not to tremble. He stepped back, just slightly.

"Boyd Crick's his name. And he's not afraid of you, mister," Clayton said.

Widow smiled and stared down at Crick.

"Damn it, Clayton! Why did you tell him?"

But before Clayton could respond, Ester came out of her bedroom carrying a duffel bag and a backpack slung over her shoulder. She ignored Crick and looked at Widow. "I'm ready."

"Go ahead," Widow said.

Ester paused a beat. "You promised," she whispered to him.

"I'm right behind you," Widow said, and he took her duffle bag for her, carried it one-handed like it weighed nothing.

Ester turned toward the door and Widow stepped backward to follow her. He kept his eyes on the two men, making sure they didn't pull a firearm on him while his back was turned.

Crick started to call after Ester. He wanted to say something. He meant to antagonize her. But Widow, sensing that was coming, stopped at the door and stared at him. Crick gulped and said nothing. He literally swallowed his words.

Widow followed Ester out of the trailer and down the porch steps. Adam stood by his friend's truck, watching them come out.

"We'll follow you," Ester said to Adam.

"How was it?" he asked.

"Let's get out of here. I'll tell you later," Ester said.

Adam nodded and climbed into his friend's truck. Ester threw her backpack in the back of her pickup and climbed in. Widow put the duffle back there and got in the passenger side.

She sat there for a moment with her hands on the steering wheel, shaking. "Thank you."

"Don't worry about it."

She started the engine, and they pulled away, following Adam.

As they drove off, Widow glanced in the side mirror and saw Crick step out onto the porch. He stood there watching them leave with his arms crossed.

Widow hoped he'd see Crick again.

CHAPTER 28

The Brasis' Cessna Citation CJ4 touched down at the North Plains Regional Airport just after three in the afternoon on Husk-Town Showdown day. It was a small facility that catered to fliers who wanted to avoid the hassle of commercial airports. But it also worked well for wealthy clients who wanted to stay off the radar and off flight logs. It was one of hundreds of small airports across the US like this. A ground crew member guided the jet with a tug to a private hangar at the far end of the runway.

Two black Cadillac Escalades waited near the hangar.

The ground crew member stopped towing the plane just in front of the hangar. The cabin door opened, and a ramp extended to the ground. Two of the Brasis' henchmen emerged first—the same men who'd pretended to be FBI at Donovan's lake house. One carried Elena Brasi in his arms down the stairs. The other carried her wheelchair. They gently set her into it. She wore all black, including a silk scarf flapping in the wind from around her neck.

Her son, Vito Brasi, followed. He took over the wheelchair and pushed her forward. The henchmen stepped aside. Elio

Brasi came next, wearing an expensive suit and sunglasses. His thick white hair blew like a field of straw in the wind.

The twins were in their mid-eighties but still sharp. Elena's body had failed her years ago, but her mind remained as dangerous as ever. Elio moved with the careful, measured steps of a man in his eighties who'd outlived most of his enemies.

Five SUV doors opened and five men stepped out of the Escalades as the jet powered down. The leader was tall and broad-shouldered, with a shaved head and cold eyes. He wore a dark suit with a sidearm holstered under his jacket. Their ties flapped in the wind, mirroring Elena's scarf. The other four men stayed by the vehicles, all dressed in similar dark suits.

The leader approached the Brasis.

"Mr. and Mrs. Brasi," the man said with a slight nod. He spoke loud to fight the jet noises from the surrounding planes. "I'm Colton." It wasn't the man's birth name. It was his alias for this kind of work. He couldn't use his real name for unsanctioned wetwork, especially the kind on American soil. Same thing went for his guys too. None of them used their real names.

"Mr. Colton," Elio said, shaking the man's hand. "You came highly recommended to us. I hope you live up to it."

"Yes, sir. My team and I are ready to execute the operation, as discussed." Colton gestured to the men behind him. "These are the best operators money can buy in this region, on such short notice. But don't let that deter you. They're all former Special Forces, with plenty of combat experience between them. We've handled situations like this before. Never had a problem before."

"How many are on your team? Is this all of them?" Elena asked from her wheelchair.

"Five total, including myself. More than enough to handle two elderly targets and deal with any complications that arise," Colton said.

"And if the local police get involved?" Elio asked.

"The local boys are a small sheriff's department. They're going to be exhausted and spread thin because of today's festivities in the town." Colton told them about the annual Husk-Town Showdown Festival going on at that moment.

"So, then we should go now?" Elena asked.

"Not yet, ma'am." Colton said. "The state police are here. We may run into too much trouble if we hit now. Better wait till midnight. The festival will be long over by then. The state cops have orders to clear out by nine p.m. Most of the tourists will be gone by then. And the local boys will be so exhausted and left busy with the stragglers that we have a good chance of no interference from them at all. For a mission like this, it's best for my team if we're in and out without interaction with the cops."

"What if they intervene?" Vito asked from behind his mother's wheelchair.

"We're prepared for that contingency. We have the equipment and training to neutralize any law enforcement response. Come. Let me show you," Colton said, and led them to the back of one of the Escalades and popped the cargo door open. Inside were military-grade rifles, sidearms, flashbang grenades, night vision equipment, and other tactical gear. It was all holstered into slits built in to hold the equipment neat for travel and storage.

The Brasi twins were unimpressed. But Vito said, "Oh. Looks like overkill. I love it!"

"We don't anticipate needing all of this, but it's better to be over-prepared," Colton said.

Elio leaned over the trunk and examined the weapons with an approving nod. "Good. This will work. Let's proceed."

A few moments later, Vito helped Elena into the back seat of the lead Escalade while Elio climbed in beside her. Colton got behind the wheel and his team divided between the other two vehicles. One of the other Brasi henchmen folded up Elena's wheelchair and stuffed it into the back of the other Escalade, where there was room. The convoy pulled out of the small airport and headed toward Tent Hills.

They drove into the early evening, through farmland and small towns, past fields of corn stubble and bare trees. The landscape was flat and empty for most of it. Every turn seemed like the kind of rural lands where people minded their own business and strangers were noticed immediately.

"The target's currently at the local hospital." Vito told Colton from the passenger seat, like he wanted to be the team leader.

"No, sir. That's negative," Colton said. "We've confirmed he's been released."

"Where is he then?" Elena asked.

"We believe his son's taken him home. The family owns a horse ranch just outside of the town. That's where we'll strike. We gotta recon the place first."

"Recon for what?" Vito asked. "I thought your guys were some kind of badass mercenaries? And you got all this fire-power? Donnie D's an old man. What do you need reconning for?"

"We can't just rush the ranch. They grow corn and raise horses. And public records show the place to be pretty big. They must have hired hands on the premises. Hired hands mean more men, and they probably have guns of their own. We don't know who they might be. Some could be ex-military or felons who know how to shoot. There could be a couple of them or there could be dozens. We just don't know for sure. Not without scoping it out first. Doing a proper threat assessment. Maybe there's no one there because it's wintertime. But we can't take the chance. We have to know what we're up against first. Then we move."

Vito grimaced disapprovingly, but he said nothing. He just stared out the window, watching the cornfields fly past.

They drove into Tent Hills and scoped out the locals, just as the festival was winding down. The parade ended, and the crowds thinned out, but the streets were still busy with people. Colton navigated through the traffic and past the downtown area, driving by Bloom in her gear, directing traffic at a blinking traffic light.

As they turned off Main Street, Elena leaned forward in her seat and pointed. "Stop the car."

The pickup behind them honked at them as they stopped.

Colton pulled over to the curb. Elena stared up at a massive billboard on the corner. The sign featured a smiling man with gray hair and perfect teeth. He wore a bright yellow corn suit with a tie. He had two thumbs up, approving of some new deal on used cars. It was an advertisement for Mitch Nicely's Automotives.

The real name of the man in the photograph wasn't Mitch Nicely. Not to the Brasis. They knew him as Mickey Fog Eyes. He was alive and well and selling cars, all things they already knew. But seeing his billboard was a slap in the face. He was a low-level rat that Enzo thought Donnie D took out sixty years ago.

Elio leaned over to her sister and looked up through the same window. He said, "Two for one, my darling sister."

"Ma'am?" Colton looked at her in the rearview mirror.

"What about him?" she asked.

Colton looked up at the face on the billboard. "Don't worry, ma'am. We'll get him first."

"Good. Continue," Elena said.

They drove out of town and headed west toward the Elton ranch. The second Escalade followed. Colton programmed the Elton's ranch address into his GPS. They followed the route along increasingly rural roads. After twenty minutes, they turned onto a long driveway that led through pastures and fenced fields. The second Escalade stayed out on the road, waiting for them to return.

A sign posted on metal read: *Elton Horse Ranch*. "This is it," Colton said. The Escalade idled.

The ranch house sat at the end of the drive. It was a large blue two-story farmhouse with a wide front porch and several outbuildings nearby. Horses grazed in a corral behind a large barn. A newer pickup truck was parked in front of the house.

Colton drove them past slowly without stopping, taking in the property's layout. No one from inside the house seemed to notice they were there. No ranch hands came out of the barn. The only life seemed to be the horses.

The house was isolated, with excellent sight lines in all directions. The nearest neighbor was at least a half mile away. It was the kind of place where gunshots wouldn't draw immediate attention.

"I don't see anyone," Elena said.

"I think you're right. If they're inside, they're preoccupied, which could be because Donnie D just got home from the hospital."

"I don't see any ranch hands," Vito said.

"Yeah, that's a good sign," Colton said. "If there are, we'll adapt." He turned the Escalade around and headed back down the driveway, back to the road.

Elena turned to Elio and said something to him. Colton glanced at them in the rearview. Elio and Elena watched the house as they drove away. Finally, he said, "What do you think, Mr. Colton? Will this be easy?"

Elena stared out the window. The sun was setting. Orange and red streaked across the winter sky.

Colton thought about the question. "Simple? Yes. Easy? Probably not. But we'll make it easy."

The sun was dying on the horizon. It bled out across the flat Nebraska plains in streaks of orange and crimson that looked like wounds in the sky. The winter cold turned the colors harsh and brutal. No soft pastels here. Just raw light cutting through bare trees and dead cornfields. Shadows stretched long and dark across the road ahead. The kind of shadows that swallowed things whole. Within the hour, full darkness would settle over Tent Hills like a heavy blanket. Perfect cover for what they had planned.

Colton paused. Checked his mirrors. Then he said, "I recommend we pick up a few more guys. Local muscle. Have them watch the road for cops, stay on the scanners, and stick around the outside perimeter for backup and support. My team handles the house. They handle anyone who shows up. Or let us know if the cops show."

Elio looked at Elena. She nodded. Elio said, "Do it. No mistakes. No survivors."

Colton drove them north of the town. The second Escalade followed. They turned into a neighborhood that looked different from the rest of Tent Hills. The homes here were run-down and neglected farmhouses. The farms gave way to trailer parks with yards cluttered with junk. Several properties had Confederate flags hanging from porches. This was another way through The Scarlands.

"Where the hell are we?" Vito asked. "It looks like something out of Texas Chainsaw."

"Local bad area. Good place to find disposable help," Colton said. He pulled up to a bar called The Outer Limits; the same place Widow and Bloom were the night before. Country music thumped from inside.

"Wait here," Colton said. "This won't take long."

He climbed out and crossed the parking lot, pulled the bar door open, and entered. Inside smelled like stale beer and cigarette smoke. It was dark, but pretty much empty. Most of the bar stools were filled, but the dance floor was empty. A jukebox near an empty stage for live music played country songs.

A dozen men sat scattered around the bar. Leather vests. Prison tattoos. The kind of guys he wanted, only he'd already arranged to meet the right guy for the job.

Colton spotted the guy at the far end of the bar. Mid-forties, scraggly beard, ink crawling up both forearms. Sitting alone over a half-empty Budweiser. Exactly where he'd said he'd be when they spoke on the phone.

Colton walked over and took the stool beside him.

"Buy you a drink?" Colton asked.

Crick glanced sideways, looking up from his beer, and sized him up. Colton was a man to be feared. Anyone with half a brain could see that by looking at the guy. But he wasn't as terrifying as the guy he'd met back at Marrow's trailer. He said, "Who's asking?"

"It's me. You Crick?"

Crick's eyes narrowed; he listened to the guy's voice. He set down his beer. "Colton, good to meet you. I'm surprised to hear from you. This job's short notice. I rarely do short notice. Not for cheap anyway."

Colton glanced around the room. No one watched. He reached into his coat pocket and showed Crick a banded stack of hundreds, currency strap still intact. "Satisfied?"

"Yes. I'm happy."

"You'll need at least one other guy. You got someone?"

"I can find someone."

Colton took out a notepad and grabbed a pen from the bartender. He wrote the Eltons' address, tore the paper from the pad, and stuck it in front of Crick. "Be there. Bring another guy. Follow orders. Keep your mouth shut after."

"I can do that." Crick nodded. "When?"

"You know anyone else?"

"Yeah. I know a guy who ain't doing anything tonight."

"Good. Be here at eleven thirty p.m. We'll pick you up." Colton left him sitting there. Crick took out his phone and texted Trent. He knew boy would do it for money. He couldn't use Clayton, who was still high and passed out in his chair. Clayton was useless.

Colton left the bar and rejoined the Brasis. He got in and told them he'd found their lookouts.

Elio nodded and looked at his sister. "Good. Donnie D goes down tonight for what he did to our brother."

Elena gazed at the darkening horizon. "Time to go car shopping."

Vito frowned. "What, Mama?"

"Mickey Fog Eyes," Elena said. "Might as well finish what we started."

Colton put the Escalade in gear. "I know just the place. Mitch Nicely's."

Elena nodded.

Colton drove them out of The Scarlands and back toward Tent Hills. They passed the same billboard where Widow first encountered John Elton. In it, Mickey Fog Eyes smiled down at them in that yellow corn suit, flashing perfect teeth and a smug expression.

"By morning, both traitors will be dead," Elena said to Elio.

He nodded and said, "Our brother can rest easy, my dear sister."

CHAPTER 29

The sun set over Tent Hills at nearly the exact moment the Elton family left the hospital. They discharged John into Matty's care with instructions for round-the-clock supervision and more tests to come down the pipeline.

The Tent Hills hospital was good, but it was a small-town facility with limited resources. Dr. Russell had told them he would research doctors in Lincoln who would be better suited to diagnose and treat John. His current pending diagnosis was dementia, likely Alzheimer's disease, with severe nighttime confusion. Russell couldn't explain the midnight episodes or the personality changes. Possibly dissociative episodes triggered by suppressed trauma. Maybe a PTSD component. He recommended specialists in Lincoln who might have more experience with complex cases like John's.

When the Eltons left the hospital and traversed the town, the festival had wound down, and the streets cleared out as vendors packed up their booths and families headed home. The parade floats sat abandoned on side streets, and cleanup crews had already swept trash from the sidewalks.

John Elton sat in the passenger seat of Matty's truck with the hospital discharge forms folded in his lap. He crossed his arms and stared out the window, not mad at Matty, just upset at himself. His new crutches lay strewn across the rear bench. Dr. Russell had approved his release on the condition that he stay home and rest. Someone needed to be present with him around the clock—no more unsupervised midnight wandering. The plan was rest, medication, and hope that the episodes didn't get worse. His ankle throbbed beneath the foot wrap. The doctors said he was lucky—the fall from the horse could've been much worse. The fall fractured his ankle, bruised his ribs, and gave him a black eye that had turned deep purple. At his age, bones didn't heal fast. Russell told Matty to prepare for John to look like this for a while.

"You okay, Dad?" Matty asked as they drove.

John stared out the window at the passing cornfields. "Yeah. I just want to go home."

They turned onto the long driveway. The house sat at the end; every window lit against the gathering dark. John stared at it like a man who'd been lost and finally found his way back home. This was the place he and Alessandra built, where they raised a family. The ranch was their life—Matty ran it now, and his boys would inherit it someday.

Matty parked the truck in front of the house and helped his father out. They walked up the porch steps together, John moving slowly with his crutches while Matty stayed close in case he stumbled. Each step sent a jolt of pain through John's injured ankle, but he gritted his teeth and kept going.

Inside, Elsa was in the kitchen preparing dinner. The smell of roasted chicken filled the house. T.J. sat at the kitchen table doing homework, and he looked up when they entered.

"Grandpa!" He jumped up and ran over, then stopped short, remembering his grandpa's injuries. He hugged John carefully, avoiding his grandfather's bruised ribs. "You're home!"

Elsa joined them in the foyer, offering to help John to his favorite chair near the kitchen table. John had a favorite chair in every room of the house. Everyone knew it. They had an unwritten rule: *Never sit in Grandpa's chair.* John thanked her, but wanted to move himself around.

"I'm home," John said with a tired smile. He winced as he settled into his favorite kitchen chair.

Twenty minutes later, two more vehicles pulled into the driveway. The Eltons heard the tires on gravel. They peeked out the dining room window.

Adam's borrowed truck parked next to Matty's pickup, and three people climbed out—Adam, Ester, and Widow.

The last rays of sunlight barely colored the sky, leaving just enough light to see. The cornfields, heavy machinery, barn, outbuildings, and horse pens were still visible in the fading dusk.

Widow and the kids walked toward the house. Ester moved slowly, dragging her feet. She carried her backpack. Widow carried her duffle bag. She questioned if coming here was a good idea. Adam comforted her, reminding her she needed to go somewhere, and she didn't want to go to the cops. His parents were the next best hope for her to stay away from home for a while.

They stopped in their tracks when they heard a commotion from the training pen. A bronco stood in the middle of the enclosure, tossing his head and stamping his hooves angrily like a bull about to charge. The stable door hung open behind him. The horse stared at them.

"That's the new horse," Adam said. "My dad must've forgotten to herd him back in the stable."

"Is that the one Mr. Widow punched?" Ester asked.

"That's the one," Widow said. The bronco stared him down. Even from that distance, the animal locked eyes on him.

Adam looked at the horse nervously. "I better get him back in the stable."

"I got it," Widow said, handing the duffle bag to Adam.

The kid stared at Widow, unsure about this. He asked, "You know how to get him back in?"

"You go ahead. I can handle him." Widow nodded toward the house.

Adam and Ester walked to the house while Widow approached the training pen. Elsa and T.J. came outside to greet Adam and Ester. They spoke on the porch, out of Widow's earshot. He stepped off the driveway and approached the training pen. He climbed over the fence and dropped into the enclosure. The horse watched him with wild eyes. He knew who this big man was.

Widow took a step forward. The horse snorted, kicked at the air, bucked, spun in a circle—like they had unfinished business. The horse remembered the punch from the night before. No one on earth, man or beast, ever forgot a punch from Widow. There were men out there walking around whose jaws still ached from one of his strikes.

The bronco held his ground, huffing and puffing as Widow stepped closer. There was a wide berth between them. Most men would stay away from a horse like this. But Widow kept going. Partially because he wasn't afraid. And maybe a little because he wasn't thinking straight. The pain in his cast hand still hurt.

The bronco snorted once more—a loud, threatening breath. Widow paused and said, "I'm not afraid of you!" He took another step. This time he stomped and made it a big, loud gesture, like he was the one who was going to charge the beast. The horse reared and neighed loudly. But Widow didn't back down. He stepped closer, raising his good hand high and the cast one as best he could. He made his profile bigger, like he might do to scare off a bear.

It worked. The bronco fell back to its feet, neighed once, and bolted. He ran in a wide arc around the pen. Widow followed him, circling around him to herd him toward the barn. The horse beelined for the open stable door and disappeared inside.

Widow heard hooves clattering on the wooden floor. He walked to the stable and closed the door, latching it shut. The horse whinnied from inside. Widow looked inside. The horse roamed freely in the stable. This was probably wrong. It was supposed to be tied up or shut in properly from the inside. Widow knew nothing about that. He shrugged. This seemed good enough to him. The animal was contained. Matty could worry about it later, if he didn't already have enough to deal with.

Widow climbed back over the fence and headed to the house. The sun had dropped below the horizon and the sky turned dark blue. Stars started to appear.

Widow walked up the porch steps and knocked on the door. T.J. opened it with a big grin, like he was as happy to see Widow as his grandpa. He ran into Widow, planting the same big hug he had on John, only this time, he didn't hold back because Widow wasn't old and broken from falling off the bronco.

"Good to see you too, kid," Widow said, surprised by the

hug. After a long moment of hugging T.J., they went into the house and closed the door.

The family huddled in the kitchen, talking about Ester and her situation. There was some back-and-forth about what to do. Elsa warmed up to the idea of letting her stay as long as she needed. But Matty pushed back, citing the law and their responsibility to report this to child protective services. But in the end, they agreed quickly that this was an issue they could resolve in the morning.

Adam turned to Widow and asked, "Any trouble?"

"He pretty much put himself away," Widow said.

Adam nodded.

Widow stepped further into the house. The warmth from a furnace enveloped him. The kitchen smelled great. He noticed the quiet. Last time, two big white dogs had barked at him through the doorway. "Where are the dogs?" he asked. "They're at the neighbors for a few days," Elsa said. Elsa took Widow and the kids' coats and hung them somewhere. Widow left his boots in the mudroom.

They invited him to stay the night again. He gladly accepted. Elsa reheated whatever food needed reheating and served Widow, Adam, and Ester. She sat with them while they ate.

Matty, T.J., and John stayed with them for the first half of their dinner. Matty talked about the ranch while they ate. He told stories about growing up as a kid and his parents. Widow never mentioned the names that John had said in his last two episodes. No one talked about it. No one asked John about it. That was good. He could forget all about it for a time. He could just enjoy his family.

At one point, T.J. jumped in with talk about a science project at school. The kid was smart. Adam and Ester sat quietly but close together, shoulders touching. They seemed content just to be near each other. Ester smiled nearly the whole night, like this was the first time in her life she was sitting at dinner with a normal, loving family.

Widow knew how she felt. The two of them were the odd men out.

John said a lot, too. He jumped in from time to time with a tale about raising horses and Matty's childhood and his late wife, Jane. He smiled as big as Ester every time he mentioned her.

After dinner, Elsa cleared the plates and came back with a deck of cards.

"Who's playing?" she asked.

"What game?" Adam asked.

"Rummy. Pennies this time." Elsa shuffled the cards fast. Widow and Ester stared at her in awe. They were the only two not to know she could do that. She did it again and smiled. "What? I used to be quite the card player in my day."

They played into the night. They laughed and talked. Time slipped by.

Around eleven p.m., John's eyes started to glass over and grow heavy. His words came slower. He was getting tired. They all were. Matty helped him up. John got his crutches and said goodnight to everyone. Matty helped him down the hall to his bedroom. John leaned heavily on his son.

After a long goodnight to his dad, Matty returned to the family. "He's out," Matty said. "We'll have to put a lock on his door or something. Just to keep him in at night." He sat on the sofa by Elsa.

She stroked his back and said, "He seemed better tonight."

Matty looked at Widow. "Thanks. For everything."

"You already thanked me."

"I know. Doing it again anyway."

Ester checked her phone, waiting for a text message or missed call from her dad. But there was nothing. She knew there wouldn't be. But she hoped on some level, anyway. He was a terrible father to her, but that didn't mean she didn't long for him to change.

Seeing her distress, Elsa said, "You can stay with us, Ester."

Matty glanced at Adam and then back to Ester. He said, "You can stay as long as you need to."

Ester and Adam thanked Matty and Elsa. They were ecstatic with joy at this.

Elsa added, "You sleep in different rooms. I never want to see the two of you in a room with the door closed. Got it?"

They agreed and laughed.

They played card games into the night. Eventually, the family scattered. T.J. went to bed. Elsa went to check on John. Matty and Adam moved to the kitchen with the last of the dishes. Ester and Adam stayed in the living room, talking and laughing.

Widow was glad to see it. Ester deserved a night free of worry. They all did. But he felt like a third wheel sitting on the couch next to two dating teenagers. He got up and stepped outside onto the porch to take a break.

The night air was cold and still. The ranch sat quiet except for the occasional sound of a horse moving in the stable or wind whistling through the icy cornfields. The moon hung bright overhead. Long shadows stretched across the property.

This was peaceful. The kind of peace that came from being around good people in a place far from the world's problems. Widow liked it, even though his mind kept going back to a little farm in Missouri.

Widow didn't know it yet, but that peace wouldn't last.

Out on the road less than a mile from the ranch, a large group of men loaded weapons and checked their equipment. They prepared for a night raid. The target slept thirty feet from where Widow stood.

The armed men had a timeline. They had no intention of leaving anyone alive.

Widow didn't know any of that. Not yet.

CHAPTER 30

The parking lot at Mitch Nicely's Automotives was empty. Rows of used and new pickups sat cold and silent under bright lights high on poles. A massive billboard with Mitch Nicely's face on it glowed overhead. The glow from his teeth reflected off the vehicles' windshields.

Most of the dealership had shut down a few hours earlier. All the departments were closed. The only one still open this late was sales. Mitch always believed that sales should only close late nights. "Sales is all the time. And deals are forever," he'd tell his crew over and over.

Nearly all the employees were gone. Most of the buildings were dark. The only one left with lights on was the main building. Inside the showroom in the main building, Mitch sat at his desk with his boots propped up and a toothpick between his teeth. He watched a video of himself on his phone and smiled.

Mitch smiled a lot. It was usually authentic, too. He had a lot to be happy for. He set the phone down and stared at the stump on his hand where his missing finger used to be. He thought about his good friend John Elton. If it hadn't been for Elton, he'd have died in that hole sixty years ago.

Mitch looked at his phone again. He thought about calling the Eltons. He knew John was in the hospital, something about memory problems. But he didn't want to throw a wrench into John's life.

The two men and Alessandra had escaped that life and created a new one—a good one. Mitch owed John. He knew it. Maybe he'd check on the guy tomorrow.

The festival had kept most people away from the dealership today. Not a single customer had come in for six hours now. That was fine. Tomorrow would be busy. People always needed cars.

The door to the sales floor opened and the last employee on the premises, his assistant, walked in, slipping her arms through her puffer coat. She was young, early twenties, with exactly the kind of attractive looks that made men stop and stare. Mitch hired her for that reason. Pretty girls sold cars.

"Mitch, I finished filing the rest of the parts order forms, filed the sales reports, and locked your safe for the night. Do you need anything else before I go?"

"Good work." Mitch swung his feet off the desk and stood. He walked over to her, stood a little too close for comfort. This was something he did sometimes. He never got close enough to cross the line, but just enough to push it. "You can head on home now."

She took a small step back. "Thank you."

She left, and the showroom fell quiet.

Her headlights disappeared down the street. Mitch was about to turn away when he saw more headlights approaching from the opposite direction.

Two black Cadillac Escalades pulled into the lot in convoy formation. They drove slowly past the rows of trucks and parked directly in front of the showroom windows. They kept their headlights pointed at the windows.

Mitch couldn't see past them. He fluttered with excitement for a last-minute customer. He could make a major sale and keep the commission for himself. The luxury vehicles told him this was a customer with plenty of spare cash to throw around. His night was about to go from slow to great. Black Escalades with tinted windows weren't cheap, and people who drove them usually had cash to spend.

Mitch grabbed his white cowboy hat from the desk and put it on. He turned to a full-length mirror on the wall and shot himself a smile and a thumbs-up. Then he walked to the front door and stepped through it. He wore a big smile on his face, ready to greet his new customers.

The doors of the Escalades opened and eight men stepped out. Three of them were noticeably different from the other five. The five were all big guys, dressed in dark clothes. They moved with the kind of precision that seemed like military training. The other three wore tailored suits, gaudy and over-priced. They reminded Mitch of the Chicago enforcers he used to do business with a long, long time ago.

None of his new potential customers smiled.

"Gentlemen! Welcome to Mitch Nicely's Automotives!" Mitch spread his arms wide in his best salesman pose. "I'm Mitch Nicely! What can I do you for?"

Mitch's enthusiasm faltered when the men surrounded him. Something about these men didn't feel right. They towered over him menacingly. The clean-cut military guys circled him in formation that seemed practiced, while the three suits were more sporadic in their stances.

One suit looked vaguely familiar. Not like he'd ever met the guy, but there was something about him that Mitch recognized, like he was related to someone famous. Maybe?

That same guy stepped up to him and snatched his cowboy hat off his head, fast and violently. The movement startled Mitch. He stumbled back from it, but one of the precision guys caught him and stood him upright so fast it was like he never fell back.

"Hey! That's my hat!" Mitch blurted out. The guy who took his hat put it on, mockingly. "Fellas. What is this about?"

The one wearing the hat nodded to one of the suits. "Get his attention."

The suit moved fast, crossing the distance between him and Mitch in one big stride. One of the precision guys grabbed Mitch by a tuft of hair to hold him in place.

Before Mitch could react, the suit guy's fist buried itself in Mitch's gut. The air exploded from Mitch's lungs and he nearly vomited. The precision guy released him. Mitch dropped to his knees, gasping for breath and clutching his stomach.

One of the precision guys stepped beside him and drew a handgun from his jacket. He pressed the barrel against Mitch's temple and grabbed a handful of his hair again, jerking his head back.

Mitch struggled to breathe. His lungs burned and his vision swam. He tried to speak but only managed a wheeze. He was forced to stare up. The guy who stole his hat stood over him and said, "Pay attention now." He stepped aside so Mitch had a clear view to the Escalades.

One suit went back to the vehicles and opened the rear door and reached inside. He pulled out a wheelchair and unfolded it. He rolled it around to the open door. Two older people emerged from the Escalades.

One was an elderly man in an expensive suit. He had thick, silver hair slicked back. The other was an elderly woman who looked like she'd been carved from stone. The suit guy lifted her carefully and placed her in the wheelchair, arranging a blanket over her lap. Then he wheeled her toward Mitch.

Mitch sat on his knees in the parking lot of his own dealership. As the elderly man and woman got closer, he recognized them, too. The guy wearing his cowboy hat became more familiar as well.

The elderly man walked toward Mitch with slow, deliberate steps. The suit guy wheeled the elderly's woman's chair up to him. They stopped a few feet away and looked down at him.

Mitch's blood turned cold. Even after sixty years, he recognized them immediately. The sight of them switched off his fear of vomiting to the fear of death. He had to escape. He had to find a way out of this.

The one wearing his hat said, "My name's Vito. Do you remember my uncle and my mother?"

Mitch said nothing.

"Sure you do," Vito said.

"Hello, Mickey Fog Eyes," Elio Brasi said.

The old Chicago accent slipped out before Mitch could stop it. "Oh, shit."

Elena smiled from her wheelchair. It was not a kind smile. "Oh, shit is right."

"I don't—I'm not—" Mitch struggled to find words. The gun pressed harder against his head.

"You're not Mickey Fog Eyes? Is that what you're going to say?" Elio asked. "You're not the man my brother sent Donnie D to kill sixty years ago? The man who was supposed to die but somehow lived? You're not the one who helped them murder my brother?"

"I had nothing to do with that," Mickey pleaded. "That was a long time ago. I'm not that person anymore."

"Funny how that works," Elena said. "You get to become someone new. You get to live a whole life selling cars and playing cowboy in this cornfed state. But our brother? He stays dead. Murdered. Rotting in the ground for six decades."

"I didn't kill him. That wasn't me."

"No, but you helped the man who did." Elio took a step closer. "Donnie D was supposed to kill you. That was his test. Prove his loyalty by putting a bullet in your head and dumping your body in a grave near Lake Michigan. But he couldn't do it, could he? He let you live. And you helped him escape. That's the only thing that makes sense."

Elena said, "You could've reached out to Enzo. You could've warned him. And he'd be alive."

Elio said, "Did you help Donny D plan the murder? How did it work?"

"I didn't! I swear! I had nothing to do with it!" Mickey begged.

Vito exploded forward and kneed Mickey square in the face. His nose didn't break, but it bled. Blood seeped out of his nostrils. The blow chipped two of Mickey's teeth and knocked several others loose. The chipped pieces flew out in little white slivers. He stared at them on the concrete. His smile was ruined. "I don't know nothing about that."

"Liar." The word came out like a whip crack from Elena. "That traitor FBI agent already told us everything before he died today. He helped you disappear. And he did the same thing for Donnie D and Alessandra after they murdered our brother. But you helped them reinvent themselves here in nowhere Nebraska."

Mickey's heart hammered in his chest. Donovan was dead. They'd killed him. That meant he was next.

"Please," he begged.

"Shut up!" Vito said. He punched Mickey square in the face, knocking out one of his loose teeth. Mickey spit it out. Blood trickled out of his mouth.

Elena leaned forward in her wheelchair. "My brother wanted sons. They would've been my nephews. But your friend murdered our brother, murdered those sons too. He took that away from him. Took that away from our family. And you helped make it possible."

"I didn't. I just wanted to live."

"You got sixty years." Elio nodded to the man holding the gun, like he was giving a kill order. "That's more than Enzo got."

"Wait! Please!" Mickey's voice broke, his old accent heavy. "I can help you! I know where Donnie D is! I can take you there!" He didn't want to betray his friend, but he had to buy some time.

"We know where he is," Elio said, chuckling. "You think we didn't figure that out too?"

"Don't kill me! Please!"

"We're not killing you just yet," Elio signaled to Vito. He took off the cowboy hat and slung like a frisbee. It flew like a saucer through the air, landing in a wet puddle.

The henchman with the gun stepped back and kicked Mickey in the back of the head. Mickey toppled forward. He stood over Mickey and forced him down with a boot on his back. One of the Spec Ops guys stripped a long piece of duct tape out of a roll. He pulled Mickey's hands back and wrapped the tape around his wrists behind his back. They taped a long strip around Mickey's head, covering his mouth.

Mickey tried to scream, but the tape muffled the sound, nearly gagging him. The men dragged him toward the back of one of the Escalades.

They opened the rear and spread out a plastic tarp inside the cargo area, and lifted him into it. Mickey thrashed and kicked, but there were too many of them and they were too strong. They folded him into the back like he was cargo and slammed the hatch shut.

One of the Spec Ops guys threw a dark bag over his head. Darkness swallowed Mickey. He could hear his own breathing, rapid and panicked, echoing in the confined space. The vehicle dipped down nearly at once as the guys piled in. The Brasis and Colton returned to the first one. Both Escalades started up. Mickey felt them begin to move.

They were taking him somewhere. Somewhere he wouldn't come back from. He knew it.

Mickey had survived for sixty years by staying hidden and playing by the rules. But the past had finally caught up to him, and there was no escaping it now.

The convoy headed toward the countryside, back to the Elton ranch where Donny D and his family would receive the overdue retribution that was coming to them.

One target captured.

One to go.

CHAPTER 31

The weather turned ugly as the night wore on. Snow had fallen across Tent Hills a few hours after sunset. It snowed lightly at first, then more heavily as the wind picked up and the night carried on. The snow swirled through the streets as people piled into their trucks and gathered their belongings and left town. The locals headed back to their homes. The tourists left town for the long road back to the distant parts of the corn belt they'd come from.

By ten in the evening, the snow hammered roofs and battered windows. The snowfall continued like that until near midnight, when it evened out to a slower pace. The temperature dropped, and the roads grew slick with ice. Traffic slowed to a crawl for the stragglers who finally left the county.

Far away from Mitch Nicely's Automotives, Bloom sat in her patrol SUV parked on one of the tent-shaped hills overlooking the western part of town. Her shift was almost over. Another hour and she'd be done for the night. She sipped lukewarm coffee from a thermos and watched the snow collect on her windshield.

It had been a long, busy day. She was glad it was nearly over —the sooner the better. So far, she'd not heard from Easton since the sun went down. Her radio was busted. Something to do with faulty wiring. It had been that way for nearly a week. She would've gotten it fixed by now, but the town had a limited budget. With the Husk-Town Showdown, most of the town's budget went to that. This tracked across all departments, not just the sheriff's budget. She needed a new radio, but there wasn't enough budget this month to cover repairs like that. All excess went to cover the overtime pay for her and the other deputies.

Not having a radio would've been catastrophic to her if she worked in a major metropolitan area. But she didn't. Emergencies in Tent Hills were relatively low. Therefore, Easton told her if he needed her he'd call her phone.

She sat in her cruiser, not even thinking he'd call. It was the furthest thing from her mind. Instead, she thought about another man—Widow. She wished she could call him. Hear his voice. But how? He didn't carry a phone. He didn't carry much of anything.

Bloom knew she would see him again. The last time they'd spoken, he said he would stick around. She wondered where he was now. They never arranged a meeting place. She hoped he stuck around. But she also hoped he'd found some place warm to spend the night, out of this weather. She figured the Eltons had taken him in again. After all, he'd saved John at least three times now.

Bloom glanced at her phone. The thought of calling the Eltons crossed her mind. She could check to see if they knew where Widow was. Maybe he was there.

Staring at her phone, it rang, startling her. She nearly jumped out of her skin. She scooped it off of a car phone holder, stuck to the dash and phone using magnetics. The caller ID read a number with no name attached to it. So it wasn't Easton.

"This is Bloom."

"Hey. It's me. It's Widow."

She sat up straighter and smiled widely. "Hi. I'm … so glad to hear from you."

"You are?"

"Yes. I thought you might've left town already, without saying goodbye."

"Not yet. I'm at the Eltons. It's been a day. I ended up here. They're letting me stay. We've been playing card games all night," Widow said. "What time do you get off?"

"Soon. About an hour."

"Want to come over here when you're done?"

Bloom glanced at the clock on the dashboard. "It's kind of late. Don't they have kids? They've got school tomorrow."

"They're keeping the kids out of school tomorrow. The family's spending time with John while they can. Oh, he's here. The doctor discharged him to his son's care. They can't help him. So he'll have to plan to go somewhere else. Lincoln, maybe."

Silence stretched between them for a moment. Bloom said nothing. It wasn't because she had nothing to say to him. It was because she didn't want to say too much.

"I'd really like to see you again," Widow said.

Bloom stared at the snow on the hood. Her pulse kicked up for no good reason that she'd like to admit. But he was the reason. "Yeah. I'd like that. I'll head over when I'm off. It'll be around midnight or so."

"I'll see you then," Widow said. Twenty miles between them, they both smiled and didn't know it.

They hung up and Bloom held the phone tight, like she feared he might call back and cancel on her. She stared out the windshield into the night gloom. She watched the falling snow and thought about Widow sitting in that ranch house with the Elton family, playing games like he belonged there. *Could he belong here? Could he stick around long term?* she wandered.

The phone startled her once more. It rang again. This time the caller ID read no number. It only read: *Unknown Caller*.

She answered it. "Hello? This is Bloom."

"Deputy Bloom, my name's Jerry Nicks. I'm an agent at the FBI Chicago field office. I need your help. I tried to call the sheriff, but he's not returning my calls. And the operator at the station just keeps taking my messages. I don't know what's going on, but this is urgent!"

Bloom said, "Today's been a big day for our department. There's a big festival going here. That's why he's not gotten back to you yet. He will, though. Probably in the morning. What can I help you with?"

"You called us yesterday? One of my agents told me the entire story about a man named John Elton. And the names he mentioned. Especially the name Enzo Brasi."

Bloom's stomach tightened. "Yes, Agent Nicks. I remember. Of course."

"I'm calling with urgent information..."

The call cut out, but didn't drop. Static took over the phone line.

"Hello?" Bloom asked.

"Bloom... Can you hear me?"

"Yeah. I can now. Sorry. There's some bad weather here. I guess it's affecting the phone lines."

"That's okay. I was saying, earlier today, a retired FBI agent named Tony Donovan jumped from his roof. It was four stories up. He died right in front of his whole family."

"Jesus. That's terrible."

"Yes, ma'am. It is. He was a decorated agent."

Confused, she asked, "Why're you telling me this?"

"Because I had just spoken to him on the phone before he jumped. I called him following up on your story. You see, back in 1985, Agent Donovan was the lead investigator on the Enzo Brasi murder when the body was discovered nearly two decades after the killing. Before that, in the sixties, he headed a mob task force in Chicago. So he knew all the players. He knew the Brasis very well."

"What does this mean?"

The call cut out. Static again. "Hello?" Bloom asked.

Nicks's voice came back in. "His death might've been a forced suicide."

Bloom's hands gripped the steering wheel one-handed. "What?"

"Yeah, his family says that right before he jumped, like minutes before, a group of men came to their home and visited with him in private. These men claimed to be FBI. Only I sent no agents there."

"So, what? It was the Brasis?" she asked, bewildered that the family would still be in operation after sixty years. Then again, she knew nothing about the mob.

SCOTT BLADE

"At this time, we don't know who or what. But it's better to be safe than sorry. Enzo was the youngest of three siblings. After he vanished in 1966, his siblings took over his territory. Let's just say that they became much worse than he ever was."

Bloom perked up in her chair. A sudden rush of excitement rushed through her. A real-life conspiracy and danger weren't on her radar. But this could be her chance to become something more than she'd been. She could make that detective spot. Or maybe even better. "Please, tell me more."

"This guy John Elton, the one you were calling about us about. I did some digging into him and his wife, Jane."

Bloom listened intently. She pressed the phone tight to her ear. Snow plopped onto the hood of her SUV in large, soft clumps. It came down slowly, like it was about to pick up. But it didn't.

"The two of them never existed before 1966. At least, we found no record of them. I'd have to dig more into it to be sure. However, the thing that sticks out to me is…"

Bloom interrupted. "The year. 1966. That's the year Enzo Brasi vanished."

"Right. I think John Elton's not your guy's real name. See, when Brasi went missing, so did a bunch of his guys and his wife. When we found Brasi's body in the eighties, we found several of his guys buried with him. But according to the files, there was member of his crew missing. A guy named Donnie D. But you know who else was missing?"

"Who?"

"Brasi's wife, Alessandra. She also vanished back in 1966. And her body was never found."

Bloom stared straight ahead out the window. She saw a lot of the town was dark. Power issues. Probably. The town's power lines were still above ground on poles. It was common during bad winter weather and storms for there to be some outages.

"Guess what Donnie D did for Brasi?" Nicks asked.

"What?"

"He drove for Alessandra. Brasi hired him to be her driver and bodyguard."

"That's interesting?" she said, and paused a beat. "Elton mentioned Alessandra. Do you think he could really be Donnie D?"

"That's why I'm calling you. We have informants inside the Brasi organization. None of them are a hundred percent reliable, but they're tell us the same thing. Enzo's siblings—Elena and Elio—left Chicago this afternoon on a private jet. They were supposed to touch down in LA. They never did. We think they diverted to Nebraska."

Bloom's heart raced. She said, "So what? You think they're here?"

"Yes. I do. They've wanted to find their brother's killer for decades. And trust me, Elena and Elio Brasi aren't the kind of people to forgive and forget. I tried calling the hospital where you mentioned John Elton was staying, but they told me he was discharged. We need to find him. He needs to be put under protective custody now. I can get some agents out there tomorrow to take him in. But if the Brasis are already there, tomorrow might be too late. That's why I'm calling you."

"Oh, my god." Bloom put her phone on speaker, and texted Easton to call her asap.

"Where is Elton now?" Nicks asked.

"He's at home with his family."

"Deputy Bloom, listen to me carefully. John Elton and everyone around him are in grave danger. The Brasi family doesn't leave witnesses. If they're in Tent Hills, they're coming for him tonight. It's up to your department to get over there now. Move them to a safe location if you have to. But they must be under guard for the night."

Bloom didn't wait for the end of his sentence. She threw her SUV in gear and pulled out onto the road, spraying up gravel and snow behind the tires. She switched on the vehicle's emergency lights. Blue lights danced across the surrounding gloom. Snow whipped across the windshield. She turned the wipers on. They wiped snow off the windshield, struggling to keep up. "I'm heading to the Elton ranch now."

"Be careful, Deputy. Don't be a hero. You get there and get the sheriff to send all his guys to help you. These people are dangerous. The Brasis are ruthless. They've killed before. They've killed countless people over the years, including cops. And they've gotten away with all of it. They won't hesitate to kill you, too."

"Understood."

She hung up and didn't wait for Easton to respond to her text. She dialed his number. It rang three times before he answered. The background noise was deafening—shouting, sirens, the roar of flames.

"Easton!" he shouted, like he was annoyed at being bothered. His voice was barely audible over the chaotic sounds behind him.

"It's me. Bloom. Where are you? We got a real problem."

"Tell me about it! I'm at Mitch Nicely's dealership. The whole damn place is on fire. Every car on the lot is burning, and it spread to the neighborhood behind it. There's an old folks' home back there engulfed in flames, too. The fire department's here. We've evacuated what we can so far. But we're still looking for missing residents."

Bloom drove fast, her cruiser skidded as she turned the corners hard. "Nicely's dealership?" She glanced out a side window toward the dealership. She saw the smoke. It rose black in the sky, dotting out the town lights around it.

Holy shit! she thought.

"Yes! It's hell over here! There's no telling how many are dead."

"Bill, I need you to listen to me. The Eltons are in danger. The FBI just called and—"

More static. She said, "Bill?"

Easton's voice came back. "I can barely hear you! Listen, the fire department needs us here! All hands on deck! Get over here!"

"I can't! The Eltons are in danger! There's a mob family coming for them! They might already be here!"

"What?" Easton shouted. "I really can't understand you. You keep cutting out!"

She repeated her warning, but it was no good. Static crackled over the line.

"Bloom, are you there?"

"Can you hear me?" she asked.

The line went dead.

Bloom pressed harder on the gas pedal. The SUV fishtailed slightly on the icy road, but she corrected it and kept going. She texted him instead. Only this time she noticed her messages weren't going through. She got an error message on both of them. She dialed the Elton ranch instead.

The phone rang twice before someone picked up.

"Hello?"

It was a youthful voice. Adam.

"Widow?!" Bloom said urgently. "I need to talk to Widow!"

"Oh, sure. Hold on, I'll get him." Adam set the phone down. She could hear voices in the background, laughter, the sound of the television playing. They had no idea what was coming for them.

She waited, counting the seconds. Five. Ten. Fifteen.

Finally, Widow's voice came on the line. "Bloom? You on your way over already?"

Before Bloom could respond, the line went dead again.

"Widow?! Widow?!"

Silence.

She looked at her phone. No signal. She tried to call back but couldn't get through. She tried Easton's number again, too. Nothing.

The weather must've been blocking the towers. Or something worse.

Bloom gassed the accelerator as far as she could without losing control. The SUV's engine roared, and the speedometer climbed. Snow pelted the windshield so hard she could barely see the road ahead. The emergency lights reflected off the white landscape, painting everything blue.

The Elton ranch was far away. But she had to get there.

A t the Elton's ranch, Widow stood in the kitchen holding the phone receiver and staring at it with a confused expression on his face. The line was dead.

Widow tried to call her back, but couldn't even get a dial tone.

He hung up the phone and walked to the window. Outside, the snow was coming down heavily. The wind howled and rattled the windows. Visibility approached zero.

Something felt wrong. His primal brain was speaking to him. He just wasn't sure why.

Widow couldn't explain it, couldn't put his finger on what exactly was bothering him, but his instincts were warning him. He'd learned a long time ago to trust his first instincts. They had kept him alive through combat, secret black Ops missions, and more dangerous situations than he could count.

He walked back to the living room where the family was gathered. Matty and Elsa sat on the couch. T.J. was on the floor playing with a handheld video game. Adam and Ester shared a recliner.

John was asleep in his room.

Everything looked peaceful. Normal. Safe.

But Widow's instincts said otherwise.

He walked to the front door and looked out the window. He saw nothing but snow and darkness in the gloom.

Elsa got up to bring some empty snack bowls to the kitchen. She stopped behind him and asked, "Everything okay?"

"Phone line's dead," Widow said.

"Probably the weather. Happens sometimes out here. It's pretty common."

Widow nodded but didn't move from the window. Not much was visible beyond the porch lights. He tried anyway. He just stood there, watching the darkness.

Outside, beyond the range of the porch lights and far from Widow's line of sight, eight men, armed like SEALs going on a night mission, approached the ranch through the snowy cornfields. Five of them moved in formation with military precision, their weapons ready and their night vision goggles painting the world in shades of green.

Vito and his two guys took up the rear, with the Brasis behind them. Elio wheeled Elena along the driveway. They stayed far enough back to remain out of sight; to give the men they paid to do their job first. Back a couple of acres, near the edge of the Elton's property, the Escalades were parked near Trent's old pickup truck. He hung back with Crick. They watched the road and the mouth of the driveway. They were tasked with watching for cops. The moment they saw any, they were charged with slowing them down, if they had to. But also with calling Colton's phone to warn them.

Just how they were supposed to slow the cops down, Trent wasn't sure. Crick had no problem firing at them.

Colton's guys began their approach to the house. First, he wanted to cut the power. He looked around. There were several ways to go about it. They could cut the power at the house, if the house's key box was outside. But a better way to do it was at the street. He signaled for his team to stop, and stay just at the edge of the icy cornfield. That way they would remain concealed in case someone at the house could see that far out.

Colton ordered one of his guys to cut the power. He pointed to the power line at the driveway and road. The guy nodded and took off running down the driveway to the road.

The rest of them waited. Colton checked the time on his watch.

It was nearly midnight. Nearly time to move in and kill the Eltons and anyone else who got in their way.

CHAPTER 32
MEMORY THREE

At midnight, back in 1966, John Elton was only known as Donnie D, and it would be that way for only one last night. He sat behind the wheel of a 1965 Cadillac Deville, black as an empty grave, driving north out of Chicago with Enzo Brasi in the backseat and Brasi's deadliest enforcer, Carlo, riding shotgun.

Silence followed them for most of the drive. Donnie D didn't know where they were going or why. He feared asking questions. Brasi behaved more unhinged than usual. The drugs and the business made him more paranoid than normal. His wife, Alessandra, still had not given him any sons, no children at all. She had confided in Donnie D that Brasi had been acting strange lately. He'd been distant, no longer sharing a bed with her, which didn't bother her. And it definitely didn't bother Donnie D, since he and Alessandra had become more than either of them ever intended. They'd been sleeping together for months. But it was far more than sex. There was something special between them.

Alessandra told Donnie D that whenever Brasi touched her, she closed her eyes and thought of him. It was the only way she could push through it. Everything went fine for a while. Until one day, Alessandra told him she could no longer pretend. She could no longer hide how she felt.

They were in the car when it happened. It wasn't this car, but another of Brasi's cars. They'd had sex in the backseat, parked in a secluded spot by Lake Michigan, when Alessandra said it first. She told Donnie D she loved him. It was real. He felt the same way.

That's when their real problems began. They'd turned a corner, past the point of no return. They discussed options. Escape. They could run away together although that would be hard. Neither of them had any money. Not enough to escape the grips of the Brasis.

Eventually, the conversation turned to murder. It was the obvious way out. If Donnie D killed Enzo, but made it look like a mob hit, then Alessandra would get some money. They could run away together. However, there was a big problem there. Donnie D would never be free as long as the other Brasis were still alive. Also, he brought up another point to her. There was no reason to think that Elena or Elio would let her live after their brother died.

They were at an impasse.

The thing that worried Donnie D right now, at that moment, was that their discussion was last night. Today, they still had no solution. And he hadn't seen Alessandra all day. She was gone by the time he got to Enzo's home to pick her up.

When Donnie D asked Enzo about this, Enzo told him she was driving with Mad Dom. Donnie D's stomach turned hearing that. *Why was she driving with Mad Dom?* he wondered, but didn't dare to question Enzo.

Now he was driving Enzo and Carlo out to the middle of nowhere. The job? He had no idea, which wasn't totally unusual. He was the low man on the totem pole. Often, Brasi kept him in the dark. He wasn't paid to know the plan. He was paid to follow orders.

The city lights had died behind them nearly forty-five minutes ago. They drove on a highway, turning off onto lonely roads that seemed to shrink as they continued. First, they were four lanes, then two. Now they drove on a narrow road. It grew so narrow that if they came across a car going the other way, they'd have to pull off nearly into a ditch to let them pass. There was nothing around for miles. No signs of life. No house lights. No streetlights. Nothing.

As the drive closed in on an hour, they drove through the Des Plaines River corridor. The narrow road stretched into darkness. Trees crowded both sides, thick and menacing. Large, gnarly burr oak and hickory timbers twisted and stretched all around them.

Both Enzo and Carlo stayed quiet most of the drive. Occasionally, Carlo instructed where to turn. Enzo had barely said more than two words since they got in the car.

The circumstances started to make Donnie D worry. Finally, he broke protocol and asked, "Where we goin', boss?"

"Just drive," Enzo replied, his voice cold as ice. "You'll know when we get there."

Donnie D caught Enzo's eyes in the rearview. They were snake eyes, cold and calculating.

Donnie D's hands tightened on the wheel. His revolver was in a holster under his jacket. He could probably reach it. He could shoot Carlo first. Knowing Brasi, the man was probably unarmed at the moment. He never carried. He didn't have to. His guys were always armed, and always around him.

The Cadillac bounced over ruts. Branches scraped the paint. The headlights cut through darkness and hit a clearing. Something was very wrong. Brasi would never take one of his good cars out on a drive like this. Unless, it was a ruse to make Donnie D think nothing was wrong.

Where was Alessandra? he wondered.

Just up ahead, he saw lights. The first lights in a long while. It was headlights.

Another car waited. It was Brasi's '57 Chevy Bel Air. The engine idled, and a man stood beside it smoking a Lucky Strike cigarette. The man's face was shrouded in darkness, until he puffed on the cigarette. The small burst of orange flame at the end lit up his features enough to reveal who it was.

Mad Dom smoked and watched as they pulled up. The moment he saw them; he puffed the last of the cigarette and tossed it. He reached behind him on the hood of the Bel Air and scooped up a pump-action shotgun, a Winchester Model 12. It was one of the last from off the line, before Winchester stopped producing it in '64.

Donnie D swallowed hard. His heart raced suddenly, feeling like it was going to burst out of his chest. He moved one hand from the wheel, started to slide it toward his revolver. But he froze. He couldn't go for it. It was a stupid move to go for it he figured, because he was outgunned and not totally certain what was going on.

Carlo barked, "Park here."

Donnie D parked, leaving the headlights on and the car running. The purr of the motor was muted in his ears. All he heard was silence of the surrounding men. It hit like a fist. He heard his own heartbeat.

Carlo got out. Enzo followed, straightening his suit from the long car ride. He adjusted his tie, tightening it. Donnie D stayed put, behind the wheel. He was unsure of what to do. Frozen in place.

Carlo threaded around the hood to door. Donnie D missed it, but Carlo had drawn his firearm on the walk around the front of the car. He held it down by his side and opened Donnie D's door.

"Get out, Donnie-boy," Enzo ordered. His voice sounded friendly, but wrong, like betrayal. "We got somethin' to show you."

Donnie D climbed out on shaking legs. The night air bit cold. He felt it in his bones. He smelled earth and dirt. Donnie D pulled his coat in closer to himself, like he was trying to get warm. But really he was reaching for his revolver. Carlo stopped him. He reached out fast and grabbed Donnie D's gun from out of its holster. He did it one-handed. The other hand pointed a gun at Donnie D.

Donnie D's eyes widened. He froze. "Carlo, what's this?"

They said nothing. No answer. Carlo removed Donnie D's gun and pocketed it. He kept his gun aimed from the hip at Donnie D and backed away.

They forced him to walk forward, into the beams of the '57 Chevy Bel Air. That's when he saw it. Two graves had already been dug. The shovel stuck in the ground behind them, like a temporary unmarked headstone. They were deep, black, and waiting.

Donnie D's stomach dropped. His eyes darted from side to side. *Where was she?* he wondered. She wasn't in the grave.

"Boss, what's going on?" he asked, playing dumb. But he already knew.

"You tell me." Enzo walked toward him with his hands in his pockets. Carlo and Mad Dom flanked Donnie D. Mad Dom pumped his Model 12. Both he and Carlo pointed their guns at Donnie D's chest.

"I don't know what you're talkin' about." Donnie D raised his hands in surrender.

"No?" Enzo stopped and studied him. "See, I been hearin' things, Donnie. Stories about my wife and another man. Someone close. Someone I trusted. I doubted it. Seriously doubted it. Then I started thinking. I started seeing for myself. And you know what I figured for myself?"

"It ain't true. I swear—" Donnie D pleaded.

"Shut up." The words were sharp as a razor. "You think I'm stupid? You think I don't see how she looks at you? How she smiles when you drive her around? How excited she is in the morning to get out of the house? At first I couldn't believe it. I mean it's you. Ugly Donnie D. I started to think that she was meeting a man somewhere. Right under your nose. Like maybe you were bringing her to meet this man. Maybe you were innocent in all of this. Maybe he tricked you somehow into delivering her to him. Like a doctor's visit or maybe a priest. But no. It was actually you. You've been having sex with my wife! The whore!"

"Boss, please—" Donnie D appealed, terrified.

"I said shut up." Enzo snapped his fingers to Mad Dom. "Show him."

Mad Dom walked to the rear of the Bel Air. For the first time, Donnie D realized there were noises coming from the trunk, like someone was in it, kicking and shuffling around, trying to escape.

Mad Dom fumbled about with the keys and popped the trunk. The dome light came on. He stood over it.

"Go ahead! Look!" Brasi barked at Donnie D.

Donnie D shuffled to the back of the Bel Air and saw her.

Alessandra lay curled on her side with her hands bound behind her back and duct tape across her mouth. Her dress was torn and bloody. Her once angelic face was bashed, bruised, and bloody. One eye was swollen shut and blood crusted her lip. When she saw Donnie D, she tried to sit up but couldn't.

Donnie D's world tilted. Everything went cold, then hot, then cold again. He balled up his fists and took a step toward her.

Carlo shoved the gun into his ribs. "That's far enough, cowboy!"

"She never gave you up," Enzo said. His tone was conversational, like he was discussing the weather. "We asked nice. Then not so nice. But she wouldn't say your name. Loyal to the end." He walked to the trunk and looked down at his wife with disgust on his face. "Almost made me respect her. Only then I thought, would she give me up? Of course she would." Enzo stared at his wife.

She looked at Donnie D. Her one open eye glinted at the sight of him.

"There! You see! The way she looks at you! That's how I figured it was you!" Enzo pointed at each of them accusatively.

"Let her go." Donnie D found some courage. His voice was steady now. The fear had burned away and left something else. "She's not to blame here. I took advantage of her. I tricked her. She didn't know what she was doing. I swear. It was all me."

Enzo stared at Donnie D. He looked dead serious at first. Then he started laughing. "You started it? You think I'm a stunod? No. I don't think so. I ain't like you! She's a whore when I met her. And she's still one. I don't think you get it. Those graves ain't just for you, Donnie-boy. They're for both of you. You betrayed me. She betrayed me. You wanted to be together. Now you get to be together forever."

Enzo reached into the trunk and grabbed Alessandra by the hair. He dragged her out, and she thumped on the ground hard. She let out a muffled cry through the tape. Enzo kicked her ribs.

Donnie D lunged.

Carlo shoved the gun into his spine. "Easy. You move again; I put one in your back. And you can watch yourself bleed out slowly from the bullet."

Enzo knelt beside Alessandra. He grabbed her face and forced her to look at Donnie D with her one good eye. "You love him? This… This ugly cafone! Answer me! You threw away everything for him?"

She couldn't answer, but her eye said it all. Even beaten and terrified, she looked at Donnie D like he was worth dying for.

Enzo stood, wiped a tear from his eyes with a fancy handkerchief. He reached out to Carlo, palm open. Carlo handed over his pistol. Brasi pointed it at Alessandra's head. He looked at Donnie D and said, "Say goodbye to your whore, Donnie-boy."

Time slowed.

Donnie D pictured everything in his mind. Carlo stood to his back. But his pistol was in Brasi's hand now. He still had Donnie D's gun, but he never took it out. Mad Dom moved away from Brasi and stood on the other side of Donnie D. He had the shotgun.

Brasi's finger slid into the trigger housing and squeezed against the trigger. Alessandra lay on the ground, looking at Donnie D with her one pretty eye. Her face looked painful, but the look in her eye said to him she loved him.

Donnie D dug down deep. He had one move. Maybe. It was insane, but what difference did it make now to try?

Donnie D dropped to his knees like he was begging. Mad Dom's shotgun followed him down and tracked his head.

Before his knees hit the dirt, Donnie D spun around. He grabbed Mad Dom's shotgun with both hands and pulled hard.

The shotgun went off with a deafening crack. The slug went wide, grazing Brasi in the arm. He spun and dropped Carlo's pistol.

Donnie D drove the shotgun's butt into Mad Dom's stomach and wrenched the weapon away from him. Carlo went for Donnie D's revolver, but couldn't clear it in time.

Donnie D pumped the shotgun and shot Carlo in the stomach. He dropped Donnie D's revolver and crashed back against the Bel Air's door.

Donnie D pumped again and fired into Carlo again. The slug smashed through Carlo's neck and collarbone. The windows to the Bel Air shattered behind him. Blood gushed from his neck. Carlo fell back and slid down the side of the Bel Air. He was dead.

Mad Dom tried to draw a gun from inside his coat. Donnie D pivoted, pumped the shotgun, and shot him in the face. The slug blew the back of his brains out. Red mist sprayed into the dirt behind Mad Dom's head.

Suddenly, Enzo's killer of killers was dead.

Enzo scrambled to recover his dropped pistol. If he could get it, he could kill Donnie D before the man could pump again. Only the fallen pistol wasn't there.

But it wasn't the only thing not there. Alessandra had moved away from the trunk during the commotion. She'd gotten her bound hands in front somehow and grabbed the fallen pistol and pointed it at Enzo.

She locked eyes with Donnie D, who pointed the shotgun at Brasi at the same time. He pumped once. The two of them fired together. Alessandra emptied the pistol into Enzo Brasi's chest and face. Donnie D pumped and fired, pumped and fired.

The gunshots echoed through the darkness, bouncing off the surrounding trees. Night birds flapped their wings, trying to fly away and escape the potential danger.

Enzo's body slumped beside the graves that Mad Dom had dug for them.

Donnie D stood breathing hard. Alessandra dropped the empty pistol and looked at him. She mumbled through the duct tape. He dropped the shotgun and ran to her. He untied her. She ripped the duct tape off her mouth and lunged at him. She wrapped her arms around him, hugging him tighter than ever before. He did the same.

They rocked there together, sobbing. They were alive. Barely, but they'd made it.

"You came for me," she whispered, panting.

"Always," he said.

They didn't speak after that. They rested there for a long, long time, trying to catch their breath.

Finally, they moved.

They jumped into gear and dragged the bodies to the graves. It took everything to roll them in. They tossed the guns in with them. Donnie D shoveled in the dirt and patted it down in the end.

It was hours past midnight when they finished.

They took both cars and drove them south until the Cadillac ran out of gas. They ditched it on Route 30 near mile marker 278, just past Sterling.

Donnie D drove the Bel Air west with Alessandra beside him, her head on his shoulder. They drove through Illinois, then crossed into Iowa, putting miles between them and the bodies.

At a motel near the border, Donnie D made a call from a payphone. The number belonged to a man he'd let live six months earlier. A man who owed him everything.

Mickey Fog Eyes answered on the third ring.

"It's Donnie D."

Silence. Then, Mickey asked, "What happened?"

"Enzo's dead. We need help. We need to disappear."

More silence. Mickey was breathing on the other end, weighing risks. Finally he said, "I know someone. FBI agent named Donovan. He's dirty, but he's got morals too. He'll help you."

Donnie D called Donovan next and made a deal.

Three days later, they were on a bus to Nebraska with new names and new identification. John and Jane Elton. A young couple starting fresh where nobody would think to look.

They would end up in the same town as Mickey Fog Eyes, because it was nice to have a friendly face from the past. Someone who knew what they'd gone through. Someone who understood.

The Eltons bought land outside Tent Hills and built a life. They had a son, then a grandson. They grew old together and tried to forget the violence that had brought them there.

But memories don't stay buried forever.

Not even the ones you bury in graves in the woods at midnight.

John Elton jerked awake in his bed, gasping, with his heart hammering. Sweat soaked his collar. The house was quiet, too quiet. The power was out. Strange. He figured his family was still there, safe and warm, in the living room.

But in his mind, he still heard the gunshots.

Still saw Enzo's face as the bullets tore through him.

Still smelled the earth from those graves.

The clock on the mantel read the time was shortly after midnight.

Outside, the wind howled. Snow hammered the windows.

And a team of armed men moved through the darkness toward the house.

CHAPTER 33

The power blacked out at twelve minutes past midnight.

Widow stood at the living room window, staring out at the darkness beyond the glass. Snow fell in thick sheets and the wind howled across the fields. One moment the porch lights illuminated the falling flakes, and the next moment there was nothing but black.

The house went dark around him. The TV died, the refrigerator's hum cut out, and the heating system clicked off with a final shudder, like a machine's death rattle.

Behind him, Elsa said, "There goes the power."

Widow turned from the window. The Eltons didn't seem alarmed, not even a little. It was all a normal part of life for them. Ester groaned about the TV show she'd been watching and Adam muttered something about his phone dying too soon. But that was it. No other complaints.

"Happens all the time out here. Every winter. And it'll happen several more times before the season's done with us," Matty said. He was already moving, pulling open a cabinet near the fireplace. He retrieved two battery-powered lanterns and clicked them on, filling the room with soft white light. "Winter storms knock out the lines. Sometimes it's hours before they fix it. That's why we have these."

Elsa took one lantern and set it on the coffee table. "And candles. And a fireplace." She smiled at Widow. "We're used to it."

Widow nodded but stayed quiet.

Something gnawed at him. That old primal warning system buried deep in his brainstem—the lizard brain, the part of human evolution that kept cavemen alive when predators stalked the tall grass around their camps. It fired on all synapses now, sending signals he couldn't ignore. His primal brain neurons signaled to him, like that little warning voice in a normal person's head.

Something felt wrong.

He couldn't explain it and couldn't point to any one thing. It was just his nature, his first instinct. The power outage made sense. The snowy weather made sense. It was winter. And Nebraska winters were as rough as they come. Everything the Eltons said made sense. It was all explainable. But his instincts didn't care about the explainable. They cared about survival.

Widow walked to the front door, grabbed his boots from the mudroom, and pulled them on. Then he put on the ugly puffer coat and zipped it up.

Matty watched him. "Where you going?"

"Just want to check it out for myself."

"I'll join you for a second." Matty glanced at Elsa, seeking her input. She shrugged, like to say, *What's the harm?*

Matty grabbed his own coat and followed Widow onto the porch.

The cold hit them as if they'd run into a biting ice wall. Widow's breath fogged in front of his face and snow accumulated on the porch railing. The darkness beyond was absolute —no moon tonight, no stars, just black sky and white snow.

The porch lights were dead, which made sense since no power meant no lights.

Matty pulled his coat tighter, making an audible "Brr" sound. Then he asked, "What's really on your mind?"

Widow stayed quiet for a long moment. He scanned the horizon, walking to the edge of the porch to look north, then he looked east, then south to the road, then west, taking it all in.

"You seem on edge all of a sudden. There's nothing to worry about, Widow. Really. This sort of thing happens in the winter. It's no big deal."

Widow pointed west, past the barn and stables. In the distance, maybe a mile away, a farmhouse glowed with light. The windows were bright and the porch lights were on. "Why do the neighbors have power?"

Matty looked where Widow was pointing. His brow furrowed. "Huh. Maybe they're on a backup generator. I have one, but it's busted. Been meaning to fix it."

Widow walked the porch back to the east and pointed across the road, where another farm's lights were on and bright. Matty followed his finger. Then Widow pointed to another property to the south, which showed the same thing—bright lights in windows and other signs of electricity flowing to those farms.

"Them too? And backup generators don't emit that much

electricity. Look at those ranches. They've got power. We don't."

Matty stepped to the porch railing and gripped it with both hands, staring out at the neighboring farms. His expression changed as confusion crept in.

"Huh. Well, that's weird." Matty turned and looked at the properties closer to the ranch. The nearest neighbor to the west was dark, and the one beyond that was also dark. "Look. Those are out too."

"Yeah, but aren't the others all on the same grid?"

"There's a transformer. Maybe it's out? That might only affect some of the homes," Matty said.

"Where is it?"

Matty pointed south, down the road, maybe a quarter mile away. "That way. Just past the bend. There's a utility pole with a transformer box. If something hit it—lightning, ice buildup—it could knock out power to just our house and a few others."

Widow nodded and thought about the phone call with Bloom. They'd been talking when the line went dead—not just dead, but cut off mid-sentence. She'd been saying something. It sounded important—urgent, maybe. Was she trying to warn him?

"I was on the phone with Bloom. We got cut off. But it seemed like she might've been trying to warn me."

Matty stared at him. "Warn you? About what?"

"I have no idea. The call dropped before she could finish."

Silence hung between them. The wind gusted and snow swirled across the dark porch.

Finally, Widow asked, "I know you got that shotgun and handgun. But any other guns in the house?"

"No. Just those two. Why?"

"Get them. Bring them down here near the front door just to keep them handy."

Matty's face went pale in the darkness. "You think I'll need them? What for?"

"It's probably nothing. But better safe than sorry," Widow said and paused a long beat. "I'm going to check it out—the transformer—and see what's going on."

"You want to take my gun with you?"

Widow shook his head. "Keep it. Stay here with your family."

Matty hesitated, then said, "Wait here for a minute." He disappeared back into the house and returned a moment later with a flashlight—a heavy-duty model with a black metal casing, the kind that could double as a clubbing weapon if needed.

He handed it to Widow. "Take this at least."

Widow took it and tested the switch. A bright beam cut through the falling snow. He clicked it off. "Thanks."

"Be careful."

Widow stepped off the porch and walked down the driveway toward the road. The snow crunched under his boots and the cold bit at his face. Behind him, the Elton house sat dark and silent. Ahead lay nothing but darkness and snow and whatever waited out there in the night.

CHAPTER 34

Colton watched from the edge of the dormant cornfield. The stalks were iced over from the winter. Through his night vision goggles, he stared as some big guy he'd never seen before, or ever heard of, stepped off the porch.

The world glowed green through the lenses—the farmhouse, the barn, the stables, the two figures on the porch—the large guy and the average-sized one. The snow fell green like static on an old television across his night vision.

Colton and his team held a position at the edge of the cornfield. Five men were all dressed in black tactical pants and insulated jackets, with balaclavas pulled up over their faces. Which wasn't necessary, but it instilled fear in the targets. It also provided concealment of their identities in case a witness escaped. Not tonight, though. Tonight they all would die, horrible deaths too. It was already predetermined and paid for. No question.

Each man carried an HK416 with an ACOG scope, a Glock 19 holstered on their hips, and flashbangs clipped to their belts.

No suppressors. No need for them. Not when everyone would die.

A guy named Stahl crouched in the snow to Colton's left, tracking the big man through his rifle scope. He switched the fire selector to semi auto. "Should I take the shot?"

Colton watched the man descend the porch steps. The guy moved with long strides and a kind of confidence to his walk, like someone who knew how to handle himself. Military, maybe, or law enforcement. Something about the way he carried himself suggested some kind of training. Colton recognized it because he too had it. So did his guys.

"Wait," Colton ordered.

They watched as the big man—whom they assumed was a ranch hand or farmworker—walked down the driveway. He reached the road, turned left, and walked south, away from them and nearly out of view.

The distance grew. Fifty meters, then seventy, then a hundred. The shot became less certain with each step. The falling snow didn't help, and wind gusted sideways. There were too many variables.

"He's getting too far," Stahl said.

Colton ordered, "Follow him. Take him out silently. Then meet us back at the house."

Stahl nodded and rose from his crouch position, staying low. He slipped between the frozen cornstalks toward the road, his black clothing blending with the darkness and his footsteps virtually silent in the snow.

Colton turned to his remaining men—Vance, Kreiger, and Decker. All good operators and all professionals. All killers who didn't question orders. Women. Children. The targets didn't matter to them. As long as they got paid.

"Spread out. Recon the house. I want to know how many people are inside, how many might be armed, entry points, exit points—everything."

The men moved without a word. They'd done this before, many times, in worse conditions and against harder targets. This should be a walk in the park for them.

Colton keyed his radio. "Mr. Brasi. We're in position. One farmhand left the property on foot. Stahl is pursuing and he'll be dealt with before he gets out of range. The rest of us are beginning recon now. I'll call you back when it's safe to drive up."

A voice crackled back, dim with an Italian accent. It was Vito. "Good. Keep me in the loop. My mama's eager to get this over with."

"Understood."

Colton settled in to wait. Somewhere out in the darkness, Stahl was hunting the big guy. It wouldn't take long because Stahl was one of the best—quick, efficient, and deadly.

This would all be over soon. And they could get paid, then go on to the next thing.

CHAPTER 35

At the road, before he left the Elton Ranch, Widow looked both ways and confirmed what he'd seen from the porch. The farms in the distance had power, but the Eltons didn't, and neither did their closest neighbors. A pocket of darkness in an otherwise lit landscape.

Widow walked south along the road. The snow fell heavier now, but visibility was decent. He could see the neighbors' houses from the street—some sat dark like the Eltons' property, others were lit up like a Christmas tree. A couple of them had hung early Christmas lights.

It was cold out, a lot colder than the day had been. It seeped through Widow's puffer coat. The chill numbed his extremities: his fingers, his ears, the tip of his nose. He kept the flashlight off because he could see enough to walk the road. Plus, he had a deep Navy SEAL itch that told him never advertise his position unless absolutely necessary.

Widow walked for six minutes until he saw the source of the problem. It *was* a transformer.

It sat atop a utility pole, right where Matty said it was. Even from hundreds of feet away, Widow saw the sparks—bright flashes of blue-white light, electrical discharge sputtering and crackling like the thing was dying.

But there was no storm damage, no ice buildup on the lines, no evidence of a lightning strike. Nothing at all. Which left Widow with one thought, *Someone sabotaged it.*

Widow slowed his pace, paying close attention to his surroundings. Widow wasn't superhuman. He wasn't born with any kind of powers. But he was trained. And better than most. Right then, he got this feeling that he was being watched.

His primal brain warned him. He wasn't alone out here and he could feel it—that prickling sensation on the back of his neck, the weight of hidden eyes following him. Someone was tracking him.

Widow glanced left toward the cornfields, then back over his shoulder at the empty road behind him.

Nothing was visible, just snow and darkness, but something was out there. He knew it. If he was wrong, better to be alive and wrong, then right and dead.

Widow kept going forward. Just around the bend, he saw headlights. Not on the road. They weren't driving toward him. They came from a vehicle parked off the road, deep in the cornfield. As he got closer, he realized it was multiple vehicles. Their lights were switched on and cutting through the darkness like beacons. Three sets of headlights. Three vehicles. It was a small convoy, parked and waiting.

Waiting for what? he wondered.

Widow stepped off the road and into the cornfield, smashing cornstalks under his bulk. The frozen stalks crunched around him as he pushed through. He needed concealment. He needed to see what he was dealing with before they saw him. The only thing was, he had already been seen. He just didn't know it yet.

Behind him, in the darkness he'd just left, Stahl cursed under his breath.

"Damn it."

He'd had the shot. The big guy's back was turned to him—right there, center mass, an easy kill. Then the guy stepped off the road and vanished into the corn.

Stahl moved to the spot where the big guy had been standing. He could see the footprints in the snow, obvious tracks leading into the cornfield. He followed them.

The cornfield swallowed him up in seconds. Dead stalks rose seven feet high on either side and ice clung to everything. His night vision goggles painted the world in shades of green. The footprints were harder to see in here because the snow had drifted and the ground was uneven.

Stahl pushed forward. Fifty meters, then a hundred. The tracks disappeared in a section where the wind had blown the snow clean.

Then he froze because of something up ahead of him. Directly in his line of sight, a light bounced through the stalks ahead. The big man's flashlight. He'd switched it on finally. The beam swept left, then right, then left again, like the big guy was walking slowly, checking his path carefully.

Too bad being careful wasn't going to save him, Stahl thought and smiled. *What an amateur.*

Stahl raised the HK416 and sighted through the scope. The flashlight beam danced across the stalks, like a bright green orb. It was maybe forty meters ahead. He saw it waving through the green glow of his night vision goggles. The wind howled through the stalks. The flashlight beam swept across his face once, but he didn't flinch.

Stahl aimed right below the arc of the swing, timing his shot from the moment he squeezed the trigger to where the bullet would hit the big guy holding the flashlight. The bullet would go right under the light at the perfect moment the big guy was standing at that spot. It should hit his center mass. Actually, without an act of God, it should hit the big guy in the heart, killing him instantly.

Stahl fired a single shot, suppressed only by distance. The crack echoed across the field. The shot was dead on target. But nothing happened. The flashlight kept moving.

Stahl frowned and fired again, a quick squeeze of the trigger, a two-round burst this time, center mass right behind the light source.

Nothing happened. No spray of blood, no thump of a body hitting frozen ground, no screams of agony from being hit.

Nothing.

Frustrated, Stahl switched the fire selector to full auto. He fired again. Several more rounds rocketed out of the gun's barrel. Two of them hit the flashlight beam directly. It shattered, and the beam died away.

Stahl released the trigger and advanced, fast but cautious. He covered twenty meters in seconds, his rifle sweeping left and right, ready for a wounded target trying to flee. But he assumed the guy was dead. He had to be.

Stahl stopped cold at the kill spot. His boot crunched on shattered glass from the flashlight. And he found the flashlight. It hung from a bootlace, tied to a cornstalk and swaying in the wind. No body, no blood, no dead big guy.

It was a decoy.

The realization hit him a half second before Widow did.

The stalks exploded on his left and a massive shape burst through. Widow punched him with a colossal left hook to the jaw. It rocked Stahl like a freight train. The impact drove Stahl sideways nearly off his feet. He lost balance. His rifle swung wildly through the air. He tried to bring it around, tried to get the big guy on the business end of the gun. But Widow was too fast. He was already inside Stahl's circle, already behind enemy lines.

Widow grabbed the rifle barrel with his left hand. His right hand—the one in the second cast—drove forward, and the hard plaster connected with Stahl's throat. It crunched the cartilage in his throat, along with fracturing the cast in several spiderweb cracks.

Stahl gagged and his grip loosened on the rifle. Widow ripped it away, reared back, and swung the stock into the side of Stahl's head. A deafening crack reverberated through Stahl's skull as it cracked from the impact. The man dropped to one knee. Blood trickled from his ear.

Widow didn't wait. He didn't hesitate. He reversed the rifle, flipping it in the air one-handed, catching it with the same hand. Then he jammed the barrel against Stahl's forehead. The man's night vision goggles had been knocked askew and one eye stared up at Widow, wide and terrified.

"Who're you with?" Widow asked. He was only going to ask once. And the guy knew it. Widow saw it in his one exposed eye.

If the guy answered, Widow would knock him out, but let him live. But the guy did something stupid.

Stahl's hand moved toward a Glock 19 in a hip holster.

So, Widow answered the only proper way. He pulled the trigger. The weapon was still switched to full auto, so more than one bullet came out before Widow released the trigger.

The shots rang out loud, echoing across the cornfield like thunder. Night birds, stragglers that hadn't flown south yet, scattered across the dormant cornfield. The muzzle flash lit up the night.

Blood spattered across Widow's ugly puffer coat and his face. Stahl's body crumpled backward. His face would be unrecognizable to anyone who used to know the guy. His corpse smashed down a couple of cornstalks and settled in a heap in the snow.

Widow stood over him, breathing hard. Steam rose from his mouth and his hand throbbed beneath the cast from the impact to the dead guy's throat. The guy was dead. No question. Widow couldn't ask any more questions. But he still needed information. He'd have to get answers another way.

Widow knelt beside the body. Rifle stock planted in the snow beside him, he searched the dead guy. No wallet. No identification, which Widow expected. In his experience, guys dressed in night time wet work gear rarely carried their wallets on them.

Widow found an earpiece in the guy's left ear. Not good. An earpiece told Widow a lot. It said that this guy wasn't alone. He was part of a team. Even worse, they were some kind of professional crew, like a hit squad. Judging by his gear and weapons, they were some kind of crew with former military training and experience. And they were well funded. Night vision goggles of this quality and flashbangs and a HK416 rifle weren't cheap items.

The earpiece consisted of the receiver and a thin wire running down to a radio clipped to a belt. Widow pulled the earpiece free and inserted it into his own ear.

He listened and continued to search the guy. He took the Glock 19 and pocketed it. He found a flashbang clipped to the belt on the opposite side of the radio. He took it too, stuffing it into another pocket.

Suddenly, static crackled over the earpiece. Widow listened. A deep voice came through, the leader of the group. It had to be.

"Stahl. We heard a lot of gunfire. Is it done?"

Widow stared down at the dead man. Stahl was his name. One bullet Widow fired had entered just above Stahl's right eye. It exited out the back of his head, along with bone and brain matter. Both stained the snow behind his head in a mess of crimson blood.

"Stahl? Respond!"

Widow didn't want to alert them he was still alive. So he keyed the radio, dropped his voice low, and added gravel to it. He rubbed his thumb over the receiver to add static. "Yes. Here. The target's down."

A pause. Then: "Damn it, Stahl! You shot your gun too much. The Eltons probably heard it. We did! You probably blew our element of surprise. They're probably aware something's happening now. Get back here. We're going in now. I'll tell the Brasis to drive up to the ranch now."

The radio went silent.

Widow grunted an affirmative sound and nothing more. He clicked off the radio.

The Brasis, he thought. The name that John had mentioned in his state of midnight dementia. Enzo Brasi was the name of the guy he mentioned during both episodes. The first night Widow saw him, Enzo Brasi was the name of the guy John was shooting at.

Who are they? Widow wondered. The answer didn't matter. All that mattered to him was they were here, and they were here to kill the Eltons. He couldn't let that happen.

Widow moved fast. He took Stahl's radio and earpiece so he could listen in.

He checked the HK416. Twenty rounds remained in the magazine. Good enough.

Through the cornfield, he heard an engine start, then heavy tires crunching on snow. A vehicle was moving fast, heading toward the road, toward the Elton farm.

He was out of time.

Widow started to move back through the corn, back toward the house. But then he heard something else—music, thumping bass, coming from deeper in the field, from the direction of engine and tires he'd just heard. There was another vehicle still parked there.

He hesitated.

One vehicle had already left, and he couldn't catch it on foot. But if there was still another out there? That meant there were more men waiting behind. A backup team. He could take them out and commandeer their vehicle to get back to the Eltons' faster. It was a gamble, but it made sense in a two birds, one stone kind of way.

A backup team wouldn't be the A-team. They'd be the guys on the bench. They'd probably be smaller in numbers. He could take them out fast, steal their wheels, and drive back.

Widow pushed through the stalks toward the headlights and the music.

Less than a minute later, he emerged at the edge of a small clearing. Two vehicles sat parked on a dirt access road. Just under the transformer. It sparked overhead. Widow knew why it went out. They'd shot it. Sparks spit out of a couple of bullet holes.

He turned his attention back to the two vehicles. One was a black Escalade, empty with its engine off. The other vehicle made Widow's jaw clench. He knew it.

It was Trent's pickup truck. The same rust-bucket crew cab from outside The Outer Limits and the bookstore. Music thumped from inside, some kind of death metal. The bass vibrated the truck's side panels.

A figure leaned against the front bumper—a big guy with a buzzed head and a leather jacket—Crick. The guy who'd tried to sexually assault Ester at her trailer. Widow had promised not to hurt him. But that was back at the trailer. *What was the shelf life on a promise like that?* he wondered.

Crick smoked a cigarette. It dangled from his mouth. He held a phone in his hand. He was texting someone, oblivious to his surroundings. His phone worked. But not the others. Widow realized it was some kind of sat-phone. Maybe given to him by the Brasis to keep in touch, while everyone else in town was disconnected from their phones.

Next to Crick there was another HK416. It leaned against the truck's grille, within arm's reach.

Widow let his HK416 hang by the sling over his shoulder. He drew the Glock from his pocket and circled wide, using the Escalade for cover. He approached from Crick's blind side, the music masking his footsteps and the darkness hiding his approach.

He came up behind Crick, stepped out into the headlights, and shoved the Glock into Crick's face. "Stand up!"

Crick froze. The cigarette fell from his lips and his phone clattered to the ground. He raised his hands slowly and pushed off the grille, standing on his feet. His eyes went wide at the sight of Widow. Blood spattered across Widow's face, making him more terrifying than usual. Fear flashed across Crick's face, then confusion, then strangely, amusement. The whole things seemed like a show, like improv. And it was. Widow knew instantly he'd made a mistake. Especially when Crick started chuckling.

"You know, I didn't think you'd fall for it," Crick said.

Widow frowned. "Fall for what?"

Then he felt it—cold metal pressed against the back of his ear. The same thumping bass that masked his approach had also stopped him from hearing someone sneaking up behind him. Stupid mistake.

"Drop the weapon." A familiar voice said. It sounded young and cocky, full of false bravado.

Widow didn't move. He calculated angles, distances, and options. The gun at his head was too close and the man holding it was too confident. Confidence made people careless, but it also made them reckless, which was dangerous.

"I said drop the weapons!"

Widow opened his hands and let the Glock fall, then let the HK416 follow. They thudded on the cold, hard ground at his feet.

Crick didn't wait. He scrambled forward, scooped up the dropped rifle, and aimed it at Widow's chest. A grin spread across his face. "Not so tough now, are you?"

"Turn around," the cocky voice said.

Widow raised his hands and turned around.

Trent Marrow stood there smiling. He held another Glock 19 —procured out of the Spec Ops guy's cache—and aimed at Widow's face. His eyes gleamed with satisfaction.

"You put my boys in the hospital." Trent stepped closer. The Glock wavered in his hand, like he'd never actually shot anyone before. But he was planning to change that. "I've been waiting for this."

Behind Widow, Crick laughed. "What should we do to him first?"

Trent's smile widened. "I got some ideas."

Widow stared at him, at the trembling Glock, at the situation he'd walked into. His cast throbbed and his body ached. He was outgunned, outnumbered, and out of time.

The Eltons were back at the house, unaware and unarmed, sitting in the dark with lanterns and board games while killers closed in.

CHAPTER 36

Trent smiled like a man who'd just won the lottery.

He backed away about seven feet from Widow, out of arm's reach. Which was a smart move on his part. He'd learned from their encounter at the bookstore. The Glock 19 in his hand was shaky, but it was still aimed at Widow's chest.

"How's it feel now?" Trent asked. His voice dripped with satisfaction. "You're not walking away this time. You know that, right? I want to see it in your face."

Widow stayed quiet. He lowered his hands to his sides, palms open, unthreatening. Quiet snow fell around them and the music from Trent's truck thumped in the background. Somewhere overhead, the damaged transformer sparked and crackled.

Crick stepped closer, shoving the HK416 toward Widow's face. The barrel hovered inches from his eyeball. Crick's finger was on the trigger, and his eyes were wild with excitement.

"Not so tough now, huh?" Crick said. He jabbed the rifle

forward, almost poking out Widow's eye. "Big man. Big tough guy. Look at you now."

Widow didn't flinch. He stared past the barrel at Crick's face, at the anticipation there, the eagerness. Crick wanted to pull the trigger. He was working himself up to it.

"Don't get close to him!" Trent barked.

Crick ignored the warning and stayed where he was, bouncing from foot to foot, excited. "Let's just shoot him! Why we talking to him?" Crick asked. "Come on, Trent. Let me do it."

"Not yet." Trent circled to Widow's left, keeping his distance. "I want him to know what's happening. I want him to feel it."

Widow tracked both men with his peripheral vision.

"You know what's funny?" Trent asked. "Those Spec Ops guys paid us to be lookouts. Backup. In case the cops come this way. Said they'd handle everything. They may be after the Eltons for some stupid vendetta, but look who caught the real big fish."

Widow stayed quiet.

Trent grinned wider. "When this is over, I'm gonna tell everyone how I took down the guy who put my boys in the hospital. How I—"

Widow didn't have time for this. He was stuck here with these two idiots while the real threat rolled toward the farm.

He needed to end this fast. So he interrupted Trent. Widow said, "Before you do anything stupid, there's something you should know."

Trent smirked. "Yeah? What's that?"

"Your sister, Ester, is inside that house. Where all these trigger-happy maniacs are headed."

Trent's smirk vanished from his face—fast.

The words cut through Trent's monologue like a Mark 3—the Navy's combat knife of choice. His grin faltered, just for a second.

"What the hell are you talking about?"

"Your sister. She's inside the house right now, with the Eltons. And your new friends, those Spec Ops guys are going there to kill everyone. Ester will die in the crossfire. Is that what you want?" Widow asked.

Trent's face went through several expressions—confusion, disbelief, concern—then forced dismissal. "Bullshit. Ester's home… Or she's at work or somewhere. She knows better than to go to Adam's house."

"She's not. In fact, she's probably going to stay with the Eltons for good."

"Bullshit!"

"It's not. It's true. I know. I took her to your father's trailer today. You live out there in that place they call The Scarlands in a trailer park. It's the last one in the park. Back corner," Widow said.

"You're lying."

"I'm not."

Trent glanced at Crick. Crick shrugged, but something flickered in his eyes. Something nervous.

Widow saw it and pressed harder. He'd worked in a secret unit for the NCIS, once upon a time. He was undercover twenty-four-seven, three-sixty-five. In all that time, Widow had learned how to exploit weakness. How to lie and make people believe it. But this wasn't a case where he needed to lie. The truth did all the heavy lifting for him. "Do you know why she left? Why she needed me to escort her?"

Trent said nothing. Crick shuffled his feet, nervously.

"Your sister left because of him." Widow nodded toward Crick. "Because of what he did to her."

Trent glanced at Crick. He wouldn't have bought it except that Crick wasn't even trying to hide it. Crick's face twisted into visible knots, like he'd just been hit with food poisoning. He shouted, "Shut up!"

"What's he talking about?" Trent asked.

"Nothing. He's trying to mess with your head, man. Don't listen to him," Crick pleaded with Trent, but both Widow and Trent noticed, Crick didn't deny it.

Widow kept his eyes on Trent. "Ask him what he did to her. Ask him why your sister can't sleep in her own room anymore. Ask him why she's never going back there."

"I said shut up!" Crick shoved the rifle's barrel toward Widow's face again.

Trent's gun no longer wavered. It was level now, and his attention shifted. He looked at Crick—really stared at him. "What's he talking about, Crick?"

"Nothing, bro. He's making stuff up. Trying to get in your head."

"Then why're you acting so weird? So nervous? Why you sweating like that?" Trent asked. Crick sweated. His forehead was slick with it, like he was being interrogated by cops who had him dead to rights.

Crick wiped his forehead with his sleeve and this time his rifle wavered. "It's cold out here, man. I'm not sweating."

Widow said, "I'll tell you what he did."

"You shut up!" Crick barked and pointed the HK416 at Widow.

Trent said, "Let him talk!"

Widow spoke anyway. He'd had rifles pointed at him before. "This guy stood in her doorway and watched your sister sleep the other night. He pleasured himself while he watched her. He thought she was asleep, but she wasn't. She was too terrified to move. Then he leaned over her bed and whispered to her. Told her he hoped they'd get to spend some time together."

Nobody spoke. The snow fell, the music thumped, and the transformer sparked. Widow added, "And this morning, he tried to keep that promise. He made a pass at her. She pushed him away, so he punched her. Good too. She's got a shiner from it."

Trent stared at Crick. He started to shake again. The Glock shook in his hand. But this time it wasn't from nerves. It was from rage. He fumed.

"She's a minor too. A child still," Widow said. "She's your sister, Trent."

"Is that true?" Trent asked Crick.

"Come on, man—"

"Is it true?"

Crick's eyes darted between Trent and Widow. He licked his lips. "Look, even if something happened—which it didn't— why would you believe this guy over me? He's the enemy here. He put your boys in the hospital. He—" Crick raised the HK416, finger tightening on the trigger. "Let's just shoot him!"

"Kill me and you've got no chance of saving Ester," Widow said.

Trent did something he never thought he'd do in a million years. He swung the Glock's aim from Widow to Crick. "Put the rifle down."

"What? No way, man. Are you nuts?"

"I said put it down! Boyd, I'll shoot you!"

Crick side-eyed Trent, saw he was telling the truth. Crick lowered the rifle slightly, but not all the way. His eyes widened, and panic set in. "Trent, she's just a whore, man. They all are. You know that."

Trent's jaw dropped opened. He couldn't believe what he was hearing.

Crick's mouth opened, like he was going to deny it. Then it closed. He was trapped, and he knew it. The truth was written all over his face. He said, "Come on, man. You've known me since you were a teenager. I'm ole Uncle Crick! I'm old pals with your dad. Your sister's teased me all these years. You must've seen it? You must've noticed? She's a woman now. That's all. It's the most natural thing in the world. Besides, what difference does it make? She's just another girl. Bros before hoes, am I right?"

A gunshot rang out—louder than the sparking transformer, louder than the music.

Crick's head snapped back and a dark bullet hole appeared above his left eye. He stood frozen for a split second with a look of pure surprise on his face, then his legs buckled and he collapsed into the snowy dirt. The HK416 clattered beside him.

Trent stood with his arm extended, the Glock still aimed at where Crick's head used to be. His hand shook and his face went pale. He'd killed no one before. Plus, thirty seconds ago, this man had been a family friend, a comrade in his beliefs in white supremacy. That was all gone now. Pulling that trigger did more than rearrange a 9mm-sized part of Crick's brain matter. It also rearranged Trent's thinking. It hit him as hard as that bullet impact. *Who have I been?* he thought. *What have I become?*

Widow looked down at Crick's body. Blood pooled beneath his shattered skull, melting the surrounding snow. Steam rose from the wound. His eyes were wide open. He stared up at the sky, lifeless.

"Huh," Widow said. "Didn't see that coming."

Trent lowered the gun. His breathing was ragged and shallow, and he looked like he might vomit.

"He was my friend," Trent said. His voice was hollow. "Since I was in middle school."

"He wasn't your friend. None of those losers you hang out with are. They're lowlives."

Trent said nothing. He stared at Crick's body for a long moment, then something shifted in his expression. The shock faded and was replaced by something different from who he'd always been.

Trent shoved the Glock into his waistband, turned toward the Escalade, and glanced at Widow. "Let's go. We gotta save her."

Widow joined at the back of the Escalade. In the SUV's cargo space, he saw a cache of the Spec Ops guys' empty weapons cases. A couple of flashbangs, ammunition boxes, and tactical gear filled the cargo area. A couple of full gas cans sat beside the weapons.

Widow noted them. Gas cans weren't standard issue for an assault team. Gas cans meant they planned to burn something down—probably the farmhouse, maybe the Eltons.

The Spec Ops guys weren't hired to kidnap them. They'd come for an execution.

Widow took stock. He grabbed two flashbang grenades and clipped them to his belt, then found a full magazine for the HK416 and pocketed it. He walked to Crick's body and pried the rifle from his dead fingers, ejected the partially spent magazine, slapped in the fresh one, and chambered a round. He kept the spent magazine as a spare.

Trent paced behind him, agitated and anxious. "Come on, come on. What're we waiting for, man? Let's go get my sister!"

Widow checked the rifle's optics and adjusted the sights. He was just getting everything right. The last thing he wanted was equipment failure in the middle of combat. Everything had to go right. He was already up against impossible odds— a highly skilled team of four left, plus the Brasis.

"Can't just go rushing the house guns blazing," he said. "Innocent people die that way. I need a strategy."

"We."

Widow looked up. "What?"

"You said I, as in you can't go rushing the house. But it's us. I'm going with you."

"You?"

"Yeah, man! Come on!" Trent stepped closer, his eyes wild. "I gotta save Ester! She's all I got left that matters. I'm not gonna sit here while those guys murder her!"

Widow studied him. The kid was scared, angry, and motivated—all useful qualities in a fight. But he was also reckless, untrained, and emotional—all dangerous qualities in a firefight, and, especially in a hostage situation.

"What about the others?" Widow asked.

"What?"

"There are six civilians in that house. You going to look out for them, too?"

Trent hesitated before answering. That hesitation was all the answer Widow needed.

"I only care about my sister."

Widow nodded slowly. "That's what I figured."

Trent stared at him, dumbfounded. He had zero clue what Widow was inferring.

"Sorry about this."

"Sorry for—"

Widow exploded from his feet, creating a surge of power. He drove his left fist with a vicious uppercut into Trent's jaw. The punch was fast and brutal, all technique and torque. That and the fact that Widow had monstrous fists, like big stones. The uppercut carried enough force that it lifted Trent off his feet.

His Glock tumbled from his waistband. And Trent flew backward with his arms pinwheeling. He slammed into the side of the Escalade with a thud, then crumpled to the gravel. He was out cold before he landed. Thank you and goodnight!

Widow stood over him and shook out his left hand. The cast

made punching with his right awkwardly, but his left worked fine.

"Nothing personal," Widow said to the unconscious skinhead. "But I can't have you shooting the wrong people."

Widow scooped up Trent's fallen Glock and tucked it into his waistband, abandoning the one he'd come into the clearing with. Then he hung the HK416 over his shoulder again by its sling. He knelt and grabbed Trent under his arms and dragged him to his pickup truck. He dropped him in the dirt at the driver's side door and leaned in and killed the music. Then he went to the tailgate, letting it down.

Widow returned to Trent and dragged him to the back of the old pickup. He lifted Trent and heaved him into the truck bed. Widow rolled Trent onto his side in the recovery position with his airway clear and stepped back.

The kid would wake up in twenty minutes with a headache and a bruised ego. But he'd live. And his sister would be alive. If she wasn't, then Widow would be dead from trying.

Overhead, the transformer sparked again.

Widow ignored it and turned and headed into the cornfield. He thought about taking a vehicle, but the element of surprise worked better on foot. They'd hear the engine coming from a mile away. The frozen stalks closed around him and the snow fell heavier now, covering his tracks almost as fast as he made them. The farmhouse was maybe a quarter mile back the way he came—five minutes if he moved fast, less if he ran. But running burned energy. He didn't want to be overheated when he got there.

So, Widow moved through the corn at a steady pace with his HK416 up and his eyes forward, every sense tuned to the darkness ahead.

CHAPTER 37

W idow made it to the edge of an icy cornfield, where he could see the farmhouse. He studied it through the falling snow. The place was dark, just as he'd left it, but now there was movement inside. Shadows passed behind the windows and flashlight beams swept across the rooms. The Spec Ops team had already breached. Both the front and back doors were smashed to pieces.

Widow had heard gunshots on his way back—several of them, muffled by distance and snow. But he figured they were handgun caliber. From the sound of it, it was probably from Matty's gun. Either way, it meant the situation inside had already gone bad. He hoped he wasn't too late.

Widow counted heads through the windows and the open doorways. He spotted at least three men moving on the ground floor, plus a fourth silhouette near the front door. Four Spec Ops guys total, one less than planned because Stahl was dead and cooling in the snow a quarter mile back.

But there were others too. Through the living room window, he glimpsed different shapes. Civilians in expensive clothes.

An older woman with silver hair in a wheelchair. A middle-aged guy in a suit pushing her around. The Brasis, but not Enzo. John had killed that one, Widow figured. That was what all of this was about. Probably was what Bloom tried to tell him. The surviving Brasis had come to Tent Hills for revenge. A revenge that had festered for decades, probably.

Widow didn't know the details. He didn't need them. He knew enough. John might've been someone else once, a long time ago. Perhaps he'd see the inside of a courtroom one day for any crime he'd committed. But what Widow knew was that Matty, Elsa, the boys, and Ester were innocent. That was good enough for Widow to kill whoever needed killing to keep them alive.

There were too many targets spread across too many rooms. If Widow went in through the back door, he'd be fighting in tight quarters with civilians caught in the crossfire. The Spec Ops guys had night vision and superior numbers. The family was probably already zip-tied on the floor somewhere, which meant any stray round could hit an Elton instead of a bad guy.

A frontal assault would get people killed. The wrong people. And Widow would be among the numbers of the dead. No question.

Widow needed a different approach. Something creative. He needed a distraction. Something to lure them outside into the cornstalks, where he had better odds.

Widow searched the cornfield surrounding him for an idea. The stalks rose seven feet high, dead and brown, coated in ice and snow. But they were plenty dry in patches, too. They'd been standing since the fall harvest, dried out by months of frigid wind. He reached out and snapped one in half. It broke clean and easy, like kindling.

They were still flammable as hell. Which made Widow smile.

A fiery idea formed in his mind. He turned and ran back through the stalks, retracing his path toward the convoy. The HK416 bounced against his back as he moved, the sling digging into his shoulder. His boots crunched through the frozen ground and his breath came out in clouds of white vapor. The cast slammed through the loose dead leaves dangling from the stalks. His injured hand throbbed, but he couldn't think about that now.

A few minutes later, he passed the dead remains of Stahl. Continuing, he breached the cornstalks and ran into the clearing and the parked Escalade and Trent's truck. Crick's body still lay in the snow where he'd fallen. The blood around his head started to freeze into a dark stain. Trent was still unconscious in the bed of his pickup, right where Widow had left him too.

Widow grabbed both gas cans from the back of the Escalade. They were heavy—five gallons each, maybe more. He lifted them by the handles and headed back into the corn. The real issue was on his cast hand. The added weight, though minor, really hurt his injury. But he had no choice.

The return trip took longer with the extra weight, and he had to slow twice because of his cast hand. The gas sloshed around in the cans as he ran. His cast hand burned and his shoulders ached, but he kept moving. When he reached the edge of the field behind the Elton house, where he'd just been standing, he set down the cans and caught his breath.

Then Widow got to work. Picking up the first can, he unscrewed the cap. The smell of gasoline hit his nostrils, acrid and chemical. He started walking in a wide arc through the stalks, tilting the can and letting fuel pour out in a steady stream. The gas splashed across the frozen cornstalks and soaked into the snow at their base. He made the circle large—

maybe fifty yards in diameter—leaving a wet trail of accelerant behind him.

Widow paused once because he heard yelling and screaming. But no gunshots, which was good. The Eltons were alive. Was it all of them? Or only the survivors of the assault on their house? Widow had no answer. Not yet.

When the first can ran dry, Widow dropped it there to mark the spot. He returned halfway through the circle he was trying to create and ran back to the other can. He grabbed it, returned to the first dropped can, and kept going. He completed a full circle, connecting two sides of the stream of gasoline. He emptied the remainder of the second can in a few interior lines for good measure, creating a rough grid pattern that would spread the fire fast once it caught.

Widow tossed the second can aside and unslung the HK416 from his shoulder. Then he pointed the rifle at the sky and pulled the trigger. It was still switched to full auto.

The shots cracked through the night—several of them, spaced seconds apart. He paused and fired again to overkill the point. The sound echoed across the flat Nebraska landscape like thunder.

Stahl's radio in his ear crackled immediately.

"Stahl?" Colton's voice was tense and alert. "Stahl, what's going on out there? Where the hell are you?"

Widow keyed the radio and dropped his voice into that gravelly register he'd used before, adding static by cupping his hand over his mouth. "Ambush! There's hostile gunfire out here! I think it's a bunch of the neighbors or something! They're heavily armed! I need backup!"

"Say again? How many hostiles?"

"Not sure! Multiple shooters! They've got me pinned down! Get out here now!" Widow released the transmit button and went silent.

Widow moved quickly to the far side of the gasoline circle and crouched behind a thick cluster of stalks. His rifle was up and ready. He controlled his breathing and waited.

Thirty seconds passed, then a minute.

Then he heard them coming.

Boots crunching through frozen corn. The rustle of stalks being pushed aside. Low voices exchanging tactical commands. They were moving in formation, just like he knew they would—spread out in a line, weapons up, night vision goggles painting everything in shades of green.

Colton's voice came over the radio again. "Stahl? We're approaching your position. Where're you?"

Widow stayed quiet and smiled.

"Stahl, respond!"

Widow gave him nothing.

Then Colton's actual voice rang out across the cornfield, no longer filtered through the radio. "Stahl! Stahl! Where the hell are you?!"

The Spec Ops team pushed deeper into the stalks, searching for their friend. Widow watched them through gaps in the corn—four dark shapes moving in a tactical wedge. Colton was on point, his HK416 sweeping left to right. The other three fanned out behind him, covering the flanks.

They crossed into the gasoline circle without noticing. Why would they? The snow covered most of the wet trail and the darkness hid the rest. They smelled the gas, but were in too much of a hurry, too much on edge, to register the danger.

Plus, their night vision would pick up heat signatures and movement, not liquid soaking into the ground.

Widow let them get to the center of the gas ring. He wanted them deep inside the ring, with nowhere to run.

"Stahl!" Colton called again. His voice had an edge now. Something wasn't right, and he knew it, but he didn't know what. *Where was Stahl? And where the hell were the supposed armed hostiles?*

All four men were inside the circle. They'd stopped moving, their heads turning as they scanned the stalks for threats. Colton held up a fist—the signal to the others to hold position.

Widow pulled the first flashbang from his belt. He yanked the pin and lobbed it in a high arc over the cornstalks. It landed ten feet from Colton's position and bounced once in the snow. Before anyone could react, Widow pulled the second grenade, then the third. He threw them to opposite sides of the circle, creating a triangle of death.

Widow turned, covering his eyes and ears. The first flashbang detonated in a hot, white flash.

The blast was deafening—a massive crack of sound and light that turned the night into day for a split second. The concussive wave flattened the nearest stalks and sent the Spec Ops guys staggering. The white hot flash exploded in a bright green flash across their night vision.

The second grenade went off directly after the first, followed immediately by the third.

The flashes blinded and deafened the team. But it did a lot more than that. The sudden bursts from the grenades ignited the gasoline.

The ring of gas lit up instantly.

Fire raced along the fuel trail like a living thing, spreading in both directions at once. Blue flames turned orange as they climbed the dry cornstalks and caught hold of the brittle leaves. Within seconds, the entire circle was burning—a ring of fire fifteen feet high, roaring and crackling as it consumed everything in its path.

One of the Spec Ops guys caught the worst of it. He'd been standing directly over both the ring of gas and the impact point of the first flashbang when it exploded. The gasoline had pooled at his feet, and the flames engulfed him instantly, climbing up his legs and torso like he'd been dipped in napalm. He screamed—a horrible, animal sound that rose above the roar of the fire.

A second one caught fire pretty quickly as well. Only he tried to run as the flames crawled up his legs, burning his inner thighs. Half on fire, he dropped his rifle and tried to run, but the flames were everywhere. He made it maybe ten feet before he collapsed, still burning, still screaming, his tactical gear melting into his flesh.

The other two were trapped. The fire had closed around them like a noose, cutting off every escape route. They spun in circles, rifles up, searching for a way out that didn't exist. The one called Colton ripped the night vision goggles from his face. He searched frantically for a way out of the flames.

The heat was intense. Widow felt it from outside the ring, pressing against his face like an open oven.

Widow stepped closer to the ring of fire. He stood outside it, just behind them. He aimed the HK416 at the two remaining Spec Ops guys. He shouted over the crackling flames. "Hey!"

Colton heard him and spun around. He squinted into the darkness beyond the fire. He saw Widow's silhouette for maybe half a second.

"You should've stayed home!" Widow shouted. Then he squeezed the trigger.

The HK416 roared on full automatic, spitting rounds at a rate of eight hundred bullets per minute. Only it didn't have nearly that many. And Widow didn't need that many. He had plenty to kill these two. He walked the barrel across both targets, stitching holes through them. The first guy took multiple rounds across the chest and throat, the impacts jerking him backward like a puppet with cut strings. Blood sprayed from his neck in a dark arc that turned to steam when it hit the flames.

The last guy, Colton, tried to return fire, but he was shooting blindly. His rounds went wide, bursting through the wall of flames, and snapping through cornstalks twenty feet to Widow's left.

Too close for comfort for Widow, so he adjusted his aim and put the rest of the magazine into Colton's center mass. The bullets punched through his tactical vest like it was made of paper. Colton dropped to his knees, his rifle falling from his hands. He looked down at the holes in his chest with an expression of pure disbelief, then toppled face-first into the burning snow and dried cornstalks.

The first man, the one who'd caught fire at the start, had finally stopped screaming. He lay curled in a fetal position, flames still licking at what remained of his charred body. The smell hit him—burning hair, melting plastic, and something worse.

Widow's rifle clicked empty.

He ejected the spent magazine and slapped in the old one from his pocket. He chambered a round and scanned the kill zone, looking for movement. There was none. Four bodies lay scattered across the burning cornfield, all of them still, all of them dead.

The fire spread fast, jumping from stalk to stalk, racing through the Eltons' cornfields. He hoped it would burn out before doing significant damage to their fields. But under the circumstances, it was better to save their lives over their cornfields.

Widow needed to move.

Suddenly, he heard it—gunfire from the front of the house. Not the heavy crack of assault rifles, but something smaller. Handguns. Multiple shooters exchanging fire in rapid succession.

Widow ignored the burning pain in his cast hand and ran along the edge of the cornfield, keeping the flames behind him. The smoke rose to the sky thick and black, stinging his eyes and coating his throat. He pushed through it, moving toward the front of the property.

The gunfire continued—pop pop pop, then a pause, then another burst.

Widow cleared the corner of the house and found a better vantage point near a barn. He dropped to one knee and raised the rifle to his shoulder and aimed over the scope. He scanned the front of the house.

Bloom's SUV was parked in the driveway, its emergency lights flashing blue through the falling snow. The driver's side door hung open, and the windshield was spider-webbed with bullet holes. Someone had lit the vehicle up pretty good.

Two men crouched behind the Escalade that the Spec Ops team had driven to the house. They wore suits, not tactical gear—the Brasi enforcers. They were firing at the SUV with handguns, taking turns popping up to squeeze off rounds before ducking back to cover.

Widow couldn't see Bloom. She had to be somewhere behind the SUV, using it for cover, but from this angle and this distance he couldn't confirm she was still alive. The enforcers were focused on her position, which meant she'd been returning fire at some point. That was a good sign.

But Widow was too far away to help. At this range, with the smoke and snow obscuring his vision, he couldn't guarantee accurate fire. If he started shooting now, he might hit the SUV. He might hit Bloom.

He moved in slowly, using the barn for cover, then crossing to the animal pens. He saw Clucky, the rooster, marching up and down in front of the chicken coop, like a general giving battle orders to the chickens.

Widow moved on, running fast. He hit one side of the main house. He lost sight of the enforcers because of the angle and the smoke. He kept moving, trying to close the distance between him and Bloom.

But it was too late. The gunfire stopped.

One enforcer shouted something in Italian and the other one responded with a laugh.

Then there was nothing but silence.

Widow froze halfway to the house and listened. No more shots, no more voices, no more movement—just the crackle of the fire raging behind him and the whisper of snow falling through the darkness.

He ran on and reached the back corner of the house and pressed himself against the wall. The window beside him looked into the kitchen. Through the glass, he could see overturned chairs and broken dishes on the floor. Signs of a struggle, but no people.

He moved to the back door. Maybe he could cut through the house and come out the front. It would be helpful for him to get a quick scan of the inside to see if any of the Eltons were dead.

The back door was broken and splintered from the Spec Ops guys breaching it.

Widow took a breath, raised the rifle, and stepped inside.

CHAPTER 38

Widow stepped through the back door and into the Eltons' kitchen.

The room was dark, lit only by the distant orange glow of the cornfield fire bleeding through the windows. Shadows crawled across the walls in shifting patterns. The air smelled like sweat and fear.

The kitchen was destroyed. Chairs lay scattered across the tile like broken teeth. Shattered dishes covered the floor in a minefield of jagged ceramic.

Blood pooled near the kitchen island, thick and dark and wet. Matty's handgun lay on the floor beside the refrigerator, fired empty. Brass casings glittered around it. Matty had emptied the gun before they'd taken him down. He'd made them work for it.

Widow hoped he was alive. He hurried through the first floor.

The house was empty. No bodies. No hostages. No bad guys. They'd moved everyone to the barn.

Then Widow heard crying, faint and distant, coming from outside.

He crossed to a window. Through the glass, he spotted the stables. A black Escalade sat parked at the doors, backed up, with its rear hatch hanging open. Light spilled out from inside the building through the gap in the main doors. And now that Widow focused, he could hear something else—voices, faint but distinct. Someone was talking in there. Not just talking, but sinisterly laughing.

Widow slipped out the front door and descended the porch steps, staying low. His HK416 was ready to use. Bloom's SUV sat in the driveway, lights still flashing, windshield shot to hell. The enforcers who'd been shooting at her were gone, inside the stable now with everyone else.

Widow crossed the yard, using the shadows along the fence line for concealment. The snow muffled his footsteps, and the strobing police lights created just enough visual chaos to mask his movement. He reached the corner of the stable and pressed himself against the weathered wood.

The voices were clearer now. A man's voice, deep and cruel, saying something Widow couldn't quite make out. A woman's voice, older and hard, barking orders. And underneath it all, the sound of children crying.

Widow circled around to the side of the building, looking for a vantage point. The stable walls were old, the planks shrunk and warped by decades of Nebraska weather. Cracks ran between the boards where the wood had separated. Widow found one wide enough to peer through and pressed his eye against it.

The first thing he saw was the horses.

They were terrified, all of them. The quarter horses stamped and snorted in their stalls, their ears pinned flat, their eyes rolling white with panic. One of them was kicking at its stall door in rhythmic thuds that shook the entire structure. They sensed the violence, and they didn't like it.

Widow shifted position and found a grimy window on the east wall. He crouched beneath the sill, raised his head just enough to see inside, and felt his stomach drop.

The Eltons and Ester were lined up against the far wall.

They were all there, zip-tied to metal rails that ran between the horse stalls—hands behind their backs, ankles bound, arranged in a row like prisoners awaiting mass execution by firing squad, which, Widow realized, was exactly what they were.

Matty was on the end, closest to the main doors. His face was a mess of blood and swelling, one eye puffed completely shut from the beating he'd taken. But the real damage was his leg. His jeans were soaked dark from mid-thigh to the knee, and someone had tied a belt around his upper leg as a makeshift tourniquet. The leather was cinched tight enough to cut off the blood flow, but the wound was still seeping. He'd been shot, probably early in the fight, probably after he shot off all his bullets to defend his family.

Elsa knelt beside him; her hands bound behind her. She was crying now, silently, her eyes fixed on her boys.

Adam and T.J. were next to her, next in line on the black railing. Adam's face was blank with shock, his mind retreated somewhere deep inside itself where the horror couldn't reach him. T.J. was worse—the eight-year-old was shaking uncontrollably, his cheeks streaked with tears, his breath coming in hitching sobs that made his whole body shudder.

Ester was at the end of the line. Tears streamed down her cheeks and she couldn't stop them. Her whole body shook against the railing, shuddering the metal.

And then there was Bloom.

She sat slumped against the wall near the stable doors, separate from the family. Her hands were pressed against her abdomen, her fingers interlaced over a spreading stain of crimson red. She was bleeding badly. It had seeped between her knuckles in a slow but steady flow. Her bulletproof vest had a crater in the center where at least one round had struck —the Kevlar had stopped it—but something else had gotten through. A fragment, maybe, or a round that had found the gap beneath the vest's edge.

She was dying. Her skin had gone pale as death. Her chest rose and fell in shallow, labored breaths. Her eyes were half-closed and unfocused, drifting toward unconsciousness.

She had minutes, not hours. Maybe less.

Widow forced himself to look away from Bloom and focus on the threat. If he kept his focus on her, rage would take over. That would be a mistake. He needed to stay sharp.

Five hostiles occupied the room. Widow felt much better about these odds than earlier. Not only were the numbers better for him than before. But these guys were dumb compared to the Spec Ops guys. They were dumb because none of them questioned where the Spec Ops guys were. It was like they'd forgotten them completely.

Two of the hostiles were young mobster types in dark suits— the Brasi enforcers. They stood near the center of the stable, their handguns drawn but held casually at their sides. They were relaxed and confident because they thought the hard part was over. They watched the Eltons carefully. But ignored the main stable doors. Amateurs.

The obvious Brasis in the room were two older people. They were much older. And they looked just alike, twins. Enzo's older siblings, only Widow didn't know that yet.

The man was in his mid-eighties, but in great shape. He had silver hair slicked back from a face that looked like it had been carved from granite and left out in the rain for decades. He wore an expensive overcoat over a charcoal suit, and something glinted on his right hand. Widow squinted through the dirty glass and saw brass knuckles, the old-fashioned kind with four finger holes and a reinforced striking surface. Blood stained the metal. He'd been using them.

The woman sat in a wheelchair near the center of the room, a wool blanket draped across her legs. She was the same age as her brother—his twin—with silver hair pulled back in a severe bun and a face that might have been beautiful once but had hardened into something cruel.

Elena and Elio Brasi. They'd waited sixty years for this moment.

And kneeling on the concrete floor in front of them, beaten and broken and barely conscious, was Mitch Nicely—Mickey Fog Eyes.

The used car salesman looked nothing like the grinning face on the billboard at the edge of town. His features were swollen and purple, his lips split, his nose clearly broken. His left hand was wrapped in a blood-soaked rag. The ring finger had been missing for sixty years—cut off when he'd faked his death. But the pinky was gone now—taken tonight.

Vito Brasi—the younger one, Elena's son—stood over Mitch with gardening shears in his hand, the heavy-duty kind with thick handles and curved blades meant for cutting through branches.

The blades were wet with blood.

"Does your family know who this is?" Vito asked. He turned to face John, who sat propped against a support beam on the opposite side of the room. The old man's crutches lay on the floor beside him, out of reach and broken in half. His face was battered—fresh wounds layered over old bruises—and his wrists were zip-tied around the beam behind his back. But his eyes were clear and lucid. The fog of midnight dementia had lifted, replaced by something older and harder within himself.

Donnie D had returned.

"Do they know who you really are, Donnie-boy?" Vito continued, his voice light and mocking. "What you did to my uncle? What that did to my mother?"

Elena spoke up from her wheelchair. Her voice cut through the stable like a KA-BAR through canvas.

"This is Mickey Fog Eyes," she said, gesturing at the broken man on the floor. She looked at Elsa and the children with undisguised contempt. "He helped your grandfather murder my brother sixty years ago. Shot him in the woods and buried him in an unmarked grave like a dog."

"That's not true!" The words tore out of John. His accent was back—that thick Chicago drawl of his day was back. He'd buried it under decades of Nebraska living. But it was here now—back from the past. "Mickey had nothing to do with it! None of them did! I'm the one you want! Let them go!"

Elio stepped forward and drove his brass-knuckled fist into John's stomach, which he'd done countless times tonight already.

The blow made a wet, meaty sound that echoed off the stable walls. John folded in half, the air driven from his lungs in a violent gasp. Before he could recover, Elio hit him again—a vicious backhand across the face that split his cheek to the bone. Blood sprayed from the wound and spattered across the concrete.

Even though Elio was in his mid-eighties, he was pretty fit. John's bones were just as old as theirs and suffered the same brittleness of age and time. Plus, brass knuckles in anyone's hands will do significant damage.

"Shut up!" Elio barked. "You'll get your turn, Donnie D. But first you're going to watch. An eye for an eye. You took our brother, so we're going to take your family. One by one, right in front of you."

T.J. sobbed harder. Elsa screamed at them to stop, to leave her family alone. The horses kicked and stamped in their stalls, driven to frenzy by the screaming and the violence.

Vito grabbed Mitch by the hair and hauled him upright, then kicked him square in the chest. The old man whimpered but didn't resist. Whatever fight he'd once had was gone, beaten and carved out of him from the Brasis' sick torture.

"Are you kids watching?" Vito asked, glancing over his shoulder at Adam and T.J. His voice was cheerful, almost playful, like a teacher about to demonstrate something interesting to the whole class. "Pay attention. This is what happens to people who cross the Brasi family."

Vito grabbed Mitch's left hand and unwrapped the bloody rag. Two stumps—the old one healed smooth, the fresh one still seeping blood. Vito examined the remaining fingers with clinical detachment, like a butcher inspecting meat.

"Two down," he said. "Let's make it three."

He positioned the shears around Mitch's index finger.

"No," Mitch whispered. His voice was barely audible, cracked and broken. "Please. No more."

"Should have thought about that sixty years ago," Vito said.

He squeezed the handles.

The shears bit through flesh and bone with a thick, wet crunch—the sound of a chicken wing being separated at the joint, only louder. Blood sprayed across the concrete in a dark arc, spattering Vito's Italian shoes and the hem of Elena's blanket. Mitch screamed—a raw, animal howl that rose from somewhere deep in his gut and filled the stable like a living thing.

He collapsed onto his side, clutching his destroyed hand against his chest, his body convulsing with agony. Blood pumped from the fresh wound in rhythmic spurts, pooling beneath him on the cold concrete.

Vito held up the severed finger and examined it in the light. The digit dangled from his grip, pale and bloody, the nail still perfectly manicured.

"Three down," he said.

He tossed the finger aside like a piece of garbage and laughed. The enforcers laughed with him.

The children screamed. Elsa screamed. Even Adam snapped out of his shock and yelled something, straining against his bonds. The horses went berserk, kicking at their stalls, their neighing mixing with the human screams adding to the chaos.

"Enough!" Elena barked from her wheelchair. Everyone fell silent—even the horses seemed to quiet, their ears pricking toward the old woman.

"Enough games," she said. She adjusted the blanket on her lap and looked at her son with cold disapproval. "We didn't come all this way to play with them. We didn't come here for fingers. We came for blood. I want more! Let's finish what we started!" The old woman's eyes were wild with bloodlust.

Widow pulled back from the window.

His mind raced through options, calculating angles and distances, and probabilities. Five hostiles—two enforcers, Vito, Elio, and the old woman in the wheelchair. The family sat bound and helpless along the far wall—Matty bleeding from his leg, John tied to a beam. Bloom bled out near the door. Mitch lay a shattered wreck on the floor.

Widow still couldn't go through the main door with guns blazing. People would die. The wrong people. Maybe. He needed to even the odds. He needed a distraction.

He searched outside the stable for something.

Bloom's SUV idled, its lights still flashing. Police vehicles had PA systems, bullhorns, and sirens. They made plenty of loud noise.

Widow loped along the side of the stable, keeping low, and crossed the yard toward Bloom's SUV. The vehicle was a mess —bullet holes stitched across the driver's side door, the windshield spider-webbed with cracks, the lightbar sparking and flickering on the roof. But the engine ran, idling roughly, but working.

He reached the driver's side and leaned in through the open door. The interior smelled like blood and leather. There was blood in droplets on the seat, blood on the steering wheel, blood on the center console. Bloom had been hit while still in the SUV.

Widow found the radio controls mounted below the dashboard. He cranked the volume dial all the way up and hit the power button. Country music blasted from the speakers— something about trucks and back roads and cold beer. He found the PA switch and flipped it, routing the audio through the external bullhorn mounted to the vehicle.

The music screamed across the yard, echoing off the stable walls, filling the night with noise.

Somewhere in the distance, the fire rose higher and higher. It consumed more and more of the cornfields, too. Smoke filled the air, climbing up into the sky.

Widow killed the SUV's interior lights, backed out, and sprinted for the stables.

He pressed himself against the corner of the building and aimed the HK416. His breathing steadied and his hands stayed calm. He'd done this before, more times than he could count.

Inside the stable, he heard shouting, not the screaming from the Eltons. This was from the Brasis.

"What the hell is that?" Elio shouted. His voice, slightly muffled by the walls.

"I don't know!" one enforcer said.

"Maybe it's Colton playing a joke?"

"Speaking of Colton, we haven't seen those Spec Ops guys in a while," the other enforcer said.

"Last I saw, they went to help one of their guys out in the field. Someone was shooting at him," the first one said.

"Well, go find out what the hell is going on!" Vito snapped. "And shut that goddamn music off!"

Widow heard footsteps crossing the concrete. The stable doors creaked open and two figures emerged, silhouetted against the light from inside—the enforcers. They had their pistols drawn, but their body language was relaxed, annoyed rather than alert. They thought this was a nuisance, not a threat.

They walked toward Bloom's SUV, their shoes crunching through the snow. One of them gestured toward the cornfield behind the house.

"Fire's getting pretty damn big out there."

"Yeah." The other one nodded. "Must be why those Spec Ops guys haven't come back. They're probably trying to keep it from spreading. Don't want to draw attention."

The other one shrugged it off. That sounded plausible enough for them.

They reached the SUV. The first enforcer leaned in through the open door and fumbled with the radio. The music died abruptly, leaving only the soft crackle of static and the distant roar of the cornfield fire.

"Must've been a power surge that turned on her radio or something," the enforcer said.

His voice boomed from the speakers outside the vehicle.

Both men froze. They looked at each other, then at the dashboard, at the PA switch that was still flipped to the ON position.

The microphone had gone hot.

They spun around, their pistols coming up, their eyes scanning the yard behind them.

Widow was already there.

He stood between them and the stables, maybe fifteen feet away, the HK416 leveled at their chests. The strobing blue and red lights from the SUV painted his face in alternating waves of color, making him look like something out of a nightmare.

The enforcers saw him. Their eyes went wide.

Neither of them had time to speak.

Widow pulled the trigger.

The first burst caught the closer enforcer center mass—two rounds punching through his sternum with the flat, meaty sound of fists hitting a heavy bag. The bullets shattered bone and shredded muscle and pulverized the chambers of his heart into red paste. Hydrostatic shock liquefied the soft tissue around the wound channels and sent a pressure wave through his entire torso.

For a fraction of a second, the enforcer stood frozen. His brain hadn't caught up to what his body already knew. Then his face went slack, his eyes rolled back, and his legs gave out. He collapsed backward, arms pinwheeling, his pistol spinning away into the snow. He hit the ground and slid for a few feet, leaving a dark smear on the snowy surface, before coming to rest against the SUV's front tire.

He was dead before he stopped moving.

The second enforcer tried to bring his weapon up. His reflexes were decent, and in a fair fight, he might have had a chance. But this wasn't a fair fight. This was an ambush.

Widow shifted his aim two degrees to the right and fired again.

The rounds punched the enforcer in the chest and throat. The chest shots cratered his lungs and sent fragments of rib bone tumbling through his thoracic cavity like shrapnel. But the throat shot was the one that did the real work. The 5.56mm round entered just below his Adam's apple and exited through the back of his neck, taking a good chunk of his spine with it.

Blood erupted from the wound in a violent spray of red mist, jetting outward in a crimson arc that painted the snow behind him in a fan pattern six feet wide. The enforcer's body locked up, every muscle contracting at once as his spinal cord was severed. He dropped to his knees, his hands flying to his ruined throat, blood pouring between his fingers in thick pulses that matched his fading heartbeat.

Staring at Widow, he tried to speak. His mouth opened and closed, but all that came out were a wet gurgle and a bubble of blood that burst on his lips.

Keeping one eye on the stable's main door, Widow walked toward him, slowly and deliberately, each footstep crunching through the snow.

The enforcer looked up at him. His eyes were full of pain and terror and the dawning realization that he was about to die. He tried to raise his pistol, but his fingers wouldn't cooperate. The gun slipped from his grip and dropped into the snow.

Widow stopped three feet away and looked down at him and shot him once—the kill shot.

The round entered just above the enforcer's left eye. It was a small hole going in—maybe the size of an eraser head on a pencil, neat and almost polite. Coming out was different. The bullet tumbled through the enforcer's brain, shredding gray matter and blood vessels, before exiting through the back of his skull in a spray of bone fragments and tissue that splattered across the snow in a Rorschach pattern of red and white and gray.

The enforcer's body pitched forward and landed face-first in the snow. His legs twitched twice, then went still.

Widow walked over to the first enforcer, who lay sprawled against the SUV's tire. The man's eyes were open, staring at the falling snow with a look of mild surprise. Widow put a round in his head anyway, just to be certain. The skull cracked open like a melon, spilling its contents onto the frozen ground.

Two down and three to go.

Widow ejected his magazine and checked the bullet count. Empty. He dropped the HK416 and drew the Glock from his pocket.

Widow moved toward the stable doors, which still stood further ajar than earlier from when the enforcers had exited. The gap was about a meter wide—plenty of room to see through, not enough to slip through quietly. He'd have to push them open, which would draw everyone's attention.

Before Widow could move, he heard something from inside. It was T.J. crying.

Then Vito said, "Think I'll start with this one!"

Widow stepped to the edge of the door and looked through the gap.

Vito had T.J. off the ground, holding the boy up by his zip-tied wrists. The kid's feet dangled in the air, kicking uselessly, his small body twisting against the plastic restraints. His face was contorted in pain and terror, tears streaming down his cheeks.

Elio stood beside them with a revolver aimed at the boy's stomach.

"Wait!" Elsa shouted. She thrashed against her bonds, her voice cracking with hysteria. "Please! He's just a kid! Don't do this!"

"Shut up!" Vito snapped. He shook T.J. like a rag doll, making the boy cry harder. "This is how it's going to be. This is what your father brought on your family. You can thank him while you watch your son die."

John shouted in that old Chicago accent, cursing and begging, but Elio just laughed.

"Save it, Donnie-boy. You're going to watch every single one of them die. Then you're next," Elio said and pressed his revolver's barrel against T.J.'s stomach. But just then, someone else caught his eye. "Or should I start with this one?" He swung the gun toward Ester, who sat at the end of the line. "Who're you, sweetheart? You family too? You don't look like the rest of them."

Widow had seen enough.

He pushed through the stable doors with the Glock up and his finger on the trigger. His cast's plaster hung in chunks from his forearm, from all the violence. It had been a long night. He ignored it. It didn't matter. The only thing that mattered in this moment was his trigger finger, and that still worked fine.

Vito saw him first. The color drained from his face—a flash of confusion, then realization, then fear. His mouth opened to shout a warning—probably. Who knew? Because no one ever will. He was too slow.

Widow shot him.

The first bullet tore through Vito's upper back, just below his shoulder blade. The bullet punched through muscle and bone and lung tissue before erupting from his chest in a spray of red mist. The impact spun him like a top. The second bullet hit square in his chest, nearly going the opposite flight path as the first. They might've collided inside Vito's lungs. Probably not, but possible. Widow shot him again in the chest, right side this time.

Vito's body jerked with each bullet impact—once, twice, three times—like a man touching a live wire. His grip on T.J. failed instantly, his fingers going slack as the nerve signals from his brain short-circuited. The boy dropped to the concrete floor and scrambled away awkwardly, his zip-tied hands clumsy beneath him, sobbing and gasping. Blood spattered across his little face.

One of Widow's rounds kept going. It passed clean through Vito's torso, losing velocity but not stopping, and slammed into the safety latch on one of the horse stalls. It was the wild bronco's stall. The mechanism shattered in a spray of metal fragments, and the sliding door rattled loose on its track.

Inside the stall, the bronco whinnied, rearing and bucking against the walls. The massive horse lunged forward, its hooves striking the air. It slammed its shoulder against the damaged door, and the door wrenched open, crashing against the wall with a bang that shook the whole stable.

The other horses reacted in various ways. Some kicked at their stall doors. Others neighed. The more docile ones just scooted to the backs of their stalls, afraid.

The wild bronco's stall stood wide open now. It saw the chance to bolt, but it didn't, not yet. It stood in the open doorway of its stall, trembling and snorting, too terrified to move.

Vito wasn't dead yet. At least he didn't know it. He swayed in the center of the room, blood oozing from his chest and back in thick streams. He looked down at himself, at the holes in his body, at the blood spreading across the concrete beneath his feet. His face wore an expression of pure disbelief, as if he couldn't comprehend that this was happening to him.

Then his legs buckled, and he toppled over, hitting the concrete face-first with a wet crunch that shattered his nose and scattered his teeth across the floor. His body twitched once, twice, then went still. Blood pooled around him in an expanding circle, reflecting the overhead lights from the ceiling.

He was dead. One dead Brasi. Two left.

Widow stared at the Brasi twins, the remaining two. Enzo's brother and sister. He smiled at them.

Elio reacted faster than Widow expected. The old man's reflexes were good, surprisingly good for someone his age. He was fast, too. Elio got his revolver up. He fired before Widow could adjust his aim. Not good.

But the shot went wild, thrown off by panic and adrenaline. The bullet rushed past Widow's head, close enough that he felt the wind of its passage, and punched through the open stable door into the night beyond. Widow heard it slam into the Escalade's rear quarter panel with a metallic thunk.

Widow didn't flinch. Flinching caused unplanned reactions. It caused a shooter in the field to overreact. In a gunfight, seconds mattered. But the thing that mattered more was keeping a cool head. Accuracy was a step ahead of speed in winning a gunfight.

To gauge how much time he had to react, Widow pivoted on his front foot, tracked Elio's muzzle, and returned fire with three shots of his own.

The first bullet punched through Elio's chest, dead center, shattering his sternum and driving fragments of bone into his heart. The second hit two inches higher, clipping his clavicle and tumbling up through his shoulder. The third hit him in the throat.

The bullet entered just below Elio's jaw and tore through his trachea, his carotid artery, and his jugular vein before exiting through the back of his neck in a spray of blood and tissue. Blood erupted from the wound in a violent geyser, painting the air in a fine red mist that hung in the light like fog.

Elio's body flew backward, the brass knuckles spinning off his hand and clattering across the concrete. He hit the ground hard, his body bouncing once before coming to rest on his back. His mouth opened and closed, gaping like a fish, blood bubbling up from his throat with each attempt to breathe.

A team of paramedics could've saved him. Maybe. If they were right there on the spot, waiting. But they weren't. Elio drowned in his own blood.

Widow watched him die. They all did. Without a medic there to save him, it took seconds. The old man's eyes stayed open the whole time, fixed on the ceiling.

Elena Brasi was all that was left. She sat alone in her wheelchair.

Her son lay dead at her feet, his blood soaking into the concrete. Her brother lay dead six feet away, his throat torn open, his eyes staring at nothing. The room smelled like cordite and copper and the sharp ammonia stench of loosened bowels.

She slowly raised both hands above her head, in surrender.

Widow walked toward her with the Glock aimed at her face. His boots splashed through the blood pooling on the concrete —Vito's blood, Elio's blood, Mitch's blood, all mixing in a dark lake that spread across the concrete floor. He stopped in the center of the room, standing directly over Vito's corpse, and looked down at the old woman.

Elena met his gaze. Her eyes went wide with fear, but there was something else there too—intense hatred.

"Do it," she whispered. "Kill me. Finish it."

Widow's finger tightened on the trigger. He was tempted. In a wheelchair or not, because of her, people were dead. Because of her, Bloom might die.

But Bloom wasn't dead. She made it known. Even on the

verge of death, she had a duty to uphold, a duty that Widow understood, but no longer had.

Weakly, Bloom whispered "No!"

Widow glanced at her.

She slumped against the wall near the door, her hands pressed against her bleeding abdomen, her face the color of old newspaper. She looked at him with eyes that could barely focus, eyes already starting to glaze over.

"She's unarmed," Bloom said. Her voice faded, the words slurred and soft. "Widow, don't. You're better than that." She coughed blood. "I know it."

Widow stared at Elena for a long moment. The Glock didn't waver.

Then he lowered it and backed away. "You're lucky she's here." He lowered the Glock and stuffed it into his pocket.

Behind Elena, the wild bronco stood in the doorway of its open stall. It recognized Widow—remembered the fist that had put it down—and cowered against the back wall, its ears pinned flat, its body trembling.

Widow turned away from Elena, turning his back to her, and crossed to T.J. first. The boy huddled against his mother, shaking and crying. Widow knelt beside him and spoke in a calm, quiet voice.

"Let me see your hands."

T.J. held out his bound wrists, the zip ties cutting into his skin.

"This is going to sting a little," Widow said. He got behind the boy, gripped the plastic ties, and wrenched them toward T.J.'s body with a quick jerk. The plastic snapped and fell away.

T.J. rubbed his wrists and looked up at Widow with red eyes.

"I need you to be brave a little longer," Widow said. "Is there a knife somewhere around here? Something sharp?"

"We keep one in the toolshed," T.J. said. His voice shook, but stayed coherent. "It's right next door."

"Go get it. Grab anything else that can cut—pliers, wire cutters, whatever you find. Then come back and help me free your family. Can you do that?"

T.J. nodded.

"Go now, and go fast."

The boy ran, his small feet pounding across the blood-slicked concrete and out the stable door into the night.

Widow stood and turned back toward Elena. Only she wasn't where he'd left her.

She'd rolled her wheelchair forward, positioning herself away from the open stall, closer to the center of the room. And her hands were no longer raised. They were under the blanket on her lap.

"Look out!" Elsa screamed.

Elena sat there, holding a gun—a snub-nosed revolver, small and silver. She'd pulled it from beneath the blanket on her lap. She raised it toward Widow, her arthritic fingers curling around the grip, her thumb pulling back the hammer with a soft click.

"You killed my son!" she shrieked, decades of hatred pouring out in a torrent of fury. "You killed my brother!"

Widow didn't reach for his Glock. There was no time. It was in a pocket. He wouldn't clear it in time. Not unless she couldn't shoot straight. The distance between them wasn't far. In these close quarters, even an amateur could hit him easy enough.

But Widow had another thought.

Instead of going for his Glock, he looked at the wild bronco. It had moved out of its open stall and stood just behind Elena's wheelchair. The horse had emerged from its stall during the chaos. It stood there now, confused and agitated, its massive body blocking the aisle, its hindquarters directly behind the old woman.

Widow hissed through his teeth, loud and sudden—the sound a handler makes to get a horse's attention. It was something he'd seen in the past. But not something he'd done before.

Startled, Elena's aim wavered. She stared at him, confusion flickering across her face. "What're you doing?"

Widow hissed again.

The bronco's ears pinned back flat against its skull. It shifted its weight, its haunches bunching, its back legs tensing. The horse spooked, overwhelmed by the blood and the noise and the bodies on the floor. All it needed was a trigger.

Widow would be that trigger. He stomped his foot, hard and heavy. The sound echoed through the stable like a gunshot.

The animal slow-walked forward, like it was gearing up to charge, stampeded Widow again. It huffed. Air punched out through its nostrils. It moved just to the left of Elena, its body massive compared to her tiny frame. The bronco lined up just in front of her, nearly blocking her shot. It stopped at a point where she was just behind its legs.

"Stop it!" Elena barked. But Widow didn't stop. He stomped again.

The bronco reacted on pure instinct. Sixty years of evolution, a million years of prey-animal survival coded in its DNA, all compressed into a single explosive movement.

The horse pistoned its hind legs backward, both hooves kicking with the force of twin sledgehammers.

The first kick caught Elena in the shoulder and chest—over a thousand pounds of force concentrated into a hoof the size of a dinner plate. Her collarbone shattered. Her ribs caved inward, the jagged ends puncturing her lung and lacerating her heart.

But it was the second kick that killed her.

It caught her in the head.

The hoof struck her temple with a sound like a baseball bat hitting a watermelon. Her skull cracked open along the suture lines, the bones separating and folding inward under the massive pressure. Her brain, already hemorrhaging from the impact, crushed against the inside of her skull and pulped into gray mush.

The wheelchair came up off the ground, tipping back on its rear wheels.

Her head snapped backward so hard and so fast that her neck broke in three places. The vertebrae separated with a series of wet pops, like knuckles cracking, and her spinal cord severed completely. Her body went limp instantly, every muscle releasing at once, the revolver tumbling from her slack fingers and clattering to the floor.

Elena slumped sideways in the wheelchair, her head hanging off her shoulder at an impossible angle. Her neck bent so far that her ear nearly touched her collarbone. Her jaw hung open, slack and loose. Her eyes stared at nothing.

She looked like a Pez dispenser with the lid broken off.

The bronco reared, its front hooves pawing the air. Then it bolted, charging out past the rest of them, through the open stable doors in a thunder of hoofbeats. On its way out, it rushed over the bodies of Vito and Elio. Its hooves crashed down on their dead flesh, shattering ribs and crushing organs, leaving hoofprint-shaped craters in their backs and chests. Blood spattered on the horse's legs.

Then it was gone, galloping across the yard and disappearing into the darkness beyond the burning cornfield. It left a trail of bloody hoofprints in its wake.

When Widow looked back at Elena, she was still slumped in her wheelchair. Blood dripped from her crushed skull, pooling on the floor beneath her. The revolver lay beside her dangling hand, unfired.

The family looked away in horror.

T.J. came running back into the stable with a hunting knife in one hand and a pair of rusty wire cutters in the other. He froze in the doorway, his eyes going wide as he took in the carnage—the bodies, the blood, the old woman with her head bent at that terrible angle.

Widow intercepted him, took the cutting tools, and sent him away. He told him to wait back on the porch to their house. T.J. obeyed readily. He ran back to the porch and waited.

Widow freed the rest of the family. Widow cut Elsa loose first, sawing through the zip ties with the hunting knife. He gave her a pair of pliers. Together, they freed everyone else. Matty was last—his leg wound needed attention, but the tourniquet had done its job. He'd make it.

John sat slumped against the support beam, his face battered and bloody, but his eyes were clear.

Elsa found a cellphone on one of the dead Brasis, tried it, but got no signal.

Widow went to Bloom. She'd barely stayed conscious. Her skin was pale and her lips blue at the edges. Her hands had fallen away from her wound, too weak to maintain pressure.

Widow knelt beside her and examined the damage. The round had struck just below her vest, tearing through the soft tissue of her lower abdomen. A bad wound—the kind that killed people if they didn't get immediate medical attention. He had to get her to the hospital.

He scooped her up like he was carrying his bride across the threshold. And brought her out to her SUV and set her in the backseat. Ester helped him load her into the back, keeping pressure on the wound. She sat back there to hold the pressure down so Bloom didn't have to.

Widow barked for others to hurry with Mitch or Matty, because they were the most injured.

Mitch was curled in a fetal position near the wall, clutching his mutilated hand. Adam helped him. Mitch asked for his finger. They found it, grabbed it, wrapped it in a rag, and shoved it in one of Mitch's pockets. Adam hauled Mitch to his feet and half-carried him to Bloom's SUV.

Adam returned to his mother and helped her bring Matty to their own truck, and then John. T.J. climbed in with them. Widow didn't stick around to watch the rest.

Bloom's vehicle was a wreck—bullet holes, shattered windows, lightbar sparking—but the engine turned over on the first attempt.

They got Mitch in the passenger seat.

Widow hit the lights and siren and floored it.

In the rearview mirror, the cornfield burned.

He pushed the speedometer past ninety and kept his foot on the gas as they booked it to the hospital.

CHAPTER 39

The fire at Mitch Nicely's Automotives spread beyond the dealership, jumping across the access road and tearing through the retirement community behind it. The flames reached several buildings and homes before the fire department contained them. No one died. That was the miracle. But ten people had been hospitalized with burns and smoke inhalation.

The small hospital in Tent Hills didn't have the capacity for a mass casualty event. They called in every doctor, nurse, and orderly off work and available. The waiting room looked like a war zone when Widow arrived with Bloom and Mitch and Ester.

Bloom's surgery took hours.

She made it through, luckily. Widow stayed in Tent Hills for two weeks after—longer than he usually stayed anywhere. He needed to make sure she was okay.

Now, four days after the surgery, he stood in her hospital room, his arm encased in a fresh cast from knuckles to elbow this time. The doctors took one look at his previous cast—

cracked and crumbling—and insisted on starting over. Six more weeks, they'd told him before he could remove this one. He'd nodded and thanked them.

Easton stood beside him, both men looking down at her in a hospital bed. Bloom was sleeping, or appeared to be. An IV line ran into her left arm.

The bullet—a 9mm round fired by one of the Brasi enforcers —had struck the lower edge of her tactical vest. The vest stopped the round from penetrating fully, but the impact fragmented the bullet, and several pieces deflected downward into her lower abdomen. The surgeons repaired the damage, removed the fragments, and flushed the abdominal cavity to prevent infection.

She'd be fine, they told her. A few weeks of recovery and she'd be back on her feet. But it had been close. Another inch to the left and she'd have bled out in that stable too fast before they could've saved her.

"If there's anything you need," Easton said, "let me know."

Widow looked at him. The sheriff's face was tired and drawn, the lines around his eyes deeper than they'd been when they first saw each other. He'd been running on coffee and adrenaline since the night of the attack, coordinating with the state police, managing the crime scene, fielding calls from the FBI.

"There is actually. I'd like to be left out of any paperwork," Widow said.

Easton stared at him. His expression didn't change, but something shifted behind his eyes.

"I'd really appreciate it," Widow said.

Easton was quiet for a long moment. Then he said, "How will I explain who killed all those Spec Ops guys? The scene out there looked like a war zone. Burned bodies, bullet casings everywhere, blood all over that stable. Someone did all that."

"Oh, those guys?" The voice came from the bed. Both men looked down to find Bloom awake, a weak smile on her lips. "I took them all out." She smiled and added, "Jack Widow? Never heard of him."

Easton moved to her bedside immediately. "Daisy. I'm so glad you're awake. How are you feeling?"

"Doped up," Bloom said. "Whatever they're giving me, it's the good stuff."

"They didn't give me anything this time." Widow held up his newly cast arm.

Bloom's smile widened. "Nice. We both got war wounds." She shifted her gaze back to Easton, her expression becoming more serious. "I killed those men, Bill. I got a warning call from the FBI. I showed up and saw what was going down, and I shot them in self-defense."

Easton frowned. "Four of them were ambushed and set on fire out in the cornfield. The state investigators will see that. They're not stupid"

"Yeah," Bloom said, nodding slowly. "That's what I meant. There were too many of them. And I couldn't reach you. I had to act. So I did..."

Widow mouthed the answer to her behind Easton's back.

She repeated it. "What they call divide and conquer. I lured six of them..."

"There were four." Easton said. His brow furrowed.

"Right, four. That's what I said. I lured them out to the corn-field and ambushed them and set them on fire. I had to. It was the only way to save the Eltons."

Easton looked at her, then at Widow. "You killed nine bad guys? *You* did that?"

Bloom stared at Widow and swallowed. "Nine?"

"That's how many we found dead on the property. Four in the cornfield, two in the yard, plus three in the stable." Easton shook his head. "The state boys are calling it the biggest police shooting in modern Nebraska history."

Easton added, "Well, there was one out in a field near the property, but Trent Marrow's in custody for that one. Apparently, he had some kind of argument with that no-good loser, Boyd Crick. He killed him."

The room went quiet after that. The heart monitor beeped steadily.

The door opened, and a doctor walked in—an attractive woman in her fifties with dark hair pulled back in a practical ponytail. Her nametag read: *Wakefield*.

She smiled at the room, but her gaze lingered on Easton. "Sorry to interrupt. I just need to check on my patient."

Easton stepped back from the bed. "Of course, doctor."

She checked Bloom's vitals and examined the surgical site. Widow smiled at Easton's interaction with the doctor. The sheriff couldn't stop glancing at her, and the doctor kept finding reasons to smile in his direction. Neither seemed aware of how obvious they were being.

"Everything looks good," Dr. Wakefield said. "If everything stays on track, we should be able to discharge you tomorrow afternoon."

She turned to leave, but Easton stepped forward. "You're Dr. Wakefield?"

"I am."

He introduced himself and she did the same back. He told her about the parking space with her name on it. Easton watched her go.

"Yes," Bloom said quietly, finishing their conversation. Though it was done already, the morphine they'd given her had her still catching up to what was happening. "I did it all. Everything you found out there—that was me."

Easton studied her face, then nodded. "Get your story straight, Daisy. The state police and FBI are both going to have questions."

He moved toward the door. "I've got to follow up with Dr. Wakefield. Ask her some questions about the other patients." He paused. "Medical questions." He left.

Widow never saw him again for the rest of his life.

"You wanna stay at my house for a while? Key's in a fake rock by the front step. Stay there until this blows over. Feed my cat." She grinned. "And when I get out, maybe we can finally explore some of that *Fifty Shades of Grey* smut you seem to be into. You know I have department issue handcuffs?"

Widow laughed. "You're never going to let that go."

"Never."

He walked out into the cold Nebraska afternoon.

CHAPTER 40

The weeks that followed brought resolution to the chaos of that night, though the process was slow and grinding.

The Eltons recovered. Matty's leg healed cleanly, leaving only a scar and a slight limp that would fade with time. Elsa threw herself into caring for the family, helping to manage the ranch, and shielding the boys from the worst of the aftermath. T.J. had nightmares for months, but children are resilient, and eventually, the bad dreams came less frequently.

John Elton's dementia worsened steadily. The trauma seemed to accelerate his decline. By spring, he couldn't remember his grandchildren's names. By summer, he didn't recognize Matty at all.

The FBI opened an investigation into John's past as Donnie D, but it went nowhere. Agents flew in from Chicago and spent weeks interviewing witnesses, digging through old records, trying to build a case against a man who'd killed Enzo Brasi sixty years earlier. But their primary suspect was an eighty-five-year-old man with advanced dementia who couldn't remember what he'd eaten for breakfast. No charges were ever filed. John Elton lived out his remaining days in a memory care facility in Lincoln, surrounded by strangers who called him by a name that had never really been his.

The Brasi empire crumbled in the wake of Elena, Elio, and Vito's deaths. FBI agents raided properties in Chicago, New York, and Miami. Bank accounts were frozen. Businesses shuttered. Every living associate was hauled in, interrogated, and charged with everything from racketeering to murder conspiracy. The Brasi assets were sold off at auction, and the proceeds disappeared into the bottomless maw of the Department of Justice.

Matty and Adam together finally broke the wild bronco. It took several weeks of patient work, but eventually, the horse accepted a saddle and a rider. They named him Widow, and he became T.J.'s personal mount. The boy and the bronco developed an unlikely bond, both carrying scars from that terrible night, both learning to trust again.

Trent Marrow went to prison, though not for murdering Boyd Crick. They couldn't make that stick. Some kind of foul-up at the sheriff's office. What sent Trent to prison was an illegal gun charge. He was a convicted felon, and possession of a firearm carried a mandatory ten-year sentence under federal law.

Prison changed Trent. He met an older inmate—a former professor convicted of tax fraud—and something about the man's quiet dignity broke through. He learned to read properly, got his GED, and started taking college courses.

Years later, he became a public defender in Lincoln—the kind of lawyer who worked for people who couldn't afford anyone else.

He spent years removing his white supremacist tattoos. The

laser treatments were painful, but nowhere near as painful as what he'd been.

Clayton Marrow was found dead in his recliner three days after the events at the Elton ranch. A needle was still in his arm. The coroner ruled it an accidental overdose, though some people whispered that the timing was too convenient.

Ester had nowhere to go after her father's death. The Eltons solved the problem by adopting her.

It was Elsa's idea, but the whole family embraced it. The paperwork took months—Ester was seventeen, almost an adult—but by spring, she was legally an Elton. She had a bedroom of her own in the house, a seat at the dinner table, and a family who loved her.

She and Adam graduated from Tent Hills High School together that May. They'd broken up romantically after the trauma of that night—too much had happened, too quickly—but they remained close friends. They chose the same university, lived in the same dorm, and took some of the same classes.

Senior year, something shifted between them. Maybe it was maturity. Maybe it was the distance they'd gained from that terrible night.

They started dating again in October. By graduation, Adam had a ring. They married the following spring on the Elton ranch, under a sky so blue it looked painted.

They raised three children of their own. The youngest was a girl they named Jane.

CHAPTER 41

MEMORY FOUR

One of his last nights, living with his son, John, had another episode.

At midnight, he dreamed of a time when he and Alessandra lay in bed in their first home. Before they went to Nebraska, they lived in Los Angeles, in a cheap, rundown house for a few years. It wasn't much, but the beach was walking distance.

They went by the name Spencer back then.

The year was 1970, nearly '71. A radio played softly in the background. It rained outside. A clock on the dresser read 11:59 p.m.

Donnie D held Alessandra in his arms. They listened to the music and the rain thumping on the window. They were running out of money and it didn't matter. They were both the happiest they'd ever been.

Alessandra pulled away from him and got out of bed. She walked naked over to the dresser. She said, "I love this song. Have you heard it?" She turned the volume on the radio up.

"You ask me that every time it plays. It's 'Your Song,' " he said.

She took it as a question. "I haven't decided if it's my favorite song or not."

"No, I mean that's the song title. 'Your Song.' I hear it everywhere now. But, darling, we have to decide on a name."

Alessandra returned to Donnie D. She sat on the edge of the bed, touched his bare chest with her hand. "You want me to decide on a new last name for us, like we're married? But we're not married." She looked at the window. Raindrops gathered on the glass.

Donnie D turned away from her to his side of the bed. He sat up, put his feet on the floor, and stretched.

Alessandra got up and walked to the window. She looked out. If she stood on her tippy toes just the right way, she could see the ocean from this window. But the rain was too thick to see it now.

Donnie D went into the nightstand next to his side of the bed. "Your Song" played behind them. He pulled out a ring box and walked over to her. He put his arms around her and handed her the box. He said, "I've been wanting to give you this."

She stared at it. "What's this?"

"Open it."

Alessandra opened it. It was an engagement ring. It had the smallest diamond she'd ever seen in her life. It didn't even compare to a shred of the one she used to wear, back when she was a Brasi. That one was long gone. They'd pawned it for the cash years ago.

"What's this?" she asked again.

"I want to marry you," Donnie D said.

She turned and looked up in his eyes. Said nothing. But her eyes glassed over.

"What? You don't want to?" Donnie D asked.

"You gotta ask me first!"

Donnie D smiled, took the ring box and got down on one knee and proposed. She accepted, and he slid the ring on her finger. He stood, and they kissed.

She whispered, "Ms. Donnie DeLuca." Then she spoke up. "Oh, I can't go by that."

"I know. That's why I've been asking you to choose a name you like."

She stared at the ring, then looked at the radio. The song ended and a DJ came on. He mentioned it as one of the top songs on the charts and named the singer.

Alessandra said, "That's it! Elton John!"

Donnie D stared at her. "You want me to go by Elton John? Isn't that kind of suspicious?"

Alessandra said, "John Elton."

Donnie D smiled and nodded. "I like it. What about you?"

"You'll be Mr. John Elton. And I'll be... Jane. John and Jane Elton." They hugged and kissed to the rain and new music.

Fifty-five years after that night in 1970, Matty visited John every weekend at the memory care facility. Elsa and his grandkids came sometimes too.

John died ten and a half months after the night he met Widow.

His last words were, "Mrs. Brasi, I'm your new driver." In his mind, he heard her voice. "Call me Alessandra."

EXCITING NEWS
FROM SCOTT

Hello Operatives!

Thank you for reading *The Midnight Memory*. I hope you enjoyed it!

This book marks ten years of writing the Widow series for me. What a ride!

Some don't know this, but I started writing Widow near a war zone, in my old life. What an adventure it's been since then!

I have some exciting news. I'll be publishing more books starting in 2026. A lot of readers have asked for more books from me. Many have asked for new series, characters, and adventures. I also have secret projects I've been developing for a long time. I want to start publishing those as well. They range from thrillers to dramas to horror to fantasy and even epic science fiction.

I will continue to publish a new Widow book every year. I'm just adding more series and standalone books to my catalog.

If you enjoy my work, I hope you will enjoy my new books as well. If some aren't your preferred genres, no problem. Widow will be here!

I will keep you updated via my Newsletter or Facebook.com/ScottBladeAuthor.

The story continues...

The next book in the series is *JACK WIDOW: BOOK 22 UNTITLED*, coming in 2026!

My first new release of a different book is coming out in 2026 as well. Check out The Secret of Lions: A WWII Epic Spy Thriller.

To find out more, sign up for the Scott Blade Book Club and get notified of upcoming new releases.

Thanks so much for all your support over the years.

Scott Blade

GET JACK WIDOW
KINDLE BOXSET

Did you know you can get a Widow book free when you buy the eBoxSet on Kindle? Buy three Widow eBooks for the price of two.

UNTITLED BOOK 22

The next Widow book's title and premise will be unveiled in 2026. Follow me at Facebook.com/ScottBladeAuthor, where I post daily. Updates will be there.

THE SECRET OF LIONS

A Brand New Historical Fiction Thriller from Scott Blade
Coming 2026

(Actual cover to be revealed in 2026)

THE SECRET OF LIONS: A BLURB

From Amazon Bestseller Scott Blade, author of The Jack Widow Series, comes a gripping WWII epic spy thriller about lost art, politics, and assassins.

A mysterious painting hides a deadly secret. A secret that could rewrite history.

One morning, a painting appears in a London gallery. No one knows who hung it there. No one knows who painted it.

They call it *The Secret of Lions*.

The truth begins in 1924, in a German prison called Landsberg. A guard. A Jewish wife. A newborn son. A political prisoner with dead eyes and dangerous ideas.

When that prisoner walks free, he destroys everything the guard loves—and takes the child as his own.

That prisoner is Adolf Hitler.

From youth, Willem's gift for painting is extraordinary—so extraordinary that Hitler, once a failed artist himself, grows jealous. He forbids Willem from ever touching a brush again.

Instead, the boy is sent to elite Nazi academies. Trained to kill. Trained to lead. Trained to rule. Groomed to inherit Hitler's reign at the seat of absolute power.

For years, Willem barely remembers his true parents. Only fragments. Only dreams. Only flashes of a life that was stolen from him.

Until 1939—when the memories begin to surface and a new assassin is born.

For fans of **Daniel Silva's Gabriel Allon, Steve Berry's Cotton Malone,** and **Ken Follett.** *The Secret of Lions* delivers a riveting mix of buried history, stolen identity, and a secret the world was never meant to know. Preorder today!

A SPECIAL OFFER

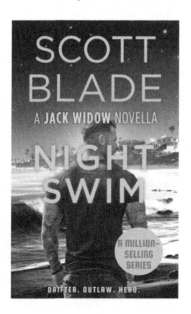

NIGHT SWIM: A BLURB

Under the cover of night, Widow swims through dangerous waters to rescue an FBI agent from a death sentence.

A blown cover for an FBI agent means a death sentence, unless Widow can stop it.

Under cover of darkness along the Malibu coast, Widow takes a night swim. It's meant to be soothing and stress-relieving.

Instead, Widow's night swim turns deadly with the echo of gunshots over open water. A covert FBI operation is blown apart, leaving only blood in the water and a lone undercover agent exposed to a den of lethal international criminals. From the quiet night swim to a high-stakes criminal party at a mega millionaire's beach house, Widow faces grave danger to warn her.

Widow, the drifter who stands for justice, emerges from the waves. With literally nothing but his resolve, he faces unbelievable odds. Time is running out, the enemy is within reach, and for Widow, stealth and cunning are his only weapons.

In this pulse-pounding Widow novella, the line between the hunter and the hunted blurs in a deadly game of espionage and survival.

THE SCOTT BLADE
BOOK CLUB

Fostering a connection with my readers is the highlight of my writing journey. Rest assured, I'm not one to crowd your inbox. You'll only hear from me when there's exciting news to share—like a fresh release hitting the shelves or a can't-miss promotion.

If you're just stepping into the world of Jack Widow, consider this your official invite to the Scott Blade Book Club. As a welcome gift, you'll receive the Night Swim: A Widow Novella in the starter kit.

By joining, you'll gain access to a trove of exclusive content, including free stories, special deals, bonus material, and the latest updates on upcoming Widow thrillers.

Ready to dive in? Visit ScottBlade.com to sign up and begin your immersion into the Widow universe.

THE NOMADVELIST

NOMAD + NOVELIST = NOMADVELIST

Scott Blade is a Nomadvelist, a drifter and author of the breakout Jack Widow series. Scott travels the world, hitchhiking, drinking coffee, and writing.

Jack Widow has sold over a million copies.

Visit @: ScottBlade.com

Contact @: scott@scottblade.com

Follow @:

Facebook.com/ScottBladeAuthor

Bookbub.com/profile/scott-blade

Amazon.com/Scott-Blade/e/B00AU7ZRS8

ALSO BY SCOTT BLADE

The Jack Widow Series

Gone Forever

Winter Territory

A Reason to Kill

Without Measure

Once Quiet

Name Not Given

The Midnight Caller

Fire Watch

The Last Rainmaker

The Devil's Stop

Black Daylight

The Standoff

Foreign and Domestic

Patriot Lies

The Double Man

Nothing Left

The Protector

Kill Promise

The Shadow Club

The Ghost Line

The Midnight Memory

Jack Widow: Untitled Book 22

Jack Widow Shorts

Night Swim

Made in the USA
Las Vegas, NV
10 December 2025